THE
HOSPITALIST

Michael Weisberg, M.D.

ISBN: 978-1-4834-1997-8 (sc)
ISBN: 978-1-4834-1996-1 (e)

Lulu Publishing Services rev. date: 12/02/2014

NOTE

In 1997, the legislature of India officially changed the name of Bombay to Mumbai.

This book is dedicated to all of the physicians who take care of sick patients in the hospital.

Thanks to Doug Ross, Seth Weisberg, and Andrew Harris for their critical readings of this manuscript and for their suggestions.

Love to Sheryl, Reid, Brent and Carly – life is worthwhile because of you.

MFW

PART 1

CHAPTER 1

Belle Glade, Florida 1955

If you were given twenty-four hours to live and a choice of where to spend your last day on earth, Belle Glade, Florida would be top on your list of places you would never want to go. Located forty-five miles due west of the jewel of Palm Beach, Belle Glade is in the middle of Florida and can best be described as a wasteland. There is one two-lane road leading from West Palm Beach to Belle Glade, and it is straight as a yardstick with no exits or rest stops. Both sides of the road are overgrown with dense brush, with an occasional forlorn palm tree sticking up through the wilderness to reach toward an unforgiving sun. The only lights in the road at night come from headlights, and one can travel miles without seeing a fellow traveler. Sitting under the brush is the swamp, not visible from the road, but lurking unseen, waiting for a motorist's wrong turn to quickly bring a vehicle to its demise. There are alligators inhabiting the swamp; they eat the small rodents and fish that occupy the swamp with them, and wait impatiently for humans whose cars run out of gas or swerve into their home.

It's hard to breathe in Belle Glade. It is oppressively hot and overwhelmingly humid. Unlike the breeze which comes off the ocean to cool the Palm Beaches, not a whiff of air is generated in Belle Glade from the nearby Lake Okeechobee. The air is heated and still; sometimes it feels like it has to be gulped into the lungs with effort. Mosquitoes are happy in Belle Glade; they must be - they are always around and a few minutes outside can result in a body covered with bites.

The main reason Belle Glade exists is sugar cane. Mile after mile after mile of the cane is grown in the Glades year after year and transported by truck to waiting vessels on the coast. The sugar cane plantations are owned by two families, the Clarks and the Dennisons, and everyone else who inhabits this uninhabitable part of the world in some way or another works for them.

****

Belle Glade is divided into three areas. First, there are two enormous plantations, each of which has a huge mansion not visible from any road surrounded by miles of sugar cane crop. Second, there is a small town where a few businesses have cropped up to provide the necessities for the people who live and work in this area. There are small homes behind the business fronts, and this is where the white people live and work. Finally, in the worst part of Belle Glade is Colored Town where all of the coloreds who work the sugar cane fields live. The homes here are more like huts - a few pieces of wood nailed together to form a square and a huge piece of aluminum as the roof, held in place by stones on top of it. The roofs leak in the almost daily rains and the one or two rooms inside the hut become soaked. Years before, a hurricane came up from the Caribbean, hit the Florida coast a little south, and then, as if divinely guided, shot like an arrow straight into Colored Town. Every hut was destroyed and all possessions lost. Thousands drowned including hundreds of children. The Belle Glade newspaper which came out every Thursday said thousands died, but they didn't bother going into Colored Town to count the bodies. Thousands of bodies were transported on the backs of flat bed trucks to be buried in unmarked graves on the banks of Lake Okeechobee where the colored buried their dead.

****

Arthur "Tank" Johnson was the foreman of the Dennison's plantation. He'd worked there since he'd gotten out of the army and he lived on the plantation in one of the two small houses Mrs. Dennison allowed to be built three miles away from her mansion. Arthur had built the house with the help of a few buddies - it had a wooden front door and a screen door in front of it. When you entered the house, there was a small kitchen directly in front with a tiny stove and icebox, and on the right side of the entrance was a living room/dining room where a small table and chairs occupied most of the space. There was an overstuffed, faded blue couch which Tank's wife's family had given them, and two almost matching blue chairs stuffed with feathers that would constantly float out from the tiny tears in the seats.

On the left side of the house was a short hallway leading to three tiny bedrooms. Tank and his wife, Elizabeth, slept in the bedroom furthest down the hallway which had a bed, two wooden dressers, blue carpet with scattered cigarette burns, and one window directly opposite the bed. Halfway down the hallway was Arthur Junior's room; it was large enough for his bed and one dresser. Arthur Junior was nine years old, and his room was where he spent most of his time when home. His few clothes were piled in dresser drawers; Christmas and his birthday were the only times when he got a new shirt, trousers, underwear, or socks. The last bedroom was a quick left-hand turn from the main hall and it had been newly painted bright yellow and was newly occupied by an old, beat-up wooden crib. It was the only almost cheerful room in the house, and when Arthur Junior wasn't in his own room playing with his toy soldiers and toy tanks, he loved to wander into the baby's room and sit on the floor and dream.

The baby's room wasn't occupied yet, but any day now a baby was coming. Arthur had heard this twice before in the last three years and watched hopefully as his mother's stomach would begin to swell, and she would wear the larger plain white dresses she had sewn for herself before Arthur was born. Each time, though, something had happened - a scream in the night followed by wails of despair and somehow, the baby was gone. His mother would stay in her bedroom for days after and when Arthur went in to see her, he saw her face red and swollen from the tears that wouldn't stop coming. Each time his father would take him outside and they would sit on the porch swing together. His father would tell him that his mother had lost the baby and it had gone to heaven to be with Jesus.

Although the news made Arthur sad - he wanted a little brother to play with so much - it was one of the few opportunities he had to spend time alone with his father, Tank, whom Arthur worshipped. Tank had been a tank commander in World War Two and had fought in the Battle of the Bulge. A German anti-tank missile had hit his father's Sherman tank directly, and the tank had exploded, killing everyone onboard except Arthur. The explosion had blown him twenty-five yards away, and he landed in soft weeds which saved him. The left side of his body had been severely burned and when Arthur looked at his father's face, he saw the scars and crevices that the burns had caused. His left eye had had to be removed - a fragment from his tank had been embedded in it and caused it to pop like a dart hitting a balloon. In its place, Tank had a glass eye with the eyeball painted blue to match his other eye.

Tank's hairline was receding, and what was left in front formed a V on his forehead. He got his hair cut every two weeks in the small barbershop in town and he always got a crew cut. Arthur Junior loved the feel of his father's crew cut and would run his fingers through his father's head to feel the stiffness of the hairs tickle his fingers. When he turned nine years old and had run his hand across his father's head, Tank had taken his massive right arm and pulled Arthur's hand from his head. "Only fags run their hands through another man's hair and I sure as hell ain't raisin' you to be no fag!" Arthur never ran his fingers through his father's hair again, or touched the huge Sherman tank tattooed on Tank's left arm. Tank had the tattoo done in France one month before the Battle of the Bulge. His enormous left biceps had been covered with a Sherman tank and below it was written 99th Tank Division. The burns on the arm had been so extensive that all that was left was the carriage of the Sherman tank with a scar running through it and the word Tank below it. His wounds had earned Tank a Purple Heart which sat on top of the dresser in his bedroom. But the explosion had burned the entire left side of his body, disfiguring the muscles so much that when in public, Tank always wore long-sleeved shirts and long pants, not willing to let the oppressive Belle Glade heat cause him to remove enough clothes to reveal his deformities.

****

Arthur attended the one small school in Belle Glade which housed grades one through twelve. He was one of only ten white students at the school, the rest were colored. It was almost three miles from his house on the plantation to the school, and each morning, Arthur's father would get him up at five a.m., give him an egg and a piece of toast and a glass of milk, and send him on his way. Arthur would watch as the Dennison children would be driven from their house on top of the only hill in Belle Glade, down the long winding road to the street in front of the plantation in a long black limousine. All three of their children went to a private school in Palm Beach, so they had to leave early in the morning and wouldn't return till close to dark. None of the Dennison children acknowledged Arthur's presence - in first grade, he used to wave at the big limousine daily as it passed him on the road, but there was never a return wave. One time in second grade, one of the car windows rolled down as the car passed Arthur, and he thought someone might say hello. He ran closer to the car and was greeted by a squirt of water from a water gun which soaked his face and then he heard laughter before the window rolled up and the limousine sped off.

At school, the nine other white children, sons and daughters of merchants in town, were all older than Arthur and wanted nothing to do with him. He ate by himself in the cafeteria and played by himself in the small clearing behind the school which contained two broken swings and a rusted jungle gym. He knew not to get near the swings or jungle gym - these were in colored territory and getting close to them would result in a bloody nose or a black eye. Arthur invented his own games; most of them were war games in which he was in an imaginary tank giving orders to his crew. He sat on the ground just behind the school and surveyed the playground. The jungle gym was the German tank he was fighting; he barked orders to his men and they rolled the tank gun around so that it had the jungle gym in its sights. Sometimes, Arthur's crew would talk back to him, asking him questions and wondering how he could be so brave while the rest of them were scared. Arthur could hear their voices distinctly; at first it frightened him to hear the imaginary voices so vividly, but then he accepted it as part of the game.

On the way home after school, Arthur would be followed by some colored boys his age and some older colored boys. They couldn't beat up Arthur as much as they wanted at school with a few teachers around, so they would follow him on his three-mile walk. They would carry rocks which they picked up along the road. They would throw the rocks at Arthur, first at his feet to make him jump. Three or four would throw rocks at a time, and Arthur would try to anticipate them and jump out of the way. Sometimes the coloreds would surround him and throw rocks at his feet and legs to make him jump. "Jumpy, that's your name," they would yell at him and "Jumpy" he became. At school, all of the coloreds called him "Jumpy" and even his teachers sometimes slipped and called him "Jumpy."

Once, in the center of eight colored boys with his body bruised by the rocks and punches he'd received, Arthur cried out, "Why, why are you picking on me?" The tallest and oldest colored boy, Clem, who was sixteen laughed and showed a smile with a few rotten teeth. "Your dad, Tank, he part of the Klan. You know the Klan, Jumpy? You know how they treat and kill colored folk? He part of that group that hung Missy Simpson's father...we sure that. Now we can't get him too easily, but we surely get you."

The Klan. Tank was the Grand Dragon of the Klan for Central Florida. He hated niggers and he hated Jews. Next to their small house on the Dennison Plantation lived the only Jewish family in Belle Glade. Isaac Greenberg was the accountant for the Dennison's business, and he also guided them on how and when and where to sell their crop. He was a typical Jew according to Tank - he knew money and that was all he cared about. The Greenberg's house was a hundred yards away from the Johnson's, and Mr. Greenberg had hired a construction crew to build it. It had two stories, bedrooms for each of their three young children, and ceiling fans in each room. It also had a beautiful wooden porch and a rocking chair which Mr. Greenberg would sit in at night as his children sat on the porch around him and listened to his stories. Greenberg had served in World War Two also, but hadn't seen any action. No, he was kept in the states in New York, helping to plan where to send supplies and weapons to the troops all over the world. He had worked with Mr. Dennison's cousin during the war who had told Mr. Dennison about his brilliant mind. When the war ended, Mr. Greenberg was immediately offered a job, a house, and a very generous salary to come to Belle Glade. There was even a rumor that Greenberg invested the Dennison's money for them and received a small percentage of the profits which Tank thought was despicable and angered him immensely. So the Klan was Tank's life and greatest joy. Even though he had a wife and child to support and a baby on the way, if a nigger ever did something to warrant it, he would call his knights together to right whatever wrong had been committed.

****

Jumpy and his mother were sitting next to each other on the blue couch in the small living room/dining room. School had ended for summer the day before. They had the rotating portable fan on the table in front of them, but still both were hot and sweating through their clothes. Jumpy jumped when his mother yelled out, "Owww, dammitt." Her body shook for a minute and then her body was covered in more sweat.

"These contractions are coming closer and closer. I need to get to the hospital so the doctor can deliver this baby." She leaned over and took a drag from the cigarette smoldering in the ashtray on the table. She slowly drew on the cigarette and then puffed out the smoke. Her lips closed around the cigarette butt again, and she closed her eyes and inhaled deeply.

"Why'd your father hafta go to Klan meetin' tonight? He knows how close I was to givin' birth. My due date is Friday. How I'm s'posed get to the hospital?"

"Momma, that hospital is in West Palm Beach - more'n hour away. You gonna git there in time to have my brother?"

"If your dad comes home soon, yes. These contractions are about fifteen minutes apart now. I told him not to go..."

"But momma, some nigga went into Casey's Barber Shop this week, sat down and demanded a hair cut. No nigga needs to act like that."

"I know. Your father tries so hard to keep them in their place when they workin' with the cane. Dumb niggers, need be taught everything."

"Do you think Mr. Greenberg could drive you? They gotta fancy new Ford car. You want me to run over there and ask?"

"Stupid fool. I'd never let that Jew drive me anywhere. Tank would kill me - he hate that Jew. Money-grubbing, fancy-talking bastard." She reached over again for a drag on the cigarette. She blew the smoke at Jumpy.

Suddenly she jumped up from the couch. The bottom of her white cotton dress was covered in water and blood, and the bloody water soup dripped down from between her legs to the floor.

"Jesus, help me! My water broke!"

Jumpy started crying, "Mama, whatcha gonna do, whatcha gonna do?" He looked down at the floor where a puddle of bloody water soaked the carpet to make sure his little brother wasn't down there.

"How fuckin' long it take to burn a cross? He shoulda been back hours ago."

Just then they heard the sound of a motorcycle engine roaring down the dirt road to their house and then there was silence. Jumpy ran to the door and saw his father on his Indian motorcycle. He'd taken off his white hood, but was still wearing his long, flowing white Klan robe which fell over each side of the motorcycle.

"Daddy, mommy's bleeding and she's gonna have my brother. Come quick!"

Tank jumped off the motorcycle and ran into the house. He looked at Elizabeth who was having another contraction.

"Shit. We needa get you to the hospital."

"Why...why the fuck you so late?"

"Cross burning lasted longer than I thought. Then we rode around Nigger Town in our Klan uniforms. I'll ride into town to Bill Wiley's - he said I could borrow his pick-up to take you to West Palm."

"Tank, there ain't no time. We gotta go now on your chopper. This baby's gonna come soon and I don't want to be stuck in the middle of the swamp when he does. You wait here, Jumpy. We'll be back in a few days with a little brother or sister for you."

Tank walked into the living room and the screen door closed behind him. He picked Elizabeth up in his massive arms and carried her to the door. He kicked the screen door open and carried her down to the Indian motorcycle. Even in the dark with the only light coming from inside the house, Jumpy could make out the red stains on his mother's white dress. Elizabeth reached around Tank with both arms and clasped them around his waist. Tank gunned the engine and they were off, and Jumpy stood alone on the porch.

****

Jumpy went back inside and closed the wooden door and locked it. He turned on every light in the house, then walked into the brightly painted baby's room. Tonight had been terrifying, yet exciting. It would all be worth it. It had taken years, but he'd have a baby brother to play with and a real person to talk to who would talk back. Jumpy went into his room, got into his bed and buried his entire body under the blanket.

There was a loud banging. It started slowly and then intensified. It woke Jumpy with a start - he thought he was dreaming, but it was coming from the front door. He went into his parents' room to get the loaded German Luger that his father kept in the back of the second drawer of his dresser, but it wasn't there. The banging grew louder, and he heard someone yelling, "Arthur, Arthur!" He crawled down the hallway to the kitchen and pulled a knife out of a drawer. He walked silently to the door holding the knife in front of him. He unlocked the wooden door and pulled the knife back, ready to stab. Through the screen door, he saw Mr. Greenberg and two policemen.

"Arthur, there's been an accident involving your parents. These policeman have come to take you to them."

Jumpy realized that he was still holding the knife back, ready to stab someone. "An accident..." The knife clanged as it dropped to the floor. "Are my parents OK?"

"Come with us, son," said one of the officers as he opened the screen door and Jumpy walked out.

****

Jumpy sat in the back seat as the siren blared and the patrol car sped down the two- lane road to West Palm Beach. After about fifteen minutes, the headlights on the patrol car illuminated an ambulance and two other patrol cars on the side of the road. The ambulance and the patrol cars all had their sirens flashing.

Jumpy and the officers got out of their car and they ran over to where the ambulance driver and policemen were working. They were pulling a motorcycle from the swamp and were working on pulling two bodies out. Both bodies had been thrown off the motorcycle and were further back in the weeds and water. Jumpy shuddered when he recognized his father's Indian motorcycle. Tears began streaming down his face. "No, no," he screamed, but no one paid any attention.

The first body they brought out was Tank's. The officers' powerful flashlights lit up Tank's face, and Jumpy saw that the glass eye was gone, and in its place was a huge clot of blood. Then Jumpy saw the other side of his father's head - he'd been shot and the bullet had gone through his real eye and then out the glass eye and the part of the nose next to it. Tank's mouth was open and crying silently for help. The mouth was so full of mud that no teeth could be seen. The Klan robe was covered in blood, mud, and insects.

"He's been murdered," one of the officers who had picked up Jumpy at his house said to the other.

"Wonder who shot him? Some crazy nigger may have seen him dressed up in his Klan get-up."

"Where's my mama and brother?" Jumpy choked on his tears, "I want my momma!"

For the first time, both policemen looked at him. The flashlights now illuminated a second body - it was Jumpy's mother. She was being carried by two ambulance workers whose white shirt and pants were covered in mud and slime and blood. One cradled her head and neck and the other carried her legs.

Jumpy ran up to her. He didn't notice or care that the one new pair of pants that he'd gotten for the start of third grade were now wet and muddy. He looked at his mother's face. Her eyes were closed and her mouth was shut.

"She's dead, son," one of the ambulance workers said. They laid her down inside the ambulance next to Tank. Jumpy crawled into the ambulance to see his mother's face.

"Momma, momma!" he shouted at her still pretty features. "Don't be dead. I need you. What about my brother?" Jumpy looked down to his mother's swollen belly where the baby had been. "My brother for nine months."

"Sorry son, nothing we can do. Baby's dead also."

Jumpy lay between his dead father and mother and never-seen dead brother and cried. He held all three of them with all of his might, as if his strength would bring them back to him. The ambulance workers tried to pull him off - he wouldn't let go. He felt the German Luger behind his father's belt and pulled it out and put it under his own belt.

"Please Jesus. I never asked for no help when those niggers beat me or white kids made fun of me. Please Jesus, Son of God, Ruler of Man...make my family alive."

"Come on son. We need to drive your parents' bodies back to the morgue in West Palm Beach so we can start working on who killed 'em. Looks like someone shot your daddy and he wrecked that motorcycle in the swamp, killing your momma. We'll drive you home."

"I wanna stay with my family."

A tall burly policeman reached down and pulled Jumpy out of the ambulance. "Son, your family is gone. You'll need to go home so we can notify your next-of-kin to come take care of you." The policeman picked Jumpy up and flung him over his shoulder. The ambulance drivers closed the back door of the ambulance and with sirens flashing, started the drive east. That was the last time Jumpy ever saw his family.

****

Neither of Tank's brothers was willing to have Jumpy come live with them - they'd always thought he was strange and didn't want him around their children. Elizabeth had been an only child raised by her mother since her father had left when she was eight. Elizabeth's mother was long dead, so no one on that side of the family was around to take care of Jumpy. Plans were quickly made to send Jumpy to live in the state orphanage in Tallahassee, Florida, and within a week, Jumpy was living in an old brick three-story building, sharing a room with seven other boys. He had a cot and a wooden dresser with three drawers next to his cot. In the drawers he put his few clothes, his miniature army men and tanks, his father's Purple Heart, and the cross that had hung in his parents' room. Under the clothes, he carefully hid the German Luger which he managed to conceal from everyone. He knew that niggers had killed his parents and unborn brother and vowed someday to get revenge. Due to circumstances, he never found out what really happened that night.

****

Six weeks after the Johnson murders, the police arrested Jeff Casey, the barber, for the murder of the Johnsons. They'd found tire tracks next to where the motorcycle had skidded off the road that matched Casey's motorcycle, and the bullet that killed Tank was from Casey's shotgun. When the police questioned Casey on his whereabouts that evening, he said he'd gone to the Klan rally and then driven home at ten o'clock. But his next-door neighbor, Bill Wiley, who'd also been at the rally said he was sitting on his porch cleaning his guns, and that Casey hadn't returned to his house until at least two in the morning. He remembered it distinctly, because Casey usually was the first one home and to bed since he opened his barbershop at seven every morning.

Jeff Casey confessed and admitted he'd killed Tank Johnson because he found out Tank was fucking his wife. He'd made plans for weeks to kill him and was parked on his motorcycle outside the plantation that night after the rally trying to decide if he should drive in and shoot him. Suddenly Tank's motorcycle had flown by with someone holding onto him, and Jeff had taken off after Tank. He caught up with him after about fifteen minutes, pulled his motorcycle next to Tank's, and shot him twice - once in the face and a second shot through the Swastika that Tank had Elizabeth embroider on the front of his Klan robe.

****

News from Belle Glade didn't reach Tallahassee, so Jumpy never found out the truth about his family's death. He was left believing it was some nigger who hated white people; more than likely the father of one of the nigger bullies at school.

****

Jumpy stayed in the orphanage for three years and then began living with foster families. In the five years before his eighteenth birthday, he had lived with eight different families, none of whom wanted him for long. They all thought he was strange and dangerous. He talked to himself all the time and talked out loud when no one was around. Three months before his eighteenth birthday, the father in the foster home where he was living in Orlando sodomized Jumpy while holding a World War Two army knife to Jumpy's throat. Jumpy ran away the next night and hitchhiked up to Georgia. He worked in a gas station until his eighteenth birthday, and then went into the local recruiting office to join the army. Two days before he was shipped to Viet Nam, he stole a car and drove to Orlando. He went back to the home of his last foster family and parked his car down the block from their home. He pulled a cowboy hat over his head and waited. When he saw the father's car pull into the driveway, he slowly got out of his car and walked down the sidewalk towards him. The father was walking from the driveway into the house when out of the corner of his eye he saw a man walking towards him in a cowboy hat and jeans. Something familiar about that man, he thought. Suddenly the man pulled a German Luger from behind his belt and shot him three times in the face.

"Don't forget me, father, I'm Jumpy." were the last words that foster father heard before he died.

CHAPTER 2

Bombay, India – 1981

The west coast of India was in the midst of one of the worst rainstorms of the past 20 years, and Bombay had been drenched. Three days of nonstop, pouring rain had flooded most of the city. There had been no night separated from day; darkness had enveloped the islands of Bombay for 72 hours, and only streaks of lightning illuminated the black skies. Power outages had robbed the city completely of electricity, and the only generators operating were in the hospitals. For the first time in years, flooding had caused the government to close the streets to all transportation except emergency vehicles. Almost 15 million people huddled inside their homes and apartments, trying to wait out the storm. Even Bombay port, the only natural deep-water harbor in west India, had been closed.

As always with natural disasters, the poor suffered the most, and this one was no exception. The slums of Bombay were covered in water and excrement as the sewers had backed up into the streets. The lucky street-dwellers who had survived the floods were huddled under blankets and coats on the streets or in the stairwells of the apartment buildings; the less fortunate were now just bodies bobbing lifelessly in the rising waters.

Vijay Givagushrai was 14 years old and lived with his father, two older brothers and two younger sisters on the seventh floor of a 20-story apartment building in the heart of the poorest neighborhood in Bombay. The apartment consisted of two rooms; one served as the kitchen/eating area, and the other was the living room where they sat, talked, studied and slept. No one had a true bed. The girls, Grace, age 12, and Julie, age 10, shared a small couch that Vijay's father had found upside down in a dumpster outside an apartment building in a nicer part of the city. The father, Prasad, slept in the corner of the room on a tiny cot which he had found in the rubble of a hospital in Bombay which had burned to the ground ten years before. The three boys, Ravi, age 18, Anjay, age 16, and Vijay all slept together on a pile of blankets in the middle of the room. The apartments were wired for electricity, but, with the deluge, they'd had no electricity in three days. The family had gone to sleep at 10 o'clock that night after eating a meager meal consisting of the few scraps that their father had managed to pick up on the streets. Prasad worked as a laborer on the docks of Bombay, but since the docks were closed by the weather, there had been no work for him and no money for the family.

Anjay hadn't eaten at all that night and hadn't been able to keep anything down earlier in the day. The smell of Anjay's vomitus and diarrhea permeated the apartment, even though Vijay had done his best to clean it up. Anjay had now been sick for three days, and Vijay was getting more and more worried about his older brother. The first two days at least Anjay had had the strength to run down the hallway to the common latrine. Today, he didn't have the energy to get up off the blankets and was constantly soiling them. One hour after going to sleep, Vijay awoke suddenly. Anjay was lying next to him, screaming in pain.

"Help me, please help me! Someone has got to do something!"

Prasad got up from his cot and walked in the darkness to Anjay.

"What is wrong, son? Tell me what is wrong."

"Everything is wrong, father. I hurt all over. I am weak. I'm going to die. I'm going to die, father."

Prasad kneeled down and put his hand on Anjay's forehead. "You are burning up. You are so hot, Anjay."

"Father, I am burning. I am burning. I am going to die."

Vijay could feel his brother trembling on the floor next to him. When the lightning flashed, he could see his brother's pale face that was covered in sweat.

"Father", said Vijay, "we must do something now to help Anjay. He needs to go to the hospital. He is very sick."

Prasad was silent for a moment. The other children had now gathered around Anjay.

"I don't have any money for a hospital," Prasad said slowly.

"But he must see a doctor. He must see a doctor now," Vijay said.

"I know you are right, Vijay. He must see a doctor."

"What about Dr. Bissel-Mozel?" asked Vijay. "He takes care of poor people. He treated me two years ago when I had the bad infection, and we had no money to pay him."

"How will we get Anjay to him?" asked Prasad. "The water is so high; how can we carry Anjay to him?"

"I will go to Dr. Bissel-Mozel and bring him back to Anjay," replied Vijay. Without waiting for a reply, Vijay stood up and pulled on the shirt and pants lying on the floor next to him.

Prasad was initially surprised by Vijay's response, but then he remembered how independent and smart Vijay was. Vijay was the only one of the three boys still in school, and his teachers had always made it a point to tell Prasad how brilliant his son was. Physically, Vijay was also very different from the rest of them. He was already 6 feet tall and had a broad, muscular build. None of the other men in the family was over 5 feet 8 inches, and they all had slight builds. Ravi was four years older than Vijay but was mildly retarded.

"Do you want me to go with you?" Ravi asked.

"No, I will be OK by myself," Vijay said. "I will go to Dr. Bissel-Mozel's clinic and bring him back to Anjay."

Vijay left the apartment and walked into the black hallway. He used his hands to feel his way along the walls to the stairwell. He opened the door to the stairwell, and it banged against a person sleeping there.

"Ow" came the loud shout from the man lying there. "Where are you going so late at night?"

"I'm in a hurry," Vijay replied and he stepped over the man. He ran down the stairs and got down to the street. The moment he stepped out of the apartment building's door, he was soaked by the rain. He was startled by a clap of thunder, and then he began to run. The brown water was up to his knees as he splashed his way to Dr. Bissel-Mozel's clinic.

The clinic was located on the very edge of the slum neighborhoods and just across from a large automobile factory and an even larger cotton textile plant. The location afforded Dr. Bissel-Mozel the opportunity to take care of workers in these factories who could afford health care and whose payments supported a practice whose primary interest was in taking care of the poor who had no means to pay. To the slum-dwellers, Dr. Bissel-Mozel was a true saint, well known for his compassion and skills.

Vijay continued running in his bare feet, and, as he rounded one corner, he stopped and fell. He scraped his knees and right elbow, but he kept going. Finally, he came to the clinic. He tried to open the front door, but it was locked, so he banged on the door with his fist.

"Dr. Bissel-Mozel, Dr. Bissel-Mozel!" he screamed.

An old man was sleeping on the covered porch in front of the clinic. He sat up and looked at Vijay. "You looking for Dr. Bissel-Mozel?" he asked in a matter-of-fact tone as if he was Dr. Bissel-Mozel's appointment secretary.

"Yes, yes, my brother is very sick. I've got to bring Dr. Bissel-Mozel to help him. Dr. Bissel-Mozel must help him, or I think he is going to die."

"Dr. Bissel-Mozel lives over there," the old man said as he pointed to the small apartment building behind the clinic. "Go around the back of the clinic to the alley, and there's a stairway that goes up to his place."

Vijay ran around to the back alley. He ran up the stairs and knocked on Dr. Bissel-Mozel's door. Within a minute, Dr. Bissel-Mozel appeared and opened the door. He was dressed in dark black pants and a white T-shirt. He carried a candle that lit up his face. Vijay had always considered Dr. Bissel-Mozel the most unusual-looking man he had ever seen, and, in the two years since he'd last seen him, nothing had changed. Dr. Bissel-Mozel was a 50-something-year-old British man who was completely bald and wore tiny gold wire-rimmed glasses. The most unusual part of his appearance, though, was that the entire left side of his face was pushed in as though a truck had run over the left half of the doctor's face. If the right and left sides of his face were each considered a separate tire, Vijay thought, it was as if someone had forgotten to inflate the left tire. The left half of his nose was pushed in, and Dr. Bissel-Mozel had to constantly push at his spectacles to keep them on his face. If that wasn't enough, the left side of the face was also covered by a huge port-wine birthmark. He had a pencil–thin gray moustache and a mouthful of broken brown teeth. As hideous as he looked, it was sometimes hard to remember that this was the man who was a hero and saint to the poor of Bombay.

Dr. Bissel-Mozel looked at Vijay, and to Vijay's surprise, remembered him immediately.

"You're Vijay, son of a dock worker. I treated you a couple years ago. Very intelligent boy. Why are you here on a night like this?"

"Dr. Bissel-Mozel, there's a bad problem with my brother, Anjay. He's been sick for three days with diarrhea and vomiting. He's been having pain. But tonight, the pain is worse, and he has a high fever. He initially could take food, but today nothing. He needs your help immediately."

"Where is he now?" asked Dr. Bissel-Mozel.

"He's lying in our apartment in the slums."

"Let me get dressed and get my doctor's bag, and I'll come with you."

Dr. Bissell-Mozel reappeared in a few minutes. He was now wearing a white dress shirt with a red bowtie and a long black coat. His bald head was covered by a black English bowler. Vijay started quickly down the stairs and looked back up the stairs to see Dr. Bissel-Mozel was still at the top. Vijay had forgotten that Dr. Bissel-Mozel was also a cripple. He remembered hearing that Dr. Bissel-Mozel had had polio as a child in England which rendered his left leg useless. He walked by thrusting his right leg out in front of him and then using momentum and upper body strength to pull the stiff left leg almost even with the right. He struggled getting down the stairs, gripping the railing with both hands as his black bag was clutched between his elbow and body.

"How did you make it here? It looks like the streets are all flooded."

"I found a way, doctor. Come with me. I will lead you."

The two walked deeper into the slums. At one point, a vicious gust of wind blew the bowler off Dr. Bissel-Mozel's head. Vijay ran to retrieve it but was unable to find it in the murky water.

"Don't worry about that hat, Vijay," said Dr. Bissel-Mozel as the rain bounced off his skull. "Let's go help Anjay."

It took well over an hour, but finally, they came to Vijay's apartment building.

"Can you make it up six flights of stairs?" asked Vijay.

"Sure, it may take me some time, but I'll make it."

Vijay opened the door to the stairway, and they were in complete darkness. Dr. Bissel-Mozel gave Vijay a flashlight from his black bag which Vijay turned on.

"Let me hold onto your arm," requested Dr. Bissel-Mozel.

Vijay extended his arm, and slowly the two of them made their way up the stairs. Vijay could hear Dr. Bissel-Mozel breathing heavily as he pulled his dead leg up stair by stair. Finally, they reached the seventh floor. Vijay pushed open the door to their apartment, and Dr. Bissel-Mozel walked in with him.

"Dr. Bissel-Mozel," said Prasad. "Thank you for coming, thank you. You've got to help Anjay."

"Your son, Vijay, has done a very good job of telling me what's going on with Anjay. Give me the flashlight, Vijay."

Dr. Bissel-Mozel used the light of the flashlight to guide him to the area where Anjay was lying. He took a thermometer out of his bag, cleaned it off with a piece of cotton dipped in alcohol and then took Anjay's temperature. "One-hundred five degrees," he exclaimed! "Do you have any ice around here?"

"We don't have any ice," replied Vijay. Dr. Bissel-Mozel took Anjay's pulse and blood pressure and then listened to his heart and lungs with his stethoscope. He pushed on Anjay's abdomen, and Anjay screamed in pain. He then gently placed his stethoscope on Anjay's abdomen and listened. "Your brother will have to be moved to a hospital as he is very ill," Dr. Bissel-Mozel said to Vijay as he struggled back to his feet.

"We have no money for a hospital," replied Vijay calmly.

"I will get him in under my name. He needs antibiotics right away. I'll give him an injection."

Dr. Bissel-Mozel pulled a syringe and glass bottle out of his bag. He drew the medicine out of the bottle with the syringe, and, then, after carefully wiping off Anjay's arm with alcohol, he injected the contents of the syringe into Anjay's arm. Anjay winced a little bit but by now was delirious, and none of his mutterings made sense.

"How will we transport him to the hospital?" asked Dr. Bissel-Mozel.

"We can carry him," replied Vijay. "Raji, father and I will carry him. One of them can carry each of his arms, and I will carry him by the legs."

Dr. Bissel-Mozel used his flashlight to illuminate Vijay and his family. He was amazed at how big Vijay was compared to his father and brothers; only age 14 and he was at least 6 feet tall and very husky.

"Yes," replied Dr. Bissel-Mozel. "If the two of them each take an arm and you carry the legs, we will get him there."

Vijay picked up Anjay's legs, and his father and Ravi picked up his arms. They followed Dr. Bissel-Mozel out of the apartment and into the hallway. They slowly trudged down the stairs and then walked almost two miles to the hospital. When they got there, they were greeted by a nurse sitting at a desk in the emergency room.

"Yes, can I help you? Oh, Dr. Bissel-Mozel, what can we do for you?"

"This is a very sick patient of mine. I've taken care of him and his family for years. He's going to be admitted to the hospital immediately under my care. We need to get an IV in him right away and give him fluids wide open. Then, take him upstairs to a bed on the ward. I will write further orders there."

Vijay picked Anjay up off the floor of the emergency room and placed him onto the stretcher which two nurses had brought. Vijay watched as one of the nurses put an IV into Anjay, and then they wheeled Anjay upstairs, and they waited outside Anjay's room. About 30 minutes later, Dr. Bissel-Mozel came out of the room.

"He's got a bad infection, no doubt. We'll give him antibiotics, intravenous fluids, and I'll have one of my surgical colleagues keep an eye on him also. He's young and strong, so hopefully, we'll be able to get him through this."

Dr. Bissel-Mozel reached up and put his hand on Vijay's shoulder. "You're a brave young man to risk your life coming out in the middle of the night to get me. You're extremely intelligent also; you explained your brother's situation quickly and accurately, and then you figured out a way to get me safely back to your apartment and then to get your brother here. Your brother owes his life to you. Like I told your father two years ago, I think that you should strongly consider a career in medicine. You're old enough now to start working in my clinic. How would you like to be my assistant on weekends and holidays? I'll pay you of course."

Vijay looked at his father, and his father nodded at him.

"I would be honored, Dr. Bissel-Mozel. I would love to work with you. Do you really think I could be a doctor?"

Dr. Bissel-Mozel smiled. "Yes, I do. And I will help you any way I can."

And so, on that bleakest of Bombay nights, Vijay helped save his first life and decided to become a doctor.

CHAPTER 3

Nashville, Tennessee – 1981

It was a chilly night in Nashville, Tennessee, that February evening, and there was still snow on the ground from the heavy snows the previous days. The temperature that Saturday night had risen to just over 40 degrees, a high for the week.

The Vanderbilt University campus was alive with parties. There had been an important conference basketball game earlier that evening, and Vanderbilt had come from behind to upset the fourth-ranked Louisiana State University team in a thrilling finish. Now at 11 o'clock, parties were going on at all of the fraternity houses on campus except one. That one house was dark and silent; it was the Alpha Epsilon Pi fraternity house.

Alpha Epsilon Pi was one of the smallest fraternities on the Vanderbilt campus and was made up almost entirely of Jewish members. There were not a lot of Jewish students at Vanderbilt, and a significant percentage of them did not want to be associated with anything Jewish. Being a small fraternity, Alpha Epsilon Pi did not have the budget to have weekly parties, and, so, tonight, the house was dark. The only lights in the house that were on were in the basement where one of the members, Aaron Bernstein, was playing ping-pong with the nephew of the house's black cook, Nate.

At 6 feet and 165 pounds, Aaron had a thin but muscular build and a head full of curly brown hair. He wore loose-fitting blue jeans and a large Vanderbilt University sweatshirt over a white T-shirt. The boy's name was Ed, and he was 11 years old. When Aaron had come over to the fraternity house an hour before, looking for something to do after studying that evening, Ed was the only one around and was watching television. He and Aaron had played ping-pong before on Saturday nights, so they decided to stop watching television and go down to the basement and play ping-pong. The basement was sparsely furnished with junky, old couches around the perimeter of the room and a ping-pong table in the middle. There were two fluorescent lights with bare bulbs in the middle of the room, and one of the lights constantly flickered.

Aaron was in a great mood. Earlier that day, he had received an acceptance letter from Baylor College of Medicine in Houston, Texas. Aaron had studied hard for four years at Vanderbilt with the primary goal of getting into medical school and becoming a doctor. No one in his family had ever been a doctor before, but it had been Aaron's dream since he was six years old. Aaron had been a sickly child and had spent a lot of time missing school and in the hospital while growing up. At least twice, Aaron had thought he was going to die, and those horrible experiences were etched in his memory. He had been very impressed by the caring and compassionate doctors who had taken care of him and had pulled him through those tough times, so he decided early on that he, too, wanted to become a physician.

Aaron had volunteered in the oncology clinic and in the emergency room at Vanderbilt Hospital for all four years there, and he loved being able to help people get better. This was his goal in life: to become a doctor and to make people better. Today, he had gotten his acceptance letter to medical school, the first step towards that goal. Unlike most of the southern gentlemen and gentlewomen who were students there, Aaron had spent his four years at Vanderbilt University working and studying. He worked as a security guard at a girls' dormitory for four years, and he had refereed intramural basketball games two nights a week for the last two years. Most of his time, however, had been spent studying. Schoolwork had not come easily for him, but he had passionately devoted himself to it and had maintained an A average. He was a creature of habit, though, and even though he had been accepted to medical school that day, that night, he had studied for several hours. It was hard to break his routine, and he did have a test coming up in biochemistry on Monday. Now, at 11 o'clock at night, he was in the basement of the fraternity house with Ed playing ping-pong and relaxing.

The noises of the campus sifted down in bits and pieces to the basement of the Alpha Epsilon Pi fraternity house, and it made Aaron even happier to know that his fellow students were having a good time. He and Ed were volleying the ball back and forth when suddenly they heard a banging on the windows to the basement. These basement windows were at ground level and were next to one of the main walkways going between the fraternity houses on the Vanderbilt campus. All the time that they were playing ping- pong, they had seen legs walking by on this walkway. They could not see the rest of the bodies due to the height of the windows.

Suddenly, a face pressed up against the window glass. "Hey, Pooh, watcha doin', Pooh? Playin' a little ping-pong on a Saturday night?"

Alpha Epsilon Pi members called themselves "Pi's" for short, but the popular southern fraternity boys degraded them by calling them "Pooh's."

Aaron looked up to the window and recognized the face of a member of Sigma Alpha Epsilon fraternity or SAE. On campus, they were known as the "E's" and their members were the most highly regarded boys on campus, all coming from extremely wealthy families. Many were great athletes, and they went out only with the most beautiful girls. The boy who was yelling into the window was the only Jewish member of Sigma Alpha Epsilon fraternity, Marty Shapiro, and Aaron knew him only casually. It was rumored on campus that SAE took in one Jewish member every few years to serve as their treasurer and to handle the fraternity's finances. Another face appeared in the window next to Marty.

"So, this is Saturday night at the Alpha Epsilon Pi house. Hell of a party," the boy shouted.

Aaron also recognized this boy whose name was Randy Wiley. He was another SAE senior.

Marty Shapiro spoke again, "I got someone out here who can kick your ass at ping-pong, Pooh. Ping-pong Pooh. I love it!"

The two boys' faces disappeared from the window. There was the sound of heavy steps coming down the outside stairs, and then there was banging at the basement door.

"Let us in, nerd," Randy demanded.

There were four of them, the two boys Aaron had seen at the window and their dates. All were carrying beer bottles, and, in unison, they took a swig.

Marty spoke, "Let's go, nerd. Marilyn here says she's gonna kick your ass in ping- pong."

Marty grabbed the blonde-haired girl standing next to him around the waist. Aaron recognized her immediately, Marilyn

Tate, one of the most beautiful and popular girls in school. A real southern belle, heavy southern accent: "Ya'll, you're so sweet." A typical member of Delta Delta Delta sorority. The Tri Delts only went out with SAE's. Marilyn was a junior at Vanderbilt, and she had been in one of Aaron's large lecture classes. She had always dressed up for class and looked like she stepped out of an Izod magazine advertisement.

"Should I let them in?" Ed asked.

"Sure, why not?" Aaron replied.

Aaron was slowly bouncing the ball on the ping-pong table with his left hand. He was a little angry but didn't want to reveal his feelings. The "partiers" walked into the basement.

Randy was tall and broad-shouldered with blonde hair and blue eyes. He was handsome enough to be a model except for the constant sneer he wore on his face. Marty was much shorter at 5 feet 5 inches and had a slender build. Marty had a large nose with a prominent hook, and his brown eyes darted back and forth as he spoke. Both boys were wearing khakis, Docksiders and SAE jackets.

Marty Shapiro spoke, "Marilyn here says she can kick any nerd's ass in ping-pong. Right, honey?"

Marilyn put her beer bottle down on the hard concrete floor. "You know it, honey. Just give me a paddle and let's go."

"Hah, hah, hah," Marilyn's friends laughed together.

The other girl with them also had blonde hair and blue eyes but was not nearly as beautiful as Marilyn. She was three inches shorter than Marilyn's 5 feet 8 inches, and she didn't have the 36C cups that Marilyn possessed or Marilyn's perfectly rounded ass. The girls were dressed identically with tight blue jeans and three triangles in a row, signifying Delta Delta Delta on their blue jackets.

Randy took Ed's paddle out of his hand.

"Leave the boy alone," demanded Aaron.

"Ooh, now I'm so scared. The Pooh told me to leave the boy alone." Randy waved the paddle menacingly in the air at Aaron as if he was going to joust with him. "Get out of the way, kid. Here, Marilyn, show him your stuff."

Marilyn took the paddle and took her position across the table from Aaron. She was truly one of the most gorgeous women Aaron had ever seen. He wondered why she was dating an asshole like Marty Shapiro. Marilyn wiped her mouth with the back of her hand. "Hit the ball to me," she demanded.

Aaron hit the ball to her, and they volleyed a few times before Marilyn hit a great spike shot that Aaron could only whiff at.

"Ha, ha, ha," Marilyn's friends laughed.

Marilyn's girlfriend said, "You gonna skunk him, right, baby? Do it for old Delta Delta Delta."

"I'm ready," Marilyn said. "Ping for serve."

"Uh, just a minute," interrupted Marty. "Just to make this a little more interesting, why don't we place a small wager on this match? We know how wealthy you must be to belong to this luxurious fraternity house." Marty pointed around the sparse basement and laughed. "Ten bucks, my money, says Marilyn is gonna beat you to 21. What do you say, big man?"

"Twenty-one, huh. OK. Let's play," Aaron replied.

"Kick his ass, honey," Marty said.

Marilyn served first. It was immediately obvious that she was the better player with great reflexes and coordination. However, she hadn't played in a while, and that combined with the fact that the lighting in the basement was far from optimal and took a while to get used to, gave Aaron a chance. Marilyn had a killer spin serve, though, the kind that came right at you, and when you tried to hit it straight back, went flying off the right side of the table. However, she netted two of her five services and ended serving, leading three to two.

"Whew, AE Pi's finest up against his true challenge. Kind of reminds me of our football game against you guys," Randy sneered. "Forty-two or was it 49 to nothin', Marty?"

Aaron began serving and served five straight points for himself. One serve landed on the back edge of Marilyn's side and jumped away, giving her no chance to return it. Two of the other services Marilyn tried to put away with spike returns, and her shots missed the table by the narrowest of margins. One of her returns hit the net, came over but flew off the table before hitting Aaron's side.

"Seven to three. Your serve now, angel lips," Aaron laughed.

Aaron didn't know why he'd called Marilyn angel lips, but it had an effect on her. She was flustered, and she took a moment to wipe the sweat off her brow and then unzipped her jacket. Underneath the jacket, she had on a bright pink Izod sweater which was stretched fully by her voluptuous chest.

The game went back and forth. Aaron was playing the best ping-pong of his life, and Ed was cheering his every point. Ed stood behind Aaron's end of the table and did his best to distract Marilyn.

"Come on, Aaron. Teach these spoiled brats here how to play ping-pong," Ed implored.

Aaron said, "Twenty to 14, my lead. You can serve." He tossed Marilyn the ball.

"I don't need any favors from you, big nose!" Marilyn yelled as she threw the ball back at Aaron, and it hit him in the nose.

"Whoa, baby, yeah. Eat his lunch, Marilyn," said Marty.

Aaron served the ball just as Marilyn turned to look at Marty. She made a swipe at the ball but hit it off the end of her paddle and out of bounds.

"Yea, Aaron. I knew you'd beat her," Ed yelled as he grabbed Aaron around the waist from behind.

"Couldn't you see I wasn't ready? Trying to cheat me? I was talking to my boyfriend."

Aaron looked across the table into Marilyn's eyes which were burning wildly with anger. This was the type of girl who wasn't used to losing. She got what she wanted in life; she always had and she always would.

"Fuckin' nerd tried to cheat her. That's the only way you could win. We're gonna play that point over," Marty said. He threw the ball back at Aaron.

"You won fair and square, Aaron," Ed said. "Don't play no more. It's almost time for me to go home."

"He's scared of you, Marilyn. He's scared you're gonna whip him. Shoot, ain't much though whippin' up a pre-med nerd," Marty said with contempt in his voice.

Aaron could hear the "partiers" as they passed by the basement windows. People all over the campus were enjoying themselves, and here he was with four people he disliked having to prove that he was…a man? He could feel himself sweating profusely.

"Twenty to 14," Marilyn stated, "let's see you get one more point off me."

Aaron served the ball, and Marilyn spiked it back.

"Fifteen to 20. Now I'll serve."

Marilyn threw her head back, tossing all the blonde curls behind her ears. She served four service winners in a row. Each serve Aaron barely got to, and the one he hit solidly flew off the end of the table. Marilyn's friends cheered every point. She smiled and bounced the ball on the table a few times.

"Come on, Aaron," implored Ed.

Marilyn served again, but this one wasn't quite as good. Aaron hit it back, aiming for the left side of the table. The ball carried back and landed near the middle of the table and deep. Marilyn hit a forehand smash which came off her paddle so quickly that Aaron could only raise his paddle in self-defense. The ball hit the top of the net, hung there for what seemed an eternity and then fell back onto Marilyn's side. It bounced, bounced, bounced. Aaron had won.

Marilyn threw her paddle down on the table. "Lucky fuckin' Jew," she sputtered. She turned to Marty. "Give me my jacket, Marty, and let's get the hell out of here. It stinks down here."

The four of them started walking towards the basement door, but Aaron ran over and blocked their way.

"I think you owe me something, Marty," Aaron said.

"I don't owe you a thing," Marty replied.

"Listen, hotshot, you bet ten bucks on your girlfriend, and I beat her. Now, you're not getting out of here until I get my money."

Marty replied, "The pre-med nerd's grown balls now. Beating a girl gave him balls. Get out of my way before I kick you out of my way. I've got a black belt in karate, and I'd just love to hurt you," Marty put his hand on Aaron's shoulder, but Aaron knocked it off.

"I want my money," Aaron demanded.

"Give him his money, and let's get the hell out of here," the other Tri Delt said.

Marty gave Aaron a long look. He reached into his wallet which was stuffed with money and pulled out a $10 bill and held it between two fingers. He then flicked it over his shoulder, and it floated slowly to the ground.

Aaron walked away from the door and picked the money up from the floor. Randy opened the door, and the four of them started walking up the stairs.

"Pleasure doing business with you folks," Aaron said. "This money will sure come in handy in medical school."

At the top of the stairs, Marty looked back at Aaron and gave him the dirtiest look Aaron had ever seen.

CHAPTER 4

1990

After four years of medical school and a three-year residency in internal medicine at Baylor College of Medicine in Houston, Aaron Bernstein moved to Dallas, Texas, where he completed a three-year fellowship in gastroenterology at Southwestern Medical School. The third year as a junior faculty member had been optional, but Aaron was uncertain if he wanted to stay in academic medicine or go into private practice, so he'd decided to use the third year to see if he liked academic medicine.

Three months into his third year of fellowship, Aaron was convinced that he wanted to go into private practice. He had been on call for emergencies every weekend and almost every weeknight those three months since he was one of the only doctors in the gastroenterology department who knew how to perform endoscopic procedures. Most of the other gastroenterologists in the department didn't have the time or inclination to do endoscopic procedures as they were too busy killing lab rats for one reason or another. They were all so caught up in their research that they ignored the fact that, to practice gastroenterology in the 1980s and 1990s, one had to be a proficient endoscopist. So, Aaron's life had been miserable as he got little sleep and was constantly taking care of critically-ill patients. Aaron felt he was an intern all over again.

Aaron decided that he would leave academics when the year was up and go into private practice. He picked out three areas in the country to practice: the Houston area, the Atlanta, Georgia area, and the Boca Raton, Florida, area where Aaron's elderly parents lived.

Aaron sent out his resume to over 100 gastroenterology practices in those three areas along with a cover letter stating his desire to go into private practice. The first practice he heard back from was a group of four gastroenterologists in Boca Raton, Florida, who invited him to come for an interview. Aaron bought his own plane ticket and flew to Fort Lauderdale where he rented a car and drove to Boca Raton.

Boca Raton was a beautiful city located on the east coast of Florida between Fort Lauderdale and West Palm Beach. It was a thriving community made up mainly of senior citizens. From the little knowledge that Aaron had of the economics of medicine, he knew this meant a large number of Medicare patients for whom reimbursement lagged far behind private pay insurance companies.

The four doctors in practice in Boca Raton were all between 45 and 55 years old. They showed Aaron their offices and the hospital at which they practiced which had been built approximately 40 years before. The hospital's architecture was elegant, but walking around inside made Aaron feel like he was back in the 1950s. Very little had been done to update the hospital, and even the equipment in the endoscopy lab was not up-to-date.

The doctors then took Aaron out to dinner at a cheap Italian restaurant with paper menus and crayons for the children. They took turns telling Aaron what a great opportunity it was for him to join their practice since they had all been successfully practicing for over 15 years, and their experience could guide him to success.

When dessert came, it was time to crunch the numbers, and Aaron asked them about his salary, how much time it would take to become a partner, and what his call schedule would be like. The leader of the group explained everything to Aaron and, at the same time, scribbled the data on Aaron's menu with a yellow crayon. Aaron would be an employee of theirs for five years and then could buy into the practice. For the first three years as an employee, Aaron would be on call every other night and every other weekend for the group, and, then for the last two years as an employee, Aaron would be on call every third night and every third weekend. They told Aaron that his starting salary would be $100,000 and would go up by $10,000 each year of employment. Aaron would receive bonuses based upon how much he collected minus the overhead he was costing. After five years, if the partners thought that Aaron had done a good job, they would offer him a chance to buy into the partnership for an amount that would be determined at that time.

Aaron thought it would be great to live near his parents in Boca Raton, but he quickly saw that this was not the job for him. He was single at the time, but he wanted to meet someone, get married and have a family. Being on call every other night would give him no time for a social life; he would either be working or recovering from the previous day's call. He could understand doing a little more frequent call for maybe six months or until he had built up his own practice, but to cover four busy doctors' practices every other night for three years seemed ridiculous. Also, there was no guarantee that, after five years, they would let him become a partner. They could decide that they didn't want him as an equal member of their group and could fire him. The head of the group mentioned that there would be a "no-compete" stipulation in Aaron's contract, saying that, if things didn't work out, he not only couldn't practice in their hospital but in any hospital within 20 miles.

Finally, the salary that they offered him was at the lower range of what gastroenterologists were being offered to start practice and was very low for someone who had done a third year of training. So, when Aaron got back to Dallas, he sent them a letter thanking them for their hospitality but rejecting their offer.

Aaron next flew to Houston to interview with three practices there. The first interview was with a large multi-specialty practice which owned its own hospital located across the street from the Texas Medical Center where Aaron had gone to medical school and done his residency. The hospital was called Houston United Hospital (HUH), and the group also owned a 15-story medical office building attached to the hospital. Aaron had seen the hospital when he was in training in Houston, but it wasn't associated with the medical school so he'd had no reason to go into it. Also, he'd never heard anyone ever mention Houston United Hospital.

Aaron interviewed with a gastroenterologist at Houston United Hospital who explained to him how their system worked. First, he told Aaron that the majority of their patients came from Mexico and South America. These were wealthy, upper-class people who weren't satisfied with the medical care that their countries offered and could pay cash to receive the care that they and their families wanted.

Second, the doctor said that every doctor's salary at HUH was based upon how much he billed. He added that a physician could bill for anything from blood work to an endoscopy to a

CT scan. The gastroenterologist told Aaron that, that morning, he had seen a wealthy industrialist from Ecuador for diarrhea who, on his review of systems, had checked yes for frequent headaches. Rather than sending him to a neurologist for an evaluation of the headaches, he had ordered the CAT scan of the brain himself, racking up approximately $3,000 in billings. The gastroenterologist also told Aaron that he rarely performed endoscopies and colonoscopies since the radiology department was so good at doing upper GI series and barium enemas. He added that he could actually bill more for these radiologic procedures than he could for doing endoscopic procedures.

Aaron thought that this was a strange and unethical way to run a practice. It financially rewarded the doctors for ordering tests, so naturally there would be tremendous incentives for the physicians to order more and more tests and to order the most expensive tests, even when these tests weren't in their own specialities. This was not only costly but also could be dangerous to the patients. So, Aaron crossed Houston United Hospital off his list.

****

The next doctor Aaron interviewed with in Houston was a solo practitioner named Bill Rosenbaum who, in his letter to Aaron, claimed that he had one of the busiest gastroenterology practices in the country. He practiced in a suburb of Houston called The Woodlands and had a procedure room right in his office.

Just as Aaron arrived at Dr. Rosenbaum's office, Dr. Rosenbaum was getting ready to start his last procedure of the morning. Aaron followed the receptionist into the procedure room where Dr. Rosenbaum was about to do a colonoscopy on a Hispanic woman who appeared to be in her mid-30s. The nursing assistant gave Dr. Rosenbaum a tourniquet which he tied around the patient's upper arm. She then handed Dr. Rosenbaum a syringe. Dr. Rosenbaum searched for a vein on the patient's forearm, and then he injected the contents of the syringe into the vein and removed the tourniquet.

"What was that you gave her?" Aaron asked.

"Versed 10 mg IV. We'll give that a minute or two to work, and then we'll get started."

Initially, the patient was talking excitedly in Spanish to the medical assistant, but, in three minutes, she stopped talking and was completely relaxed. Dr. Rosenbaum started the colonoscopy and completed it in ten minutes. Aaron had never seen a procedure done so quickly and wondered if Dr. Rosenbaum had gotten a good look at the colon. Aaron knew that he would never have been satisfied with the completeness of the exam he had just witnessed.

When the procedure was over, Aaron walked around to the other side of the table to make sure that the patient was still alive. There had been no monitors on the patient during the procedure to follow her blood pressure, pulse or oxygen saturation.

"What, worried about her breathing?" asked Dr. Rosenbaum. "I've done procedures like this for 20 years. All those monitors we're supposed to use now just add to the overhead. Young healthy people like this just need one good dose of Versed, and they're set."

"Uh, Dr. Rosenbaum," said the medical assistant, "I don't think this patient is breathing very well."

Dr. Rosenbaum made a fist with his right hand and rubbed the patient's sternum as hard as he could with his knuckles. The patient made a faint whimper and then cried out in pain and gasped for air.

"And when all else fails, there's still the trusty old sternal rub," laughed Dr. Rosenbaum.

Aaron was appalled. He'd been taught to always have an IV in the patient while doing procedures and to give sedation in small amounts. With an IV in, if the patient got into trouble, medicine could be given to reverse sedation and wake the patient up. With no IV in, one was left with the brute force of the sternal rub which, if the patient was too sedated, wouldn't work.

Aaron's concerns about Dr. Rosenbaum were further confirmed when Dr. Cruz, who was a family practitioner in the office next door, stopped by Dr. Rosenbaum's office to get a quick consult. The family practitioner was seeing a 35-year-old woman in his office who, on routine blood work, had an alkaline phosphatase level more than twice the normal value. The alkaline phosphatase was an enzyme whose elevation could signal either liver or bone disease, and Aaron knew that further blood tests could determine its origin. Dr. Cruz asked Dr. Rosenbaum if he needed to be concerned about this abnormality. Dr. Rosenbaum just laughed, patted Dr. Cruz on the shoulder and said, "Naw, we see it all the time in young women. Wouldn't think about it twice. Don't even bother sending her to me. Call me if you've got anyone that needs a procedure."

Aaron wanted to follow Dr. Cruz out the office door and tell him how to work up an elevated alkaline phosphatase level, but he restrained himself. He knew that this wasn't the practice for him. So, Aaron made an excuse that he had another appointment to go to, and he left Dr. Rosenbaum's office.

****

The final group that Aaron interviewed with in Houston was a group of eight gastroenterologists who covered six hospitals throughout the city. They had a moderately busy practice, but a large portion of their income was derived from doing clinical trials on their patients. Before new drugs could be approved by the FDA for general usage, they had to be rigorously tested in clinical trials. In the last stages of these trials, the drugs were matched against similar drugs or against placebos to determine their efficacy and risks. This group in Houston owned their own endoscopy center and employed nurses to act as study coordinators so that they could do drug trials on their own patients.

The two doctors who Aaron interviewed with told him that they got paid an average of $5000 a patient to put them on these new drugs or placebo and then to monitor them for six weeks to six months, depending on what the end point was.

Aaron bluntly asked them, "Do you think it's fair and ethical to refer your own patients to these drug studies that you're going to profit from? I mean, these patients trust you enough to let you be their doctors. Aren't you abusing that trust to make money off of them?"

One of the doctors coolly answered, "You're pretty naïve. This is how medicine makes advances, through placebo-controlled trials. Why shouldn't we conduct the trials? We're better at doing them than the medical school, and we can usually do them cheaper for the drug companies. Plus, the patient involved in the trial often gets paid and gets the medication for free."

"I'm not saying there's anything wrong with placebo-controlled trials," Aaron responded. "But, if a patient that you had taken care of for ten years had been doing well on a particular drug for ten years, would you take him off it just to enroll him in one of your studies?"

"We might, just might," the other doctor answered. "So, where else are you looking for a job?"

Aaron knew this was a signal that they were no longer interested in him joining their group. They made small talk for a few minutes, and then Aaron left.

****

Aaron interviewed with five groups in the Atlanta, Georgia, area, but, when he met Cole Stone and saw Pleasant Point, Georgia, he knew that that was where he wanted to practice.

Cole was in his early 40s but already had a full head of gray hair. Cole's hair was thick and wavy and never moved on his head. Cole had a handsome, rugged face, pockmarked by acne scars. He was always tanned, no doubt from the time he spent outside hunting which was his hobby and the passion in his life. Cole's voice was deep and projected confidence.

Cole picked Aaron up at his hotel in downtown Atlanta in his new white Mercedes sedan. The car was the top-of-the-line Mercedes and had every option imaginable including wipers on each of the front headlights, heated seats and the finest sound system available.

As they drove up to Pleasant Point on Interstate 85, Cole told Aaron the history of Pleasant Point. Pleasant Point had been a quiet town for years, located ten miles north of Atlanta. There were farms and ranches in the city and not much else. Then, in the late 70s and early 80s, "white flight" had occurred with many white families fleeing the city of Atlanta and looking for suburbs to live in. North Atlanta was the first place people moved to since it was right next to Atlanta, but North Atlanta was "landlocked" and soon there was no more room there.

The leaders of Pleasant Point had anticipated its expansion and had worked hard to have a strong infrastructure for the city. They built safe, wide roads, put a lot of money into excellent schools and supported the city's hospital, Pleasant Point General Hospital.

Initially, most of the people who lived in Pleasant Point commuted to jobs in Atlanta, but then Pleasant Point began to attract businesses which wanted to move their corporate headquarters there. Cole drove Aaron to an area in east Pleasant Point called Industrial Park where the corporate headquarters for three Fortune 100 companies were located. Out in the middle of nowhere in pastureland, these huge companies had built enormous campuses with massive buildings.

Cole assured Aaron that many more companies were in the process of moving their headquarters to Pleasant Point including companies involved in computers and technology. With regard to the telecom industry, many of these companies had already moved into Pleasant Point along Hatfield Expressway in what was being called the technology corridor, and others were now moving to Pleasant Point.

Cole drove Aaron to Pleasant Point General Hospital and introduced him to several doctors there. The hospital seemed relatively quiet, but Cole assured Aaron that, in the last few years, the number of patients had skyrocketed and that the greatest growth was yet to come. This was echoed by the hospital's administrator, John Smith, who talked to Aaron briefly and by one of the family doctors Aaron met in the hospital, Jeff Conner.

Cole then drove Aaron by the site of the future Pleasant Point Physicians Hospital which was going to be built right next to the highway in west Pleasant Point.

"Ten to 15 years from now, this will be the hospital in Pleasant Point," Cole told Aaron. "By then, we will have brought in several more partners, and we'll have satellite offices out here."

For lunch, Cole took Aaron to Peachtree Country Club which was located in west Pleasant Point. They were met there by the other two partners in the gastroenterology group. The four of them walked out of the clubhouse building and down to the huge gorgeous swimming pool where Cole said his wife and kids spent a lot of their summer. Then, they walked behind the clubhouse so that Aaron could see Peachtree's magnificent golf course.

"Do you play here often?" Aaron asked Cole.

"Nope, don't play golf. Hunting is my main hobby, and I sometimes fool around on my little boat at Lake Pleasant Point. I love to bring the family here on Friday nights though. They have family night geared towards the kids with an awesome buffet, make your own sundaes. And they have clowns, face-painting. My kids are too old for a lot of that stuff, but they still like coming here and seeing their friends."

Cole introduced Aaron to other doctors from Pleasant Point General Hospital who were having lunch at the country club. He first met Langston Harris who was the chief of pathology at the hospital. Langston was a chubby, balding man who constantly smiled. Langston was having lunch with two men, one of whom he introduced as his stockbroker, and the other he introduced as his chief financial advisor.

"So, you're thinking of joining Cole's practice," Langston said. "Well, let me tell you, you couldn't practice with a nicer, more honorable man. I couldn't imagine anyone better to practice with. This Pleasant Point area is a goldmine for a young, talented, aggressive doctor. You let me know if there is anything that my people or I can do to help you."

Cole then brought Aaron to a table where a very tall, muscular black man was sitting with a short white man. "Thomas," Cole said to the black man, "I want you to meet Aaron Bernstein. He's thinking of joining our group. Aaron, Thomas Kelly is the chief of the radiology group at our hospital."

Thomas stood up, and he towered over Cole and Aaron. He extended his arm towards Aaron, and his hand engulfed Aaron's hand. "Cole's gonna need more help," Thomas laughed as he crushed Aaron's hand in greeting. "You should think seriously about joining his practice."

"I'm amazed to see all of you doctors at a country club in the middle of the day," Aaron said as he rubbed his right hand with his left. "Who's doing all the work?"

"Today is one of my short days, Aaron," Thomas replied. "I just work a few hours, and then I take the afternoon off to play golf. I'm actually meeting with my financial advisor now – Sid Tufts. This is Cole Stone, our community's leading gastroenterologist, and his partner-to-be Aaron Bernstein." The small white male stood up, and Aaron waved to him.

When they were done eating, they left the country club, and Cole drove Aaron through some of the most exclusive neighborhoods in Pleasant Point. Aaron saw the gorgeous houses of sports stars, industrial titans and celebrities. They went through one neighborhood after another that had houses worth a million dollars or more. Aaron nodded when Cole mentioned that Pleasant Point was the wealthiest suburb of Atlanta.

"Some day, you could have a house like this," Cole told Aaron.

Aaron could only stammer, "Yeah."

Finally, Cole drove Aaron to his house. It wasn't as elaborate as many of the houses they'd seen, but it sat on over an acre of land and was approximately 6,000 square feet.

They sat in oversized, plush leather chairs in Cole's living room. Cole said, "Aaron, you're a hardworking guy, and I think you'd be a good fit for our practice. These are my terms which are not negotiable. You'll work as an employee for three years making $110,000 a year. You'll get a bonus each year determined by how much your collections exceed your overhead. After three years, you'll have five years to buy into this partnership at a cost of $500,000. That will be easy for you to come up with. Here's my last tax return." Cole took out some papers from a large brown envelope. "You can see that last year, I made over $600,000 from my practice alone, so your buy-in won't be a big deal."

Aaron was sold. The opportunities in Pleasant Point seemed limitless. It was a wealthy community with an excellent, established hospital and a new hospital being built. The community was growing rapidly, and the people moving in were young people with insurance.

Plus, being single and Jewish, Aaron wanted to practice in an area where he would have a chance to meet Jewish women. Atlanta had a large, active Jewish community with many singles.

Initially, Aaron told Cole he'd have to think about the offer, but, by the next day, he was sure Pleasant Point was the right place for him. He called Cole and accepted.

PART 2

CHAPTER 1

2003

It all started with a letter. Dr. Aaron Bernstein went through his mail as usual in the afternoon after seeing his last patient. Aaron was 44 years old and still had curly brown hair, but he had a rapidly-expanding bald spot in the middle of his head. He weighed 190 pounds but still looked athletic with broad shoulders and muscular legs. His face was boyish and unlined, making him look ten years younger. He got to the letter from Denialcare and opened it up. It was addressed to AHC Healthcare Receivable Management. It was regarding Denialcare 65 member Mary Cocha and had her dates of service from September 13 through September 17.

Dear Mr. Jackson,

Your request for reconsideration of the certification of the above-noted dates of service for the above-referenced Denialcare 65 member has been reviewed. Based on the clinical information made available for review, the patient was admitted through the emergency room on September 13, 2002, with complaints of lightheadedness and rectal bleeding. The patient's temperature was 99 degrees, pulse 85, respirations 20 and blood pressure 90/60. Her rectal exam revealed large hemorrhoids. The patient had a past history of diverticulitis. The EKG showed normal sinus rhythm. Hemoglobin was 10.5. Hematocrit was 32.1. In addition, the Red Blood Cell Tagged Scan was negative for active bleeding. Admitting orders included n.p.o. except for sips of water, continuous cardiac monitoring, IV fluids, vital signs every four hours and possible scheduling of colonoscopy. On Saturday, September 14, the patient was having no further bleeding. Her temperature was 99.1 degrees. IV fluids continued. Hemoglobin was 8.9, and hematocrit was 26.8. She continued to receive IV fluids, and she received oral preparation for a colonoscopy. On September 16, 2002, the patient underwent the colonoscopy by Dr. Aaron Bernstein, a gastroenterologist, at which time four rectal polyps were removed. There was blood noted throughout the colon attributed to significant diverticulosis. Post-procedure orders included saline lock and a full liquid diet. The patient's hemoglobin was 9, and hematocrit was 27. On Tuesday, September 17, 2002, the patient was discharged to home. Based on available clinical information, it appears that, by Saturday, September 14, the patient was no longer experiencing any bleeding, her vital signs were stable and she was awaiting preparation for a colonoscopy which was not performed until Monday, September 16. Therefore, the denial for dates of service September 14 through September 17 will be upheld due to delay of care and lack of medical necessity. The member has no financial responsibility for services denied as a result of this decision. Since this case involved a retrospective review of a benefit determination according to the Georgia Department of Insurance and HCFA (Health Care Financing Administration) guidelines, it is not subject to review by an independent review organization. This is the final decision in this matter.

Sincerely,

James Buchman, M.D.
Medical Director

The letter was copied to the patient, to the hospital, to Dr. Aaron Bernstein and to the patient's family doctor, Dr. Jeff Conner.

Aaron was stunned when he read this because it meant he would not get paid for taking care of this patient throughout the weekend as well as for the colonoscopy he had performed on her. He remembered her well even though it had been six months since the patient had been in the hospital. She was a 75-year-old woman who appeared older and was extremely scared when he saw her in the emergency room. She had been bleeding for approximately 12 hours when she finally came to the hospital in an ambulance, and the fact that she had a significant drop in her blood pressure and a significant increase in her pulse when standing told him that her bleeding was significant. Sure enough, her blood count had dropped two full points by the next day with just IV fluids.

Aaron sent back a letter copying it to the hospital and to the patient as well as to the patient's family doctor.

Dear Dr. Buchman,

I strongly ask you to reconsider your decision not to pay the hospital's fees as well as my charges for patient, Mary Cocha, from Saturday, September 14, until Tuesday, September 17, 2002. There was no way of knowing when the patient had been in the hospital less than 24 hours that she was not going to have further bleeding. As you stated in your letter, her blood count had dropped two points from hemoglobin of 10.5 to hemoglobin of 8.5 just with intravenous fluids. How was I going to know that the hemoglobin was not going to continue to drop and that the patient would become more and more anemic? As you are aware, acute anemia in the elderly can be associated with strokes and heart attacks. The patient needed to be watched carefully over the next few days. Of course, if I had a crystal ball and could have seen into the future and known that the patient was not going to continue to bleed, I would gladly have sent her home after she had been in the hospital for less than 24 hours. However, no crystal ball was available to me at the time, and, after seeing a significant drop in blood count in a patient who had significant orthostasis on admission, I felt that she needed to be watched carefully for several days in the hospital prior to having the diagnostic procedure of colonoscopy to determine where she was bleeding from. I strongly ask you to reconsider your decision. I am sending a copy of this letter to the State Insurance Commission so that they will also be aware of what is going on in this case.

I look forward to hearing from you shortly.

Sincerely,

Aaron Bernstein, M.D.

Aaron felt better after completing this letter. Previously, he had sent letters off for reconsideration of payment but had never received a positive result. But this time, he knew he had a strong case. He waited two weeks, and, finally, a letter came back from Dr. Buchman, Medical Director of Denialcare.

Dear Dr. Bernstein,

We have received your recent letter. However, as we stated in our initial review, there is no evidence that this patient needed to be kept in the hospital beyond Saturday, September 14, when she was no longer experiencing any bleeding. As mentioned in our previous letter, her vital signs were stable, and the only thing that was done for her was preparation for a colonoscopy. We will not send you any further correspondence regarding this decision.

Sincerely,

James Buchman, M.D.
Medical Director, Denialcare

Aaron made copies of all of the correspondence and sent them with the following letter to the State Insurance Commission.

Dear Sirs,

As you can see, the hospital and I were denied payment for taking care of a critically-ill patient from the time of September 14, 2002, through September 17, 2002. I feel this is grossly unfair. If your mother or father went into the hospital with severe lower GI bleeding and was sent home less than 24 hours later because they had no further bleeding, you would feel that they had received improper care. People with significant lower GI bleeds can re-bleed. They can re-bleed massively. These people need to be watched closely, the source of the bleeding found if possible and treated appropriately. I would greatly appreciate your prompt attention to this matter.

Sincerely,
Aaron Bernstein, M.D.

When Aaron heard back from the State Insurance Commission, this was their reply:

Dear Dr. Bernstein,

We have reviewed your case regarding patient, Mary Cocha. At this time, we do not feel anything further needs to be done regarding Denialcare's denial of payment for this patient. No further correspondence will be sent on this case as we have closed our file on it.

Sincerely,

Joseph Minor
Georgia State Insurance Commission

Aaron opened the bottom left-hand drawer of his desk where he had set up a folder for insurance claims denied. What had initially started as a thin folder containing two or three forms was now overflowing with unpaid claims. Inside this folder were ten identical letters from the State Insurance Commission refusing to look further into denied claims. Aaron dropped the latest letter into the folder, slammed the drawer shut, picked up his stethoscope and walked out of his office to begin rounds. On his way out the door, he passed by his office manager and said to her, "Wendy, from now on, I will no longer see Denialcare patients. Take me off the Denialcare 65 plan."

Wendy looked at him, raised her eyebrows and said, "OK. But pretty soon, there's not going to be any insurance companies left for you to see patients." She walked back to her desk, pulled out the book that had all the insurance plans in it and scratched off the Denialcare 65 under Aaron's name.

CHAPTER 2

Dr. Vijay Givagushrai felt like the luckiest man in the world. He was making a great living taking care of patients and had time for dating nurses he met in the hospital. Who would have thought 36 years ago when he was born a poor boy in India that he would have achieved this success? But now, he was a "hospitalist," and, as a hospitalist, there was a steady stream of patients for him to take care of. He smiled and hung up the phone after speaking to Aaron Bernstein. He'd consulted Aaron on a patient that he had admitted to the hospital, a patient of one of the family doctors in Pleasant Point, Georgia, named Jeff Conner. Jeff Conner, like many of the family doctors and internists in Pleasant Point, had decided no longer to take care of hospital patients, and they turned these patients over to doctors like Vijay. Aaron had been a little upset on the phone talking to him, mainly because the patient had already been in the hospital for a couple of days. Vijay explained that he had tried to consult Aaron's partner, Cole Stone, yesterday, but Cole had refused to see the patient, saying that Vijay had to do several more diagnostic tests before he would agree to see the patient. Vijay had just laughed at Cole's request, and, when he found out that Aaron was going to be on call the next day, he decided to save the consult for him.

The patient was a 58-year-old white male named Jumpy Johnson with abdominal pain. He'd come in and the emergency room doctor had put him on a morphine pain pump, done some x-rays and labs, and nothing had shown up. They'd ordered a CAT scan of the abdomen and pelvis which was normal and had admitted him to Vijay's service.

****

Vijay was the only one of the five children in his family who had pursued an education. Vijay's brothers and sisters were all common laborers in India with high school educations or less. Vijay went to college and medical school in India and then came over to the United States and did a residency in Arkansas at the urging of Dr. Bissel-Mozel who wanted Vijay to experience American medicine. Arkansas was the only place in the United States that would take him, but it came with a catch. After he did his internal medicine residency, he had to spend four years working as the sole doctor in the small town of Fort Springs, Arkansas.

Very few people had insurance in Fort Springs, Arkansas, and Vijay scraped by financially. He took care of patients in his office and in the hospital, and, sometimes in the 20-bed hospital, eight to ten of the patients would be his. There was a surgeon in the next town and a general practitioner within 50 miles who came in to deliver the babies, but Vijay was responsible for everything else. He'd worked hard his four years, but, after four years, his net worth was less than $50,000. He had no house; he rented a small duplex. He owned his own car, but it was a six-year-old Chevy Impala he had trouble fitting into due to his size. Despite his deprived childhood, Vijay had grown to 6 feet 3 inches, and he now weighed 240 pounds, giving him an imposing presence. The people in the town liked him and seemed to respect him even if he was a "furner," but they wanted nothing to do with him socially.

Then in late 2001 came the call that changed Vijay's life. One of his buddies from residency, Sirha Khan, had opened up an internal medicine practice in Pleasant Point, Georgia, and had been a spectacular failure until he gave up the practice to become a hospitalist. Hospitalists were a new breed of doctors who just took care of patients in the hospital, he had told Vijay. They took care of walk-in patients admitted through the emergency room or the patients of other doctors when those doctors didn't want to come to the hospital. Vijay, at first, thought it was a strange setup. In Fort Springs, he'd always felt that the most rewarding part of being a doctor and being an internist was the hospital work. In the hospital, he got to see really sick patients, take care of them and get them better. In the office, it was only a matter of dispensing pills and listening to neurotic people. How internists and family doctors could give up this rewarding part of medicine he couldn't understand, but he could understand the financial aspect of it. These doctors obviously could see more patients in the office and make more money that way, so it was no longer financially rewarding for them to go to the hospital. Internists used to see ten to 15 people a day in the office; many now saw 30 to 40 patients a day. Plus, there were the headaches of taking care of hospital patients: the unpredictable hours at which they showed up, the constant pestering from the floor nurses and the increased liability that went with taking care of truly sick people.

Dr. Khan was keeping a census of 20 to 40 patients in the hospital at Pleasant Point General Hospital and Physicians Hospital of Pleasant Point, and he told Vijay that there were many more patients for him. Vijay drove to Pleasant Point, looked around and was very impressed. Pleasant Point was one of the fastest-growing cities in the country. Dr. Khan took him out and showed him all the restaurants. There were Indian restaurants, and Dr. Khan assured him that there were plenty of single Indian women. Vijay gave notice in Fort Springs that he was leaving, and everyone seemed sad to see him go. There was no internist to replace him right away in Fort Springs, although Vijay understood that they were going to be bringing in someone else from India soon.

Vijay had moved his few things to Pleasant Point and started as a hospitalist one year before. The first thing he had done was to go to the two emergency rooms and meet the emergency room doctors. He told them he was willing to take all the unassigned internal medicine and family practice patients. This usually brought him at least two to three patients a day, many of whom did not have insurance. Next, he went to the doctors who did ER call for internal medicine and family practice and told them that he would be willing to take their call for them. Enough of them were willing to let him do it that he was on call for the ER an average of ten days a month at Pleasant Point General Hospital and five days a month at Physicians Hospital of Pleasant Point. As more and more internists and family doctors heard about him, they called him over the next few months, saying that they no longer wanted to have a hospital practice and asking him to take care of their hospital patients. He happily agreed because these were all insured patients. Over a year's time, he'd built up a practice where he now carried a census of 20 to 30 patients in the hospital. His overhead was the 6 percent that his collection agency took to collect his bills. He did absolutely no office work and, upon discharge, sent the patients back to their internists or family doctors.

Vijay laughed as he closed the chart on Jumpy Johnson. He liked getting to consult the specialists as this was the trick to hospitalist care. The larger his census of patients was, the less time he had to take care of each one. Vijay had a rule that each patient had to have at least one consultant on the case to actually take care of the patient, and, on most patients, Vijay had several consultants. Vijay had no idea what was going on with Mr. Jumpy Johnson. He'd been yelling in pain for 36 hours now. He hoped that Dr. Aaron Bernstein could figure it out.

CHAPTER 3

Jumpy Johnson knew that he'd been a bad boy. He also knew that, at the age of 58, he shouldn't think of himself as a boy anymore. But he did, especially when his wife, Sue Ellen, went away and left him alone for the weekend. She left him alone with instructions for him to stay in the house. She'd already made him dinner and all the meals he would need. The one thing that Jumpy knew he shouldn't eat was the one thing he had a terrible craving for: barbeque. The last time he's eaten barbeque, he had gotten sick as a dog. He'd gone to Junior's Barbecue Restaurant with Sue Ellen and spent the next day at home puking his guts out and having diarrhea and belly pain. That had been a year ago, and, for the next year, Sue Ellen kept him from eating barbeque. But now she was away, so Jumpy got into his pickup truck and drove to the barbeque restaurant. He'd eaten two pulled pork sandwiches plus an order of barbequed sausage and then headed home. That night, Sue Ellen came home, and he'd been asleep. So, she lay down next to him and went to sleep. In the middle of the night, he woke up screaming. His insides were on fire. He was sick. Sue Ellen's first question was, "What did you have for dinner?"

Jumpy replied, "I just ate the food you made me, honey."

"Then why are you so sick?"

"I don't know." He ran to the bathroom and began vomiting.

"I'm getting scared," said Sue Ellen. "I'm calling 911."

"Call Dr. Conner first."

Sue Ellen called Dr. Conner's office and received the following recorded message: "Dr. Conner's office is closed now. Our regular office hours are Mondays to Thursdays from 9:00 a.m. to 5:00 p.m. with the office being closed for lunch from noon to 1:00 p.m. On Fridays, we are open from 9:00 a.m. to noon. If you have an emergency and need immediate medical assistance, hang up the phone now and call 911 or proceed immediately to the nearest emergency room. If you have a routine matter, call us back during office hours. Have a pleasant day."

Sue Ellen hung up. "I'm calling 911," she said. "All I got at Dr. Conner's office was a recording."

****

The paramedics came to their house and found Jumpy hunched over the toilet. He was red, covered with sweat and was squirming in pain.

"We're taking you to the hospital," they said.

"No, I'm not gonna go… I'm not gonna go!"

"Ma'am, your husband needs to go to the hospital."

"You're going!" said Sue Ellen as she packed a bag for him.

"Wait a minute… If I'm going, I'm gonna pack my own bag."

Jumpy stumbled to his bedroom, opened the closet door and pulled out some clothes. He could barely move and had to crawl over to the dresser to get some underpants. He picked out his favorite shoes, his slippers, and then he picked out a bathrobe. The last thing he picked out he put at the very bottom of his bag. It was his father's loaded German Luger revolver.

Wherever he went, the gun went, and now was not going to be an exception.

****

When they arrived at Pleasant Point General Hospital, the emergency room doctor was shocked at how dehydrated Jumpy was. They drew his blood and started an IV.

"We're gonna admit you to the hospital, sir," the ER doctor said.

"I'm having tremendous pain," Jumpy said. It was now 3:00 a.m. "Call my doctor, Dr. Conner."

The ER doctor went back to his list of doctors and saw that Dr. Conner did not do his own admissions. All of his admissions were directed to Dr. Givagushrai.

He called Dr. Givagushrai on the phone. "We got a 58-year-old white male here. He's got severe abdominal pain. He's been vomiting. He's got diarrhea. It may be just a bad case of the flu or some kind of food poisoning, but I think he needs to come in. Labs look OK, mildly elevated white count at 13,000. Liver tests, amylase, lipase all OK. Two-view abdominal x-rays are normal. Conner is his family doctor."

"No problem," said Vijay. "Put him in under my service. I'll see him later today."

So Jumpy was admitted to Vijay Givagushrai's service. Because he continued to writhe in pain, the ER doctor came into his room and said, "I'm going to CAT scan your abdomen and pelvis."

They sent Jumpy on his stretcher to the radiology suite for the CAT scan. When he got back, he was still having such severe pain that the ER doctor called Vijay Givagushrai and said, "Listen, this guy, Johnson, is having such severe pain, I think he needs to be on a morphine pain pump."

"Go ahead and do it," said Vijay. "And I'll see him first thing in the morning."

Jumpy had never been on a pain pump before. It was the most wonderful feeling he'd ever had. They instructed him how to give himself morphine. He just pushed the button and injected more and more morphine until he went to sleep.

****

They wheeled his stretcher up to the fourth floor. Mrs. Johnson had gone home an hour before after being assured by the ER doctor that Jumpy was stable.

"Mr. Johnson, I'm your nurse, Eve," said a large black woman. "What medications do you take at home?"

Jumpy was in a morphine-induced fog. "I'm on Cardizem and Lasix for my blood pressure and Synthroid for my thyroid." The one thing he didn't tell her was the medications he was on for schizophrenia. He'd been a paranoid schizophrenic for years. He was treated at the VA Hospital in Atlanta for his schizophrenia by Dr. Fried, whom he saw once every other month for five minutes just so he could convince that Jew that he wasn't going to kill himself or anybody else before he could get his prescriptions refilled.

Jumpy took his schizophrenia medicines faithfully because he was scared not to. Ten years before when he'd not taken his medicines, he'd ended up almost shooting his son-in-law. A couple of nights in jail had cured him of that. Now he took his medicines all the time. But the only people who knew about his paranoid schizophrenia were Jumpy, his family, the doctor at the VA Hospital, Dr. Fried, and his family doctor, Dr. Conner. And

Jumpy fully expected Dr. Conner to be there when he woke up to get him back on his medicines.

****

Jumpy was surprised to wake up and be face to face with a tall, burly man who was a foreigner. The man said, "Hi, Mr. Johnson. I'm Vijay Givagushrai, and I'm going to be your doctor while you're in the hospital."

Every time the foreigner said something to him, Jumpy pushed on his button to activate his pain pump and put more morphine into his system. He felt great. He felt like he was floating. He wasn't having any more diarrhea or vomiting. The pain was still there but wasn't as bad as it had been. But he'd continued to moan and groan. What was that Indian man saying? He said my blood work is OK, and my CAT scan is OK. But he feels like he needs to have a specialist come and take a look at me. He's going to have a Dr. Cole Stone come in and see me. The Indian doctor did a brief exam, and Jumpy hated to be touched by him. He wondered when Dr. Conner would be in to take over his care.

Well, at least Stone sounded like an American name, he thought. It wasn't an Indian, and it wasn't a Jew. If there was one thing that Jumpy hated as much as niggers, it was Jews. He didn't want them to be his doctors which was why he picked a doctor like Dr. Conner – a good Protestant man. He always resented having to see that Jew, Dr. Fried, at the VA. He didn't want Jews to be his doctors or lawyers; he didn't want to have anything to do with them.

****

Jumpy ate the Jell-O and juices they gave him that day and sat waiting for Dr. Stone. Any time any nurses came in, he would grab his belly and complain about how much pain he was having. Then, when the nurses left, he laughed. He kept his suitcase under his bed, and, every few hours, he would pick it up and look through it, making sure his gun was still in the bottom. He always kept it loaded with all six chambers filled with bullets.

That afternoon, they brought a new patient to the bed next to him. He was a man named Bruce Herman who, the recovery room nurse loudly informed the floor nurse, had just had a penile prosthesis placed. Because of his other medical problems, his doctors were going to observe him for a few days. Jumpy thought that was OK although the man with the manufactured dick did look a little suspicious to him.

"Why are they putting someone who has a phony whacker in the bed next to me?" Jumpy thought out loud.

Sue Ellen came in that afternoon to stay with Jumpy, and she missed seeing Dr. Givagushrai. She waited at bedside for Dr. Stone, but he never came. Neither she nor Jumpy knew that Dr. Givagushrai had called Dr. Stone, asking him to come by and see Jumpy, but Dr. Stone had replied that it didn't sound like Mr. Johnson needed a gastroenterology consult. Dr. Stone said he was too busy and that Dr. Givagushrai should do other tests first, and then he would see him if still necessary.

Jumpy couldn't sleep that night, so he gave himself an extra shot of pain medicine.

****

The next afternoon, Dr. Stone wasn't there to see him, but there was some Jew doctor there in his place, a Dr. Aaron

Bernstein. Jumpy had now been off his schizophrenia medicine for over 36 hours and was starting to get a little more suspicious.

"Why the hell is a Jew here in the room with me?" he thought.

Anytime Dr. Bernstein asked him a question, Jumpy would pretend to cough and would cough through the words "Jew, Jew." He grasped the pain pump button tightly between his fingers and pressed it as often as he could.

Dr. Bernstein said, "I'm going to examine you."

Jumpy didn't want him to lay his dirty Jew hands on him. He had to close his eyes and grit his teeth as the doctor examined him. When Dr. Bernstein pushed on his belly, it really didn't hurt Jumpy, but Jumpy knew if he said it didn't hurt, they'd stop the pain medication. He was feeling too good on his pain medicine, so he screamed and yelled, "Shit, oh, shit!" when Dr. Bernstein pushed on his belly.

"I don't know what's going on," said Dr. Bernstein. "Everything so far looks normal. I guess this could be something involving your colon or small intestine. Do you think you could take a bowel prep? In other words, drink some laxatives to clean out your system so that we could look up and down with scopes?"

"Look up with a what?" asked Jumpy.

"Do endoscopic procedures, where we put you to sleep and look with scopes at your esophagus, stomach, intestine and colon."

"How in the hell are ya gonna do that?"

"After we make you sleepy, we numb your throat with a spray. We place a tube with a camera and light on it through your mouth and look at your esophagus, stomach and intestine. We then use another tube and go in through your rectum…."

"Through my butt hole?"

"That's right, up through your rectum and examine your colon."

"You sure as shit ain't doin' anything like that to me! You keep your dirty, stinking hands off me!"

"Maybe I'd better talk to your wife."

"She ain't gonna let you do nuthin' like that to me."

"It was nice to meet you, Mr. Johnson." Dr. Bernstein got up and left the room. He immediately called Dr. Givagushrai from the nursing station.

"Vijay, there's something strange about this Mr. Johnson. His pain seems so out of proportion to his findings. And he seems so angry and suspicious. I'd like to scope him and see if anything is going on."

Vijay replied, "I think he's sundowning, got his nights and days confused from being in the hospital and being on pain meds. I agree with endoscopy and colonoscopy. Maybe call his wife and get the OK."

Aaron called the patient's wife. There was no one home, so he left a message on the answering machine asking her to call him back. He wrote bowel prep orders in Mr. Johnson's chart to start the next day. In the meantime, Mr. Johnson was growing restless and more and more agitated. He reached again under his bed and made sure the suitcase was where he had left it.

CHAPTER 4

After leaving Mr. Johnson's room, Aaron hurried back to his office. There was something about Mr. Johnson that really worried Aaron, but he wasn't sure what it was and didn't have time now to analyze it. Aaron was hurrying to finish work because his oldest son, David, had his first violin recital that night. Aaron knew there was a good chance he'd have to miss the recital due to being on call, but he wanted to make every effort to go.

Aaron walked into his office and saw a stack of ten patient charts on his desk, all with detailed messages attached to their fronts written by his medical assistant, Pamela. He dialed Pamela's extension, and ten seconds later, she walked into Aaron's office.

Pamela was 28 years old and had been Aaron's medical assistant for three years. She had never been married, but she had three children with three different fathers. Despite the number of pregnancies, Pamela was in great shape. She always wore the tightest-fitting scrubs to work including a pair of hot pink scrubs through which, with very little effort, one could see the outline of her tiny bikini underwear. She'd gotten a boob job from one of the local plastic surgeons two years before and now proudly sported 36Ds. Pamela often brought catalogs to work which sold bathing suits or lingerie, and she loved to loudly discuss with the other employees which tiny bikinis, thongs or teddies she would be purchasing. Aaron noticed that a lot of these conversations seemed to get louder when he was in Pamela's vicinity, but, now that he had been happily married for over ten years, he did his best to ignore them.

There was also the rumor that Pamela was having an affair with Dr. Cole Stone. Aaron had first heard about this months before when one of the orthopedic surgeons told him that he'd seen Cole and a tall, sexy, blonde woman who matched Pamela's description fooling around on a boat docked next to his boat on Lake Pleasant Point. Aaron remembered that Pamela had come to work that following Monday morning and had talked about what a great time she'd had that weekend on the lake. She said she was glad that she went for her twice weekly tanning sessions at the tanning salon because they had given her a "base tan" that protected her from being burned from the sun reflecting off the lake. Of note, Cole had come to work that Monday with a deeply-sunburned face. Aaron noticed that Cole and Pamela always smiled at each other and seemed to have a lot to say to each other.

As a medical assistant, though, Pamela was very intelligent and efficient, and the patients loved her. She could get to the crux of the patients' problems quickly over the phone and always provided Aaron with the necessary information to make proper decisions regarding their care. The patients trusted her and sometimes were even willing to share thoughts and feelings with her that they were embarrassed to mention to anyone else.

Aaron and Pamela had already gone through a stack of 25 patient charts a few hours before, and the ten remaining charts were all from calls that had come in during the last two hours. The five charts on top were women in their 20s and 30s, all of whom had irritable bowel syndrome and had been Aaron's patients for years. One with chronic constipation was now calling with two days of diarrhea; another with chronic diarrhea hadn't had a bowel movement in four days. The third patient with daily abdominal pain was now complaining of nonstop nausea and vomiting, and the fourth patient, who usually had nausea and vomiting, now had abdominal pain. The fifth patient with chronic lower abdominal pain now was calling with upper abdominal pain.

Aaron looked through each of the patient's charts carefully and made sure their entire history was fresh in his mind. For each patient, Aaron asked Pamela if they had mentioned any symptoms of grave concern such as fever, vomiting up blood, severe unrelenting pain or feeling dehydrated. None of the five had such symptoms, and so Aaron made little tweaks in their irritable bowel syndrome medications and told them to go on just liquids for the next day or until they felt better. He also added that, if they felt they were getting worse instead of better, they should go to the emergency room immediately.

Of the other five patient charts, two were patients with Crohn's disease who were doing poorly. One was a young woman in her early 20s, Cynthia Harberry, whose Crohn's disease never went into complete remission and who had devastating complications from her Crohn's disease every few months. She would develop fistulas which were connections between her intestines and the skin from which her feces would leak. She always had bloody diarrhea, abdominal pain and weakness. She was on chronic high-dosage prednisone, a steroid which helped the Crohn's disease but had horrible side effects. Cynthia was calling today, complaining of a new fistula with stool leaking out from her belly button. Aaron added Flagyl, an antibiotic which was good for treating fistulas, to her regimen and told Pamela to have Cynthia call him back in a couple of days.

Pamela replied, "I just want to tell you that Cynthia sounded very depressed on the phone. She said that her husband left her last week and told her he was divorcing her. He told her he couldn't live with her anymore."

Aaron thought a moment. "Poor lady. Let's double her dosage of Prozac and, instead of calling me, have her come see me in the office this week."

The next Crohn's patient who had called him was a man in his late 20s who was now having five to six bloody, liquid bowel movements a day after months of doing well with one to two formed stools a day. He felt like he needed to go back on prednisone which he hadn't been on in over two years.

"Mr. Black has had Crohn's disease for eight years," Aaron said as he read through the chart. "When he says he needs to go back on steroids, he's always right. Call in prednisone 60 mg a day to his pharmacy for him."

After they'd finished the last three charts of patients with assorted GI ailments, Pamela left Aaron's office to make the calls, and Aaron signed his dictations. When he finished, he left the office and walked down the stairs to the doctors' parking lot. He got in his car and drove home.

****

On the drive home, Aaron couldn't get Jumpy Johnson out of his mind. What was he missing? What was going on with Mr. Johnson? Maybe Ms. Johnson would provide some answers when she called Aaron back. One of the diagnoses Aaron now considered in Mr. Johnson was ischemic bowel. This was a condition usually seen in elderly people with atherosclerosis where there was not enough blood flow to the intestine. It was a "heart attack" of the bowels. The patients complained of severe pain in the abdomen, especially with eating when more blood flow was required by the intestinal tract. These patients usually had normal exams of their abdomens but would lie in bed writhing in pain like Mr. Johnson.

****

Thinking of ischemic bowel now made Aaron remember the time he'd missed this diagnosis in a patient. It had been 15 years ago when Aaron was one of the internal medicine ward residents at Ben Taub Hospital in Houston. He was trying to manage a team of two worthless rotating interns and three third-year medical students who were on their first clinical rotation. During that particular 24 hours of call on a Saturday, Aaron had gotten 20 "hits" or new admissions and had not slept. At 6:00 a.m. Sunday, one hour before his shift was supposed to end, the emergency room medicine resident called and said there was another admission for Aaron. Aaron protested over the phone to no avail, as the emergency room doctor was more concerned with leaving any patients without dispositions for the doctor taking his place than he was with giving Aaron one last hit.

Aaron walked down the back steps of Ben Taub Hospital which stunk from urine and feces and came into the emergency room. He stared at the floor as the emergency room doctor told him the patient's story.

"This is a 75-year-old Mexican male who speaks no English. He's come in with 24 hours of abdominal pain and has spent the last 12 hours on the surgical side of the emergency room. He's been cleared by surgery, but they feel he needs admission and evaluation by the medicine service for nonsurgical causes of abdominal pain. He's had normal blood work, urinalysis, abdominal x-rays and CAT scan of the abdomen and pelvis.

They've medicated him with Demerol and Phenergan, and he's had good pain relief. He just got over to our side of the emergency room about 20 minutes ago."

"Where is he?" Aaron angrily demanded.

The emergency room doctor pointed to the fourth stretcher in the front row and shoved the patient's chart at Aaron. Aaron took the chart and slowly trudged to the patient's stretcher. Around the patient's stretcher were standing his wife, his son and his son's wife. None of them spoke English, but Aaron was able to communicate with them using his high school Spanish. The patient's last shot of Demerol had been given 30 minutes before, and he lay sleeping quietly on the stretcher.

Aaron reviewed the vital signs, labs and x-ray reports, and then he examined the patient. The physical exam was entirely unremarkable. The last thing Aaron did that morning as the on-call resident was to write the admission orders for that patient. Aaron left the hospital 30 minutes later since there were no attending rounds on Sunday, and all new admissions would be presented to the attending physician on Monday.

When Aaron got to work that Monday morning, he was able to find 20 of his 21 admissions. The last patient whom he'd admitted at 6:00 a.m. was nowhere to be found. Aaron finally tracked down the head nurse on the medicine ward who went through her list of the previous day's admissions.

"Oh, Mr. Rodriguez, bed 42," she said scanning the list. "He was coded at 3:00 a.m. this morning and died. He'd been calling every four hours for pain medicines, and then the nurse didn't hear from him for eight hours. She went to his bed and found him dead."

Aaron felt a cold chill through his body and knew he was visibly shaking. "Is there going to be an autopsy?" he managed to stammer.

"Yes," she replied, "family agreed to autopsy. Dr. Martinez was the ward resident on call last night; he's always able to convince those Mexicans to get autopsies."

That afternoon after finishing most of his patient responsibilities, Aaron went down to the morgue and watched the autopsy. The senior pathology resident opened the patient's abdominal cavity with a scalpel and pulled out his intestine. Twenty feet of the small intestine appeared normal; the remaining ten feet was dead and gangrenous. The pathologist showed Aaron the completely-obstructed mesenteric arteries which normally supplied blood flow to the intestinal tract. The patient had died from dead bowel from this lack of blood flow to the intestine. Aaron felt sick, knowing that the patient could have lived if the problem had been diagnosed and treated sooner.

Ever since that day, Aaron always considered ischemic bowel a diagnosis in patients with unexplained abdominal pain like Mr. Jumpy Johnson. He decided that, if the endoscopy and colonoscopy were negative in Mr. Johnson, he would order a mesenteric arteriogram to check for ischemic bowel.

****

Aaron turned from McCoy Road into the development he and his family lived in, Lakeview Estates. Aaron, his wife, Marcy, and their three children lived in a contemporary-styled 4000 square foot home which they had custom built six years before. The house was dwarfed by all the houses which had been built after theirs was completed. Many of the houses were owned by doctors who worked in the Pleasant Point hospitals and ranged from 5000 to 8000 square feet. The largest house in the development belonged to the CEO of Pleasant Point General Hospital, John Smith. His Mediterranean-style home was over 10,000 square feet and had the prime view of the man made lake which gave the neighborhood its name.

****

Aaron opened the door and was immediately greeted by his wife, Marcy, and his two younger children, Saul and Chloe. All three gave Aaron hugs and kisses.

Marcy kissed Aaron and then said, "Come on, now, we've got to sit down for dinner. We've got David's violin recital tonight, and you're late."

Aaron kissed Marcy again on the lips. "I know. I had a busy day on call today. Hope I don't get called in tonight. I'll change real quick and come to the table."

Aaron walked into his bedroom and changed clothes. He thought about his nine-year-old son David's violin concert that night. David had been playing the violin for a year, and, as far as Aaron could tell, he was lousy. David had been miserable at every sport they'd tried, from soccer to basketball to tennis. David had enjoyed playing soccer, but in the highly competitive sports environment in Pleasant Point, if you didn't show talent in a sport by age eight or nine, no one wanted you on their team. Marcy had decided that David needed to do something he enjoyed and was good at, and she'd picked the violin for him. Thus far, he'd shown little talent for the instrument and didn't practice until Marcy yelled at him. Once he decided to practice, David always wanted an audience. He would follow Aaron around the house with the violin and bow in one hand and the music stand and music book in the other hand. Whichever room Aaron settled in, David would set up shop and start playing. It was torture for Aaron; he could only compare the sound to the sound of hearing a loud cat screeching as it was choked to death. Aaron refused to criticize David or to move away from him but, instead, always encouraged him and told him how well he was playing. However, when Aaron took David to his lesson the previous week, he made it a point to talk to his teacher after the lesson.

"Wait outside for me a minute," Aaron had told David as he pulled the teacher, Mr. Dumbrowski, aside. "Mr. Dumbrowski, I know that you've signed David up for the recital next week, but I've heard him practice his pieces, 'Allegro' and 'Far, Far Away,' and he's terrible. He's been trying and practicing, but it's brutal. I'm afraid he's going to embarrass himself, and then he won't want to play anymore."

Mr. Dumbrowski smiled at Aaron. "Don't worry," he said. "I'll work with him one more time before the recital. Have him keep practicing. He's going to be accompanied by one of our other teachers on the piano, and that always makes the violin sound better. Kids like David usually rise to the occasion. And don't worry. It's the first recital for many of our other students also." Mr. Dumbrowski patted Aaron on the shoulder and walked away.

****

Aaron walked into the kitchen. Marcy and the kids had already started eating. Marcy had prepared chicken, couscous, salad and rolls. Marcy made it a point to cook nutritious, healthy foods so she couldn't understand how she'd gotten so obese over the last ten years. Aaron knew, though, that the three pregnancies had put the weight on, and then Marcy would defeat any weight-loss attempts. She would eat well all day and not snack and then would devour a gallon of chocolate chip ice cream before bedtime. Or she would eat fiber cereal with low-fat milk for breakfast and then down a 64-ounce cherry Coke Big Gulp at the 7-11 after dropping the kids at school. She was now obese, not very attractive, and looked like a caricature of the woman Aaron had married. But Aaron was more concerned by the long-term effect that obesity would have on Marcy's health than he was by the change in her appearance. She was a great mother and a great wife, and Aaron wanted her to be alive and healthy for a long time.

David, of course, was eating with chopsticks. Although David was a failure at sports and music and was only an average student, he was a genius when it came to using chopsticks. He had first used them when he was five years old and they had taken him out to a Chinese restaurant. David had been fascinated by the chopsticks, and he'd taught himself how to use them by imitating the Chinese people at the next table. Over the last few years, David had become a master at eating with Chopsticks and was far better than either of his parents. He held them like the Chinese did at the very top and could deftly use them to pick up any food and put it in his mouth. He was now showing Saul, who was seven and worshipped David, how he could pick up a single grain of couscous and put it into his mouth. David refused to eat any kind of food with silverware but had to have a new pair of chopsticks at his place setting every night. Aaron had determined that David was an idiot savant when it came to chopsticks, but it gave him some satisfaction to know that his son was a genius at something.

"How was school today, David?" Aaron asked.

"Good," came the reply.

"What did you learn today?"

"Nothin."

"Did your teacher say anything to you?" Aaron continued.

"Don't remember," David answered.

Aaron was about to ask another question when Marcy said, "I saw an advertisement in the newspaper for that weight-loss doctor, Dr. Shanamadel. You know, the one that always advertises on TV and the radio. He does that lap band surgery. I called his office and made an appointment to see him next week. First, I'll go to a seminar where he has patients that he's operated on previously talk about their experiences with the surgery, and then I'll have a one-on-one consultation with the doctor. By going to the seminar first, I get $200 off my fee."

"Which doctor is he?" asked Aaron.

"You've heard his ads," replied Marcy. "He's the foremost weight-loss surgeon in the country. He does the lap band surgery with the highest success rate and the lowest complication rate of any doctor in the country. He's taught hundreds of other doctors how to do the procedure. It says that right in his newspaper ad." Marcy got up from the table and got the newspaper off the counter and showed it to Aaron. "This woman pictured before and after surgery lost 120 pounds," Marcy continued. "She says Dr. Shanamadel saved her life. She had high blood pressure and diabetes, and her health is much better after losing all that weight. It says he's done thousands of these surgeries. I think this is the way for me to lose the weight."

"I haven't heard of him except for his ads," replied Aaron. "Where's this guy from? I know most of the local lap band surgeons, and he's not one of them."

"His secretary said he's from Scottsdale, Arizona. She said he goes all over the country performing surgery but spends one day a week seeing patients and operating here in Pleasant Point."

"He comes to Pleasant Point one day a week? Who takes care of you after the surgery?" Aaron asked.

"The secretary said that, after the surgery, which is done in a surgical center and not in the hospital, you go home the same day. She said there's really no need for much follow-up since all of his patients do so well."

"What if there's a complication?" Aaron persisted, "and he's in Houston or New Orleans or wherever else he operates?"

"I'm sure I could get one of the surgeons at your hospital to take care of me if there's a problem," Marcy replied.

"I know the weight-loss surgeon at my hospital," Aaron said, "and it's hard enough getting him to take care of the complications from his own surgeries. He'd never see you if someone else operated on you."

"Aaron," Marcy said firmly, looking him in the eyes, "I need to do something. I'm fat, and, as much as I try to diet and exercise, I can't lose the weight. You know how I follow the diet like I'm supposed to. All this will involve is outpatient surgery where they'll put a little band around my stomach, and then they'll place some controls just under my skin that can be used to make the band tighter."

"I've read through the literature on the lap band surgery. I agree with you – it's relatively simple to put in and doesn't require a lot of surgical training. But there are a lot of possible complications. The band can erode into the stomach; you can get leaks or infections. It's not uncommon that they have to go back in surgically and remove it. I don't think it's the best weight-loss surgery; the roux-en-Y gastric bypass is. It's a more complicated surgery, but it has better long-term results. And I certainly don't want you to have surgery done by a doctor who only comes to Pleasant Point one day a week. He's not going to do an adequate preoperative evaluation, and he's not going to take proper care of you after the surgery."

Marcy had tears in her eyes. "I'm not going to talk to you about it anymore. I can see it's a hopeless situation with you. I'll just research it myself." She wiped the tears from her eyes and turned to David. "It's time for you to get ready for your recital. Get dressed in the clothes I laid out on your bed, and we'll get in the car and go."

Aaron cleaned the dishes off the table, rinsed them and then loaded them into the dishwasher. He poured the leftover food into Tupperware containers and put them in the refrigerator. Marcy had left the room to put on more makeup, and, when she returned, Aaron could see that she was still upset. He put his arms around her.

"Honey, you know I love you and want what's best for you. As a doctor, though, I see what's out there. This weight-loss surgery is amazingly profitable for the surgeons who do it. Since this lap band surgery is so easy to do, a lot of surgeons do it who don't have the skills to do it and who don't do the necessary preoperative evaluation of the patient. If it's weight-loss surgery you want to have, let me research it further and find the best surgeon for you."

Marcy looked up into Aaron's eyes. "I know you will, honey. I love you." She put her arms around him, and they kissed.

****

The Pleasant Point School of Music was located on the second floor of a large strip shopping center in Pleasant Point. Aaron, Marcy and the kids walked into the school and were greeted by the owner of the school who handed them programs.

On the front of the program was printed

PLEASANT POINT SCHOOL OF MUSIC 2003 RECITAL PRESENTED BY SHAPIRO AND GOLD LAW ASSOCIATES

Listed inside the program were all 45 students who would be performing that evening and the instruments they played and the pieces they were playing. The back of the program was an advertisement for Shapiro and Gold Law Associates:

HAVE YOU BEEN THE VICTIM OF
MEDICAL MALPRACTICE?
HAVE YOU SUFFERED AN INJURY CAUSED
BY A DOCTOR'S INCOMPETENCE?
HAVE YOU TAKEN A MEDICINE
THAT RUINED YOUR HEALTH?
IF SO, CALL SHAPIRO AND
GOLD LAW ASSOCIATES
(404) 442-8877
WE'RE HERE FOR YOU.

SHAPIRO AND GOLD
PROUD SPONSORS OF PLEASANT POINT
SCHOOL OF MUSIC 2003 RECITAL

Aaron knew the Shapiro from this ad was his "buddy" from college, Marty Shapiro. Marty and his partner advertised everywhere, all the time. Aaron thought it was disgusting, but he'd heard Marty was amazingly rich now.

David walked off with Mr. Dumbrowski while Aaron, Marcy, Saul and Chloe walked into the recital room. Even though they were right on time, the only seats open were in the very back row. They got to the seats, and, as soon as they sat down, Chloe announced that she had to go potty.

"We just left the house." Marcy angrily said. "Couldn't you have gone then?"

"I'm sorry, sorry," answered Chloe, putting her head down.

"I'll take her," said Aaron. And he picked Chloe up and carried her to the bathroom.

Aaron and Chloe got back to their seats just as the recital was about to start. The entire back row had to stand up to let them in. When they sat down, Aaron noticed that in front of him was sitting a black couple in their 30s. The mother was holding a baby boy who looked less than a year old and who was squirming around. Aaron smiled at the baby, and the baby smiled back and stopped squirming. Aaron read through the program. David was the next-to-last performer. He hoped he wouldn't get beeped...Just then, he felt the beeper vibrating.

It was a nurse on the fourth floor at Pleasant Point General Hospital calling about one of the patients Aaron had seen in consultation that afternoon. After the first performer finished her piano piece, Aaron stood up and started to walk out. Again, the entire back row had to stand up to let him out. Aaron mouthed, "Got beeped," to Marcy as he passed her. He left the recital room and made his way to the walkway outside the music school. He called the hospital.

"This is Dr. Bernstein returning Sheila's call regarding Mr. Lewis."

"Dr. Bernstein, this is Sheila. Mr. Lewis had a 6:00 p.m. hemoglobin of 8.1. You left orders to transfuse if hemoglobin is less than 8. What do you want us to do?"

"How's he doing," Aaron asked. "What are his vital signs?"

"Blood pressure 120/70, temperature 98.7 and pulse 85," Sheila replied.

"Has he had any more bloody bowel movements?"

"No bowel movements since I came on at 3 o'clock."

"Well, he is 80 years old. He'll do better with a higher blood count. Go ahead and give him two units of packed red blood cells. Give each unit over four hours and give 20 of Lasix in between units. Recheck a STAT blood count 30 minutes after the second unit is in and call me if it's less than 9. OK?"

"Thanks, Dr. Bernstein. Have a good evening."

Aaron walked back inside the music school and waited outside the recital room until the current performance was done. He then quickly walked to the back row and made his way to his seat as everyone in the row stood up to let him pass.

Aaron sat down and looked in front of him. The little baby now had a pacifier in his mouth and was asleep with his head on his mother's shoulder. That's great, Aaron thought, maybe he'll sleep through the whole recital.

The recital went on and on. Six performances before David's turn, Aaron was beeped. This time, it was from a patient who was supposed to have a colonoscopy the next day and was vomiting up her laxative prep. Aaron called in some Phenergan for her nausea and vomiting and told her to take one and then wait an hour before resuming the bowel prep.

When Aaron got back to his seat, the performer was the cellist right before David. The baby in front of Aaron was now awake and was squirming and crying. Aaron made funny faces at the baby, and the baby stopped crying and began to smile at Aaron.

The owner of the music school announced, "Our next performer is nine-year-old David Bernstein on the violin. David will be performing 'Allegro' and 'Far, Far Away' with our own Kitty Nichols accompanying him on piano."

The piano accompanist entered the room and sat down on the piano bench. Then, David entered from the side door and walked onto the stage carrying his violin. David bowed to the middle of the room and then to the right and to the left. The crowd laughed. Just as David lifted his bow to begin playing, the baby in front of Aaron spit out his pacifier onto Aaron's lap and screamed at the top of his lungs.

"Oh, shit," Aaron whispered. "Oh, shit."

David started to play 'Allegro.' He missed the first note but then played perfectly. Mr. Dumbrowski had been right; David was rising to the occasion, and the piano accompaniment made him sound even better. The baby continued to scream as Aaron tried to put the pacifier back into his mouth. The baby's mother snatched the pacifier out of Aaron's hand and tried to put it into the baby's mouth but was unsuccessful. David finished 'Allegro' and started 'Far, Far Away.' He played it perfectly. Just as he finished the piece, the baby took the pacifier from his mother and stopped screaming. The entire audience cheered when David finished, and he again bowed in all three directions.

After the last performer was done, the audience made its way out of the recital hall and into the large waiting room which was now the reception area. Aaron saw Dorothy Dickman, the wife of one of Pleasant Point's cardiologists, Peter Dickman. Her teenage daughter had played the piano in the recital, so Aaron congratulated her and then asked, "Where's Peter?"

"Your guess is as good as mine," Dorothy replied flatly. "He doesn't live with us anymore."

"Oh, sorry," Aaron awkwardly stammered. "Oh, there's my son. Gotta go."

Aaron went over and picked David up and hugged him. "David, I'm so proud of you. You did an incredible job."

"Thank you, Dad. I knew I could do it."

"That was the best I've every heard you play those songs. I'm so proud to be your father, and I love you so much."

"Thanks. I love you, too. Where's Mom?" David asked.

"I don't know. I thought she was right here behind me." Aaron scanned the room. He finally spotted Marcy at the refreshment table. She was eating one large chocolate chip cookie with her right hand while, with her left hand, she held a large cup of punch. Aaron sighed and hugged David again.

****

When they got back to the house, Aaron and Marcy tucked the kids into their beds and turned out their lights. Marcy went to check her e-mails while Aaron got ready for bed. He was about to turn off the lights when his beeper went off. It was the emergency room at Pleasant Point General Hospital. Aaron quickly dialed the number and was connected with the emergency room doctor. "Aaron, this is Don Rose. Sorry to bother you this late at night. Gotta 47-year-old man who I think can be sent home, but I want him to be seen by someone tomorrow. Probably gotta ulcer: epigastric pain, usually better with eating, much worse tonight, nausea but no vomiting. Vitals stable and labs normal. Gonna send him out on some Nexium. By the way, guy's been taking eight Advil a day for a bum shoulder; probably how he got the ulcer."

"Sure," Aaron replied. "Have him call the office after 8:30 in the morning, and one of us will see him. Bye."

Aaron turned out the lights and lay down in bed. He had just drifted off to sleep when the beeper went off again. This time, it was the sixth floor at Pleasant Point General Hospital calling.

"Dr. Bernstein, this is Rebecca calling from Pleasant Point General Hospital. Mrs. Virginia Smith in 611 is a patient of yours."

"Yes, yes. Mrs. Smith...she had an upper GI bleed, what - seven days ago? I signed off on her a few days back. I didn't even know she was still in the hospital. What's going on?"

"She pulled out her IV accidentally a few hours ago. I wanted to know if we could leave it out. She's not getting any medication through the IV; she's just getting Ringers lactate at TKO."

Aaron felt warmth inside his chest as he became angry. He looked at the clock – 12:36 a.m. "I'm not sure why you're calling me," he said, trying to stay calm. "I'm not her attending. I signed off several days ago. I'm surprised she's still in the hospital. She's been stable for days."

"Oh, I already called her attending, Dr. Givagushrai, and he said it was OK with him to leave the IV out but to make sure it was OK with you."

"It's fine with me," Aaron said, clenching his teeth. "And do me a big favor. With something like this that can easily wait until the morning, please wait until the morning to call me."

"But, Dr. Givagushrai told us to get your OK…"

"Goodnight," Aaron said, and hung up the phone.

Aaron walked into the bathroom and took two Tylenol PM and gulped them down with some water.

He got back into bed and fell asleep after a few minutes. He began to dream that he was sitting in a patient's room at Pleasant Point Hospital. He got up from the chair he was sitting in and looked into the hospital bed, and there was his wife, Marcy. She was intubated and on a ventilator. Somehow, Aaron knew that she'd had the lap band surgery and that she'd had major complications leading to her current predicament. Aaron walked around the room with his arms in the air.

"Where is Marcy's surgeon? Where is her surgeon? Doesn't he know how sick she is?"

All of a sudden, an Asian man dressed in surgical scrubs walked into the room accompanied by a tiny woman who began to speak.

"Dr. Bernstein, this is your wife's hospitalist surgeon, Dr. Yellow Saki. He doesn't speak any English, so I am his interpreter."

"Hospitalist surgeon, what do you mean hospitalist surgeon? I want the surgeon who operated on my wife to take care of her."

"Oh, that surgeon is not available. He does not come to the hospital to take care of patients. He makes big bucks in private practice. This is the only surgeon who is here now. The hospital pays him a good salary to take care of sick patients."

"Well, what's wrong with my wife? What is Dr. Yellow Saki going to do?"

"He says your wife has an infection from where the band had eroded into her stomach. He will treat her with antibiotics and have other hospital specialists come and see her. Do you have further questions?"

"Yes, how long will she need to be in the hospital? Will she need another surgery? Do they need to take the band out?"

The interpreter conferred with Dr. Yellow Saki in hushed voices. She turned back to Aaron. "He says your wife will be OK. You just need to be patient. He wants to give you his card so that, when you admit patients to this hospital, you can call him."

"Yeah, right," Aaron muttered under his breath. "Hey, why is my wife on the ventilator? She must be very sick if she is intubated."

The interpreter turned her back to Aaron and conferred with Dr. Yellow Saki again. She turned back to Aaron and said, "Dr. Yellow Saki says you must talk to the pulmonary specialist. He must leave now. Goodbye."

Great, Aaron thought. That means Greg Segal will be in. He's a good competent doctor… Just then, a very handsome man who looked like the actor Antonio Banderas entered the room. He, too, was followed by a tiny woman who wore large glasses.

"Who are you?" Aaron asked.

The tiny woman said, "This is your pulmonary hospitalist, Dr. Jose Gonzalez."

"Pulmonary hospitalist?" repeated Aaron. "What do you mean? Greg Segal is the pulmonologist and critical care specialist at this hospital."

The interpreter and Dr. Gonzalez both smiled. "Very funny," she said. "We now have hospitalists in every specialty to take care of the patients."

"Do any of them speak English?" Aaron asked.

"Now you insult me," said Dr. Gonzalez in a thick Spanish accent. "I understand every word you say."

"Then why won't you answer my questions?" Aaron asked.

The little interpreter smiled. "He won't answer your questions because that's not his job. His job is to get your wife well."

"What about dealing with me? I'm her husband. I need to know what's going on with her. I need to be able to tell our children how their mother is doing."

Dr. Gonzalez smiled and whispered something to the interpreter who laughed and then said, "He says your wife will be OK. He's got 30 other patients to go see now. He'll be back… if she gets worse."

Dr. Gonzalez left the room followed by his interpreter. Aaron could feel himself getting madder and madder. His face was red and hot. He looked back at his wife who, even though she was intubated, was now able to talk to him.

"Aaron, you've got to help me. You've got to help me. Don't let these hospitalist doctors who don't know anything about me treat me!"

"Don't worry, honey, I'll get you a doctor I know."

Another doctor walked into the room followed by a small woman.

"This is Dr. Jacobs from India," the interpreter said. "He will be your wife's cardiologist. He speaks no English, so I will interpret for him."

"Why does my wife need a cardiologist?" Aaron asked. "There's nothing wrong with her heart, is there?"

Both Dr. Jacobs and his interpreter laughed. Dr. Jacobs whispered to the interpreter, and then she said, "Dr. Jacobs says you're right, there is nothing wrong with your wife's heart. However, his hospitalist colleague, Dr. Givagushrai, consulted him as he does on all patients admitted to the hospital just in case there is a problem with the heart later on. Not to worry, though, Dr. Jacobs is around and will keep close watch on your wife."

Just then, the monitor above Marcy's bed began beeping wildly as her heart went into ventricular fibrillation.

"Do something, do something!" Aaron screamed. "Get Peter Dickman in here. He's the cardiologist I want. He's the one I want! Do something!"

Dr. Jacobs pulled defibrillator paddles out of a small briefcase that he had brought into the room. He walked up to Marcy's bed and put the paddles on her chest and shouted out some words in Hindi.

"All clear," the interpreter interpreted.

Aaron jumped back from the bed as the electrical impulse coursed through Marcy, and her entire body jerked. The monitor now showed normal sinus rhythm.

"You see," said the interpreter. "Dr. Jacobs will stay on top of things."

Dr. Jacobs put the defibrillator paddles back into his briefcase and walked out of the room with his interpreter in tow.

Aaron looked at Marcy who was now smiling at him. "I'll be OK, honey. I'm just scared."

"I've got to get you doctors I know. I've just got to," Aaron replied.

Just then, Vijay Givagushrai came into the room.

"Vijay, good, you're here. At least you speak English."

Suddenly, a tiny woman entered the room.

"Uh, he no longer speaks English. He speaks Hindi, and I'm his interpreter."

"Vijay, tell me about my wife. Tell me what we need to do."

Vijay talked to the interpreter who then told Aaron, "Dr. Givagushrai says your wife isn't really sick…she's just fat."

Vijay walked up to Marcy and pulled the breathing tube out of her mouth. Marcy sat up in bed and asked, "What's going on here?"

Vijay's mouth was moving, but the words were coming from the interpreter. "She's just fat. We expect this after surgery. You don't need…"

"Listen to me!" demanded Aaron. "I just paid $15,000 in cash to a surgeon for Marcy to have this surgery. I want that surgeon here now."

Vijay and the interpreter laughed heartily and then walked out of the room.

Aaron sat down in the chair next to Marcy's bed. Marcy was now sitting up in bed eating.

"You see," Marcy said, "now that I've had the surgery, I can cat whatever I want." Marcy gobbled down mouthful after mouthful of food.

The door to Marcy's room opened, and in walked the lawyer, Marty Shapiro. He was carrying a notebook that was the size of a small table. He sat down next to Aaron and put the notebook on the table between them.

"OK, Bernstein. This notebook contains the names of all the doctors involved in your wife's care. You just put an X by the ones you want to sue, and we'll sue them."

"Sue them?" Aaron asked incredulously. "Why would we sue them? They're all trying their best. Look at her. She's eating and doing much better."

"You need to leave these doctors alone," Aaron continued, "you're ruining medicine. Medicine is a noble profession. Your lawsuits are making doctors practice medicine in ways they wouldn't practice and making the patient the doctor's enemy."

"Yeah, right, right," replied Marty. "All right, watch here." Marty swept his hand across the page in the notebook and X's appeared next to all of the doctors' names who were taking care of Marcy.

"You're crippling medicine," Aaron screamed. "Don't you understand that you're crippling medicine? Let the doctors help my wife."

Marty laughed. "We'll have our day in court," he said. "Look, your wife is going flat line." Aaron looked up and saw Marcy's EKG was now flat line, and the monitor was beeping loudly. At that point, Aaron's half-conscious mind told him that it was his beeper going off, so he reached over to the nightstand and picked it up.

CHAPTER 5

Marie loved looking at herself in the mirror. Her body and face looked a lot younger than the 47 years which was her true age but which no one suspected. All the time she spent working out was worth it, and the breast implants and Botox injections hadn't hurt either. It was 4 o'clock in the afternoon, and she looked in the mirror at the reflection of her latest sexual conquest lying in her bed.

"That wasn't much of a pickup line you used yesterday at the hospital."

Peter Dickman laughed. "Yeah, but you seemed kind of lost. And I figured that asking you if you were an agency nurse could get things rolling."

"Of course, I was an agency nurse. Why do you think I was wearing the badge that said 'Advanced Health Agency'?"

Peter laughed again. "You had a good time this afternoon, also."

They had made love twice, first with Peter on top and then with Marie on top. Peter's turn on top had been extremely enjoyable with both of them having intense orgasms, but he had to admit that the session with Marie in control had been incredible.

Marie had slowly thrust herself up and down on his penis while he fondled her enormous breasts. Then, Marie turned around with Peter still inside her so that he could see her fabulous, tight ass gyrating as she went up and down on him. She had a tattoo on each of her butt cheeks. The left cheek was covered by a huge, angry-looking blue shark with a half-eaten man in his mouth and had the word "Maneater" beneath it. On the right cheek, there was a black Winchester rifle drawn in exquisite detail with the words "The Law" written in old English script beneath it.

Marie then turned back around, and, after putting Peter's penis all the way inside her, she began doing slow pushups on top of him. Each pushup ended with Marie's pelvis crashing into Peter's pelvis with a soft thud. After doing 25 pushups, Marie did one-arm pushups with her right arm, and, with her left hand, she massaged Peter's scrotum. After five one-arm pushups, Peter couldn't hold out any longer, and he orgasmed with Marie soon following.

This was Marie's life, and it had been like this for the last 15 years. Sure, she'd been married when she was in her 20s for a couple of years to a cop, but he was like her: an adventurer, always on the prowl, always looking for new conquests. The day she came home with a man to go to bed with and found her husband already in their bed with a girlfriend made her realize that there was no reason for them to stay married. They'd divorced, and then she had a hysterectomy a few years later for pelvic pain which took away any notions of ever having children. From then on, her life had been devoted to two things: as many sexual conquests as possible and keeping her body in as good a shape as possible. She was proud to admit she'd done a great job of both.

The 80s had been scary for Marie with the AIDS epidemic, and she'd almost gotten through it unscathed. However, seven years before, she'd had a brief fling with a resident at Emory

Hospital who it turned out was bisexual and had AIDS. Marie contracted the HIV virus from this resident but only learned about it two years later when she went in for routine blood tests for a physical examination. Marie continued to have countless sexual partners and never informed any of them about her HIV status.

Marie had found out a lot about her latest sexual conquest in the last 24 hours. Peter was a cardiologist at Pleasant Point General Hospital, and he was a player. He had a wife and five children, but he told her that he was separated from his wife. This information was all relayed within the first five minutes of meeting Peter. It had been Marie's first day at Pleasant Point General Hospital, and she was working on the cardiology floor. It was hard enough getting used to the four patients she was taking care of, but this good-looking doctor wouldn't leave her alone. She'd been informed by one of the other nurses that Peter had dated at least three or four of the other nurses on the floor, some of whom had been married. She was told he had fathered one child out of wedlock and that he was always on the lookout for new pussy. That's just my kind of man, Marie had thought. When Peter came back to see her a little bit later in her shift and asked her if she'd like to get together the next day, Marie didn't hesitate to invite him over to her apartment.

Peter got to her apartment at about noon, saying he'd just finished his morning rounds and didn't have to go back until he had to see some patients later in the day. She greeted him at the door wearing a black thong and a black bra. They had immediately gone into the bedroom and made love. Peter was good…he'd obviously had a lot of partners, and he had no inhibitions. After making love, they went swimming in the apartment's pool with Marie wearing a tiny pink string bikini.

Then, they came back inside and made love again with Marie taking charge.

Now, Marie was admiring herself in the mirror, and Peter was admiring her body also.

"Quite a body you've got there. How often do you work out?"

"Every day. If I don't lift weights, I run at least five miles."

Marie glanced at the clock on her dresser. "Shit, I was supposed to be at work at 5 o'clock. You've got to get out of here. I've got to shower and change. I've got to be on a new floor today…up on the fourth floor."

"You working at Pleasant Point General Hospital again?"

"Yeah, I'm on the fourth floor there."

"Can I come by and see you later?" Peter asked.

"Sure. If you want to come by and visit me, that's fine."

Peter quickly put on his clothes and left the apartment.

****

Marie showered, dressed and then drove to Pleasant Point General Hospital. By the time she got there, it was 6:40, so there wasn't much time for orientation. As an agency nurse, she worked wherever the agency told her to go. One day it could be Pleasant Point General Hospital, the next day Emory Hospital, the next day North Decatur Hospital. This was her second straight day at Pleasant Point General Hospital but the first time she'd worked on a unit other than the cardiac step-down unit. She was assigned six patients, and she listened to a very abbreviated report about them. She started off her evening rounds and brought the patients their 7 o'clock medications. Everything went well, so she stopped for a break and to have dinner. There was an occasional call from a patient, and the man in 427B, Mr. Jumpy Johnson, seemed a little bit upset when she saw him. She called his doctor, Dr. Givagushrai, who told her to give him an extra dosage of Ativan if she felt it was indicated. She read through her midnight medications and began distributing them.

The man in the bed next to Mr. Johnson, Mr. Herman, had just had a penile prosthesis placed and was on a testosterone patch. For some reason, when Marie went into the room this time, she got confused. It may have been because she was thinking at the time what would happen with a stud like Peter Dickman if she were to put a testosterone patch on him. Whatever caused it, she got the A bed and the B bed confused, and instead of placing the testosterone patch on Mr. Herman, she put it on Mr. Johnson. Mr. Johnson appeared asleep, lying on his side facing away from her. She pulled up his pants and put the patch on his leg.

"Here's your testosterone patch, Mr. Johnson. Have sweet dreams, Tiger." She walked out and closed the door. Marie went back to her duties and finished up the 12-hour shift without any other mistakes. The next morning, the only thing she had to report to the morning nurse, Krystal, was the surliness of Mr. Johnson. However, she didn't report to Krystal what Mr. Johnson had growled when she left he room because Marie hadn't heard it:

"Hum. Now you're trying to take over my mind and get control of my dick...puttin' me on testosterone. This is gonna stop. The next pussy who comes in here is gonna pay for this!"

CHAPTER 6

"Why, you're the most beautiful girl I've ever seen in my life," said Mr. Brown in Room 425.

Krystal didn't blush or think twice when she heard this, she'd heard it all her life.

"Thank you, Mr. Brown. Now roll up your shirt so I can give you your morning insulin shot."

"Happy to oblige you," he said and rolled up his shirt.

Krystal gave him the shot and then gave him his blood pressure medicine. "How are you feeling today?" she asked.

"I feel much better after seeing you. Why can't all the nurses look like you?"

Krystal smiled. She ran her hand through her long blonde hair and pulled it back. She put her hand on Mr. Brown's leg. "You have a good day. You call me if you need anything."

"I'll call you even if I don't need anything," laughed Mr. Brown.

Krystal walked out of the room. It had always been like this for Krystal. She was someone who had been born beautiful. Her father had been the captain of the football team at Kansas State University. He'd married the captain of the cheerleaders and then had gone on to medical school and had become a cardiovascular surgeon. He now had the largest cardiovascular surgery practice in Kansas. Krystal had been born 25 years ago and had followed in her mother's footsteps – first becoming a cheerleader and then going to nursing school. All along, she'd modeled and won beauty pageants. She'd won Miss Kansas and finished in the top ten for Miss America. With her long blonde hair, blue eyes and Playboy model figure, men melted before her everywhere she went.

Krystal had moved to Pleasant Point three years before when she had graduated from nursing school and had gotten a job at Pleasant Point General Hospital. Her boyfriend, Quinn Bridgewater, was out in Hollywood. He, too, had been a model and was the most handsome man she had ever seen. He was now trying to become an actor in movies. She only got to see him one weekend a month, but she knew that, once he'd established himself as an actor, she'd move out to Hollywood and they'd get married. In the meantime, she worked at Pleasant Point General Hospital in two jobs. One was two 12-hour shifts a week working on the wards as a floor nurse. She enjoyed interacting with the patients, and, even more, she enjoyed having all the doctors lust over her. No doctor ever passed her by without looking back at her a second time. She'd been asked out by every single doctor and most of the married doctors on the staff. She always politely declined and explained to them that she had a very serious boyfriend.

The other two days, she worked eight-hour shifts doing utilization review for the hospital. This was a position that the CEO of the hospital, John Smith, had recommended her for, and he had done it mainly because she had to wear regular clothes and not just her scrubs. Mr. Smith admitted that he loved to see Krystal wearing dresses, tight pants, low-cut blouses and black leggings. Whenever it was one of her days for utilization review work, Mr. Smith could be found on the wards finding some business to attend to so he could check Krystal out.

Krystal loved her life. She loved the fact that she worked to make people well, and she loved the fact that she was so beautiful that, just by walking into a room, she immediately grabbed everyone's attention. She was a tall girl at 5 feet 10 inches, and she stayed at her college weight of 125 pounds. She now walked into the next room, Room 427. She'd heard from the previous nurse, Marie, that the man in B bed had seemed a little anxious during the evening but otherwise had done well. Dr. Bernstein was planning on starting a bowel prep today to clean him out for his procedures, and she knew that prepping Mr. Johnson would keep her busy. She decided to see him second and first went in to see the patient in the bed next to Mr. Johnson, Bruce Herman, who'd had a penile implant.

"Mr. Herman, good morning. How are you doing? I'm your nurse, Krystal."

"Wow!" said Mr. Herman. "I thought maybe they sent you in here to see if this thing was working or not."

Krystal laughed. "No, I'm sorry. I think that's something you're going to have to try out with your wife."

"Oh, no, no, no…" said Mr. Herman. I was talking about my IV…whether or not it was working."

Krystal blushed. "Let me see. Let me just straighten this out. There. It's working."

She gave Mr. Herman his morning medicines and then pulled the curtain back from Mr. Johnson's bed. "Good morning, Mr. Johnson." She pulled back the curtain further. It appeared there was a body under the blanket, but even the head was covered up.

"I'm Krystal, your nurse. Good morning."

Still no reply.

She went and pulled the blanket from over his head. The next thing she knew, the patient was sitting up and pointing a gun right at her breasts.

"Good morning…good morning…good morning!" Mr. Johnson said. "Is that all you can think about? I know what you're trying to do. First you try to take over my mind and then my body and then all my functions. Well, I'm not standing for it. You're going to stay here with me until I get some satisfaction." He pointed the gun at Krystal's head, and she began to cry.

"What do you want? What do you want?" she cried.

"I don't know what I want yet, but you are going to help me get it. You sit down in that chair over there."

Mr. Johnson kept pointing the gun at her. He ripped the sheets off his bed and used them to tie Krystal into the chair.

"Now, don't you move an inch, Honey."

Krystal protested, "But, but…"

He stuffed a pillowcase into her mouth, and she couldn't say anything. He reached under the sink and took the surgical tape out and wrapped it around her face.

"What's going on over there?" asked Mr. Herman who couldn't see due to the curtain.

"Justice!" yelled Jumpy Johnson. He went to Mr. Herman's bed with the gun and tied him into bed. He rolled Mr. Herman's bed against the door so that no one could get in.

"We'll see now if you are gonna get away with stealing my brain, stealing my body and turning me into some kind of homosexual," Mr. Johnson said.

"Krystal, room number. Krystal, room number." The head nurse was looking for Krystal over the intercom.

"Buggrrrha…" came the muffled sounds from Krystal.

Jumpy sat down between his two prisoners and took his time pointing the gun at each of them.

CHAPTER 7

D r. Cole Stone loved to spend time on the fourth floor when Krystal was working. He'd had his eye on her for six months and was just about ready to ask her out. It was true he was married and had a couple of kids, but that didn't stop him from occasionally playing around. He'd been sitting at the desk at the nurse's station making small talk with her, asking her how her modeling career was going. He was just about to ask her to spend the weekend at the lake with him when Krystal had to go on her morning rounds. She'd gone into the second patient room and hadn't come out yet. Suddenly, he heard a tremendous bang on the door of that room, and he thought he could hear someone screaming for help. He thought to himself, I guess I better wait until later to ask Krystal out… I better get out of here before I get involved in something.

Several of the nurses ran from the nursing station to see what was going on. They tried to open the door to the room, but there was no way they could get in. Cole watched them attempt to open the door, and then he opened the door to the stairwell on the fourth floor. He walked down to the third floor and across the walkway to where his office was. Something is going on there that's not good, he thought. Glad I got out of there quickly.

Cole went to his office and sat down. He wondered whether the patient in that room, who he'd been consulted on a couple of days before, was doing something bad. Hah, he thought to himself, I'll let Bernstein worry about that. He picked up that consult. Just then, his nurse, Mary, came into his office carrying a slip of paper detailing a patient that a referring physician wanted him to see. He read it. It was a 35-year-old woman with alternating diarrhea and constipation, severe abdominal pain, occasional nausea and weight loss.

He said to Mary, "Sounds like another irritable bowel syndrome. You know I don't want to see any of those nuts. Give it to one of my partners to see."

After Mary left his office, Cole laughed to himself. He had known that he wanted to be a gastroenterologist from the time he'd gotten out of medical school and done his residency in internal medicine. He wanted to be in a field where he did procedures, but he didn't have the temperament or the patience for surgery. He had settled on gastroenterology and had followed three rules in his career. Rule #1: Make a lot of money no matter how you do it. Rule #2: Never get sued. Rule #3: Never take care of any nuts or sick patients because taking care of nuts and sick patients got you sued and brought nothing but aggravation.

He thought back about #1: Make a lot of money. He'd found that the quickest and easiest way to make money was to bring in new partners. Every few years, he brought in a new gastroenterologist as a partner. Each of them worked as his employee for a couple of years and then bought into the practice by paying $500,000 over five years. He figured that, from three partners, he'd made approximately $2,000,000. He'd also made money in every venture that was open to doctors. When the hospital had offered to give the doctors a piece of the imaging center where they did the outpatient x-rays, he got the largest piece possible. When some other doctors had gotten together to form a medical equipment leasing company, he'd bought into that also and had made a tidy sum. Now, he was a multimillionaire, and he saw only patients that needed procedures. He never saw any difficult cases or any sick patients. That brought him to Rule #2: Never get sued. He'd been working for 25 years. By avoiding sick patients and nuts, he had never been involved in a lawsuit, and he felt certain he would finish his career without being involved in a lawsuit.

Rule #3: Don't take care of any nuts or any sick patients. Anytime a sick patient came around with Crohn's disease, ulcerative colitis or cirrhosis, he made sure that the nurses knew not to give that patient to him. Doctors would call specifically asking for him, but he would say he didn't have an opening to see those patients and all those patients went to Dr. Bernstein and his other partners. He hadn't taken care of a patient with irritable bowel syndrome in years because, for him, there was nothing to do to help those people. They were all nuts.

Cole started leafing through his mail. He was surprised to see a letter that had a law firm's return address on it. He quickly opened the letter with his letter opener. It said that the lawyer, Marty Shapiro, was requesting all of the records on a patient of his that he had taken care of in the hospital, Rhea Walmsley. He remembered Rhea very well as he'd done a procedure on her within the last month. Cole wondered why they were requesting his records on her, but he was certain that it didn't have anything to do with him because all he had done was put in a gastrostomy tube to feed the patient.

It was a very sad case. Rhea was a 27-year-old mother of two who had a ruptured aneurysm of the brain. She'd been in a coma in the intensive care unit, and no one expected her to survive. They'd consulted him after she'd been in the hospital for months to put a feeding tube into her stomach. The consult had come in on a day when he was on call, so he couldn't avoid it. But he told them at that time he didn't feel it was appropriate to put a feeding tube in her because she had a fever and pneumonia, and he didn't want the gastrostomy tube to get infected. Cole thought he had dodged a bullet because he felt certain the neurosurgeon was going to get sued, and he felt that, if he did anything on the patient, he would get sued also. He didn't even write his name on the chart or leave a consult note. He only read through the chart and talked to the neurosurgeon.

However, a month later, another consult on Rhea for a gastrostomy tube placement came in on a day Cole was on call. This time, she was doing a lot better and was about to get out of the ICU. Her doctors felt they needed a more comfortable way to feed her than a nasogastric tube which went in through her nose. She was now awake enough that the nasogastric tube was bothering her, and, because her rehabilitation looked like it would take months and months, it would be easier to feed her through a tube going directly through the skin and into her stomach. Cole was still concerned about a lawsuit but didn't see any way he could dodge the consult. She wasn't having any fever now, she was starting to improve and she really needed the tube to continue to get better. So, he set it up to do the next day with his associate, Dr. Aaron Bernstein.

Aaron had passed the endoscope through Ms. Walmsley's mouth and into her stomach and insufflated the stomach with air. Cole found the location on the skin where the light from the endoscope shined brightest, and he anesthetized the skin here with lidocaine. Cole then made a small incision in the skin and passed a catheter through the skin directly into the stomach. Through the catheter, he passed a guide wire which Aaron grasped with forceps which he had passed through a channel in the scope. Aaron then pulled the guide wire and the scope out of the patient's mouth. Over the guide wire, the feeding tube went down the mouth and ended up coming out of the stomach and then through the skin. Everything went well, and, after the procedure, the patient went back up to the ICU. Unfortunately, she got sick again two days later. This time, her fever and white blood cell count got higher and higher. She became septic, and she ended up dying.

Cole had only seen her the day after the gastrostomy tube was put in, and, at that time, she looked like she was doing pretty well, so he'd signed off her case. He'd refused to go back even though the neurosurgeon, Georgio Circelli, had called several times to ask him to reevaluate her.

Now this lawyer's request for records. Cole was sure they were going to be suing the neurosurgeon. It was a shame because the patient had started to look better, and it looked like she was finally going to be able to get out of the hospital and go to a rehabilitation facility.

Cole called his malpractice attorney to tell him what had happened and also to tell him that he was sure they didn't have anything to worry about. Cole told his attorney he would probably initially be included in any proceedings because his name was on the chart, but then he would be dropped from the case before it got too far along.

After finishing going through the mail, Cole looked at his phone messages. There was a message from the pathologist, Langston Harris, to call him at home. He called Langston who was an old friend of his and was another of the wealthiest physicians in Pleasant Point.

"Hey, Langston, this is Cole. How are you, buddy?"

Langston answered, "Cole, are you sitting down?"

"Yes," said Cole.

"Cole, I just want to tell you we got back a report on the autopsy on Rhea Walmsley, that lady that had the aneurysm of the brain that you put the gastrostomy feeding tube in."

"Uh-huh," said Cole.

"Cole, that tube went right through that lady's colon into her stomach. She had a huge abscess in that area, and she died from the complications of that abscess. Everything else looked OK in her. I've never seen one of those feeding tubes go through the colon into the stomach. Sorry to have to be the bearer of bad news."

Cole couldn't believe it. After 25 years of avoiding sick patients and nuts and anyone except for straightforward colonoscopies and endoscopies, someone's death had been caused by him, and he was about to get sued for it.

Cole said goodbye, hung up the phone and then buried his head in his hands. He thought back to when Georgio Circelli had called him after the patient had started getting sick, asking him to come back and reevaluate her. When he'd asked Circelli what was going on, Circelli replied that she was septic and had a hard abdomen.

Cole had replied, "Just watch it. That happens after we place those feeding tubes."

Dr. Circelli called later saying that her belly was getting more and more distended, so Cole told him to put in a nasogastric tube and watch her more closely. Cole had never gone back to see her, and, when he'd heard she'd died, he figured it was a neurological event. Now he knew her death was due to him, and some lawyer named Marty Shapiro was going to try and make him pay for it.

CHAPTER 8

Langston Harris was the pathologist at Pleasant Point General Hospital and was the richest doctor in Pleasant Point. His father and his grandfather had been pathologists before him. When it came time for Langston to select a career, there was no doubt he was going to go to medical school. He had ideas about helping people and saving lives, but, one day, his father sat him down and set him straight.

"Langston," he said, "when you become a medical doctor, you can either make patients better or make patients worse. A pathologist, on the other hand, makes money whether patients get better or worse. You're going to become a pathologist just like me and granddad."

Langston went on to become a pathologist and never regretted his decision. He inherited $25,000,000 from his father, but, on his own, he'd made millions and millions of dollars more. He got tremendous fees for reading pathology specimens on every surgical procedure done in the hospital, many times getting much more than the surgeons who had done the surgery at 3:00 or 4:00 in the morning. Langston laughed when he thought of them operating at 4:00 in the morning and making $600 for taking out a hot appendix when here he was at 9:00 a.m. just looking at the slides of that appendix, drinking his coffee and making at least that much money or more.

Langston also received a "clinical fee" which was why he had two doctors coming to his house this morning. Many of the insurance companies were now talking about doing away with his "clinical fee." Langston needed the doctors who were on the negotiating team for the physicians' organization to make sure they defended his clinical fee. The clinical fee was a cut that Langston got for every lab test that was done in the hospital. It was pretty amazing when you really thought about it, and even Langston admitted to himself that it was robbery without a gun. Essentially, for every CBC, SMAC or any blood test done in the hospital, Langston got a fee ranging anywhere from $10 to $50. He never had to look at the blood work or do anything about it, but, just because he was the pathologist and supposedly in charge of the laboratory, he got that money. About 500 lab tests were done daily at Pleasant Point Hospital, and, with an average clinical fee of $30, Langston made $15,000 a day just from his clinical fees. Translated over a month, that was over $450,000 a month and almost $5,500,000 a year. Add that to the almost $3,000,000 a year that he got from reading pathology slides, and one could see how Langston had gotten so incredibly wealthy very quickly.

Langston spent most of his days on the phone with his stockbroker. He got to work at about 9:00 a.m., and there were slides for him to read that took up about four hours of his time. He had three junior pathologists who worked for him and who each got paid salaries and varying small percentages of what they read. Langston spent the rest of his time talking to his broker and working on his ever-expanding portfolio which now showed a net worth of over $150,000,000. He owned three homes – one in Pleasant Point, one in upstate New York and one in Scottsdale, Arizona. Each of the homes was worth over

$5,000,000. It was to his Pleasant Point home that he now welcomed Drs. Jeff Conner and Bert Clark.

Jeff Conner was a family practitioner who had been in Langston's class in medical school. Unlike Langston, Jeff became a doctor to take care of patients and make people better. Over the years, he'd soured. First, he'd gotten divorced from his wife who was also a physician. Then, he'd come to see how much money other physicians made who didn't work nearly as hard as him. The real eye-opening experience was the first time he'd been to Langston's house ten years before. Just driving up to it was incredibly impressive. It was a huge house, over 20,000 square feet, sitting on three acres of land. It had eight bedrooms and seven baths and was built on different levels. The artwork was incredible.

Jeff had said to Langston, "These are fine reproductions of impressionists' works."

Langston replied, "These are the real works themselves."

Jeff had left Langston's house that night ten years before and vowed that he was going to make money, too. He'd done everything he could to streamline his practice, turning it into a money-making machine, but there was only so much that a family practitioner could do. And now with the insurance cuts and the PPOs and HMOs taking more and more out of his paycheck, he had to work harder and harder to make money. That was why he no longer worked at the hospital or took care of hospitalized or sick patients. Everything he did was in the office. He wanted to see people with colds, he wanted to give people pills for blood pressure, and he wanted to do cardiac stress tests on healthy people. He'd known when Langston had called him over to his house that there was something that Langston had wanted. He loved to see the house – its marble floors, its basketball gymnasium, its indoor tennis court – so he'd decided to go.

Bert Clark, on the other hand, was a successful ear, nose and throat specialist who had given up part of his practice time to negotiate contracts for the Pleasant Point Physicians Council. He'd really done absolutely nothing to help the physicians in their contracts. Each year, the insurance companies lopped off 10 percent more from the physicians' fees. However, Bert was getting paid $250,000 a year, and he had to justify his salary somehow. He knew what Langston wanted. He knew that the laboratory clinical fees were now a bone of contention with many of the insurance companies because they couldn't understand paying someone for doing nothing which was exactly what was happening.

Bert and Jeff went into Langston's massive study and sat down. There was a huge mahogany desk and a giant seat behind it. Rather than wallpaper, the walls were covered in leather, and Bert's and Jeff's chairs were also leather.

Langston said, "Listen, United Healthcare and Aetna are taking away my clinical fees. That's why I wanted to talk to you guys on the council."

"But, Langston, you're getting paid for doing nothing," said Jeff. "Look how hard other doctors are working. They're ratcheting down their fees every year. They haven't ever touched your clinical fee. They haven't ever cut back on it."

Langston just smiled and said, "Jeff, once they hit me, they're going to hit you guys even harder. You guys know how hard I work to keep the laboratory going. I'm the one who bought the biggest stake in the Pleasant Point Physicians Council when we set this up. I gave you guys $100,000. I haven't got a penny back for that $100,000. I expect you to work for me. And, Bert, I fought for you to get that last pay raise from $225,000 to $250,000. You know you haven't done jack-shit to help any of the physicians at all. This is an easy one, a no-brainer. These insurance companies shouldn't mind paying the clinical fee; they should be used to paying it. I want you guys to get back there and fight to get them to pay this to me."

All of a sudden, Langston's wife came into the room. She was a pretty blonde woman in great shape in her late 40s, and she held a portable telephone.

She said, "Langston, there's a call here from Jeff's wife for him."

Jeff got on the phone. "Yes, honey, what is it?"

"There's been a terrible problem at the hospital. One of your patients, Jumpy Johnson, is on the news. They're saying he kidnapped a nurse and has taken her prisoner in the hospital along with another patient. They're mentioning your name on the news. I guess his wife told them about you. You've got to get over there and help."

"My goodness. I've got to get to the hospital right away," said Jeff as he hung up the phone. "One of my patients has taken two people hostage at the hospital."

"Just remember what I said about my clinical fee," said Langston, "and, by the way, make sure the hospital doesn't get any bad publicity from your crazy patient."

****

Jeff got into his car and drove out of Cherokee Creek Estates. He passed by the mansion of an Atlanta Hawks' basketball star and then by the mansion of one of the top executives from Home Depot. He turned left onto McCoy Road. He started thinking about Mr. Johnson. He'd been his patient for over 20 years. He'd been to Mr. Johnson's daughter's wedding and the baptism of his granddaughter. Mr. Johnson had always been a good patient. However, there was that paranoid schizophrenia that had generally seemed to be under good control. He'd been treated by a psychiatrist at the Veterans Hospital, Dr. Fried, who saw Jumpy every other month.

Jeff wasn't sure what he could do when he got to the hospital, but he knew he had to get over there to see if he could help. He thought a little bit about how he had changed his practice and how, in the old days, he would have been on top of things and would have taken care of the patient himself. Twenty years ago, he would have been the admitting doctor and probably wouldn't have gotten that many consultants involved. Starting ten years ago, it seemed that the only thing he did when he admitted someone to the hospital was to call consultants to take care of them. So, it had been no fun taking care of the patients in the hospital anymore. All the glory, all the work was done by the consultants…what was the point? He didn't pay any alimony since his first wife was a successful doctor, but he still had two kids in college and now had two children with his new wife. He thought he'd made the right decision giving up his hospital practice, but he could only wonder now what had happened with Mr. Johnson.

****

Jeff saw news vans all around the hospital. There were policemen directing traffic, and they didn't want to let him turn into the doctors' parking lot. Jeff showed him his ID and said, "I'm the doctor for the patient that took the hostages." The policeman looked at him and laughed.

"You are joking. That patient's doctor came in about half an hour ago – Dr. Givagushrai."

"He's his hospitalist," said Jeff. "I'm his real doctor."

"You're his real doctor! How could you be his real doctor if there's another doctor taking care of him in the hospital?"

"I take care of him in the office, and, when he gets sick and goes to the hospital, Dr. Givagushrai takes over."

The policeman thought for a moment and then said, "So, I walk a beat until there's a crime, and then I turn it over to a real policeman to catch the criminal…kinda like that, huh?"

"Yeah, I guess so," Jeff sheepishly replied.

The policeman waved him into the parking lot, and he parked his car. As he walked into the hospital, he saw Cole Stone muttering and shaking his head as he was leaving the hospital.

"Hey, Cole, what's wrong?" Jeff asked. "You upset about my patient?"

Cole shook his head. "Shit. After 25 years of practice, I'm getting sued."

"You're getting sued…for what?"

"Don't even ask," said Cole. Cole shook his head, and he walked out the door.

Jeff got on the elevator and, on the third floor, he was joined on the elevator by Vijay Givagushrai. The two of them got out of the elevator on the fourth floor, and Vijay explained what was going on. They walked down the hallway escorted by four policemen. All the other rooms on the floor had been evacuated. There was a police negotiator trying to talk to Mr. Johnson.

"Here, let me talk to him," said Jeff. "I'm his doctor."

Jeff knocked on the door. "Mr. Johnson, this is Dr. Conner. I need you to come out right now."

A scream was heard from the other side of the door.

"Where were you when I needed you, Dr. Conner? You let these foreigners and Jews take away my manhood. You let them steal from me everything that I had. I needed you, and you were nowhere around. After 23 years…after paying my bills on time…after paying everything that I owed you, you were nowhere around. I don't want you. You get out of here! You're just like the rest of them…don't care."

One of the policemen said, "Dr. Conner, you and Dr. Givagushrai better get away from here. It sounds like he's really mad at you, and he's got a loaded gun."

Jeff Conner slowly walked down the hall to the elevator. He got off the elevator on the first floor and walked to his car and drove to his office. It had been his first visit to the hospital in over a month, and he'd spent less than five minutes there.

CHAPTER 9

Marc Fried pulled into the parking lot of the VA Hospital after his usual hour drive. He parked in parking space #23 which was reserved for a staff psychiatrist. As he crossed the parking lot and entered the building, he glanced around him. The Georgia Veterans Hospital was old and showed its age. Certain areas had been redone that were high profile including the area for spinal cord injuries, the operating rooms and the emergency room. The psychiatry area, which consisted of a group of locked wards as far away from the main hospital as possible, had never been redone after being built in the 1950s. Marc didn't go up to the locked ward today since it was his clinic day but kept walking down the first floor.

As he walked into the clinic area, he saw the short, fat, black secretary for the psychiatry clinics, Pearl, running towards him.

"Dr. Fried, Dr. Fried!" she was shouting.

He ignored her at first. She was too efficient for the VA. She had to keep things running on time. He knew it was a busy clinic day with at least 20 patients in this paranoid schizophrenic clinic.

"Dr. Fried, Dr. Fried, come quick, come quick. There's someone on the phone to talk to you.

Marc hated the way she said everything twice. Oh, boy, who could it be on the phone? He walked through the waiting area to the door which led to the back area where the exam rooms were located. The waiting area was packed with the schizophrenic patients and their wives. Some motioned at him; some just stared.

"Who's on the phone for me?" he asked.

"It's Mrs. Johnson, Mrs. Jumpy Johnson. She says it's an emergency."

Jumpy Johnson. Fried ran the name through his mind for a second, and quickly Mr. Johnson's image appeared. Mr. Johnson had been a paranoid schizophrenic patient of his for 15 years. He'd inherited him from a previous psychiatrist at the VA Hospital, Charlie McCoy. He remembered that he had had to hospitalize Jumpy years before after he tried to kill his son-in-law.

"Mrs. Johnson, this is Dr. Fried. How can I help you?"

"Dr. Fried, there's big trouble with Jumpy. We tried to get ahold of his doctor, Dr. Conner, for days but couldn't get ahold of him. They put Jumpy in the Pleasant Point General Hospital, and now he's gone berserk."

"What do you mean gone berserk?" asked Dr. Fried.

"I thought he was acting kind of strange; he seemed to get more and more upset. I don't think they gave him his medicine that he needed...his psychological medicines that you prescribed for him and we get down there at your hospital. Those medicines that calm him down. I think he's hearing those voices again."

"Why didn't they give him his medicines?" demanded Dr. Fried.

"His doctor, the doctor that they gave him in the emergency room, was some big Indian man. That Indian man didn't know nothing about him, and Jumpy didn't trust him."

"So, what has Jumpy done?"

"He's taken two people hostage in his hospital room. One of 'em was a nurse, and the other was his roommate. He's locked the door, and he's got his gun."

"Oh, Mrs. Johnson, can't they get in there and give him his medicine and give him a shot of Haldol? Can't someone talk to him?"

"He won't listen to anyone now. I tried, the police tried. You know him. Can't you come talk to him? Please, please, Dr. Fried, you're our only hope. They could hurt Jumpy; he doesn't know what he is doing. He might hurt someone or get hurt himself."

"Mrs. Johnson, I'll be there as soon as I can."

Marc Fried sighed. It was over an hour drive to Pleasant Point General Hospital. Today was a heavy clinic day. Twenty paranoid schizophrenics were already signed in. Just then, ten minutes late, in walked his worthless resident, Halle Saffre. Halle was from somewhere in the Caribbean. It amazed Marc that they could not get any American-trained residents in their psychiatry programs anymore, so they had to get all of their residents from out of the country. They all shared one common trait, he thought: they're all lazy.

"Halle, good to see you," Marc said.

"Ha, mon," Halle replied.

No manners either, Marc thought.

"Listen, Halle, I've got an emergency."

"Oh, mon, whachew wan' me to do?"

"I've got to drive up to Pleasant Point General Hospital. There's a patient of mine up there, Mr. Johnson, who apparently has used a gun to take two people hostage in a hospital room. They need someone to talk to him and probably inject him with some Haldol. The lives of three people are at stake. So, you're going to have to do clinic yourself today.

"Uh-uh, mon. No fuckin' way. We must haf 20 fuckin' patients today, mon. No good. Need you heah. Sheet, git police talk 'em out of dat."

"Listen, Halle. You're a resident. A first-year resident. If you want to make it to your second year, you're just gonna have to work harder and see those patients today. Twenty patients. You spend ten minutes with each one. You get out in four hours."

"Mon, listen. I tole my wife I'd be home by 2 o'clock to take care our kids. I ain't gonna see no 20 patients. You gonna hafta cancel some if you leavin'."

Pearl walked back into the office. "Dr. Fried, are you going somewhere?" she asked.

"Yes, I've gotta go see Mr. Johnson up in Pleasant Point. Can you do me a favor? Our resident doesn't feel that he can see 20 patients all by himself. Can you call Sheila Marks from the ward team and see if she can see a few patients to help out?"

"Mon, I see ma ten patients, and I'm gone. Whatever left is left."

"What dedication," said Marc. "If you want to have a job tomorrow, you'll see 15 patients. I'll get Sheila to come down and see five, and that's it."

"Mon, ya ain't fair to meun ya never do da work. Naw fair at all."

****

Marc left the clinic and started walking back to his car. How had he ever gotten into a situation like this? Residents who didn't care, couldn't speak English, and spoke to him like he was a piece of shit. He got into his car and drove it out of the parking lot.

Twenty years before, Marc had been one of the most promising researchers in psychiatry in the country. He'd done some of the pioneering work looking at twins with paranoid schizophrenia. Twins who'd been raised in the same environment and both were schizophrenics, those who were raised in the same environment and only one was schizophrenic and twins who were raised in different environments where one was schizophrenic and one wasn't or both were schizophrenic. He'd been able to publish articles in prestigious journals and had written several book chapters. It had taken him only five years to be promoted to associate professor, a record in the department of psychiatry. He was on his way. He worked hard, saw patients and had a passion for his job. It was a mission then to eradicate schizophrenia from the world. He'd gotten married to another psychiatrist in private practice. She was willing to work and make money while he climbed the ladder of academic success.

Then, his life changed. Over a period of two weeks, he'd come across a very interesting phenomenon. In his clinic at the VA, three of the paranoid schizophrenic patients mentioned auditory or visual hallucinations they'd had while at salad bars. All three had been doing well until eating at the salad bar; they'd then all had acute psychotic breaks. They'd had problems with the lettuce. It seemed too disorganized and all chopped up. There no longer existed any head of lettuce, the semblance of order they were prepared for. One had additional problems with carrots not being kept in their bowl properly and "flying" all around the salad bar. Another patient had had problems with the salad dressings being mixed in with each other and creating a vast array of colors. Marc was sure there was something going on with salad bars causing paranoid schizophrenics to break. He researched it but could find nothing in the literature. He developed a comprehensive questionnaire which he gave to all of his patients. Then he sent them on trips to a salad bar he'd designed and built in the psychiatric area of the VA Hospital. He spent thousands of dollars of research money and over a year of his time on the project and came to the conclusion that it was the color arrangement of salad bars, especially the vividness of the colors and the arrangements of greens and yellows that caused the patients to have psychotic breaks.

He published his data in *Psychiatry Today* - the most prestigious journal - and then presented his work at the annual psychiatric meeting. He was one of the keynote speakers of the conference which was covered by the national press. When his talk was through, the audience laughed and jeered. The next month, *Psychiatry Today* was filled with letters to the editor saying that Fried's work was "absurd," "ridiculous" and would "push research into schizophrenia back 50 years." Comedians learned of the research, and Marc heard his work satirized in skits on the Tonight Show and on Saturday Night Live.

That was the last time Marc presented at any meeting. After that, he followed the mantra of the typical VA Hospital doctor. Do as little work as possible, get noticed as little as possible and spend as much time at home and on vacation as possible. The VA provided him with six weeks of vacation a year plus every federal holiday off, which amounted to another two weeks of vacation a year. He got an additional two weeks of sick leave, giving him a total of two and a half months of vacation a year. His responsibilities as an associate professor were easy. One day a week, he had clinic where he saw ten of the stable chronic schizophrenic patients. Six months a year, he was in charge of the locked wards for the schizophrenic patients. There were 20 inpatient beds, and they were always full. His responsibilities included rounding with the resident for one to two hours on the new patients each day and then doing chart rounds on the old patients which took another one to two hours. On those days, he would get to the hospital at 8:00 a.m. and get out by 1:00 in the afternoon. On the months when he wasn't the inpatient attending, he could come and go as he pleased. He would get to his office by 9:00 or 10:00 a.m., read his journals and mail, talk to his colleagues over coffee, sometimes stick around for a free lunch in the doctors' cafeteria and then go home by noon.

He turned on the car radio to WSB 750, the 24-hour news station.

"Today's big story is that at Pleasant Point General Hospital, a patient has taken a nurse and another patient hostage. His name is Jumpy Johnson, and he is a 58-year-old man who was hospitalized a couple days ago for undisclosed reasons. Apparently, the patient became agitated and had a gun. This morning, he was able to overpower a nurse and his roommate. He has barricaded the door to his hospital room. Pleasant Point police are on the scene. So far, no injuries are reported. We will keep you updated on the breaking developments."

Marc turned the radio off. He knew Mr. Johnson well, and the more he thought about him, the worse he felt. He'd seen him once every other month for the last 15 years. He was one of the "stable schizos" he'd booked into his clinic to fill up a space that could have been taken by a more challenging patient. Mr. Johnson was a true oddball; he'd never worked but was on disability due to his illness. His wife, who did work full-time as a secretary, always accompanied him to his appointments. Mr. Johnson was never totally trusting and had expressed concerns over the last few sessions that people were trying to turn him into a woman. He had also heard voices that told him to rape women to maintain his manhood, but, as long as he took his antipsychotic drugs, he claimed he could ignore them. He'd had other wild ideas. A couple of months before, his wife said that he told her he wanted to impregnate all the women in their family. Marc doubled the dosage of Jumpy's medication at that point, and this desire hadn't resurfaced in their subsequent ten- to 15-minute sessions. Mrs. Johnson claimed their family doctor, Dr. Conner, was also aware of the problems because she'd taken her husband to see him several times. Dr. Conner's only comment to her was, "Make sure he keeps his psychiatrist's appointment."

At their last session one month ago, Mrs. Johnson was extremely concerned.

"He's starting to have wild thoughts again. You've gotta do something. Maybe lock him up in the ward."

Mr. Johnson had looked at his wife angrily. "I don't need to be in no locked ward. I know what's going on. I know who I am, what date it is and all those questions you always ask me, doctor."

Marc had asked, "Are you hearing any voices?"

"Not hearing any voices now except for yours."

"Your wife thinks you're having some more strange ideas, like people trying to hurt you again. That true?"

"Nah. Sometimes, I may do that…not usually. Just got too much time on my hands, doc, just got too much time on my hands."

Marc hadn't pursued it any further. Instead, he documented in the chart what both Mr. and Mrs. Johnson had said, refilled the prescriptions and said he'd see them in two months. He could tell Mrs. Johnson wasn't satisfied with the outcome. Looking back at it now, he realized that she had been right and that he should have paid more attention to what she said. The problem was that he was a VA doctor. He had no fear of lawsuits since the government couldn't get sued without giving its permission, and it wasn't about to do that. Also, there was no quality assurance, peer review or anything to try and maintain high standards of medical practice at the VA. Once you were faculty, you were faculty for life until you retired with your substantial government pension. There was no incentive to work harder or to become a better doctor. But when something bad happened to one of his patients, Marc's conscience would start to get the best of him. He worried that he'd gone down the wrong path years before when he decided to become what the students and residents called a "troll doc."

His wife had left him years ago, taking their two kids with her.

"I'm ashamed of you," she said. "Don't you have any pride anymore? Don't you want to be a better doctor? Don't you want to make more money? I make three times the salary you make…"

"Yeah, but you keep patients hospitalized longer than necessary in your psychiatric hospital until their insurance runs out. They're gonna put you in jail. I may be lazy and not care, but you're a criminal," Marc interrupted.

"It's within the law. It's what everyone does. We keep them there until they're better. At least I earn a living. You're still making $120,000 a year, and you're still just an associate professor. You're the butt of the jokes of your colleagues."

She'd left and moved to Richmond, Virginia, leaving him alone in his life as a "troll doc." He had enough money to do what he wanted and travel where he wanted. He dated infrequently and spent most of his time by himself either at home or at the VA. No one ever said anything to him about doing more research or trying to get grants. They were happy to have him there to see the patients – to "move the meat." To the staff at the VA Hospital, what he did was enough. They didn't feel that his only working an average of 15 to 20 hours a week was ripping off the government. Hell, many of them worked less and were paid more. He had to admit that to work like he worked without call or emergencies and to make what he made was a pretty sweet deal.

****

Marc got out of his car in the parking lot at Pleasant Point General Hospital and walked into the hospital's lobby. There was a policeman standing by the elevators.

"Sorry. No one is allowed on these elevators. We have a hostage situation."

"I'm Dr. Marc Fried. I'm here to see…"

He heard a voice shouting from down the hall, "Dr. Fried, Dr. Fried."

He looked down the hall and saw Mrs. Johnson running toward him. "Thank goodness you're here. You've got to help Jumpy. Please talk some sense to him. You're the only one who can help us. Please. Officer, this is Jumpy's psychiatrist."

The policeman allowed Marc into the elevator, and he rode it to the fourth floor. Marc walked with a policeman on either side of him down to Mr. Johnson's room. One of the policemen knocked loudly on the door with his nightstick.

Marc shouted, "Mr. Johnson, it's me, Dr. Fried. I'm here to help you."

"Don't want your help, don't need your help," came the reply from the other side of the door.

"Mr. Johnson, Just open the door and talk to me."

"I've got a gun. You guys try something funny, I'll kill your bitch."

"We won't try anything funny." Marc tried to say reassuringly.

"Get all the policemen to back way back. Way, way back. I'm coming to the door with the bitch's neck in my arm."

Dr. Fried motioned for the police officers to back up, and they retreated down the hallway. Suddenly, Marc felt important and powerful. He could hear a heavy piece of furniture being moved away from the door. Slowly, the door opened and he could see Mr. Johnson's face and a little bit more of his body, and then he could see one of his arms wrapped around a beautiful blonde woman's neck and the other hand holding a gun to her head.

"Doc, I know you're trying to control my mind. I know you tried to do it for 15 years. Now this is enough. Let me tell you one thing. I'm staying in here with this girl. When I get ready, I'm gonna impregnate her, and we're gonna have a whole set of new children who can take over this world and keep people like you out of our way. You gotta problem with what I'm saying? I don't want you, I don't need you around me, and, if you don't disappear in ten seconds, I'm gonna put a bullet through your Jew skull."

Jumpy slammed the door shut in Marc's face. Marc stood there bewildered, uncertain what to do. One of the police officers came up to him.

"OK, Dr. Fried, good try. Let's get you out of the way. We've got some real professionals to help out in these types of situations."

Marc walked down the hall and took the elevator down to the first floor. Mrs. Johnson was waiting for him when he got off. "Did you see him? Did you help him? Is he OK?"

"He wouldn't let me help him. Maybe the police can help him. This is their kind of situation. Gotta go."

Marc walked away from Mrs. Johnson without waiting for a reply. He got into his car and thought for a couple of seconds about returning to the VA Hospital, and then he drove home.

CHAPTER 10

D r. Jeff Conner was glad to get back to his office. What a morning it had been. First, getting called for an early meeting with Langston Harris to make sure Langston was making enough money and then finding out that a patient of his had taken two people hostage in the hospital and now wanted nothing to do with him. He was running an hour late to the office, but, since this morning he'd scheduled ten echo stress tests on healthy young adults with chest pain in his practice and was otherwise scheduled light, he knew he'd catch up quickly.

Echo stress tests – one of those loopholes in medicine that allowed primary care doctors like him to make an enormous amount of money with no work or risk. All he had to do was to be present in the office while the test was being done, and the insurance companies paid him $600 to $1000 a test for the facility fee. This was another good reason not to waste his time seeing sick patients in the hospital. Anyone who had chest pain in his practice over the age of 21 was immediately scheduled for an echo stress test. He'd put an extra page on his new patient questionnaire which dealt solely with questions about chest pain. Many of the questions were so vague that most people had to answer yes. For example, "Have you ever had heartburn but weren't certain it was heartburn?" Any yes answer on this page of questions automatically bought the patient an echo stress test. There was no reason to do these tests ever in men if they had a normal EKG since a regular treadmill test without echo was just as sensitive. In women, there was still debate about whether a regular treadmill test was accurate. So many experts felt that, if a stress test was done in women, it should include echo. But not many would agree with Jeff that a 21-year-old woman with heartburn who ran marathons should have an echo stress test.

Jeff ignored the facts, and at least half of the patients he scheduled for echo stress tests were men with normal EKGs who had answered yes to one of the 35 questions on chest pain. He didn't interpret the studies as he had a cardiologist do this who billed the patients his own interpretation fee. No, it was so sweet... Jeff got paid a facility fee of $600 to $1,000 simply for having these tests done in one room of his office and only had to be in the office if there was a problem. In order to ensure no problems, he only scheduled patients for the study who were 20 to 40 years old and had absolutely no cardiac history or family history of cardiac disease at a young age. He now had enough patients with chest pain to bring in the equipment and technician two days a week.

While the echo stress tests were being done, Jeff would schedule other patients to see but not quite as heavy a load as usual. He still saw new patients every ten to 15 minutes and follow-up patients every five minutes. He advertised in the *Pleasant Point Gazette*, a monthly Pleasant Point magazine, as well as in the Pleasant Point newspaper to attract as many patients as possible. He always mentioned that he diagnosed and treated chest pain in the ads. He also advertised that varicose vein injections were done in his office. A year before, he'd hired a woman who'd previously worked as a nurse anesthetist and had taken a course in treating varicose veins with sclerotherapy. She worked in Jeff's office full-time and treated ten to 20 patients a day for fees ranging from $200 to $400 – all cash. Jeff received 40 percent of all the revenue she generated for having her in his office, so he made sure to do good leg exams on all the women who came to his office.

"Hi, Jeff," said his wife as he walked in.

"Hi, Kelly," he replied. He was so glad he'd divorced his first wife and married a trophy wife. He loved to look at Kelly. She was a petite blonde with big, sparkling blue eyes who kept herself in great shape. She was 20 years younger than Jeff and had a lot of energy, especially in bed. He first met her when she'd interviewed to be his medical assistant. They had had a torrid affair, and he'd gotten divorced and promoted Kelly to office manager the same day. Kelly had never been a stay-at-home wife. She knew enough to know that she'd better be in the office with her husband to keep an even younger woman from grabbing him. Jeff hadn't wanted more children after having had two with his first wife, but Kelly had convinced him to have two more children with her. This kept him from thinking of retiring for many more years.

"What's going on, Sweetie?" he asked her.

"We just saw the news; they had on Mrs. Johnson."

"What did she say?"

"She said it was a terrible situation…mentioned your name. Said something about how they had tried to call you, but you weren't around. And she wasn't sure that the doctors who were taking care of her husband knew what to do to take care of him."

Jeff frowned. "Hm, not good publicity, huh. Well, let's get started. Time to start making some money. Is the first treadmill test ready?"

"Already going on. I went ahead and started it since you were late."

"Honey, you know there's supposed to be a doctor here… What if something had happened to the patient during the treadmill test?"

"Oh, come on, Jeff. The first stress test was John Thomas. That guy runs ten miles a day. He's not going to have any problem with the stress test."

Just then, Mr. Thomas came out of the room where they did the echo stress test. He was 30 years old and was in great shape.

"Couldn't find anything tougher to challenge me, huh, Dr. Conner?" he asked and slapped Jeff on the shoulder.

"I'll get that interpreted for you, and holler back at you," said Jeff.

"The technician who did it with me said everything looked fine," said Mr. Thomas. "But I guess if you tell me to go down from running ten miles to eight miles a day, I'll have to do it," he laughed.

"We've got nine more echoes today," said Kelly, "and you've got a bunch of patients to see."

Jeff walked to the first patient's room. He'd whittled his practice down to taking care of those that could be seen in five minutes or less. People with problems that required more than a few minutes of thought had to be sent to a specialist. He treated colds, uncomplicated infections, stable hypertensives and stable diabetics. He'd cut pediatrics out of his practice since it wasn't a big income generator. He was mainly interested in taking care of healthy young to middle-aged people with insurance and running as many of them through his office as he could.

He saw a new patient first. The patient was a 32-year-old man with chronic abdominal pain. He started telling Jeff about all of the previous doctors he'd seen and the tests that had been run. He'd seen this doctor at Emory Hospital in Atlanta and that doctor in Decatur. Jeff quickly went into his "dumb doc" act.

"Ya know. I'm just an ole country doc up here in Pleasant Point. You sound real complex. Ya ever been to one of them gastroenterologists?"

"Yeah, I've been scoped every which way."

Jeff rifled through the patient's questionnaire and scowled when he saw that every chest pain question had been answered no. Then, he saw that the man had a history of depression and was taking several antidepressants.

"Ya ever been on medication that helped with your abdominal pain?" Jeff asked.

"Nothing helps for long. They all help at first," the patient answered.

"Nuthin' I can do to help you today. We get you to see a gastro doctor; we gotta few good 'uns in this town. We got their cards out atta front desk where ya check out. My girls getcha taken care of."

Jeff coded the face sheet on the front of this patient's chart as a moderately complex visit. He hadn't even put a hand on the man's body.

The next patient was a young woman who complained of a headache. Jeff took a quick history and determined it was a sinus headache and gave her medicine for her sinuses. He also gave her a neurologist's card and told her that, if she didn't get better, she needed to contact the neurologist immediately.

The next patient was an older man who'd been hit in the eye by a tennis ball while playing tennis that morning. Jeff was concerned that he could have a corneal abrasion, so he called his ophthalmology colleague, Dr. Wu, who said he'd see the patient that day.

Jeff continued through his patients at a frantic pace, and, by noon, he'd seen 20 patients. Some of the patients tried to volunteer unnecessary information about their lives in general and their families, but Jeff fought to gain control of the conversation and made sure they didn't talk very long. Nine other stress echoes were completed by noon, and there were no problems. More importantly, Jeff had found an additional six people to sign up for echo stress tests among his morning patients.

"Gotta keep generating the income...gotta keep generating the income..." he told Kelly.

In between seeing patients, calls came in from two television stations and the *Atlanta Journal-Constitution* asking Jeff questions about Mr. Johnson's situation. All he would say was, "No comment."

The very last patient was an add-on who was a 35-year-old woman. Jeff read on her chart that this was a patient he'd last seen a few weeks before, and she was Mr. Jumpy Johnson's daughter. He'd last seen her for a cold, but, on the extensive chest pain questionnaire, she had said that, once three years before, she had had mild chest pain. Therefore, Jeff set her up for a stress echo which she was scheduled to have next week. On her chart, Jeff's nurse had written that she'd come in now for chest pain. When Jeff went into her room and started to talk to her, he realized that it was a ruse; the only reason she'd come in was to yell at him.

"I can't believe what you've done. You abandoned my father. You were supposed to be his doctor..."

"Now wait a minute, miss. I had people set up to take care of him – hospitalists."

"That's nothing. Those people knew nothing about my dad and that he was a paranoid schizophrenic. If you'd been there to take care of him, you'd have made sure he stayed on his medicine. He wouldn't have been so suspicious. You could have helped him. If anything happens to him, my family and I hold you responsible."

She stormed out of the exam room and walked quickly down the hallway. On her way out the door, Kelly reminded her, "That will be a $10 co-pay, Ms. Hoskins."

"Take the $10 co-pay and shove it up your ass!"

Kelly was a little confused, but she smiled sweetly and said, "And don't forget about your stress test next week."

"You just shove that right up in there after my co-pay!" shouted Ms. Hoskins as she slammed the office door shut.

CHAPTER 11

"Come on in, Thomas," said John Smith as he walked out of his office and into the small waiting area. "How are you doing?" he continued.

"Pretty good," said Thomas Kelly as he followed John into his office and sat down in a leather chair in front of John's huge desk.

John Smith had the most impressive office Thomas had ever seen. John was the CEO of Pleasant Point General Hospital, but his office rivaled those of the CEOs of Fortune 500 companies. There was wood paneling covering every wall with very expensive built-ins and even an elegant glass bar. John's chair was an enormous swivel chair made of the same oak as his desk. Its seat was higher than usual, making John appear taller than his 5 feet 6 inches. Even with the heightened chair, John still looked small next to Thomas's 6 foot 6 inch frame.

"Where'd you get that painting, John?" Thomas asked, pointing to a painting hanging on the wall behind John's desk.

"Oh, wife and I picked that one up in Laguna Beach about three weeks ago. Was out there for a little conference," he chuckled. "Went into a gallery. Corporate said I could spend 10 grand on a painting, but, with Pleasant Point General Hospital being their top national money-producer, they never argue with my purchases. This is by some famous French artist who is either dead or gonna die. Only $25,000, but they told me it'll be worth 50 grand once he kicks the bucket."

"Really looks beautiful," said Thomas. "Hey, heard the hospital has been having big problems today. What is going on? People taking hostages. Everyone is talking about it. There's policemen all over the place. We're not allowed to go up to the fourth floor. What a mess, huh?"

"Yeah, what a mess," John repeated. "Some crazy patient that no one knew about took Krystal – that gorgeous nurse with the long blonde hair and blue eyes…"

"Everyone knows Krystal," interrupted Thomas.

"Well, took her and some other patient hostage in his room. It's a police matter, and I'm gonna let the police handle it. Just gives the hospital a black eye. Like we should know if a patient is schizophrenic when he walks in the door? So, I'm just keeping things low key down here and answering the press' questions. Mainly, I'm saying, 'That's a police matter, and you need to direct that question to them.' Between you and me, I have no fucking idea what 's going on. Oh, yeah, and I've told the press that these hostage situations occur all the time. They're a way of life, and we have a company policy on how to deal with them. That's what corporate told me to say. Of course, when I asked corporate what the company policy was, they said, 'How the hell you let that happen?' What they expect, I'm supposed to keep an eye on every single patient? Anyway, Thomas, I have got another problem for you."

"What is it?"

"One of our doctors, you'll never guess who, has been complaining about the radiology department. He claims you have got a monopoly, and he thinks it's affecting patient care."

Thomas laughed. "Of course we have a monopoly. Why else would we pay you $50,000 a month under the table not to let any other radiologists practice in this hospital? We've been doing that for well over 20 years now. We did it for your predecessor, and he retired rich and young. And now, we're doing it for you."

"Well, it's Aaron Bernstein who is complaining," said John.

"Figures," said Thomas. "He's always a complainer." Thomas's eyebrows furrowed.

"Let me tell you what he said. He came to me with three cases in which he claims his patients' x-rays were misread by people who did not have the qualifications to read them." John looked down at the legal pad in front of him.

"The first one was a 60-year-old man who was having some swallowing problems. Aaron said he specifically asked for you or Arnold Goren to perform the barium swallow on this man because he was concerned that this man might have something unusual going on. He said that, instead, you had a brand new lady radiologist by the name of Lizzy Chen do the study, and she read the swallow as completely normal. He claims that, when he did this patient's endoscopy and put the scope into his esophagus, he almost went straight through a Zenker's diverticulum which, I didn't know this, is a pocket in the top of the esophagus. Bernstein said this diverticulum should have been seen on the barium swallow exam. He claims she completely missed it, and, if he hadn't been paying attention, he would have gone right through that pocket and put a hole in the esophagus."

"Shit, those things can be missed even by the most experienced radiologist. He needs to pay attention when he puts that scope into someone's esophagus," Thomas said angrily. Thomas felt himself losing his cool. He reassured himself by remembering the check for $50,000 in his pocket. No matter what John said, he thought, once he took that check, everything would be OK.

"The second case Aaron brought to my attention was a 50-year-old man who he said he did an upper GI small bowel follow-through on because they found a little blood in his stool. He said the radiologist who did the test was a radiologist you had hired to be one of your MRI radiologists."

"Oh, come on," said Thomas. "You know all of our radiologists are well trained. They can all do upper GI series."

"Yeah, but this one didn't do a real good job. Aaron says that this radiologist, R.C. Blackburn, read the x-rays out as being completely normal. But, when the patient came back to see Aaron three months later with nausea and vomiting and dilated small bowel on x-ray, he repeated the small bowel series, and the patient had a small bowel cancer the size of a baseball. Aaron said that tumor had been there three months earlier. Aaron said that Blackburn missed seeing it three months before and that he wasn't qualified to do GI series. Aaron also said that he had requested you or one of the senior radiologists to do the exam."

"I don't have time to read all of his stinking x-rays," said Thomas. "I've been here for 20 years. Shoot…you know half the time, I'm on vacation."

John laughed. "Yeah, what are you up to, about six months a year vacation?"

"Yes, I do take six months off now," said Thomas. "But you know when I started, the first couple of years when it was just me and Arnold, I took one or two weeks vacation a year. Arnold and me, Carson, Jerry and Perry, we built up this radiology department. We all need some time off now. Hell, I'm 50 years old. I gotta have time to golf, to go watch my son play basketball. I gotta see the world now."

"You are the chief of the radiology department, and you have to be aware of these complaints. I'm afraid Bernstein is going to take it to corporate if you're not careful."

"Well, I know that the money I've been paying you through the years is going to help protect me, I mean us, against corporate. Listen, the radiology department runs better as a monopoly. It's true we've got radiologists reading studies that aren't in the field where they did a fellowship, but they're all good general radiologists."

"Bernstein claims that you hire them just to fill a chair… that there's so many x-rays to be read that you have to find warm bodies."

"They are all from good certified programs…"

"But Bernstein says that some of them are right out of their training and reading some of the most difficult studies that they may not have done in a couple of years. He told me about a third case where someone came in with lower abdominal pain, and the only person you had on that weekend was Al Ross."

Thomas chuckled. Al Ross was one of the few radiologists they'd ever had to fire. Al was a 50-year-old alcoholic who was willing to work the weekends when no one else would. Al would even work the deep night shift from 11:00 p.m. until 6:00 a.m. Thomas knew the case John was going to talk to him about because Bernstein had been by to see him about it a few weeks earlier.

"Anyway, Bernstein says that Al Ross read this CAT scan on a late Saturday night as being completely normal. But Bernstein was so concerned that he asked Ross to please have someone else look at it. Al told him that there was no one else around, and that was final. Bernstein claims he called and called and finally had a copy of those x-rays made because the patient was in such agony. He took the films to another hospital and had the radiologist there read them, and he was told the patient had…let me read this now… He said, 'Portal vein thrombosis.' Bernstein says he had the patient operated on immediately by a vascular surgeon, and the patient lost 70 percent of his small intestine. Had to be taken out, he said. It was rotten."

"We had to fire Al but not for that," Thomas said coolly. "He was an alcoholic. Portal vein thrombosis can be a real difficult pickup on CAT scan. I looked at those films myself, and, yes, I would have seen it, but I'm not blaming Al or anybody for missing it."

"You know how Bernstein is," said John. "He's a conscientious mother fucker when it comes to his patients. He told me that anything that interferes with the care of his patients interferes with his life. He said that, in every other field whether it's surgery or internal medicine or pulmonary, he has a choice of who he wants to consult and have help with his patients. Except for radiology. He said, and I wrote this down, 'The radiology department here is set up as a monopoly. Five men on top who are here about half the time. They have young radiologists and sometimes older radiologists doing most of the work, some of which they are not capable of doing. And, when I want one of the senior doctors to look at the films after hours, they're either not available or not able to get back to me for days. It interferes with the care of my patients, and I don't think it's fair that I can't choose who I want to have read my patients' x-rays.'"

"Let's go over this again," Thomas said slowly. "My group and I pay you $50,000 a month to keep things status quo. The radiology department in this hospital is set up as a monopoly. There are five of us at the top who either started the practice 20 years ago when the hospital opened or became partners in the practice in the first two or three years after the hospital opened. No one else will ever become a partner. Everyone else we hire will always work for us. We have on our payroll between 20 and 30 radiologists who we pay salaries anywhere from $150,000 to half a million dollars. Most of them are really good. The few that aren't, we can usually weed out and convince to find employment elsewhere. All the money for the procedures performed and the x-rays read comes to the five of us. I make a little more than the other four just because I'm the medical director. We always have a radiologist available whether it's 3 in the morning or whether it's 6 o'clock on Christmas Eve. We provide excellent radiology coverage. I can't be here all the time. I need to be gone about six months a year. There's always someone available. I think that most people would say that we provide excellent coverage and excellent service for the hospital. And I know you're going to say that since you get paid a pretty penny by us."

John sensed that Thomas was taking control of the conversation. "What do you want me to tell Bernstein?" he asked.

"You tell him to come talk to me. I'll tell him everything I just told you, and I'll also explain to him what it took for a poor black boy like me to come to Pleasant Point, Georgia, from Birmingham, Alabama, set up this department and run it for 20 years. That fool's got no idea about the work that was involved."

"Don't you think you should be a little kind and compromising with him? You know what I mean? Just kind of stroke him a little bit."

Thomas was mad, but he knew that John was probably right. If he were to talk to Bernstein now, he'd tell him to go fuck off and might be tempted to hurt him physically. Thomas was an imposing physical specimen. He knew that he could easily intimidate Bernstein with his 6 feet 6 inches and 250 pounds of muscle. But John was right; there was no sense in stoking the flames further. Thomas knew that Bernstein was a good doctor. He was conscientious and cared about his patients. It was only yesterday that Thomas had had his weekly x-ray rounds with Bernstein. One day a week, Bernstein came down to the radiology department, and all the films that hadn't been read by a senior radiologist were reviewed by Thomas and one of the other senior radiologists, Arnold Goren, with Bernstein present. The rounds took 30 to 60 minutes, and the first year or two he'd done it, Bernstein hadn't been happy about this extra demand on his time. But now, he just kept his mouth shut and went over the films with Thomas and Arnold.

"You know, now that I think about it, I remember a few years ago Bernstein stirring up the pot a little bit with me. He was unhappy with how his films were being read, and he said something like, 'Hey, my office has to get these x-rays precertified with the insurance companies. We have to do all the work. All you guys have to do is sit down and read the x-rays and collect your money. And yet, I still can't get the doctors who I want to read the films to read them.' You know what I told him then?" asked Thomas.

"What?" asked John.

"I told him that I would personally meet with him and look at any of the films that he wasn't comfortable with the readings. I'll just do that again. I'll meet with him and tell him I'm sorry. If he's worried about emergency coverage when patients come in on the weekends or after hours, I'll give him all of our home phone numbers and tell him to feel free to call us. That will quiet him down."

"Thomas, I knew you'd come up with a good solution. You got my check?"

Thomas handed him the check for $50,000.

"John, don't you ever, ever even think about letting another radiologist set foot in this hospital!"

John put the check in his wallet. "I'd never do that, Thomas, never."

****

Thomas left John's office and walked down the hallway of the hospital. He passed a couple of police officers talking on walkie-talkies. When he got back to the radiology department, he called his wife on the telephone.

"Sugar, what time is Thomas's game tonight?"

"It's at 6 o'clock, sugar," she replied. "It's the first game of the tournament, and so they're starting at 6. By the way, your brother called. He said he wanted you to pick him up, and he'd go to the game with you. He was telling me about when the two of you played basketball together in high school."

"That was a long time ago," said Thomas cutting her off. "Talk to you later, sugar. Goodbye."

Thomas hung up the phone and began to daydream. He thought about his son, Thomas, who, as a freshman, was a starting guard on the Pleasant Point High School varsity basketball team. He was 6 feet 3 inches and reminded Thomas a lot of himself.

Thomas had grown up in Birmingham, Alabama. His mother was a cleaning woman, and his father worked in a local factory. They'd both worked long hours to make sure there was always food on the table and a house to live in. Thomas had four brothers and sisters, and all five children had gone to an all-black high school and then to college. Thomas had been a great student and a very good basketball player. He was a starting forward on his team which lost in the finals of the Alabama State High School Basketball Championship. He was the team's leading scorer and rebounder and made second team All City. Thomas knew that he was a good ballplayer, but the times he'd gone up against the top players in the state, they had dominated him. That's why he decided Harvard and the Ivy League were the best options for him. Harvard didn't have athletic scholarships, but they offered him a full academic scholarship, and he accepted.

He played his freshman year and was voted to the Ivy League All Freshman Team. He had a successful sophomore year also. However, at the start of his junior year during a game against Yale, he awkwardly landed on an opposing player's foot with a rebound and tore up his knee. He never played another minute of college basketball but concentrated his last two years on making the grades and getting into medical school.

He'd excelled at Harvard Medical School, and, when it came time to choose a residency, he'd talked to one of the few black doctors on the faculty. This doctor was a radiologist and had a teaching position as well as a private practice. He described to Thomas how he was the chairman of the department of radiology at a big hospital in Boston and how he got paid a percentage of all the x-rays that were read at that hospital. "It's a quick way to become a millionaire," he told Thomas, "and you don't have to work hard. And 20 years from now, when you're 50 and your classmates who went into internal medicine and surgery are still working their asses off, you'll be able to have as much free time as you want."

So, Thomas had done a radiology residency at Harvard, and then he looked around the country for a job. He thought he'd go back to Alabama, but there was a hospital opening in Pleasant Point, Georgia, that needed radiologists to work there. Thomas had signed up along with Arnold Goren, and they had been the two original radiologists at the hospital.

Just then, Arnold tapped Thomas on the shoulder. "Hey, you want to look at this case?" he asked.

"Sure." Thomas got up from the chair, and he towered over Arnold.

"What's the story?" Thomas asked as he looked at the CAT scan.

Arnold gave him the history, and then Thomas gave him his interpretation.

Arnold nodded his head. "Thomas, you're right. It's amazing how you can see things that we can't."

It was true. Radiology was a gift. A talent of reading shadows, and Thomas had the gift.

"Let's go over to my office and talk a minute," Thomas said.

He and Arnold walked down the hallway through the radiology department to Thomas's separate office. They went in and closed the door.

"We've got some trouble on our hands," said Thomas.

"What's up?" asked Arnold.

"Bernstein is trying to break up our monopoly at this hospital. He claims we don't have the right people reading his x-rays and that he should have the opportunity to consult whoever he wants as a radiologist rather than the person that we've hired who's working that shift."

"He had some similar complaints a few years ago, didn't he?" Arnold asked.

"Yeah. I'll need to talk to him. But I wanted you to be aware and be on your guard and be extra special nice to him. Make nice." Thomas laughed, and Arnold did also.

Thomas said, "And we've got another problem. I got a certified letter today from Corcoran's attorney. He's suing us for $10,000,000. He claims we hired him under false pretenses."

Albert Corcoran had been an interventional radiologist who had worked for the group for three years. He had asked them about becoming a partner, and they'd given him the standard line: he had to pay the equivalent of one partner's salary and work a total of ten years as an employee in order to become a partner. What they didn't tell him was that each partner's salary was $3,000,000. When Corcoran found this out after three years, he said that there was no way he could pay that amount and that, when he was hired, he'd been given no indication that the buy-in would be so steep. Albert had complained to the hospital administration as well as to various doctors in the community and was starting to generate some support from some of the younger physicians in the community when he was abruptly fired. Thomas and the other partners in his group maintained that Corcoran was fired due to incompetence, citing several patients who had died after Corcoran had done procedures on them. However, all the doctors knew that some deaths were to be expected in an interventional radiologist's practice since he did risky things on very sick patients. Arnold had played the part of the bad guy, telling Albert what a terrible job he'd done and all the problems he'd caused and that the hospital administration was on their backs to fire him. Thomas had played the good guy role and had promised Albert a good recommendation and told him that he'd help him find a job. Thomas had kept his word, finding Albert a job at a hospital in Waco, Texas. But Albert had been pissed off, and now it was coming back to bite them.

"It's coming back to bite us in the ass," said Arnold. "From now on, why don't we just lay it out from the start what it takes to become a partner?"

"You know if we do that, we'll never get anyone who's interested in becoming a partner to work for us," said Thomas.

"No one will ever accept employment for ten years and a $3,000,000 buy-in."

"Yeah, we gotta come up with something different," said Arnold. "Hey, by the way, how was Australia? You have a good trip?"

Thomas smiled. "It was one of the best months of my life. We just had so much fun down under in Australia. We saw the whole country, traveled around, took that three-day train ride across the country... Aren't you going to China next week?"

"I'll be gone for the next three weeks," said Arnold. "Gotta get back to work now."

"Arnold, I'll be cutting out early today. I'll probably be leaving about 1:00 or 1:30. Thomas Junior's got a basketball game, and I want to hit the driving range before the game."

"No problem," replied Arnold. "We'll just keep getting work out of these young eager radiologists."

They both laughed.

CHAPTER 12

When Thomas Kelly got to Peachtree Country Club, he grabbed a couple of his golf clubs and headed straight to the pro shop. He spotted Roger Powers working behind the counter at the pro shop. He'd grown up with Roger in Birmingham, and somehow both of them had ended up in Pleasant Point, Georgia, Thomas as a very successful physician and Roger as the head groundskeeper for the Peachtree Golf Course. Roger had been a good high school football player and still maintained an imposing physique with thickly-muscled arms and a huge, powerful chest. He did a lot of the necessary physical labor on the golf course, but, at times, like today, worked the counter in the pro shop.

"Hey, Rog," said Thomas, "how's life treatin' ya?"

"Doing great, doc, doing great. Gonna hit some balls at the range?"

"Yeah, gimme a large bucket. Gonna hit those, then go see Junior play in a tournament tonight."

"That boy of yours is a helluva ball player, you know," said Roger. "You gotta lot to be proud of, you know."

"He's growing up well," said Thomas. "Good boy, too. Already receiving recruiting letters from the colleges."

"Remind you of yourself when you were the superstar back in Birmingham?"

"No, I think he's gonna be a lot better than I ever was. Better ball handler, more mobile, much better shooting touch."

"Don't sell yourself short," said Roger. "You were a legend at that high school, you know. And to think, you know, now they got that high school named after you. The Thomas Kelly High School, wooee!"

Thomas laughed. "The renaming of the high school had nothing to do with my being a ball player. That had to do with me giving them a big fat check."

"I know, I know," laughed Roger. "Just incredible. You gave them like $5,000,000 two years ago, didn't you?"

"Yeah, $5,000,000 is what I donated. Enough to build a completely new library and to update the chemistry building so that they'd have laboratories for the kids to do experiments in."

"Fuckin' incredible," said Roger. "You're the only black man I know still livin' that has a high school named after you. You know, my sister's kids go to Thomas Kelly High School. She told me you helped raise another $5,000,000 to improve that school."

"I did organize the fundraising for the school. I got black celebrities and sports stars to give the school money and merchandise to be auctioned off to raise more money. It was quite an undertaking. But, hell, to know that your nieces and nephews and my relatives and other black kids benefit from attending a superior high school makes it all worthwhile. You know, that high school library has more books now than any other high school in the state of Alabama."

"Jes amazin', jes amazin'," said Roger. "Here's your bucket of balls. Oh, by the way, thanks for sponsoring the country club's inner city teen golf tournament again. What's this, like the tenth year you've sponsored it? It's the only time I see any black kids out here who aren't working here."

Ten years before, Thomas had come up with the idea of a golf tournament for minority teenagers at Peachtree with scholarship money to be given to the winners and gifts given to all the participants. It was a way to expose black children to golf and to reward those who were excelling. Thomas learned that many of the better players needed help just buying the basic golf equipment, so everyone who entered the tournament got at least a $500 gift certificate to purchase golf clubs. Thomas had given $100,000 ten years ago to get the tournament rolling, and, by now, he had sponsors who every year matched his $100,000.

"I'm hoping my son, Jess, can play this year," said Roger.

"Has he been practicin'?" asked Thomas.

"Sure, he's been hittin' balls at the range and putting in our backyard. He's convinced he'll be the next Tiger Woods, you know. This will be his first time playin' on a course, you know."

"Well, get him out here and let him start playin'. He can come out and hit some balls with me if he wants."

"I might have 'em do that," said Roger. "He could learn from you. What you got, like a five handicap now?"

"It's between five and eight," said Thomas. "When I play more, it's five, and, when I play less, it's eight. I got to get Thomas Junior out here after basketball season ends. He can hit the ball a mile."

"Speaking of Thomas Junior, you ever hear anything from your boy in Atlanta?"

Thomas frowned for the first time since he'd left the hospital. "No, haven't talked to him since I saw him two years ago in Birmingham. Gotta go, Roger. See you later."

"Good to see ya, doc. Thanks for all you do."

****

Thomas carried the bucket of balls out to the driving range and poured ten balls out of the bucket in a straight line. He picked up his driver and stood over the balls but didn't swing the club. Roger had asked about the other Thomas Junior who Thomas had fathered out of wedlock 32 years ago when he was a high school senior.

Thomas's girlfriend in high school was named Shirly. She was tall, very attractive and was one of the school's cheerleaders. She was also the star of the high school's track team and set school records in the 100-yard dash and long jump even though it turned out later she was pregnant with Thomas Junior at the time. Unlike Thomas whose skin color was light brown, Shirly was dark black. Thomas and Shirly would have sex several times a week in the apartment in the projects that Shirly shared with her sister and her sister's family. The apartment had only one bedroom, so Shirley slept in a makeshift bed in the hallway closet that she and Thomas could barely fit into together. Shortly after Thomas arrived at Harvard, he received a call from Shirly telling him she was pregnant. She delivered Thomas Junior over Thanksgiving, and Thomas first saw his son that Christmas. He brought back matching crimson T-shirts with HARVARD on the front for the baby and Shirly. He spent a few days with Shirly and his son that holiday but had to leave the day after Christmas because Harvard was playing in a holiday basketball tournament on the West Coast.

The letters and phone calls from Shirly decreased after New Years, and Thomas found out from his brother that Shirly had become a heroin addict and was strung out all the time. He saw Shirly when he got home from school that summer, and she looked terrible. She'd lost a lot of weight, and her eyes sunk into her skull. A grotesque-looking scar was engraved on her left cheek. Even though it was summer, she wore a long-sleeved sweatshirt to hide her track marks. Thomas confronted Shirly about her drug addiction and how it was affecting their child, and they'd had a vicious argument. Shirly called Thomas "whitey" and told him that he didn't care anything about her or their baby. The argument ended with Shirly telling Thomas that she never wanted to see him again, and he could never see his son again.

During his sophomore year, Thomas' brother sent him a newspaper clipping from the front page of the *Birmingham News*. The largest drug house in Birmingham had been raided by the police, and 25 people had been arrested. The large picture on the front page of the newspaper showed a year-old black baby boy who had been rescued from the drug house and was wearing a Harvard T-shirt.

Shirly died in jail two years later, and Thomas Junior was raised by her sister. Thomas saw his son a few times when he was home from college, but then he'd gotten married and the visits ended. He didn't see Thomas Junior again until he was in high school. Thomas was in Birmingham over the Christmas holidays seeing his family, and he read in the newspaper that his high school had a basketball game that night. The article previewed the game and detailed the accomplishments of his high school's center, the 6 foot 8 inch Thomas Kelly, Jr.

Thomas went to the game that night and saw his son for the first time in 14 years. Junior was an imposing presence on the court; he was about 250 pounds of solid muscle. His game, though, was very undisciplined. On one play, he skied above everyone to grab a spectacular rebound and then dunked the ball. He took his time getting down court after that play, though, and his man scored an easy lay-up with Thomas hacking him from behind. Later, Thomas got called for a technical foul for throwing the ball at an opposing player, and his coach had taken him out of the game. Their team was far ahead at the time and ended up winning easily.

When the game was over, Thomas left the bleachers and walked over to where his son was standing on the court.

"Hi," said Thomas to his son, "great game. Do you know who I am?"

Thomas Junior looked at his father intently. His face was a copy of his father's but a few shades darker. Then, he smiled. "Don't you tell me you're my fuckin' father," said Thomas Junior. "You look just like me but whiter. I feel I'm looking in the fuckin' mirror."

"I am your father. I just wanted…"

"Where the fuck you been the last 18 years? I always heard you're a fuckin' rich man. How cum I ain't never seen any that money?"

"Let me try to explain…"

"Lissen, man, you wanted anything to do wif me, you'd been here years ago. You can give me some money, but I don't want anything else from you."

Thomas Junior walked off, and Thomas remembered standing there alone in the gymnasium among hundreds of people.

Later that year, Thomas received a newspaper clipping from the Birmingham newspaper from his brother. Thomas Junior and two of his teammates had been arrested after robbing a small Korean grocery store and murdering the owner and his wife. Thomas Junior was later found guilty and sentenced to life in prison.

****

Thomas visited his son in jail for the first time when he went to Birmingham for his high school renaming. His wife and children knew nothing about his first son, so he went alone to see him in the penitentiary.

The guards led him to the visiting area, and he sat down and waited behind the Plexiglass wall. Junior was led out in handcuffs and was wearing a bright orange prison jumpsuit. He was even more muscular than when Thomas had seen him in high school and looked to have grown a couple of inches. His head was shaved, and he had tattoos covering his entire body except for his face.

"So, my fuckin' dad, come to see me again, huh…"

"Junior, I mean Thomas, I just wanted to come and say hello. I don't know what else to say…"

"Yeah, what the fuck do you want to say? Where the fuck were you? I had to rob and kill to get you to come out and see me." Thomas Junior started to laugh. "You gonna get me outta this fuckin' hole? You gonna hire some fast-talking lawyers to get me outta here?"

"Thomas, I don't know that there's much that I can do to help you. Is there anything I can get you that you need in prison?"

"Shit, man, I never needed anything from you. My auntie tole me 'bout you. You were a smartass, went to Harvard. Didn't want anythin' to do with us once you gotcher college education. Now you're a rich doctor, and they're naming my high school after you. You gave them $5,000,000. Where was some money for me? Where were you when I needed you growin' up? Only man I had was Uncle Cedric. He taught me how to play ball, and only he spent any time with me. When Uncle Cedric was killed when I was ten, you know who was there for me…no one. I was the man of the family. So, you know what I did… that's right, mother fucker, I robbed and I robbed and I ended up killin' someone tried to stop me. I don't think of you as my daddy, never have."

Thomas Junior got up from his chair on the other side of the glass and waved his handcuffed hands at Thomas in disgust. "Take me back to my cell," he said to the prison guard. "I don't want any more this bullshit."

****

Thomas began hitting the golf balls but couldn't get Thomas Junior out of his mind. While he was outdoors on this beautiful day in Pleasant Point, Georgia, his son was rotting in a dark prison cell in Birmingham, Alabama.

CHAPTER 13

Vijay Givagushrai walked into the emergency room at Pleasant Point Physicians Hospital and glanced at the clock. It was 1:30 p.m. It was time to start call at Pleasant Point Physicians Hospital. This was a hospital on the west side of Pleasant Point approximately ten miles from Pleasant Point General Hospital. It was new, approximately ten years old, and, whatever reputation it had developed so far wasn't good. However, it had been a fertile source of patients for Vijay, and almost all of them had insurance, so Vijay and his partner took as much emergency room call there as possible. Today, Vijay was on call for both internal medicine and family practice and had been called by the emergency room doctor and told there were three admissions waiting for him.

The first patient was a 55-year-old black man who had no insurance and was only being admitted to try and detoxify him from alcohol. He'd come to the hospital because of a cut on his arm which the emergency room doctor, Dr. Riley Burbank, said needed suturing which would be done before Vijay got to the emergency room. Other emergencies had come in, however, and Dr. Burbank hadn't gotten around to suturing the cut.

Vijay waved to Dr. Burbank.

"Come with me, Vijay," Dr. Burbank said. I'm just getting ready to sew up Mr. Sanders's arm."

Vijay smiled at him. He figured he'd meet Mr. Sanders, do a brief history and physical on him and move on to the insured patients. Five to ten years ago, patients like this never were admitted. It was only with the advent of hospitalists that patients who had almost no reason to be admitted were now being admitted. Because the hospitalists made their living taking care of patients in the hospital, there was no reason for the emergency room doctors to take the liability of refusing anyone admission. Therefore, the percentage of patients who came to the emergency room and were admitted had skyrocketed.

Vijay walked into emergency room #4 with Dr. Burbank.

"This is gonna be your doctor in the hospital," Dr. Burbank said to Mr. Sanders. "His name is Dr. Givagushrai, and he's gonna watch you for a couple of days so you can withdraw safely from alcohol. You also had a couple of blood tests for your liver show up abnormal, and Dr. Givagushrai is gonna take care of that."

Vijay wrote the first order on the order sheet to consult Dr. Aaron Bernstein, gastroenterologist, regarding abnormal liver tests. He looked at the liver test abnormalities on the lab sheet and recognized the classic picture of alcoholic liver disease. He needed to have at least one consultation on every patient, though, and Aaron was always a good one to start with.

"Mr. Sanders, come sit down on this stretcher so I can take a good look at that arm," said Dr. Burbank.

Mr. Sanders was a black man dressed in brown pants and a brown shirt which was covered in mud. He was carrying a torn brown overcoat. He had an IV in his left arm, and his right arm was caked with blood. There was a trail of blood droplets from the entrance to the room all the way to the stretcher he was on. Around the upper portion of that arm, a T-shirt had been tied. Mr. Sanders held his right arm with his left arm. He had a scraggly gray beard streaked with black, and his hair had the same mixture of colors in wild disarray. He moved from his stretcher to the one Dr. Burbank was at. Dr. Burbank untied the T-shirt at the top of the right arm.

Vijay asked, "How'd this happen, Mr. Sanders?"

"I don't know," came the high-pitched reply.

"Looks like someone took a knife and gutted your arm. Were you trying to kill yourself?"

"Kill myself? No, doc. Some dude took a beer bottle and did this."

"You must have done something to him…"

"No, doc. I didn't do nuthin' to him. I was jus mindin' my bizness, sittin' on the street when this crazy dude come and cut me up."

"You don't know who it was?"

"No, doc. I dunno."

"You smell like you've been drinking a lot. What have you been drinking?"

Dr. Burbank interrupted, "Now, we're gonna clean this arm off so we can look at it." He poured water and Betadine into a basin.

"Wait a minute, doc…"

"Just a little soap and water. Best medicine for…"

"Jes wait a minute, doc. This gonna hurt me."

"Not half as much as that beer bottle. You'll see…"

Mr. Sanders screamed, "Shit. That sting. Take it off. Please, doc. Take it off."

"We gotta clean you up real good now," said Dr. Burbank. "Put that arm back down there."

"You hurt me. Wait a minute, doc. Wait a minute, doc." Mr. Sanders began singing, "Wait a minute, doc. Oh, won't you wait a minute, doc. Please wait a minute, doc."

"You're still drunk," said Dr. Burbank.

A nurse came into the room.

"Bring me a suture tray and ten of Valium," Dr. Burbank told her.

Then, Dr. Burbank returned to cleaning off the arm, and Mr. Sanders began to scream. Suddenly, Mr. Sanders reached out with his left arm and pulled the tray holding the basin of soapy water onto the floor. There was a loud crash, and the floor was covered with soapy water.

"Now why the hell did you do that?" demanded Dr. Burbank.

"You hurt me, man!"

"I was only trying to help you. You want to lose this arm? It's going to get infected now, pus up, and you're gonna lose it."

"Sheet, I'm sorry, Mr. Doctor. You got anything for me to drink? My nerves need calmin' real bad. Look at my hand shakin'."

The nurse brought in a syringe containing Valium 10 mg and gave it to Mr. Burbank. He immediately injected the contents into Mr. Sanders's IV.

"I'm giving you a shot to help your nerves. Give it a couple of minutes to take effect, and I'll be back. I'm gonna let Dr. Givagushrai ask you some questions and get you admitted to the hospital." Dr. Burbank left the room.

The floor of the room was now a mixture of blood and soapy water.

"I hate this mother-fuckin' place!" screamed Mr. Sanders. "Hey, bro, ya gotta drink on yer?"

"Sorry, I don't."

Mr. Sanders farted loudly. He grinned. "Ooh, I'se foul, ain't I? My arm gonna fall off. Ha, ha, ha. I don't care. Don' make no mind to me. Sheet. I ain't ne'er gonna let no doctor touch me. I'se feel tired. Gonna lay down. Don' chewse be botherin' me now, doctor. You a big boy. You a big, big nig. Ha, ha. You a big, big nig. Only you brown, not black." Mr. Sanders laid down on his stretcher.

"Can I ask you some quick questions? Do you have any other medical problems?"

"No, doc."

"Any other surgeries?"

"No, doc."

"You take any medicines?"

"No, doc."

"You're healthy, huh?"

"Yeah, doc. I healthy."

"We're gonna put you in the hospital, give you some vitamins and give you some medicine to help you withdraw from alcohol and let that arm start to heal up. Get a gastroenterologist to see you about your liver tests. Let me examine you real quickly."

Vijay took out his stethoscope and listened to Mr. Sanders's heart and lungs. The Valium was starting to take effect, and Mr. Sanders was drifting off to sleep. Vijay then examined Mr. Sanders's abdomen. Mr. Sanders had some right upper quadrant tenderness on palpation, and his liver seemed a little enlarged. Vijay finished writing the orders and went back out to see Dr. Burbank.

"Where's the next one?" Vijay asked.

"You got one in Room 7 over there. That's the black woman that overdosed on Tylenol."

Tylenol overdose, thought Vijay. That meant three days in the hospital for 17 doses of glutathione. The story that Burbank had told him over the phone was that this patient was schizophrenic and had had a schizophrenic break. She'd fought with her husband, locked herself in the bathroom and had taken 100 Tylenol pills. Her Tylenol blood level was well into the toxic range, necessitating admission. She'd already received the first dosage of glutathione in the emergency room. Vijay knew that the two issues in this case were to treat the patient for her Tylenol overdose with glutathione and also to get her therapy for schizophrenia with psychiatry. On his way to Pleasant Point Physicians Hospital, Vijay had called the psychiatrist on call that day for the hospital. However, the psychiatrist's secretary said that the psychiatrist didn't come to the hospital anymore, but a psychiatric nurse from Yellow Pine, the psychiatric hospital, would be by to see the patient.

Vijay thought about how worthless psychiatrists were since none were willing to help on hospitalized patients. All they wanted to do was sit in their office for eight hours a day, see patients for 15-minute appointments, charge them at least $150 and prescribe medicine for them. None of them even did counseling or psychotherapy anymore. So there was no reason for psychiatrists to go to medical school, concluded Vijay, since all they needed to do was to go to pharmacology school and learn about the few drugs that they prescribed. Psychiatry was a disgusting profession and had deteriorated from the 1980s and 1990s when psychiatrists had owned their own hospitals and kept patients in them until their insurance had run out. There had been a series of scandals back then, but the psychiatrists had gone through them relatively unscathed. Now, rather than helping people, all they did was prescribe drugs. This was a patient who had tried to commit suicide, who had tried to kill her husband, who was acutely schizophrenic, and he was going to be left with just a psychiatric nurse coming by to help with her.

Just then, Vijay saw a young, pretty blonde woman with a bright blue ribbon tied around her ponytail walk into the emergency room. He recognized her from his prior dealings with her as a psychiatric nurse from Yellow Pine Psychiatric Hospital. He went up to her and put out his hand.

"I'm Dr. Givagushrai. We've met before."

"Yes," she said. "I'm Stacy Swift, the nurse from Yellow Pine Hospital."

"You're here to see Mrs. Young."

"Yes, I'm here to interview her for Yellow Pine. Of course, we won't be able to take her until she's medically cleared, but she does have insurance, so once you give her clearance, we'll admit her to Yellow Pine."

"I haven't met her yet," said Dr. Givagushrai. "Do you mind if I come in with you when you see her?"

"Sure, come on. It'll be a good chance for both of us to get to meet her."

Dr. Givagushrai accompanied Stacy to Room 7. There were two police officers sitting with Mrs. Young.

"Hello, officers and Mrs. Young. I'm a nurse from Yellow Pine, the psychiatric hospital, and my name is Stacy. Do you officers think you could wait outside the door while I talk with Mrs. Young?"

"OK. We'll be right here if you need us. We'll keep the door open."

"Mrs. Young, I'm Stacy Swift from the Yellow Pine Hospital, and this is Dr. Givagushrai who is going to take care of you while you're in this hospital."

Stacy pulled up a chair and sat down five feet from Mrs. Young. Vijay stood in the doorway in case he needed to leave.

"Now, Mrs. Young. Why don't we start by you telling me a little bit about what happened to your eye?"

Mrs. Young had a black eye. "None of your mother-fuckin' business, whore."

"I'm sorry…"

"None of your fuckin' business."

"Were you in a fight? The doctor said you were in a fight. Did someone hit you?"

"Did someone hit you, fuckin' whore? What happened to your eye, blonde bitch?"

"Were…ah…are you having trouble with your thinking lately?"

"You having trouble with your thinking lately, you little slut?"

"Do you feel someone is trying to control your thoughts or put thoughts into your head?"

"Your mother!"

"You feel my mother is putting thoughts into your head?"

"Your mother and your father."

"How do you know them? What kind of thoughts are they putting into your mind?"

"That you a slut. A stinking whore who be talkin' down to me."

One of the policemen walked back into the room. He shook his head and slowly walked back out.

"Tell me about your relationship with your husband."

"None of your mother-fuckin' damn business, slut."

"Why do you think I'm a slut?"

"Cause you a whore."

"Do you have anything against me personally?"

"Do you have anything against me personally? You're a cunt, and your mother was one, too."

"How do you know my mother?"

"Cause you're a fuckin' slut."

"Were you angry with your husband today?"

"None of your fuckin' business. Course I was angry, whore. That fuckin' bastard hit me in the eye."

"Were you having an argument with him?"

"Were you having an argument with him? What do you think, dumb slut, talkin' down to me like that?"

"Would there be any possible reason that you'd want to kill him?"

"No, slut. I don't want to kill him, slut."

"Is there any reason you don't like me?"

"No, ain't no particular reason I don't like you, whore."

"Are you hearing any voices now?"

"Your mama want…"

"You hear my mother?"

"Yeah, slut."

"What's she saying to you?"

"She ain't sayin' nuthin' 'cept you a whore."

"Do you know where you're at now?"

"I don' give a shit, slut. When you gonna leave me alone?"

"I'm only trying to help you. I'm a psychiatric nurse, and my job is to try and help people who are having problems with their thinking. I understand that your husband filed a complaint with the police stating that you were saying all kinds of unusual things, that you accused him of fooling around. Then, you came after him with a knife. Do you remember that?"

Silence.

"Have you taken any drugs lately?"

Silence.

"Do you ever take drugs?"

"I want out of this place."

"I'm almost finished with my interview now, Mrs. Young. A few more questions. Do you know where you are?"

"No."

"Are you in a hospital, a jail or a school?"

"A hospital, you slut."

"Do you know what today's date is?"

"Ain't talkin' to you no more, slut. Get the hell out of my room." Mrs. Young put her head down.

Stacy got up from her chair and walked out of the room. Vijay could hear the policemen laughing and talking to her outside the room. Vijay joined them outside the room.

"Is there anything you can recommend to help me take care of her while she's here in the hospital?" he asked Stacy.

"I'd just put her back on her usual psychiatric medicines that she's been on," Stacy replied. "Make sure she gets them. Twenty-four hour suicide precautions. Maybe give her some tranquilizers." Stacy laughed. "Good luck. Thank goodness when you call us in three days, I'll be off. It's your problem now."

Vijay grinned at Stacy but was angry. That's the way it was with the psychiatrists. All of their patients became his patients and his problems. He went back into Mrs. Young's room and told her, "I just need to examine you. I know why you're here, and we'll take care of you while you're here. If you cooperate with me, we'll get you out of here as soon as possible."

Mrs. Young's exam was unremarkable with the exception of her black eye and a few teeth missing which had been knocked out recently. He admitted her to the medical surgical floor and wrote for her doses of glutathione. He kept her on her psychiatric drugs but added Haldol as needed. He checked her blood tests, and one of her liver tests was two points above normal. He wrote an order to consult Dr. Aaron Bernstein, gastroenterologist, for abnormal liver tests.

"Two down," said Vijay as he walked back out to where Dr. Burbank was standing. So far, Vijay had spent about 30 minutes in the emergency room.

"Got another one for you over here," said Dr. Burbank. "Lady having seizures. Family brought her in…apparently hasn't been taking her Dilantin."

Vijay followed Dr. Burbank to Room #19. Dr. Burbank opened the door, and Vijay saw that the room was filled with people. There were ten people in the room, and lying on the stretcher was a woman who was convulsing. She was a white woman in her early 20s, and her convulsions were unusual. She was doing pelvic thrusts as though she was having sex, but she was also shaking her head and flailing her arms wildly.

"We can't seem to break her seizures," said Dr. Burbank. "Her Dilantin level was below the therapeutic range, so I loaded her with Dilantin IV. Now, I'm going to need you to take over and admit her."

"Absolutely," said Vijay. "How long as she been seizing?" he questioned the ten people in the room.

"I'm her mom." A woman came forward who appeared to be in her 50s. "She's been doing this for at least three or four hours."

"Shit," Vijay whispered louder than he wanted. Status epilepticus. Got to break it or possible brain damage. "I'll be back," Vijay said.

Vijay went out to the doctors' area of the emergency room and looked up the telephone number for the on-call neurologist for the emergency room, Keith Newton. He called Dr. Newton's office and told the receptionist to get Dr. Newton immediately for an emergency.

Dr. Newton came to the phone and sounded annoyed. "What is it?" he asked gruffly.

"Keith, I need you to come down to Pleasant Point Physicians Hospital emergency room right away. I've got a young woman in status epilepticus, and we've gotta break her out of it. They've loaded her with Dilantin and haven't touched her. She's got these seizures; it's terrible."

"Vijay, I've got an office full of patients. I can't get over there now."

"This lady could have permanent brain damage. You're on call for neurology for the emergency room. She needs you. I don't know what to do to break it. Burbank and I have been working on her. Nothing we do seems to help. You've got to get here STAT."

"It's my whole afternoon. I've got ten patients...OK. I'll come down there. I'll cancel things. If you're sure she's in status epilepticus."

"I'm sure."

Vijay hung up the phone and went back into Room 19. The young woman was still seizing. He got the history from the patient's parents. She had a history of seizures and had been very upset the last few days about boyfriend troubles and hadn't taken her Dilantin. She had lost her job about a week before and had been depressed about that also.

"She woke up this morning seizing and hasn't stopped," her mother said. "She vomited twice before we got here."

The patient was rolling her eyes back and forth now and shaking her head wildly from side to side. Her arms were taut and then limp.

Vijay tried to examine her, but it was nearly impossible. He wrote admission orders which included a GI consult with Dr. Aaron Bernstein for nausea and vomiting. Then, his beeper went off. It was the Intensive Care Unit at Pleasant Point General Hospital. Dr. Greg Segal, a pulmonologist and critical care specialist, was calling him. He left Room 19 and went out to the doctors' area and dialed the Intensive Care Unit.

"Yes, this is Dr. Givagushrai. Dr. Segal, please."

Greg Segal came to the phone. "Vijay, I saw this case of pneumonia you asked me to see in the Intensive Care Unit."

Vijay looked through his patient cards. He'd asked Greg to see Bitsy Collins, an 83-year-old woman who Vijay had taken care of on the fourth floor the last three days and who he'd had to move to the Intensive Care Unit this morning. She'd been admitted with a urinary tract infection and fever from a nursing home. Today on rounds, she'd seemed very short of breath to Vijay, so he'd ordered a chest x-ray. The chest x-ray showed both lung fields were "blossomed out" with infiltrates, so he transferred her to the Intensive Care Unit with presumed pneumonia. He'd done cultures and put her on a more potent antibiotic than the one she'd been on for the urinary tract infection. He hadn't really examined her at all because she was one of the 25 patients he'd had to round on that morning. He knew that all he really needed to do was to get her to the Intensive Care Unit and get a pulmonologist to see her.

"Yeah, I don't think she's got pneumonia," said Greg. "Vijay, I think you overloaded her with fluid. She's in heart failure. Those infiltrates you're seeing on chest x-ray are from congestive heart failure. I went through her intakes and outputs for the last three days that you've had her in the hospital, and she's plus almost ten liters."

"You've given her ten more liters of IV fluid than she's put out. I've just given her some Lasix, and she's already breathing better. I hope we can turn her around with Lasix, but I may have to intubate her if she doesn't continue to improve. I just wanted to update you on her condition."

"Oh, Greg, that's fine," Vijay replied. "You just do what needs to be done. I'll talk to you later. Bye."

Vijay hung up the phone. It was amazing how he didn't feel badly that he'd completely missed the diagnosis and almost killed Mrs. Collins, but it didn't really bother him at all. His job was to admit and discharge the patients, get the proper consults and let them do their thing. The more patients under his care, the more money he made. And, if he made mistakes in patient care, there was always someone around to straighten things out. He walked back to Room 19 just as Keith Newton, the neurologist, arrived.

"Is this her?" Keith snarled.

"Yes," Vijay replied.

Keith walked into the room. The first thing he said was, "Everybody leave except for the patient." The family and friends looked at Keith and Vijay, frowned and grimaced. "We don't want to leave," said the patient's mother.

"You've got to leave so I can examine her," said Dr. Keith Newton. Everyone in the room filed out slowly.

Keith turned to Vijay. "OK, Vijay, now is this the patient you think is in status epilepticus?"

"Look at her, Keith. She's seizing. They've loaded her with Dilantin."

"Miss, how are you feeling now?" asked Keith.

The young woman stopped seizing immediately. "Oh, I'm terrible. I don't know where I am, what's going on…"

"Open your mouth," demanded Dr. Newton.

She opened her mouth. There were no bites on her tongue and no bleeding.

"OK. Can you tell me who's the President of the United States?"

"Uh…I don't know, but I know it's someone, Bush, Clinton, I can't think of his name."

"So, you've been seizing for about three or four hours?"

"Yeah."

"Vijay, come with me." Keith and Vijay walked out of the room and down the hallway.

"Vijay, this lady is having pseudoseizures. Any medical student could see that. If she was having true seizures, she'd be postictal now. She wouldn't be able to talk to me. She wouldn't be able to do anything. This lady doesn't need to be loaded with Dilantin; she needs a psychiatric consult. Next time before you call me and ruin my whole day, you need to examine these patients more closely!" Keith shook his head in disgust and started to walk away.

"Hey, Keith, Keith. Wait a minute. I still want you to consult on this patient and follow her with me. I'll get a psychiatric consult, but you need to see the patient, too."

Keith shook his head again. "OK. I'll follow the patient while she's in the hospital."

Vijay added an order to the chart to have the patient evaluated by psychiatry even though he knew it would do no good since it would just be that same blonde nurse coming to see her.

Vijay went back and talked to the patient's family and told them what Dr. Newton had said. The family wasn't happy with this diagnosis and were openly skeptical.

"Now that we have her loaded with Dilantin, we'll see how she does," Vijay said. "We'll have the neurology and psychiatry services keeping an eye on her also. Maybe she can go home in a few days."

"You know something?" asked the patient's father, speaking for the first time. "Our daughter has been to four or five other hospitals for these seizures also. These aren't fake seizures. These are real seizures. I don't think you know what you're doing. I'm gonna call around, and, the moment I can get her transferred to another hospital to another doctor, I'm gonna do that."

"Sir, that's your right," said Vijay. "But as long as she's here with us, we'll take as good care of her as we can."

Vijay left Room 19 and returned to the doctors' area of the emergency room. It was time to call consultations on the three patients he'd admitted. The first call he made was to Dr. Bernstein, the gastroenterologist.

CHAPTER 14

Aaron Bernstein got back to his office, sat in his chair and put his head in his hands. He had just undergone the worse nightmare of a gastroenterologist. He had missed a lesion on colonoscopy the year before and now had found it on follow-up. The day had started out so shitty with Mr. Johnson going crazy and taking hostages in the hospital. Aaron blamed himself for not picking up on Mr. Johnson's illness and potential for disaster. Aaron's last procedure today had been a follow-up colonoscopy on a 60-year-old woman who was a prominent attorney's wife. A year before, she had had five polyps that Aaron had removed from her colon, some of which were adenomatous polyps which were precancerous. Aaron had brought her back for a one-year checkup and easily advanced the scope around to the end of her colon. However, at the very end of the colon, the cecum, there was a small amount of liquid stool covering the lining. It appeared to be covering something, and, when he washed it off, he found a large, flat polyp at least 5 cm in size. It was so flat and so large that he couldn't remove it through the scope but could only biopsy it. The only recourse for a polyp this size would be surgery. He could wait for the biopsy results to get back, but, if it was cancerous or precancerous as he suspected, this patient would need to undergo removal of the right side of her colon.

Certainly, a polyp of that size had been there a year before when he'd done her original colonoscopy… or had it? Everyone now expected a gastroenterologist to be perfect. The public felt that, if they came in for colonoscopies, their polyps would be discovered and removed in a timely fashion. This would save them from getting cancer and also save them from having to undergo major surgery. This would not be the case in this patient, and Aaron was kicking himself for it. But maybe the polyp had sprung up in the last year. All the literature suggested that no, a polyp that size had been there a year ago. What if the lesion had been too flat for him to detect a year ago? Aaron kept giving himself ways out. But his mind kept rejecting them. After he found the polyp, Linda, his endoscopy nurse, had said, "Didn't you just scope her a year ago?"

Aaron felt terrible. He'd had to tell the patient's husband what he'd found. The husband was very upset to hear that there was now a large polyp in his wife's colon a year after her colon had supposedly been cleared of all polyps.

Aaron thought about being a gastroenterologist. He'd always compared being a gastroenterologist to the famous saying from Julius Caesar in Shakespeare's *Julius Caesar* play: "Cowards die many times before their deaths; the valiant never taste of death but once." Aaron felt that the updated quote should say: "Gastroenterologists die many times before their deaths…" because there was constant concern among gastroenterologists about missed lesions in the colon. There didn't seem to be a day that went by where Aaron didn't get a call from a patient who was now having rectal bleeding that he'd done a colonoscopy on in the past year or two. Of course, the patient was now concerned that he or she was now bleeding from colon cancer. Or a call from a doctor's office saying that a patient now presented with anemia and was Aaron sure that, when he'd done the colonoscopy, no cancer had been missed that could now be slowly bleeding. Just a week before, he had gotten a call from a female internist in Pleasant Point who had referred a patient a few years back for a colonoscopy. Now, that patient had shingles, and the internist was concerned that the shingles were related to an underlying malignancy, possibly in the colon. It was a constant battle. Gastroenterology was not a clean field at all, in fact, it was a field in which you could never to 100 percent certain. In his 13 years of practice, Aaron did not know of any cancer that he'd missed on colonoscopy. However, he had heard reports of other gastroenterologists who had patients turn up with colon cancer a month or two after their colonoscopy. Anytime he was called with anemia or rectal bleeding in a patient that he'd done a colonoscopy on, a chill went through his body. That chill was what he was experiencing now.

Aaron glanced at his office wall and saw his diploma from residency. One of the signatures on the diploma was Dr. Ekram Barbosian. Dr. Barbosian had been Aaron's ward attending during residency at Ben Taub Hospital in Houston. Dr. Barbosian had always said that, in medicine, there are three categories of doctors. First were technicians or surgeons who did procedures on patients and corrected immediate problems but really did not take care of the patient long term. The next group he called physician orderers. These were the internists and family doctors who ordered tests like x-rays and labs but then had to rely on other doctors to interpret the tests and to treat the patient. These doctors never truly took care of patients either. The final category of doctors, according to Dr. Barbosian, was the healers. These were not technicians or orderers but rather doctors who worked to actually heal patients throughout their lives. Dr. Barbosian had said that Aaron and the other residents should always strive to be healers; no matter what specialty they went into, they shouldn't allow themselves to be merely technicians or orderers.

****

Aaron was so upset about what was going on that he felt he was going to boil over. He needed to talk to someone, someone who could give him a different perspective on what he was going through. He leafed through his Rolodex, found Dr. Barbosian's number at Ben Taub Hospital in Houston and dialed it.

"Dr. Barbosian's office. This is Chantella speaking. May I help you?"

"Yes, this is Aaron Bernstein calling from Pleasant Point, Georgia."

"Yes, Dr. Bernstein. I remember when you were here at Ben Taub Hospital years ago. We haven't seen you in a long time. How are you?"

"I'm fine. Actually, maybe I'm not so fine. I wanted to talk to Dr. Barbosian if he's not too busy."

"I know he's never too busy to talk to you. There's a doctor in his office, though, so let me call in."

Aaron was on hold for a moment, and then he heard Dr. Barbosian's deep voice on the line.

"Aaron Bernstein, haven't heard from you in a few years. How are you?"

"I'm doing OK in general, but I'm having a rough day and wanted someone to talk to. Are you busy now, or can you talk?"

"Oh, I'm not too busy. I'm just sitting here trying to teach one of our bright interns the difference between respiratory alkalosis and metabolic acidosis, one of those basic things in medicine that we try to drill into your heads in residency so that you can go out and practice stellar medicine when you leave the nurturing confines of Ben Taub Hospital."

Aaron laughed. He envisioned Dr. Barbosian's office full of smoke from the pipe which never left Dr. Barbosian's lips and the intern and Dr. Barbosian sorting out the mysteries of medicine in between clouds of smoke.

"You know I'm still in practice in Pleasant Point, Georgia. You may have heard that one of our patients took two people hostage today; it's been all over the news. He was a patient I was consulted on yesterday, and, unfortunately, I didn't know he was a schizophrenic."

"How long had he been in the hospital?" Dr. Barbosian asked.

"A couple of days, but I'd only seen him once, the night before."

"Aaron, you're always too hard on yourself. You need to let go sometimes. You're not perfect. None of us is…"

"I know, I know. But I also did a colonoscopy on a patient today who had a huge polyp that I had done a colonoscopy on a year ago, and I hadn't seen anything in that area."

"Aaron, you and I know that colonoscopy, like any other diagnostic tool in medicine, is not 100 percent accurate. The way medicine promotes colonoscopy now, you'd think that we would find every polyp before it had a chance to turn into cancer. Impossible. Mammograms can't do it for breast cancer, and CT scans can't do it for lung cancer. Colonoscopy is just a tool. It helps people, but it's not perfect no matter whose hands are on the scope.

"I just want to do a good job. I just want to do my best," Aaron said. "I still want to be a healer."

"You are a healer. You were always interested in helping people and saving lives. The money and power of medicine were never your motivations. I think you've always remembered why you went to medical school and became a doctor. The first day of your residency when I asked you why you were here, you said, 'to help people.' You said you hated to see people suffer. Do you remember what I said to you then? Try to ease people's suffering and make them better if it is possible. Don't ever let the outside distractions bother you."

"That's part of the problem," Aaron said. "There's these outside distractions. The hospitalists, doctors who don't even know the patients, taking care of them. There's always the threat of malpractice and lawsuits…"

"Aaron," Dr. Barbosian interrupted, "medicine and the outside world have changed dramatically in the 40 years that I have been a doctor, and they will continue to change. Many times, unfortunately, the changes aren't for the better. You must stay committed to helping people. And when you've done everything that you can, remember, you are human. You are not God. People will die in spite of your best efforts. It happens in Ben Taub Hospital, and it happens in Pleasant Point, Georgia. Diagnoses will be missed despite your diligence. It happened today to my little intern friend here in my office. It will happen to you, and it will happen to me. Don't let it make you sick. A sick Aaron Bernstein can't help anyone. There were times during your residency when your patients weren't doing well, and you seemed so down that I didn't know what I was going to do with you. Remember, Aaron, keep balance in your life. Enjoy your wife and family and cherish the love they have for you. You know you can always call me. I have been teaching doctors for 40 years now, and you will always be one of my favorites. Keep your chin up."

"Thanks, Dr. Barbosian. You've helped keep things in perspective for me. I'll stay in contact."

****

There were two phone messages on Aaron's desk. One was a message from his wife. He wouldn't call her now because he didn't want to worry her with how upset he felt. His eyes wandered to the pictures on his desk of his wife and three children. Marcy's picture was from just after they'd gotten married when she'd been a petite, 5 feet 4 inches, and 115 pounds. She'd refused to let Aaron have a more recent picture of her in his office. The children's pictures had been taken at last year's Thanksgiving dinner, with all three children sitting at the table devouring turkey with chopsticks.

The other message was from Aaron's sister who only called when she had a problem. Aaron's sister was ten years younger than him. She'd been married for a few years and had just had her first baby. Aaron dialed her number, and she answered the phone and immediately started complaining.

"I just got a bill from your hospital. We owe them more money."

"I thought you told me you'd paid your deductible, and everything else was going to be paid for by your PPO."

"Yeah, but guess what? The nurse anesthetist who put in my epidural wasn't on my insurance plan. They're out of network; their bill was $1,200. My insurance says reasonable and customary is $500, so I'm out $700."

"Did you have a choice?" asked Aaron. "Could you have gotten a different nurse anesthetist on your plan?"

"Are you kidding? This guy just showed up in my hospital room and said, 'I'm here to put in your epidural to make this delivery pain free.' Do you think I was going to turn him away?"

"That's not fair. That's going on in my own hospital, right?"

"Yeah, your hospital is running a racket. They're letting anesthesiologists and nurse anesthetists who aren't on anyone's insurance plan do their procedures on unsuspecting patients and then bill the patient for the difference between what they charge and what the insurance pays. We patients have no choice in the matter. I'm going to call the insurance commission."

Aaron chuckled in spite of himself. "Lot of good that'll do you. Anything else?"

"I got another bill from the pathologist at your hospital."

"Pathologist? Why would a pathologist send you a bill?"

"I had some lab work done while I was there for 24 hours – an SMA7 and a CBC. The pathologist sent me a bill for $50 for interpreting my lab work."

"Oh, my goodness. That's right. The pathologists have what they call their clinical fee for supposedly keeping the machines in working order in the laboratory. They actually have nothing to do with how the machines work, and they don't even see the lab results they billed you for."

"Can you talk to them? Can you talk to the anesthesiologist about giving me a break? You know, we don't have much money. We're just starting out, and Shawn is just getting over his heart attack."

"Listen, Cindy, I've had a really rough day, but I'll just put it on my list of things to do, OK, and I'll send you guys some money. Bye."

Aaron hung up the phone.

****

Aaron kept thinking about his sister and her husband, Shawn, and what they'd been through in the last several months. They didn't need the bill collectors hounding them. They'd had the ultimate high of having their first child one month ago, but they'd also had to endure what could have been a devastating tragedy.

Shawn was a 37-year-old car mechanic with the appearance of an outlaw but a heart of gold. He was over 6 feet tall, thin as a rail, and had blonde, stringy hair and a scraggly, unkempt beard. His many vices included smoking and drinking to excess. He admitted to smoking two packs a day but Aaron never remembered seeing him without a cigarette in his hand or one in an ashtray next to him. Shawn wouldn't smoke in Aaron's house, but the smell of cigarette smoke on him was enough to send Aaron's asthmatic sons into paroxysms of coughing.

Six months ago, Shawn began having chest pain. He treated himself for heartburn with Maalox for a month but got no better. He saw an ad in the Pleasant Point newspaper for chest pain sufferers and made an appointment to see Dr. Jeff Conner. Dr. Conner spent less than five minutes with Shawn and then signed him up for an echo stress test which was done the following week. Shawn exercised for seven minutes but had to stop because he was so out of breath. He never heard from Dr. Conner again, but he got a call from Dr. Conner's office one week later saying that the test was normal. Shawn called Dr. Conner's office one week after that, still complaining of the chest pain, and was told by Dr. Conner's nurse to take some over-the-counter Zantac and, if that didn't help, to see a gastroenterologist.

The chest pain became more frequent and more painful. One Sunday morning, Shawn called Aaron at home just as Aaron was walking out the door to work out at the gym. Aaron could tell from the sound of Shawn's voice that there was trouble.

"What's going on?" Aaron asked.

"I'm having severe chest pain, and it won't go away. I've had it since last night at 9 o'clock. I couldn't sleep. I've had pain like this before, but it never lasted this long."

"What does it feel like?" asked Aaron.

"It's right in the middle of my chest. It feels like someone is squeezing my chest with a wrench, tightening and tightening it."

"Didn't you get that evaluated by your family doctor?"

"Yes, I saw...oh, it hurts...hold on a minute. I saw that doctor that advertises in the magazines and newspapers for chest pain, and he did that stress test which I had to stop 'cause of my breathing. But they said my heart was OK, and it must be heartburn, so I should call a gastro doctor if it didn't go away. That's why I'm calling you."

"Have you called Dr. Conner today?"

"I jes...hold on...shit, this is a motherfucker pain...called their answering service, and I got called back by another doctor taking calls for Dr. Conner this weekend. He told me to go out to the store and buy me some more Maalox. Aaron, I'm not a pussy, and I'm just miserable. I can't stop sweating. Help me!"

Aaron thought to himself that this didn't sound like typical heartburn and needed further evaluation immediately. "We'll get this figured out," Aaron said. "Have Cindy drive you to the emergency room at Pleasant Point General Hospital. I'll call ahead and tell the emergency room doctor to be expecting you."

Aaron called the emergency room doctor and told him briefly about Shawn's symptoms and negative evaluation. He drove to the emergency room, and, when he walked in, Ron Rose, the emergency room doctor, waved him over to the desk where he was sitting.

"Hey, Aaron, bad news. Your brother-in-law isn't having heartburn. He's having a heart attack. An acute inferior MI."

"You're not joking?" asked Aaron incredulously.

"I'm serious as a heart attack, hah, hah," replied Ron Rose. "He came in here with a blood pressure of 151/105 and a pulse of 110 and was diaphoretic and pale. Hooked him up to an

EKG – here it is – he's having an acute inferior myocardial infarction."

Aaron looked at the EKG and saw the marked ST elevation in the inferior leads II, III and AVF. There was no doubt about the diagnosis.

"Who's on cardiology?" Aaron asked.

"You lucked out there. It's Peter Dickman. I already called him, and he's on his way."

"What room is Shawn in?" Aaron asked.

"Room 1," Ron replied, pointing to the room right across from the doctors' station.

****

Months later when Aaron asked Shawn what he remembered about his experience in the emergency room, Shawn replied, "White. The color white. Everything and everybody was white."

Sure enough, when Aaron walked into Room 1, Shawn was lying on a white cot covered by a white sheet up to this chest with a nurse dressed all in white injecting morphine into his IV. Cindy was sitting in the chair next to the bed wearing a white T-shirt with BABY ON BOARD written across the belly.

Cindy got up from her chair. "Aaron, what's going to happen to Shawn? You heard he's having a heart attack."

"Cindy, he's going to be OK." Aaron walked over and stood next to Shawn's head. Shawn was pale as a ghost, just as white as the sheet he was lying on. His teeth were clenched. Sweat was running down Shawn's face, so Aaron took a washcloth from the cabinet, soaked it in cold water and wiped the sweat off.

"Aaron, I'm so scared. I'm pregnant and Shawn's been having this chest pain for months. Why didn't they find it was a heart attack? Why couldn't that family doctor have found this on that stress test?"

"I don't know," replied Aaron. "But none of those tests are 100 percent."

"Shit. I'm still hurtin'," Shawn moaned.

"How much morphine have you given him?" Aaron asked the nurse.

"He's gotten three injections since he got here. I'll go ask…"

Just then the door to Room 1 swung open and in walked Peter Dickman. He was wearing violet scrubs with Peter Dickman, M.D., written in cursive over the pocket on his chest. The white clogs he was wearing made him appear much taller than his usual 6 feet 3 inches. His brown, wavy hair was perfectly in place, and his blue eyes brimmed with confidence. When he opened his mouth to speak, every tooth was perfectly aligned and dazzlingly white.

"Aaron, didn't expect to see you today. This is your brother-in-law, huh? Shawn, sorry to have to meet you and your lovely wife under these circumstances. I just looked at your EKG and blood work. You're having an acute inferior myocardial infarction which means that the bottom of your heart isn't getting enough blood flow. Kind of like stopping up the pipes that supply water to your house so, when you turn on the hot water, nothing comes out. We're gonna fix that for you right now and get you feeling better. We'll take you over to our cath lab and put a catheter up to your heart through your groin. We'll inject dye into the artery supplying your heart and find the one that's blocked. We'll open that artery up for you, and there's a good chance we'll leave a little stent or tube in there to keep that artery open. We'll take good care of you and get you feeling better right away."

Aaron glanced at Cindy and saw that the scared, overwhelmed look on her face had been replaced by a look of calmness and optimism. She was nodding her head in agreement with everything that Peter was saying.

"Any questions that you or your wife have?" Peter asked.

"No," Shawn replied through clenched teeth. "Just get rid of this pain. This is the worst pain I've ever had in my life."

"Don't you worry," Peter answered. "When you come out of our cath lab, that pain will be gone."

Three nurses from the cath lab walked into the room.

"Great to see you guys. This is Shawn. Shawn, these gentlemen are going to wheel you over to the cath lab, and I'll meet you over there."

****

Aaron sat with Cindy in the waiting room outside the cath lab. Forty-five minutes later, Peter Dickman walked out.

"We got the artery 100 percent open," Peter said as he showed Aaron and Cindy the pictures from the cath. "This is where the blockage was in the right coronary artery. This picture shows how we opened it up, and this picture shows the stent we put in. Your husband is going to do fine. We're just going to have to get him to stop smoking and do some things about his blood pressure and cholesterol, and he'll be fine. I'll let you see him for a minute, and then we'll take him up to the intensive care unit where he'll stay until tomorrow."

Peter led Aaron and Cindy to where Shawn was lying in the hallway outside the cath room. Shawn was laughing and joking with the nurses standing around his stretcher.

"You did a great job, Peter," said Aaron. "Thanks."

Peter put his hand on Aaron's shoulder. "Anything I can do to help you or your relatives is a pleasure. Why don't you take your sister and get something to eat? Gotta keep that baby healthy." Peter laughed, turned around and walked away.

****

Aaron thought about Dr. Barbosian at Ben Taub Hospital again. Be a healer. Take care of patients. Dr. Barbosian didn't consider pathologists, radiologists, or anesthesiologists to be doctors; they couldn't even make it to the categories of technicians, orderers or healers. Dr. Barbosian had labeled those fields as something else which Aaron couldn't remember. Something about specialists who specialize in making money. Another thing Barbosian had always said, "You'll never get rich as a healer, but there will always be a place for you because very few people want to take care of sick patients anymore. Everyone wants to have a little niche – something easy they can do to make money. If you're a healer, you'll be dependent on insurance companies to pay you. And insurance companies will reduce their payments over time as they get more and more control of the medical profession."

Dr. Barbosian had been right, Aaron thought. But Dr. Barbosian also said that, although there wouldn't be a lot of money to be made as a healer, there would be tremendous satisfaction to be derived from working with human beings at the worst possible time in their lives and helping to restore them to their best.

At this point, Aaron wasn't sure. It had been such a rough day. A missed lesion – his worst nightmare; Mr. Johnson taking hostages in the hospital. Aaron shook his head again. It was time to go to the hospital and make rounds. Just then, his intercom beeped.

"Dr. Bernstein, it's Dr. Givagushrai on the phone for you. He says he's got a few consults."

Not again, Aaron thought. "Transfer him back."

Aaron picked up the phone on the first ring. "Hey, Vijay, what's up?"

"Hey, Aaron, I've got three more consults for you."

Aaron shook his head again. "All right, Vijay, what are they?"

CHAPTER 15

S tacy Swift had just crossed Jefferson Davis Freeway in her new Mercedes Benz sports car when her beeper went off. It was the office calling. She wondered why they were calling; they knew that today she finished early so that she could go down to Sports Clinic to play her weekly game of tennis. That was the advantage of being the boss's wife; she could make her own schedule and do what she wanted to do. As she dialed in the office number, she thought about her husband, Sloan. He was off playing tennis at the country club now. He worked half-days three days a week including today, took one full day off and worked one full day a week. He was 25 years her senior, just having had his 56th birthday.

Stacy Swift had been a popular sorority girl at the University of Georgia and then had gone back to nursing school for two years and gotten her nursing degree. At the age of 24, she started working as a psychiatry nurse at the Yellow Pine Hospital in Pleasant Point, and there she met Sloan Meacham. At the time they met, he was 50 years old, had been married for over 20 years and had two kids. He'd been attracted to her immediately, telling her she was the most beautiful woman he'd ever seen. Gradually, they became more intimate, and eventually he left his wife and children and married her. They'd been married for four years now and Sloan took good care of her. He'd made a fortune in the 1980s. He'd been one of the owners of Yellow Pine Hospital, and the 1980s was the time for psychiatrists to cash in big time. Sloan had told her how they had done things. They would admit patients to Yellow Pine Hospital for almost any reason at all and keep them there until their insurance benefits ran out. As soon as their benefits ran out, the patients miraculously got better. Sloan told her that there had been case after case of schizophrenics, manic depressives and even neurotic patients who'd been admitted to the hospital, charged thousands and thousands of dollars in fees, and then, when their psychiatry benefits ran out, they had been discharged. He sheepishly admitted to her that very few of them had gotten better; but, even better than that, he said he had gotten rich. He'd made millions. Sure, there had been congressional investigations, but it had all gone away. It was swept under the rug just like Sloan knew it would be. Sloan had paid a $50,000 fine, served no jail time and had to sign a letter stating he would never do anything like that again. Stacy had asked him if he felt bad hurting scores of patients, changing their lives and taking their insurance companies' money away. Sloan laughed. "It was only business," he said, "and, until everyone realizes that medicine, including psychiatry, is only a business, they'll keep coming after entrepreneurs like me."

When she called the office, Barbie, the receptionist, answered. "There's a consult for you to see at Pleasant Point General Hospital."

"I'm off this afternoon," Stacy replied.

"Hold on. Let me let you talk to Dr. Meacham." The phone clicked three times.

"Honey, I need you to see one more consult."

"But, honey, it's my tennis day. You know I've got tennis with the girls. I can't ruin their game."

"It's a special situation. They're calling from Pleasant Point General Hospital. They've got a guy there who's taken over a hospital room and two hostages on the fourth floor. He's apparently a schizophrenic who's gone crazy off of his medications, and no one recognized it. They've been calling Yellow Pine Hospital, and the hospital has been calling us, too. The police have called also, wanting a psychiatrist to come over."

"Why don't you go over then?"

"Stacy, you know we doctors don't do hospital consults. That went out a long time ago. Psychiatrists do not see patients in the hospital. No exceptions. If we start doing it for this guy, they'll expect us to do it for everybody. No way I could see this patient. You need to go see him. Please, honey, as a favor. Let the girls find someone else to play."

"All right," Stacy said angrily.

"I'll make it up to you. You know that Caribbean vacation we've been planning? Instead of one week, how about two weeks?"

"Things are sounding better all the time, Sloan. I'll talk to you later. I'll go see that patient. What's his name?"

"Jumpy Johnson, fourth floor. You can't miss him – he's in the room surrounded by 50 policemen."

"All right, honey. Bye, bye."

****

Stacy turned the Mercedes around and drove north on McCoy Road back up to the hospital. She drove to Pleasant Point General Hospital and parked in the doctors' parking lot using Sloan's parking pass to get in. When she walked into the hospital, everyone looked at her. The policeman in front of the elevator greeted her. "Wow," he said, "who are you?"

"I'm psychiatry, and I've been called to see that patient on the fourth floor," Stacy replied in a business-like tone.

"You're psychiatry? You look like a model."

"Yeah, well, I'm the psychiatry nurse." Stacy pulled out her identification.

"I'll escort you upstairs."

The policeman got into the elevator with Stacy, and they went up to the fourth floor.

"Who's she?" asked the police chief on the fourth floor.

"She's psychiatry," Stacy's escort answered.

"You're a psychiatrist?" asked the police chief.

"Well, I'm the nurse from Yellow Pine. I'm the one who talks to all the patients. I've had experience doing it…"

"How long have you been doing this?"

"I've been doing this for many years now."

"Many years? This guy's a maniac. He's gone crazy. He's psychotic. You think you can talk to him?"

"Let me give it a try. Take me down to his room."

Fifteen policemen walked Stacy down to the hospital room and didn't take their eyes off of her. They got down to Room 427, and Stacy knocked on the door.

"Mr. Johnson, I'm psychiatry. Let me talk to you for a minute. See if we can straighten this thing out."

There was a loud grunt on the other side of the door, and then they heard a gunshot. A bullet exploded into the door and was trapped there.

"Maybe we, uh, better, uh, go down to the nursing station," Stacy said, obviously shaken. "I can call into his room from down there using their intercom system."

Fifteen policemen escorted Stacy back to the nursing station. Stacy sat down at her desk and crossed her legs, and the tennis skirt hiked higher up her legs. She used the intercom to call Mr. Johnson's room. "Mr. Johnson, are you there?"

"I'm here. Who wants to know about it?"

"Mr. Johnson, my name is Stacy. I'm the nurse from Yellow Pine Psychiatric Hospital. We can help you."

"You psychiatrists stink. You never helped me or did anything for me. Come down here, little cunt, and let me teach you something."

"Now, Mr. Johnson, listen…"

"No, you listen, you slut. There's nothing you can do or say that's gonna change things. I'm gonna rape and kill one and then kill the other one. There's nothing you can do. All you ever wanted to do was take away my male sexuality and make me into a woman. Well, now, now I've got control. And I'm gonna kill two people and kill myself, and that's it. And, if anyone gets in my way, they're gonna die, too."

"How long have you had these feelings?" asked Stacy.

"Feelings, schmeelings, feelings. What you talkin' about, lady? You don't know nuthin' 'bout nuthin'!"

"Can you tell me, is there something that you're mad about?"

"I'm not mad. I'm crazy. My mind has been taken away from me. And you're part of the problem, bitch. You come back down here again so I can shoot you in the leg. Then I'll shoot you in the ass, then I'll shoot you in the cunt, you cunt."

"Hmmm. We have a hospital named Yellow Pine Hospital where we take patients…"

"Shut the fuck up. Do you really think I want to listen to your shit? You leave me alone. If anyone else comes back and bothers me, I'll kill them, and I'll kill you too." They heard a loud crash as Mr. Johnson yanked the intercom system out of the wall, ending their ability to communicate with him.

"Well," said Stacy, "I gave it my best shot." She looked at her watch. She could still make the last half hour of her tennis game. "Listen, guys, good luck to you. Hope you can help that guy. And could one of you be a honey and bring me the face sheet off his chart? That's the one that has all the insurance information. I need it for my billing."

A police officer brought her Mr. Johnson's chart, and she scribbled a couple quick lines in the progress notes and tore a face sheet from the chart.

"Take care, guys. Bye, bye."

****

Mr. Johnson was getting more impatient. He'd retaped Krystal so that she was now spread-eagled on the bed. At some point, he would have sex with her, but, now, he turned his attention to his roommate. He had virtually ignored him since he'd taken over the room but now he was curious.

"What's your name?" Mr. Johnson demanded.

"Wahhgabber," the muffled sound came from the taped mouth.

Mr. Johnson went up to his roommate and roughly pulled the tape off his mouth.

"What's your name, buddy?" Mr. Johnson asked.

'Bruce Herman."

"Bruce Herman. Tell me straight. What are you here for?"

"You gotta let me go. I'm a diabetic. I've got high blood pressure. You've got to let me go or I'll die."

"Oh, you'll die all right. I'll kill you. You a sick man, huh? How they operated on you? You got bandages all over you."

"Please don't ask me. It's so personal. You just got to let me go. I know you're mad. I know you're crazy, but I don't have anything to do with it or anything to do with you. Please let me get out of here."

"Let me see what's under these bandages." Mr. Johnson went up to Mr. Herman's bed, pulled back the blankets and ripped off the bandages which covered his lower abdomen and groin. Mr. Herman screamed in pain. Underneath, Mr. Herman's penis was taped to his abdomen.

"How come you got such a big pecker?" Mr. Johnson demanded.

"OK. I'll tell you. I was here…I'm in the hospital for penile implant surgery. I'm impotent, OK?"

"You're impotent. Ha, ha. What does that mean?"

"I can't get an erection. You know what an erection is?"

"Oh, a hard-on. You can't get a hard-on. What are you, a fag or something?"

"No, I'm straight, but I've been diabetic for 20 years, and I've got blood pressure problems and I've got heart problems. So, I couldn't get a hard-on. So, they put a pump in me."

"Pump?"

"Yeah, it's a penile implant. They've got two of what they call these reservoirs in my penis." Mr. Herman pointed them out and then pointed to his scrotum. "Down here, they put a pump. I can pump it up and then give myself a hard-on so I can have sex with my wife."

"You no-good bastard. You put that in you so that you can have a hard-on and fuck my wife, didn't you? You've been fucking a lot of women, huh?"

"I don't want to have anything to do with your wife. This is just for me. This is just to help me with my wife. Listen, I'm an insurance salesman. I've been selling insurance for 35 years. I'll help you when I get out of here. I'll give you some money.

You gotta untie me and let me go. You gotta let them give me my insulin."

"Show me how that pecker works."

"I can't. The doctor said I'm not supposed to use it for six weeks or else I could have problems with it."

Mr. Johnson pointed the gun at Bruce Herman's head. "You show me how that pecker works, son of a bitch, or you'll be cold and hard like your pecker should have been."

"OK, look." Mr. Herman reached down to his scrotum. "This is the pump. If I push on it…"

"You push on it right now. Let me see. And if it gets hard enough, maybe I'll let you fuck that little piece of ass over there." Mr. Johnson pointed at Krystal with his gun.

Mr. Herman pushed on the pump in his scrotum. Slowly, almost magically, he began to have an erection. His penis ripped the tape off his abdomen and became about six inches long.

"Man, you got a big pecker, huh?" said Mr. Johnson. "How come I never got one of those?"

"It was surgery. They helped me with surgery, don't you see?"

"All right. Masturbate now," Mr. Johnson demanded.

"Oh, please, I can't. Please. Leave me alone."

"Let me see you come, bastard."

"Oh, my."

Mr. Herman began fondling himself. "I can't do it. I can't, please."

"All right. Put that pecker back down."

"Oh, thank you, thank you."

Mr. Herman reached to his scrotum and pushed on the bar above the pump to make the water leave the reservoirs in the penis so that it would get smaller. Slowly, the penis got smaller and smaller.

"Did that feel good when you had that thing up?" asked Mr. Johnson.

"I'm just so sore. Please let me go. Leave me alone."

"Put that pecker back up again. Let me see that thing work again. Hey, I want to see Krystal work it."

Mr. Johnson walked over to Krystal and pointed the gun at her. Then, he untied her and said, "If you try anything, I'll kill you." He pointed the gun at her head. "You try that pecker!"

"Please leave me alone. Let me out. I'm so scared," cried Krystal.

"Do it or half your brains will be outside that window there."

Krystal walked over to Mr. Herman's bed with Mr. Johnson behind her holding the gun to her head. She reached down to Mr. Herman's scrotum.

"Do I have to?"

"You work it or I'll kill you!"

Krystal began to push the pump, and slowly Mr. Herman's penis enlarged.

"How's that feel?" asked Mr. Johnson. "Having a pretty young twat working on your pecker? Does that make you feel better?"

"Please, I'm so sore," Mr. Herman begged.

"Make him come," Mr. Johnson demanded.

"Please leave me alone."

"You make him come. Here's some lube." Mr. Johnson poured some K-Y Jelly into Krystal's hand. "You work on that thing 'til he comes."

"Please leave me alone," Krystal whimpered.

"I'll kill you. You do it."

Krystal began rubbing the penis with the K-Y Jelly.

"It's too sore. I can't. I can't come. Please let me go back down," begged Mr. Herman. "Oh, my, I'm having chest pain." Mr. Herman gasped for air. "Please, I can't breathe."

"Put the pecker down, bitch," demanded Mr. Johnson.

Krystal reached down to the bar in the scrotum and pushed it. The penis slowly deflated.

"OK, bitch. Get back in your bed." Mr. Johnson pushed her back into her bed and used the towels and sheets to tie her up.

"I'm having such severe chest pain. I think I'm having a heart attack. Please, you've gotta do something to help me," whispered Mr. Herman.

"What's wrong with you?"

Mr. Herman gasped for air. He was sweating profusely. "I couldn't take it…with my diabetes and high blood…I'm…I'm having chest pain. I feel like someone is standing on my chest. Please…you've got to get me my heart doctor."

"You do look pretty sick, mother-fucker. All right, I'll let you see a heart doctor, but, if anyone tries anything funny, everyone dies."

CHAPTER 16

Marty Shapiro laughed out loud. "Listen, Harry," he said into the phone, "this is one of the most slam-dunk medical malpractice cases I've ever seen. I don't take many cases anymore. I've got more money than I'll need to spend in this lifetime or 20 more lifetimes, but this is a case that's so easy. We'll settle it for $20,000,000 or more."

"You're right, Marty," said Harry Gold. "It does look like an easy case. How do you think we should proceed?"

"Look at it this way," said Marty. "A 27-year-old healthy woman comes into the hospital with a bad headache. The neurosurgeon correctly diagnoses her as having an aneurysm of the brain. Then, he operates on her and leaves her with severe brain damage. Something went wrong with the surgery, obviously. We just have to figure out exactly what that was and get our experts to verify it."

Marty paused to collect his thoughts and then continued, "But then, the lady is in the hospital for several months getting better, and, when she finally gets better and is about to be moved to a rehabilitation hospital, they put a feeding tube in her and put it right smack through the colon before entering the stomach where it was supposed to go."

"How did they miss that?" asked Harry.

"We'll get some experts to figure that out. But this guy, Cole Stone, the gastroenterologist, he buries himself. Georgio Circelli, the neurosurgeon, wrote several notes on the chart saying he called Stone and wanted Stone to come back to look at the patient. She was having high fevers, abdominal pain. But Stone never came back. He never saw the lady. I think we can get him for abandonment. According to the notes that Circelli wrote, Stone said that the patient's problems had nothing to do with the feeding tube. The feeding tube was functioning fine, and there was no reason for him to see her. And Circelli waited three days before he consulted a surgeon…"

"Yeah," said Harry," and by that time, the cows were out of the barn, right?"

"Absolutely," Marty continued. "When the surgeon saw her, he ordered a STAT CT scan which showed a large abscess in the abdomen. Then, on the way from the CT scan back to her room, she became hypotensive, coded and died. They should have had better supervision with her at the CT scanner. They should have had her in better condition before they sent her down there," said Marty.

"What do you think was going through this guy Stone's mind?" asked Harry.

"I don't know. But if you look at the progress notes from a month before, it looks like the neurosurgeon wanted Stone to put in the feeding tube way back then. He waited and he waited, and, then, when he finally did put it in, he wrote a note saying, 'I'm being consulted only to put in this feeding gastrostomy tube. I will not be taking care of any of this patient's gastrointestinal problems or managing the feedings once the tube is put in.' The guy sounds like an arrogant asshole. And not to come back and see the patient after he'd done a procedure on her?"

"Yeah, I mean, what else could he have thought was going wrong?" asked Harry.

"I don't know," answered Marty. "But one of the other great things about this case is who helped Stone put that feeding tube in this lady. We're going to nail him, too."

"Who's that?" asked Harry.

"Aaron Bernstein. Went to Vanderbilt University with him. He was always a goody two-shoes. Always had to help people – that's what he thought life was all about, helping people. Premed from the start, premed nerd in a nerdy fraternity. Our fraternity used to beat up on his fraternity in every sport. Then, he came out here to Pleasant Point and became a doctor. Has a practice, pretty successful, I guess. At least, I've never had a chance to sue him before. I couldn't stand guys like him at Vanderbilt, those premed nerds. I'm going to nail him to the wall on this one. These guys probably each have about $3,000,000 malpractice coverage maximum. I'm going to go for $5,000,000 to $10,000,000 from each of them – try to bankrupt them."

"Wow," said Harry, "this sounds personal."

"Yeah," said Marty, "any more this medical malpractice stuff is personal."

"What do you think we'll clear total?" asked Harry.

"The neurosurgeon is going to have to pay us $5,000,000 to $10,000,000. Each of these gastroenterologists $3,000,000 to $5,000,000; the hospital $5,000,000 to $10,000,000. Heck, we got the hospital on negligence for taking his lady down to the CT scan without proper supervision. We may end up with a $20,000,000 to $30,000,000 settlement, and, if a jury gets to see it, we may end up with double or triple that."

"You think you'd want it to go to a jury?" asked Harry.

"The more misery I can cause these doctors, the better. These guys were negligent. All this guy Stone had to do was go by and see this lady a couple of times after he put that tube in. He needed to see her and make sure she was doing OK. He could have felt her belly, felt that there was something wrong, saved her life. A 27-year-old woman could have survived an abdominal abscess treated quickly enough."

"This guy Stone must be an arrogant, uncaring asshole," said Harry. "Not to go back and check on a patient…that just blows me away. I mean, it's malpractice. It's abandonment. We can get him for all of that."

Just then, there was a loud knock on the door to Marty's study.

"Hold on one second, Harry," Marty said. Marty put the phone down. "Come on in."

The door opened, and in walked Ballory, Marty's butler. Marty had imported Ballory from London eight years before.

"Sir, the reporter from *Forbes* magazine is here to interview you."

"OK, thanks, Ballory. Tell him I'll be right down."

Marty picked up the phone. "Listen, Harry, I've got to go now. But I want you to let me handle this case. I know since I took over the medication class action work seven years ago, I've let you handle most of the medical malpractice. But this case is so open and shut and so personal for me that I want to do it myself."

"You got it, Marty. By the way, I couldn't help hearing Ballory's booming voice. What's *Forbes* magazine interviewing you about?"

"They're doing an article on the five wealthiest lawyers in the country as the cover story for the next issue, and they want me in it."

"You're one of the five wealthiest attorneys in the country?"

"Uh-huh. Gotta go now. Bye."

Marty hung up the telephone in his study. He walked out of the study into his bedroom. The bedroom was enormous, 3000 square feet. He walked through the bedroom into his closet. He and his wife each had their own closets off the bedroom, and each closet was 1500 square feet of cedar. In his closet, Marty had 48 suits, 24 navy blue and 24 black. He had over 500 ties to go with the suits. He changed into one of the navy suits, put on a red tie, then walked out of the closet through the bedroom into the main hallway on the second floor of the house. He walked to the main stairway and began walking down the marble stairs. The chandelier which hung over the staircase from a 40-foot high ceiling was 20 feet in length. It weighed one and one-half tons and was made of the finest Austrian Strauss crystal. It had cost 2 million dollars.

Marty walked down the stairs to the gigantic entry foyer. Even he had to admire it, after living in the house for two years. The floor was rare Italian marble, and the paintings on the walls were all by masters. He greeted the reporter from *Forbes* magazine and led him into the living room. They sat down on one of the French-made 16-foot sofas in the room. Ballory appeared.

"Is there anything I can bring you, sir?"

"Yes, why don't you bring afternoon tea," replied Marty, "and some biscuits."

"Very good, sir," said Ballory, and he left.

The reporter glanced around the walls of the room. "Incredible art collection you have."

"Yes. My wife and I have always favored the impressionists. That's a Renoir over there. Those two in the corner are Bonnard's. One of our Piccasos is over there...it's one of five Piccassos in our collection."

"Incredible. Well, as you know, we certainly appreciate you letting us interview and photograph you for this story. Through our discussions with attorneys and people in the know throughout the country, we've identified the five wealthiest attorneys in the United States. Two are in California, one is in Florida, one is in New York and then there is you in Atlanta, Georgia. We'd like to complete the interview and pictures today."

"Sure," answered Marty. "I made sure my wife is around, too, so you can get pictures of both of us if you like."

"That's great. Tell me, Mr. Shapiro, how did you become interested in law?"

Marty thought for a moment. "My father was a malpractice attorney. He was one of the first big malpractice attorneys in this country. As a matter of fact, he practiced in New York. In the 60s and 70s, he won the largest malpractice suits in each of those decades in the state of New York."

"So as you grew up, it was in your blood," the reporter offered.

"That's right. It's something I always wanted to do. I started off as a medical malpractice attorney, and that's how I made the first part of my fortune. Besides having my dad in the field, one incident in my life made me realize that that was what I wanted to do. When I was 16, I had an attack of appendicitis, and my parents took me to the hospital near where we lived. It was supposedly the best hospital in Long Island. But when they found out who my father was, none of the surgeons at that hospital was willing to take care of me. It was a tremendous embarrassment for my dad and for my whole family. And it could have killed me. Finally, they arranged to transfer me by ambulance to a teaching hospital in New York City, and that's where I had my surgery. I have to tell you that, from that point forward, I hated doctors with a passion. I decided that I would seek out and destroy those doctors who were only in it for the money, who could care less about their patients and who committed malpractice."

"I saw from your biography that you went to college at Vanderbilt University."

"That's right. I was at Vanderbilt from 1977 to 1981. I could have gone to an Ivy League school…my dad was a Harvard man…but I decided I wanted to strike out on my own and go to a school in the South. I was in a fraternity there, Sigma Alpha Epsilon, and actually made a lot of connections that helped my career."

Marty paused for a moment and thought: one of those connections was Aaron Bernstein, the gastroenterologist in Pleasant Point, Georgia, that he was getting ready to sue. He laughed to himself.

"And after Vanderbilt, you went to law school at Emory University?"

"Yes, that's what brought me to Georgia. I went to law school at Emory, and I realized then that there weren't any outstanding malpractice attorneys in Atlanta. I don't mean that there weren't any good ones, just no big-time ones. I set up my practice, and I began advertising more and more and more. Radio, television, newspapers - you name it. I would take any case that I could… big, small. I eventually hired ten other attorneys to work for me. We kept working and working."

"And then you got into class action suits involving drugs, right?"

"Yes, after I'd been in practice for a while and had made more than enough money to retire, I represented a woman whose endocrinologist had prescribed the weight loss drug Fatoff for her. It damaged her heart valves, and she developed heart failure. I won $2,500,000 for her, but, more importantly, I realized that there had to be hundreds if not thousands of other people who had been affected by Fatoff. I advertised on radio, television and in the newspapers, and I was able to accumulate over 3000 patients that I put together in the class action suit. We won the largest judgment ever for a class action suit involving medications and ended up putting that drug company into bankruptcy. From then on, it was easy; anytime any drug was implicated in causing harm, we immediately would advertise for plaintiffs and then hire doctors to assess the damages."

"Yes, it became quite a business. Most of these cases you didn't take to court, right?" asked the reporter.

"Most of the cases we were able to settle out of court," Marty agreed.

"Do you have any idea how much money you've made in medication-related claims?"

"I can't say for sure, but I'm going to estimate that, just with my class action practice in the last seven years, I've made between $500,000,000 and $1,000,000,000."

"That you personally have cleared?" asked the reporter incredulously.

"Yes, that's right, at least that much."

"And along the way, you've gotten married and had three children."

"I met my wife on a trip to Israel. She was the reigning Miss Israel as well as the reigning Miss Universe. I met her in Tel Aviv, and she showed me around the country. Then, I brought her back to Atlanta, and we were married. It all occurred within a two-month period."

"An incredibly romantic story. Any advice that you could give to young lawyers?"

"There's always going to be crooks out there. There are always going to be doctors who don't take care of patients properly. My advice for a young attorney would be to find these doctors and nail them to the wall. Or find other people who don't do what they're supposed to be doing – businessmen, drug company executives, whatever. Stay ambitious, work hard, always be true to your clients."

"I've heard that you're semi-retired now."

"I have a firm of over 500 attorneys, so they don't need me on a day-to-day basis. I pick and choose. I handle some cases. I'm getting ready to work on a medical malpractice case, and I haven't worked on one of those in seven years. But the doctors at fault in this case are so totally incompetent and vicious that I feel that I personally need to be involved."

"Can you call your wife so we can take picture of you both now?" asked the reporter.

"Sure." Marty reached for the phone on the table beside him and dialed the number to his wife's office. "Honey, can you come down now?"

A few minutes later, they were joined by a stunningly gorgeous brunette with big green eyes.

"Let's take pictures of the two of you together," said the photographer from *Forbes* magazine who had just come into the room. "Why don't we start with the two of you in front of that fireplace?"

In the living room was an enormous fireplace made out of granite. Marty walked over and stood next to his wife.

"She's quite a bit taller than you, isn't she?" asked the photographer.

It was true. Marty had married a woman who was almost half a foot taller than him. Of course, being 5 feet 5 inches, most of the women he dated had been taller than him.

"Now you see how I got the nickname 'Little Napoleon,'" said Marty with a laugh. The photographer didn't say anything.

Marty continued, "But I have this to help me out. He'll just have to shoot us from the waist up." Marty pulled over a large wooden box that he stood on which put him at equal height with his wife. He put his arm around her, and the photographer took the picture.

CHAPTER 17

Of all the four-letter words that Aaron Bernstein had ever known, the word "CALL" repulsed and disgusted him the most. "Shit", "hell", "fuck" grabbed others' attention but did nothing to Aaron. If he was asked what was the worst thing in his life, he would say when he was on call two days in a row. Being on call for the group meant being on call for the emergency rooms, and there was a deluge of critically-ill patients with gastrointestinal disorders waiting for him there.

The numbers sometimes got ridiculous. Here in the middle of the afternoon, he was already five down; he had three consults to see at Pleasant Point Physicians Hospital. He was on call every fourth day and every third weekend since Cole had refused to take weekend call, and Aaron dreaded every second of it. The day before call, he would begin getting nervous, and he would have problems sleeping the night before call and almost always took two Tylenol PM.

****

It hadn't always been like this. Call as a medical student had been fun and something to look forward to. It was an exciting time, filled with teaching and new experiences. You weren't required to spend the entire night at the hospital as a student, with many of the rotations letting you go home after you had worked up one new patient.

It was always exciting because, every month or two, you switched to a different rotation and would be exposed to a completely different area of medicine. One month, you could be setting a fracture in orthopedics, and, the next month, you could be starting an IV in the scalp of a six-month-old in pediatrics.

As a student, you weren't expected to have much mastered but just to show a willingness to learn things and to help out. Aaron laughed when he remembered that some of your grade as a student was based on picking up dinner for the doctors on call, especially on the internal medicine rotation. The students would be given an order for food and sent out to a restaurant in Houston. There would sometimes be 10 to 15 people whose dinner would be ordered, including students, interns, residents and key doctors in the emergency room. The emergency room doctors determined which patients were admitted and who they were admitted to, so it was important to stay on their good side and keep them well fed. Yes, Aaron looked back at this call as a medical student as a fun learning experience that was exciting.

****

Residency was when call started getting tough. Residents were required to spend the night in the hospital. Aaron took call at Ben Taub Hospital which was the county hospital in Houston, and he also took call at the Veterans Hospital in Houston.

When he was the third year internal medicine resident on one of the ward teams at Ben Taub Hospital, Aaron would get an average of 20 new patients admitted to his service in a 12-hour period. He had two interns to help him, but one was usually a rotating intern who was required to do a month of internal medicine. These interns were going into fields like neurology or ophthalmology and were generally worthless. Aaron would have to spend a lot of his time teaching these interns how to do basic things. Things like taking blood cultures, doing lumbar punctures and doing a microscopic exam of the urine which these interns were supposed to do, Aaron himself ended up doing due to these interns' incompetence.

There had been two rotating interns Aaron had worked with at Ben Taub Hospital who had had breakdowns during their internal medicine rotation. One was a cute, petite, Mexican-American woman going into ophthalmology who wore way too much makeup and flirted with everyone. Every call night, she would end up at the doctors' desk in the emergency room with mascara streaking her face as she cried about how impossible the rotation was and how there was no one to help her. The last two weeks of the rotation, she'd had to leave the team and was admitted to a local psychiatric hospital. Aaron got no one to replace her but had to act as the intern on her patients as well as their resident.

The next month, Aaron had a neurology intern who seemed very suspicious of Aaron. Aaron knew there was something wrong when he noticed that this intern devoted most of his admission history and physical exams not to detailing the patient's condition but to giving his opinion that everything that was being done to the patient (by Aaron's direction) was wrong and that, if they followed the orders written, the patient would surely die.

Aaron confronted this intern about these comments and tried to explain to him that certainly they could discuss the patient's treatment plan before orders were written, but, once the treatment plan had been established, it was the intern's job to carry it out and not to point out that the resident was an incompetent idiot. Aaron also tried to explain that he was now in his third year of residency in internal medicine.

Aaron's speech didn't work, and the intern wrote harsher and harsher critiques of Aaron in his notes and became more and more belligerent. It came to a boiling point one night when the intern admitted an AIDS patient with altered mental status who needed a lumbar puncture. An hour after the lumbar puncture was supposed to be done, Aaron came by to see how it was going. Aaron found the neurology intern standing behind the patient's stretcher while the patient was sitting in the stretcher leaning over the table in front of him. The long spinal needle was still in the patient's back.

"How's it going, Marc?" Aaron asked. "Getting the LP done?"

Marc forcefully yanked the needle out of the patient's back and wheeled around to face Aaron. "What's it look like? Do you see any fluid? Does it look like I got the LP?" Marc shook the long needle menacingly at Aaron. "Get away from me, asshole! I know what I'm doing. Get away!"

Luckily, there was a police officer Aaron knew working security in the emergency room who witnessed the incident. The police officer convinced Marc to give him the needle, and Marc ran out of the emergency room. Aaron never saw Marc again, but he heard that Marc had transferred to a less stressful program after taking a year off.

****

On other rotations in internal medicine, the call was easier: you could finish your work at 9 or 10 at night and then go up to the call rooms on the top floor of the hospital to sleep. Each of the resident's call rooms was equipped with only a single bed and a telephone lying on the floor next to it. There was a small common room down the hall from the sleeping rooms which contained a black and white television that had survived the 1950s and on which you could get two local stations. Aaron rarely watched TV as he felt that any opportunity to sleep couldn't be passed up.

****

Call worsened as a fellow although it no longer required spending the night at the hospital. However, when you were on gastroenterology call for the Parkland Emergency Room in Dallas, Texas, you might as well have lived there as you were constantly being called in.

There was one GI bleeder after another, usually bleeding from ulcers or from esophageal varices due to liver failure. There were nights when Aaron would get home from work at 8 o'clock, get called back into the emergency room at 11 o'clock and then stay there until the next morning scoping bleeders.

One night stood out for Aaron although it wasn't that different from a hundred other nights. Aaron was called in at the very beginning of his second year of fellowship to scope an AIDS patient who was having a massive bleed. There was a procedure room on the medicine side of the emergency room where they did the endoscopies, and, by the time Aaron got there, the patient had already received four units of blood and still had a blood pressure of only 90/50.

Aaron put on a surgical gown as well as protective boots which came all the way up to his knees. He put on goggles and two pairs of gloves. As he put the scope into the patient's mouth, the patient vomited, and Aaron could feel the warmth as the blood soaked his gown. Aaron looked down and could see a puddle of blood next to his feet.

The patient had hepatitis C as well as AIDS and had cirrhosis of the liver due to the hepatitis C. He was bleeding from huge esophageal varices which were blood vessels that had formed when the blood, which couldn't flow through the damaged liver, backed up into these vessels. Aaron could actually see blood spurting from one of these vessels.

Aaron spent over an hour injecting these blood vessels with sodium tetradecyl, a sclerosing agent which would make the varices scar down and stop bleeding. When Aaron was finished, there was no further bleeding. The patient's stomach was full of fresh blood, so Aaron used the scope to suction out as much of this as possible. By the time Aaron was finished, the patient had received eight units of packed red blood cells as well as four units of fresh frozen plasma and ten units of platelets which were needed to help the blood clot.

The procedure room was covered with blood. The floor around Aaron was now covered with towels to begin soaking up the blood. Everyone's shoes had blood on them, so it had been tracked throughout the room. The patient's stretcher was covered in blood, and blood had even splattered onto the walls near the stretcher when the patient had vomited. Aaron removed his protective goggles, and these were streaked with dried blood.

It had been dangerous to be a GI fellow at a big-city hospital in the 1980s and 1990s due to the AIDs epidemic, and few places were more dangerous than Parkland Hospital. The gastroenterology department at Southwestern Medical School, which staffed Parkland Hospital, had a rule that no faculty member ever came in on emergencies. So that night, just barely into his second year of training, Aaron had been the senior doctor treating that dying AIDS patient. Every decision he'd had to make himself, and one wrong decision could have been fatal for the patient. Also, one needle stick to Aaron from a needle stuck in this patient, or one microscopic drop of blood from the torrential storm of blood flowing from this man's body onto an unprotected mucus membrane of Aaron's, could have led to Aaron's demise from AIDS.

****

When Aaron had started private practice, he was on call every fourth night during the week and every fourth weekend. This was much less call than Aaron had at Parkland, so he loved it. Over time, things changed.

First, Aaron had gotten married and had a family. Naturally, he wanted to spend more time with his wife and children. He'd missed his oldest son's first steps due to being on call, and, although Marcy videotaped them, it wasn't the same. Aaron often thought about all the holidays and weekends he'd missed spending with his family. Many beautiful summer days when he would have loved to have taken his children swimming, he was in the hospital relieving fecal impactions in 90-year-olds or trying to stop bleeding in alcoholic cirrhosis patients.

Second, over the years, call had become more and more onerous. When Aaron started practice, he would round on four or five patients in the hospital, then get two or three new consults for an entire call weekend. Now, there were 20 to 30 patients to round on in the hospitals and an average of ten new consults for the weekend. Most of these patients were extremely sick and demanded a lot of time and careful thought.

Finally, the supporting doctors weren't there to help. With the advent of hospitalists, most of the patients were now admitted to the hospital by a doctor who had never seen them before and usually knew nothing about them. It was up to Aaron to obtain the proper history and often to chase down medical records needed from outside doctors or hospitals. Most of the time, the hospitalists would just admit and treat the patient for whatever diagnosis the emergency room doctor told them the patient had. Often, these emergency room doctors had spent less than five minutes evaluating the patient, and their diagnosis was based solely on one elevated lab result or one abnormal x-ray study.

It didn't seem fair. All the things in medicine that had been exciting as a student, resident and fellow were no longer exciting but just plain scary. Permeating everything was a tremendous liability from being on call. Unlike in the office when everything was scheduled and you knew walking into the room what you were dealing with, everything on call was unpredictable. You could get awakened at 3:00 a.m. from a deep sleep to deal with a complex, sick patient whose life depended on your decisions in the next 60 minutes. If your decisions were right, you were a hero; if they were wrong, the patient might die, and you could get sued.

****

Aaron walked into the intensive care unit at Pleasant Point General hospital to see his first consult of the day.

The first patient was an 80-year-old man from Pakistan, Mr. Canaan, who was on the ventilator. Mr. Canaan had come to Pleasant Point from Pakistan a week before, and his family took one look at him and felt he didn't look or sound right, so they brought him to the emergency room. A chest x-ray in the emergency room revealed a huge, cancerous mass in the right lung, and a CAT scan of the head showed several brain metastases. Right after the CAT scan, the patient's son tried to give his father some homemade soup to drink to build up his strength, and the patient aspirated it into his lungs. Before the emergency room doctor's eyes, the patient's oxygen saturation went from normal to less than 50 percent, and the patient had to be emergently intubated and a nasogastric tube placed into his stomach. The intubation had been very difficult, and the patient's oxygen saturation was very low for several minutes.

Now the patient had been on the ventilator for a week, and the nasogastric tube's aspirate had changed over the course of the days from soup colored to bile green, and, today, to coffee grounds. The coffee grounds signified internal bleeding which was why the hospitalist, Sirhah Khan, had called Aaron.

Aaron obtained the whole history from the patient's chart; the patient was intubated and comatose. The patient's wife, who sat at the bedside, spoke no English and only nodded her head up and down to Aaron whenever he looked at her. Aaron did his exam and then wrote orders. He put the patient on a medicine to treat ulcers, and he ordered blood counts every eight hours with instructions on what to do if the count dropped below certain levels.

Aaron walked out of the patient's room and was immediately stopped by Colleen, the patient's nurse. Fifteen years before, Colleen had started working in the ICU as an attractive, shapely brunette with a sharp wit. Fifteen years and 50 pounds later, Colleen had lost her attractiveness as well as her shape but had retained her sense of humor. She was plump, not well groomed and wore granny glasses that made her look older than 40.

"So, you gonna fix him, Dr. Bernstein?" Colleen loudly asked. "You gonna stop that bleedin' today?"

Aaron stopped dead in his tracks. He wanted to snap an answer back to Colleen, but, over the years, had gotten to know her well, and he knew she meant no harm.

"I think the bleeding is the least of his problems," Aaron replied. "He's got metastatic lung cancer, and it sounds like now he's got no hope of neurologic recovery from his anoxic event. We'll just put him on some IV Protonix, watch his blood counts and see how he does."

"I'm sure his son is going to want to talk to you," Colleen said. "He's up here at least two to three times a day, making sure everything is done for his dad."

Aaron looked at Colleen again. "Hasn't anyone spoken to the family and told them the grim prognosis?"

"Oh, yeah, the neurologist has talked to them, and the critical care doctor has spoken to them also. The family still wants everything to be done. They still think they're gonna bring Daddy home."

Aaron walked to the sink and washed his hands. He then called the neurologist on the phone to make sure he had the patient's story right.

"Why did they ask you to see him, Aaron?" asked Keith Newton, the neurologist.

"He's having some GI bleeding now," Aaron replied.

"Shoot. They gotta let that guy go. His situation is hopeless," said Keith.

"That's what I thought," said Aaron. "All right, well, we'll do everything conservatively to try and get the bleeding to stop. I think, if it came down to doing an endoscopy on this guy, I'd elect not to do anything. Is that the way you feel, Keith?"

"Absolutely. The family needs to make some decisions, and we need to get him out of our hospital into one of those long-term care hospitals where he can die. Talk to you later."

Aaron hung up the phone just as the patient's admitting doctor, the hospitalist, Sirhah Khan, walked into the ICU. Dr. Khan was a small, bald, dark-skinned man with a large broad nose and eyes which darted all around behind gold-framed glasses. He wore a pin-striped suit.

"Oh, chief, so good to see you," Dr. Khan said. He walked up to Aaron and shook Aaron's hand vigorously. "You are going to get this gentleman's bleeding stopped?"

"Sirhah," Aaron said, looking directly into his eyes, "the bleeding is the least of this guy's problems. He's got metastatic lung cancer; he's aspirated and now his brain function is nil. What are we going to be bringing back in this guy?"

"Oh, oh," Sirhah replied. "The family wants everything to be done. They are still convinced that he is going to get better."

"Have you talked with them?" asked Aaron incredulously. "Have you had a talk with the neurologist?"

"Well, I talked with Keith Newton a little bit, and I sat down with the family when the patient was first admitted."

"I think you need to review the chart again," said Aaron, "and talk to the family again."

Just then, Colleen came out of the patient's room and announced, "He's having a huge bloody stool. He's filling that bed with blood."

Sirhah turned from Colleen to face Aaron. "You've gotta do something to help this guy, chief. We can't let him bleed to death."

Aaron sighed. "Let's watch and see how he does with conservative care. I've written for a Protonix bolus and then a continuous infusion of Protonix. In the meantime, I really think you need to get together with the patient's son and talk to him. This gentleman needs to be allowed to die."

"When I talked to them, they said they didn't want anything but the best possible care for their dad. They brought him over from Pakistan for a visit, and they told me they were shocked when he arrived in such bad shape."

Aaron glared at Sirhah. "Sirhah, I've been at this hospital a long time. Do you know how often we see these patients come over from Pakistan, India, Korea, etc., brought over by their children and then immediately brought to the hospital because they didn't 'look right'? Don't you understand? These people are sick, and something terrible is wrong with them. Their children bring them to this country so that they can get free medical care which is the best medical care in the world. This poor guy didn't come here just to visit. He was very sick, and his son brought him over from Pakistan for us to take care of him. Unfortunately, this man is beyond help, and his family needs to understand that, too."

"No, no, no," said Sirhah. "My job is to try and get these people well and out of the hospital. And that is your job, too, chief. I don't ever need you to tell me what my job is."

Aaron realized there was no point in talking to Sirhah further. Aaron started walking out of the Intensive Care Unit. A small, dark-skinned man rushed by him as he approached the door and then stopped to look at the name on Aaron's lab coat.

"Are you Dr. Bernstein?" the man asked with a thick accent.

"Yes, I am," Aaron answered.

"I'm Mr. Canaan's son. I've been waiting all day to talk to you. I understand that he's started bleeding internally. You've got to do something to try and help him."

"Mr. Canaan, it's nice to meet you. They did consult me to see your dad. Are you aware how sick he is…?"

"Of course, of course, I know how sick he is!" Mr. Canaan shouted, interrupting Aaron. "I know he has problems, but I need you to help him. His main problem they tell me now is the bleeding."

"Who told you that?" Aaron asked.

"Dr. Khan told me on the phone. He said, if we can get the bleeding to stop, my dad can get better. He said he called you and that you were one of the best gastroenterologists at this hospital."

"You need to understand that there is a lot more going on with your dad. Your dad has cancer all over his body; it's in his lungs and in his brain…"

"Oh, I know that, I know that! I know that he has cancer, but we can treat the cancer once we get him better."

"The neurologist has written in his notes that your dad has no significant neurological function now, and, after this period of time, he doesn't anticipate any recovery. Your dad had an anoxic episode when he aspirated. He didn't get enough oxygen to his brain for a period of time, and now his brain isn't working anymore."

"Oh, I read about that. I looked it up on the Internet. I've looked up many things on the Internet about my father. I found cases where these people's brains can come back after a year, two years or three years. With this anoxic injury, you just never know. And by the way, you are a gastroenterologist, right?"

"Yes."

"Well, your part should be the bleeding. You need to take care of the bleeding."

"Listen, Mr. Canaan. Right now, your dad's blood pressure and pulse are OK. He does have old blood coming out of the nasogastric tube, and he's putting out blood from his rectum which is probably old also. The thing to do now is to treat him with medication and see if we can get the bleeding to stop. We'll follow his blood counts and transfuse him if necessary. If it looks like the bleeding is increasing or is not stopping within the next 12 to 24 hours, with your consent, I'll do an endoscopy on him to try and stop the bleeding."

"Oh, yes, we want you to do it. We want everything. You need to understand that I have lived in this country for 20 years. I'm an American citizen. My wife is an American citizen, and our children are American citizens. My father, he just came to visit. We all wanted to see him. And now, he is so sick. You need to understand we want you to get him better so we can take him home."

Aaron didn't feel like discussing things anymore. Everyone knew the situation was hopeless except for the patient's son and the hospitalist, Dr. Khan. But at this point, there was no convincing either of them. The son could only think about getting back his healthy father, and Dr. Khan would never see the big picture. He saw medicine as a series of isolated problems that each had to be fixed in order to get the patient well. Dr. Khan couldn't grasp the concept that there could be overlying, larger issues involving the patient which dwarfed the significance of these individual problems and indeed rendered them meaningless.

Aaron walked back to where Colleen was standing outside Mr. Canaan's room.

"Colleen, make sure I get called with all of those blood counts for the next 24 hours. Page me directly on my beeper. If there are any changes in his status, call me immediately. While the son is here, go ahead and get him to sign a permit for me to do an endoscopy on his father. I have the feeling we're going to be doing something on this patient in the next 24 hours."

Colleen nodded her head and winked at Aaron. "Have a good day, Dr. Bernstein," she said.

Aaron mumbled something under his breath and walked out of the Intensive Care Unit to go see his next consult.

CHAPTER 18

Vijay drove his Chevy Impala down the highway towards Atlanta. He looked at his odometer – 125,313 miles and counting. It was time to get a new car – he could afford it and doctors around the hospital who saw the beat-up Impala were starting to kid him about it. He had his eye on a sports-car – something fast and sexy – but hadn't started the process of looking. One of the surgeons at the hospital had a friend who was in the car leasing business and Vijay had his card in his wallet.

It was six p.m. and Vijay was heading to a meeting of the Greater Atlanta Indian Singles Group held at a Holiday Inn just outside Atlanta. He'd been hearing about these gatherings for over a year and had wanted to go before, but had never been able to get away from work early enough. He'd decided that it was time to break out of the shell that the hospital had created over his life and meet new people. He would still send most of his money home to support his family and to help Dr. Bissel-Mozel's clinic, but he was well over thirty years old and it was time to think about finding a wife and having a family. Ultimately, his plan hadn't changed although it had undergone evolution. First, he had come to the United States for residency training so that he could get the best medical training in the world, and then he would go back to help Dr. Bissel-Mozel in his practice. Then the obligation to work in Arkansas had to be fulfilled, so he'd decided to work hard in Arkansas to gain experience and to send money home. He still planned to take over Dr. Bissel-Mozel's practice some day. After fulfilling his obligation and making very little money, he'd moved to Pleasant Point, still planning an eventual return to India, but now with the opportunity to send more money home both for his family and to make some real positive changes in the clinic. Now, after a year as a hospitalist, he realized how much he enjoyed America and liked working in their medical system. He would still return to India eventually to work with his mentor, but he'd decided he'd find an American wife and start his family first.

Dr. Bissel-Mozel had been in constant correspondence with him. He wanted to know how his favorite assistant was doing, and wanted Vijay to know how proud he was of him. He sent Vijay information about his family since none of them could write. Vijay's father had suffered a stroke six months before, leaving him with difficulty talking sometimes, but he was back to work at the docks. His brothers all did manual labor: two had married and each of them had one child. Above all, Dr. Bissel-Mozel's letters stressed that he was getting older and slowing down. He rarely made house calls now. Each letter ended with the statement that he couldn't wait for Vijay's return to what was now called Mumbai, but he was happy that Vijay was gaining so much experience and sending back more and more money that was helping to expand their clinic.

Vijay pulled into the parking lot of the Holiday Inn. The lot was packed with Mercedes, BMW's, and even a red Porsche 911 Turbo. Vijay parked his old Impala at the back of the lot away from the other cars, looked into the rear-view mirror and adjusted his tie, and then put on his suit jacket. He checked himself out in the mirror again, smiled to make sure there was no food caught between his teeth, and then walked into the Holiday Inn. He was so excited to meet new people that he forgot all about the Jumpy Johnson saga.

A long table was set up outside the Banquet Room at the Holiday Inn, and a pretty young Indian woman was sitting behind it. Her name tag said Adhira-President Atlanta Area Indian Singles.

"Hello and welcome to our dinner party. I'm Adhira. I haven't seen you at one of our functions before. You must be new. Tell me your name."

"Vijay Givagushrai."

She looked up and down the sheet of papers in front of her and then looked back at Vijay. "I don't see your name listed. Did you RSVP?"

"I didn't. I didn't think I would make the dinner, but I got my associate to cover for me for a few hours so I came. Is there room for me?"

"Well, you are a big man," Adhira laughed as she looked up and down at Vijay, "but people who have RSVP'ed don't come all the time. We'll seat you at table thirty. I'll need twenty dollars and then I'll make you a name tag and you can go in."

Vijay took the backing off his name tag, put it on his jacket, and walked into the Banquet Room. Everyone was already seated; the program was about to begin. Vijay found table thirty at the back of the Banquet Room and sat down. There was only one other person sitting at his table – an older man who looked fifty and who extended his hand to Vijay as he sat down.

"I'm Narendra," he whispered.

"I'm Vijay, nice to meet you."

A woman appeared on the small podium which had been set up in front of the room. She was of medium height and was wearing traditional Indian garb. Vijay looked around the room and noted that almost all of the people were wearing traditional Indian evening clothes, although some women were dressed in American dresses and some men wore slacks and button down shirts. No one else was wearing a suit; he'd overdressed.

"Tonight we have a treat as our speaker. As you know, every year the Indian Singles Group raises money to give to a worthy Indian high school senior to help him or her pay for their college education. Tonight, we have the winner of this year's ten-thousand dollar scholarship."

"Aarav Joseph's name may sound familiar to many of you. Last year's scholarship was awarded to her sister, Aaryan, who is now completing a successful first year at Harvard. By the way, Aaryan's program to provide soccer balls and create soccer fields in India for the poor has almost doubled in the past year."

"Aarav has followed in her sister's footsteps and maybe even gone a step further. First, she is a straight A student at Huckleberry, the all-girls prep school here in Atlanta. She played first chair violin for Huckleberry and was selected as the concert master for the Greater Atlanta High School Orchestra. She pursues fencing as a sport, and has won several tournaments and is nationally ranked. She has played chess since age five, and is ranked number seven nationally in the eighteen and under age group."

Vijay looked at Narendra and whispered, "How could one child have time to do all this?"

Narendra smiled and whispered back, "I'm a widower with two children in college. It's all a game now – getting into these prestigious colleges – it is so competitive! Unless you are incredibly wealthy and can buy your way in, or are so talented as an athlete that they want you for their sports' teams, or have a father or mother who attended these schools and are a legacy, there is no way in hell to get into the Ivy League schools or

Stanford unless you do something spectacular that makes your application jump out at them. The parents start them on the road at a young age – sixth or seventh grade may be too late. By the time they finish high school, their accomplishments outweigh those of three ordinary students. Start a soccer program, feed the hungry. Next thing you know one of them will start an orphanage somewhere. I didn't push my kids…wife died and just wanted them happy, healthy, ordinary kids."

"But what sets Aarav apart," continued the woman on the platform, "is the work she did outside the classroom and away from the sports fields and other fields of competition. Over the last four years, Aarav has set in motion the building of an orphanage in Chennai, India. She has raised money both from her own ingenious projects and from some incredible fund-raisers which our organization has joined other Indian organizations in supporting. She has spent each summer in Chennai – finding land for the orphanage, recruiting volunteers to work there, and even designing the buildings. And ladies and gentleman, I am overjoyed to report that as of one month ago, the homeless children of Chennai will no longer have to live dirty and disease-infested lives. There is now a home for them – the Aarav Joseph Orphanage. Twenty-two children have taken up residency there, and there are already plans to work on the expansion of the facility and improvement of the existing housing and classrooms this fall as she joins her sister and starts her first year at Harvard. Aarav, we congratulate you on your accomplishments. Please come up to the podium."

From the back of the room, Vijay saw a small, unattractive girl with glasses approach the podium. She wore a simple white dress and her hair hung behind her head in a long braid. Vijay noted that her gait was very masculine with arms swinging with each step and no swaying of the hips. Everyone in the audience stood up and began clapping loudly. Vijay stood up, too, so that he could watch the girl ascend the steps to stand next to the emcee. She walked with a strength that showed confidence, Vijay decided. She shook the emcee's hand vigorously, and then the emcee grabbed her in a tight hug.

"Aarav, it is my honor to present you with this check for ten thousand dollars to go towards your tuition at Harvard. We understand that you have already been awarded a full merit scholarship to Harvard, so we hope you will use this money for other expenses including travel. Now if everyone will sit down, Aarav will give us a brief presentation on the orphanage as the waiters start to bring you your dinner."

Everyone sat down and the lights dimmed. A screen came down from the ceiling and Aarav pulled out her personal computer to begin her power point presentation. She used her laser pointer to highlight the original plans for the orphanage, and then slide after slide showed how the financial backing for the orphanage had been achieved and then actual pictures of the various stages of building were shown. The last picture was a view of the entire orphanage from above, and there were twenty children in front of the orphanage waving. The power point went off and the lights came back on, and everyone again stood and cheered.

"Amazing, amazing," was all Vijay could mutter over and over again. He turned to Narendra. "I was born and lived in Bombay, now Mumbai. I was lucky to have a father but so many children had no parent and wandered the streets as beggars."

"Yes, yes, yes. Very honorable and commendable. It's always great to help out your own people and country," Narendra replied. "But this is too contrived, so orchestrated. A fourteen-year-old girl is going to plan and execute an orphanage in India from thousands of miles away? Her father is an architect and her mother is an anesthesiologist. They started this project undoubtedly and certainly did most of the work. Listen, I may be cynical – it helped orphans – but it also got her into Harvard."

Vijay looked at Narendra. He was a short chubby man who obviously had bad acne as a child leaving gaping pockmarks. His eyelids drooped over sad eyes.

"Your children are successful now, I hope."

"Oh, they're both OK. My son is an engineering student working for Texas Instruments in the summers, and my daughter is in nursing school. Normal, ordinary children who grew up in to be normal ordinary adults. They didn't go to Harvard, didn't start orphanages, but turned out to be good human beings. Their mother, my wife, died when they were pre-teens, so they grew up in their formative years with me as their only parent. I'm an accountant and I had to work hard to support them, so I never got to spend time with them that they deserved. But they never complained or whined. They just did their school work, helped take care of the household, and grew up normally. In my opinion, they're just as big of heroes as Aarav."

Vijay nodded his head. He was realizing as he got older that heroes come in many shapes, sizes, and even ages. One must work to help his fellow man no matter what the cost. But seeing the pictures of Chennai and the orphanage made him suddenly home-sick for Mumbai and his family and Dr. Bissel-Mozel. He was enjoying his life in America, but maybe it was time to go back and start his life's work.

All of the other twenty-nine tables were filled with eight people except for the one Vijay and Narendra occupied. They were in a dark corner in the back of the room; the spotlight which should have lit their table had burned out. They sat and talked as they ate the vegetarian meal together. Narendra worked as an accountant for himself, and when he found out

Vijay was a doctor, he immediately reached into his pocket and handed him one of his business cards.

When dinner was over, Vijay stood up. He noticed that most of the people had now left their tables and were talking in the front of the room around the podium and next to the bar. Vijay walked up to the bar and ordered a Seven-Up. He towered over everyone else in the room – no one was within four or five inches of his height. He stood there sipping on his Seven-up, wondering how he could meet a girl and what he would say once he did. Suddenly he heard a loud clacking of shoes on the wooden floor. Everyone else walked around in silence, but the clacking got louder and louder until he looked to his left and saw the most beautiful woman he'd ever seen standing next to him. She was tall, but was also wearing high heels so that she could almost look at Vijay eye to eye. She wore a tight-fitting black dress and her straight black hair was combed dramatically to the side and held in place by a gold pin. Around her neck was a gold chain with a large gold cross.

"I haven't seen you here before. My name is Preeti, what's yours?"

Vijay had just swallowed a sip of Seven-Up and now began to choke. Oh great, he thought, now I can't talk when I finally have a chance.

Preeti patted him a couple of times on the back, and the choking stopped. "Sorry to get you all choked up. I can have that effect on men. Did you just move here? I certainly would have seen you if you'd come before. You're far taller than any of the other men here, and more handsome."

For the first time in his life, Vijay blushed. He extended his right arm. "I'm Vijay Givagushrai. It is my pleasure to meet you. I've lived here for a while, but this is the first singles party I've attended. Oh, and you probably know this, but you are the most beautiful woman I've ever seen."

"Thanks for the compliment. What do you do for a living?"

"I'm a doctor at Pleasant Point."

"What field?"

"A new field – a hospitalist. I take care of patients whose doctors don't want to take care of them when they get sick and have to be hospitalized."

"That seems strange; a doctor who doesn't want to take care of his patients when they are sick. My father is a doctor, also. He is an orthopedic surgeon, although he calls himself an entrepreneur. With all of his business dealings, I don't know if he sees many patients anymore."

"And what do you do?"

"I'm a buyer for Neiman Marcus. I buy their fine jewelry. The ring I'm wearing is one of ours." She held her right hand up to Vijay, and he admired the large, perfectly cut round ruby surrounded by small diamonds.

"Beautiful ring. Is it yours or are you just borrowing it for tonight?"

"It's mine. My parents give it to me last year for my twenty-eighth birthday."

"You're so pretty and seem smart. Your father must be very successful. Why haven't your parents arranged for you to be married yet?"

Preeti laughed. "You have a direct way of asking questions. I could give you the long answer or the short one. Which would you prefer?"

"Why don't we start with the short answer, and if that isn't enough, I'll ask you to move on to the longer one."

"OK. At age twenty-three, my father arranged for me to meet fifty Indian men from all over the country so that I could pick one to marry. I traveled from New York to Miami to San Francisco. I met some wonderful men from great, wealthy, established families. I spent at least three days with each of them, going out with the men and their families first, and then the men alone. A couple of them even kissed me."

"When I returned home, my father told me that of the fifty men, forty-nine had sent him letters asking to marry me. The one who didn't lived in Chicago and seemed rather feminine to me." Preeti's large almond eyes radiated as she laughed.

"My father asked me who I wanted to marry, and I said that I picked none of them. First, I'm 5 feet 8 inches, and the tallest of them was my height – I could never wear my heels like tonight without towering over them. No, but seriously, I felt no spark, no great love. Maybe it was the system my father said, maybe you didn't have enough time to formulate a decision. I told him I didn't think that was the case, but he insisted that I rank the top ten of the men I'd met. He flew them all, at his expense, to Atlanta, and I spent more time with each of them. I started to like one man a little, but he had this annoying habit of calling me "Pretty Pet" as a nickname. And when we kissed, his lips felt so hard and his tongue went so deep into my throat that I felt like he was trying to touch my tonsils. No, no, no, I said to them all, so here I am, twenty-eight, single, and going to Indian Singles Events which seemed hopeless until tonight."

Preeti looked into Vijay's eyes and he looked into hers. It was happening quickly and before he'd expected it, but was he falling in love with this brash, beautiful woman standing next to him? His only experience with dating had been a few Indian nurses at his hospital, but he quickly realized it was a bad idea to, as his partner said, shit where you eat, so he hadn't dated in a while.

Just then another man walked up to where he and Preeti were standing.

"I'm Madanapal," he said, extending a hand to shake Vijay's.

"I'm Vijay. It is a pleasure to meet you."

Madanapal was 5 feet 5 inches tall and weighed over two-hundred pounds. He wore gold glasses and had curly, almost kinky hair. He wore a jacket without a tie and had a large gold ring on his right hand. He turned away from Vijay towards Preeti, and maneuvered his body between Vijay's and Preeti's.

"Preeti. I'm glad to see you. I really enjoyed our date last Saturday night."

"Madanapal is a partner with my father in one of his businesses. Madanapal has opened four Indian fast food restaurants in the city – "Curry in a Hurry" – and he has been very successful. My father is his business partner."

"Very successful doesn't begin to cover it. Business is up two-hundred percent over last year. Someday, we'll be as big as McDonald's. We have plans to open four more restaurants throughout Georgia. There's no competition. Preeti and I have been dating for the last six months – western style dating – not pre-arranged although her father did introduce us. I want to show you my new toy, Preeti. Come outside with me; the party is breaking up anyway."

"Excuse me one moment." Preeti reached into her Prada purse. She took Vijay's hand, "It was so wonderful to meet you, and I hope to see you more. Good-bye for now."

Vijay looked at his hand and saw that it now contained a business card with Preeti's home and cell numbers.

"It was good to meet you, Preeti, and you as well, Madanapal. Do you need a ride home, Preeti?"

"No, I have my car here."

"Come, Preeti, let me show you my new toy," said Madanapal.

"I want Vijay to come also." Preeti gently tugged on Vijay's sleeve. The three of them left the hotel and walked out to the parking lot. They walked towards the Porsche 911 Turbo which occupied two parking spots in front of the hotel. It had a fire engine red paint job and black leather interior. Madanapal pushed on the key chain and the car honked and the lights went on and off.

"What do you think? Care to go with me for a little drive?"

"It's beautiful," said Preeti. "But I'm tired tonight. I'll take a rain check. My car's parked on the other side of the lot. Vijay, would you mind walking me to my car?"

"A pleasure," replied Vijay, "good night, Madanapal." Vijay stuck out his hand but Madanapal turned away and got into his Porsche.

Vijay and Preeti walked over to her baby blue BMW 325 in silence. When they got to the car, Preeti pulled the keys out of her handbag and turned to Vijay. "There's something about you that I really like. I can't put my finger on it yet, but I have to get to know you better." She put her arms around Vijay's neck and kissed him. They stood there kissing for five minutes.

"I've got to go now...call me."

Preeti got into her car and drove off. Vijay stood there in the Holiday Inn parking lot with a smile on his face.

CHAPTER 19

Peter Dickman pulled into the West Pleasant Point Soccer Field's parking lot. There were four soccer fields next to each other with huge stadium lights around each field. All the lights were on even though it was only 6 o'clock at night and still not dark. The fields were beautifully manicured with green grass divided by perfect white lines and professional goals on each end. Each field was being used for practice. Peter walked over to the second field where his son, Josh, was playing. Josh was on a select soccer team. He'd been on the same team since he was six. At age six, he'd played on a team with buddies from school, but then he'd been recruited to play on this select team made up of the best players in the league. He'd been with this team for two years now. They practiced two times a week for three hours and had games every weekend. Some weekends, they traveled to tournaments located in other cities in the Southeast. It had taken a tremendous commitment by Josh and the family to keep him on this select soccer team, and Peter wasn't sure if it was worth it. Peter's wife had been very into it at first, but, now that they were separated, she seemed less enthused about spending her weekends driving Josh and his teammates around to different tournaments.

Tonight was Peter's night to pick up Josh. Josh and he would have supper together, and then Josh would spend the night at

Peter's apartment. The tiny apartment was a lot smaller and less glamorous than the mansion that Peter's estranged wife occupied.

As Peter got to the field, he saw Marc Simple, the father of Donnie, who was by far the best player on the team. Donnie was a year-and-a-half older than the other boys; not only was his birthday early, but his parents had held him back a year in school. So, he was a ten-year-old third-grader. He was a head taller than any of the other boys on the team and better coordinated. His father came to every practice.

"Hey, Marc, how ya doing?" asked Peter.

"Peter, good to see you. Josh is playing pretty well today."

"That's good to hear. All that money the team is spending on those professional skills coaches is paying off, huh? They almost done?"

"Yeah, probably just another few minutes."

Peter looked out at the field and saw that Josh was on the same team as Donnie. They were scrimmaging with other boys on the team. Josh made a good play and kicked the ball to Donnie, and Donnie dribbled past two defenders and kicked the ball into the goal.

"Way to go, big boy!" yelled Marc. He turned to Peter. "So how's business?"

"Oh, pretty good. Staying steady."

Peter knew that Marc was in his family's commercial real estate business and that he was loaded with money. Marc worked when he wanted to, so he could go to all of his son's practices and games.

"When this is over, I'm taking Donnie to a roller hockey game," Marc said.

"You've got a game after this? Won't Donnie be tired?"

"Yeah, but it's the time of year when he's on all these different teams, and they're all select teams and he wants to play all these sports. And he's great at all of them. He can do his homework in the car. Just another coupla hours of roller hockey tonight."

"Wow, that's a big commitment. We only let Josh play one sport at a time."

"That's probably a good idea," replied Marc. "But the boy wants it, and you only get one childhood, so we got to get him into as many sports as we can. Hey, you wanta hear something funny?"

"OK," answered Peter.

"A couple of days ago, I ran into the wife of one of your colleagues, Aaron Bernstein."

"Sure, Aaron, he's a gastroenterologist at my hospital," said Peter.

"Well, his wife, I don't know if you know her. Her name is Marcy. Big, fat lady. Anyway, she's asking me about why her son can't play on a soccer team with our kids. She says her boy knows our kids from school and pals around with them at school. Wants to know why her boy, David, can't play on our team. I tried to tell her that our team was closed, that we already had enough boys, but she wouldn't listen. She was raising hell with me, saying, 'It's not fair since the boys are in school together and are friends that they can't play soccer together.' Finally, I just had to come right out and tell her that her son wasn't good enough to play. I mean, he's played on a couple of regular league teams in the past, and he plays kind of like a little baby, you know?"

Peter looked at Marc. He realized how important Marc's son's athletic success was to him. "Yeah, I know what you're saying. It just seems a shame; Aaron's son seems like such a nice kid..."

"He'd be lost out here. He'd get killed. We've got all these extra coaches, these skills coaches, who come in and help the boys. That stuff would be lost on him. The kid is slow. I think he's got asthma or something. Can hardly run. We don't want kids like that cluttering up our team. This team's got a chance to win like a championship. I'm talking about a national championship. They finished fifth in that tournament in Oklahoma out of 120 teams."

"Yeah, I guess you're right," Peter conceded.

"And you know something that kills me? These parents whose kids aren't any good but they want to get them on our select teams, they don't show any commitment. They wouldn't be out here with us helping coach the team. They wouldn't help drive the kids around. I coached these boys when they were six years old. Just before they became select soccer players. I'm the one who got the ball rolling."

Peter nodded his head. He knew Marc thought that Donnie was going to be a professional athlete when he got older. Donnie played baseball, football, basketball, soccer and in-line hockey. He was the oldest, biggest and most coordinated boy now, but Peter knew that children matured and developed at different rates. Peter himself hadn't been much of an athlete until age 21 when he'd gotten involved in karate. He'd eventually achieved a black belt.

The practice finished, and the boys began to run laps around the perimeter of the four fields. Josh waved to Peter, and Peter waved back. He wanted to take Josh to dinner and then get him back to the apartment and to sleep quickly. He had a rendezvous planned tonight with one of the nurses from the hospital. He'd been having sex with her for some time, and he hadn't screwed her in a couple of weeks. Suddenly, his beeper went off. He was surprised because he wasn't on call. He pulled out his cell phone and called the answering service.

"It's Dr. Dickman. I just got paged. Don't you know I'm not on call tonight?"

"Dr. Dickman, the call came specifically for you. It's from Pleasant Point General Hospital, and it's an emergency. The call is from Pleasant Point's Chief of Police. This is the callback number."

Peter disconnected the phone and then dialed the number he'd been given.

"This is Peter Dickman, cardiology."

"Peter, this is Police Chief Farris. I'm here at Pleasant Point General Hospital. I'm sure you are aware that we've got a hostage situation on our hands. A Mr. Jumpy Johnson here has taken a nurse and another patient hostage, and the patient may be having a heart attack. He's having severe chest pain, and we wanted to get someone in there to see him and help him. Mr. Johnson says you're his personal cardiologist, and you're the only person he would allow into the room to help out this other man. This other man is a diabetic, has high blood pressure and is now having severe chest pain, sweating and is short of breath. That's at least what Mr. Johnson has told us. But, like I said, Mr. Johnson said only you could come in to help because he trusts you. It's dangerous, I know, but we really need you to get over here right away."

"OK. I'll be there as soon as possible," said Peter. He put down the phone. "Marc, do you think you could possibly take Josh home tonight? I've got an emergency at the hospital I need to go back for."

"Well, we've got our in-line hockey game next."

"Oh, right. Hold on one second." Peter dialed his wife's number.

"Hey, sugar, it's Peter…"

"Don't hey, sugar, me. What's going on?"

"I've got an emergency at the hospital tonight…"

"OK. Who is she? Who are you having the fling with tonight?"

"No, no seriously. They've got this hostage situation at the hospital, and one of the hostages is having an MI and he needs someone to help him. The guy that's taken the hostages is apparently my patient and will only allow me to come in. I need to go right now. Can you pick Josh up?"

"Peter, I was doing something else with our daughters tonight. I told them I would take them out to dinner and then shopping."

"Please, sugar. You gotta help me out this time. It's an emergency."

"All right. Just tell Josh to wait there, and I'll be right over."

Peter waited for Josh to come close to him and quickly explained the situation to Josh. He then ran to his Porsche and drove back to the hospital.

****

Peter wheeled the EKG machine down the hallway. He'd been briefed by the Chief of Police as to what he was supposed to do, and now he was outside Room 427. He knocked loudly on the door.

"Mr. Johnson, it's me, Peter Dickman, your cardiologist. Let me in so I can help your roommate."

The door opened a little bit, and Peter could see Mr. Johnson's eye.

"All right, Dr. Dickman, come on in. Don't you try anything funny, though, or I'll kill you and these two."

Peter had been briefed by the Police Chief not to try anything foolish. He had brought the EKG machine to see what was going on with Mr. Herman's heart. On top of the EKG machine, he had sublingual nitroglycerin, nitroglycerin paste and aspirin. He also had a syringe of morphine to inject into Mr. Herman's IV to help relieve the pain. The instructions from Chief Farris had been simple: try to get the sick hostage out of the room as soon as possible with Mr. Johnson's consent. No heroics.

All Peter wanted to do was to get the patient stabilized and down to the Intensive Care Unit. When he walked into the room, he was shocked. He saw, on the far bed, Krystal, the most beautiful nurse in the hospital, tied up in a spread-eagle fashion with towels, sheets and surgical tape. Her head was propped up on pillows, and Peter could see that her face was covered with a creamy liquid which looked like cum.

Mr. Herman was tied to his bed also. He was sweaty, pale… Peter was sure from looking at him that he was indeed having a heart attack. The door slammed behind him.

"Don't you try anything funny, mother-fucker," Mr. Johnson growled. "If you do, I'll kill you. You understand that? Only reason I'm letting you in here is you took care of me once when I had chest pain. So, I'm gonna let you take care of this slob. Then, I'm gonna let you go. You take care of him, I'll let you out of here. But he stays here."

Peter hooked Mr. Herman up to the EKG machine. Sure enough, it showed "tombstones" which meant an acute heart attack.

Peter smiled at Mr. Herman. "Don't worry, sir. We'll get you better." He took some of the nitro paste and squirted it out of the container onto a strip of paper and placed this on Mr. Herman's chest. "This will help relieve the pain." He then took out the syringe of morphine and began to inject some into Mr. Herman's IV.

"What's that you're injecting?" growled Mr. Johnson. He was now behind Peter watching him intently. "What you tryin' to do to this man? You gonna make him more of a man than me?"

"This is morphine, Mr. Johnson. This will just help his pain. Please, you've gotta let me give it to him."

"No fuckin' way. You don't give that shit to him." Mr. Johnson moved closer to Peter.

Peter saw the opportunity. Mr. Johnson was so close. Peter cried, "OK," and he turned around quickly and squirted the syringe into Mr. Johnson's face. As Mr. Johnson fell back, Peter hit him as hard as he could with a karate chop to the left side of the face. The blow broke Mr. Johnson's jaw and knocked him out. He fell backwards, and his head crashed against the wall as he slumped to the ground. Peter pushed the bed away from the door and opened the door. He called into the hallway, "Come on in. I've got him. He's taken care of."

Peter began to untie Krystal as the police stormed into the room.

"Oh, my gosh. Look at all the blood here," said one of the policemen.

Peter saw blood on the wall where Mr. Johnson's head had hit and on the floor around Mr. Johnson. Blood was dripping from Mr. Johnson's nose and mouth.

"All right," said Chief Farris. "Let's get some doctors here to help Mr. Johnson. Let's get Mr. Herman to the Intensive Care Unit as soon as possible and untie this lady so that we can take care of her." The Chief noticed that Peter was already untying Krystal and had his back to Mr. Herman who lay motionless.

CHAPTER 20

Wendy Trotter smiled as she drove down 75 to Forest Park, Georgia. It had been a good day even though she knew it was one of her last days on earth. She was dying of liver cancer; the doctor three months before had given her three months to live. But here she was at her job working as a reporter for CNN. No one knew her diagnosis or bleak prognosis. Today had been a big day for her; the first story on the wires nationally had been the hostage taking at a hospital in Pleasant Point which was her territory. Normally, if there was a big national story coming from the Atlanta area, they would allow "pretty boy" Dan Williams to take over as the lead reporter on the story. No one had expected this to be the big story of the day, but it had been a quiet day for news nationally and internationally. Plus, one of the hostages taken had been a gorgeous white woman which always piqued the national interest. So, CNN had started off three straight hours of its news with reports directly from Wendy. Now that it was later in the afternoon and nothing else more newsworthy had occurred, good old Dan Williams had driven up from Atlanta to take over. But what exposure she'd gotten! This was the most she'd been on television in one day in her 35 years of reporting.

Now, Wendy was trying to dig up new information to keep herself on the air. With Dan firmly planted at Pleasant Point

General Hospital, she had tried to locate and interview Mr. Johnson's psychiatrist. Earlier in the day, she'd interviewed Mrs. Johnson who had told her of her husband's schizophrenia and that he was being treated at the Georgia Veterans Hospital. She'd tried for two hours to get in touch with Marc Fried, his psychiatrist, but her calls to Dr. Fried's office at the Veterans Hospital and to his home were not answered. During a call to the VA Hospital, however, Wendy had gotten a lucky break. She talked to the secretary for the psychiatry department, Pearl Williams, who gave her the name and number of one of the psychiatry resident physicians who had been somewhat involved in Mr. Johnson's care. His name was Halle Saffre. When Wendy called his home, he wasn't there, but his wife said that he was moonlighting at a hospital in Forest Park. Wendy thought this was strange; how could a resident be moonlighting in the middle of the day when he was supposed to be at the Veterans Hospital taking care of patients? She called the emergency room at Forest Park Hospital and was connected to Dr. Saffre. He had a thick Bahamian accent and seemed happy to talk to her. He said he would love to talk about Mr. Johnson and the psychiatric care he had received. Wendy had immediately contacted one of the CNN cameramen at Pleasant Point General Hospital, and now he was driving in his truck loaded with camera equipment down I-75 just in front of her.

Wendy had led a lonely life. She'd been an only child and never married. At the age of 55, she really had no one – both of her parents had died ten years before. She'd had a few affairs including one boyfriend she dated for five years. But, for the last ten years, she'd had no meaningful relationships. It was sad, but she hadn't known what lonely was until she'd received the diagnosis of liver cancer. You were so lonely when you were diagnosed with a terminal illness because you were set apart from the rest of the world. Everyone else was so caught up in their own minuscule problems and in the meaningless concerns of their community; how they looked, whether or not the latest school bond issue passed, etc. None of this mattered to Wendy anymore or to anyone with a terminal illness. All that mattered was getting up in the morning and making it through that day. She had been sad and consumed by grief the first couple of weeks after her diagnosis. Then, she had vowed to live the last few months of her life to the fullest and to do what she enjoyed most, being a reporter and asking the tough, hardnosed questions that she was known for.

****

The hospital in Forest Park was tiny. Wendy parked next to her cameraman's truck and walked into the emergency room. There was a nurse sitting at the front desk under a sign marked "Triage," and, as Wendy found out later, there was only one additional nurse in the emergency room itself. The one patient who was sitting in the waiting room was a woman in her 20s who appeared to be bleeding from a cut above the left eye. Wendy showed the triage nurse her credentials and said that Dr. Saffre was waiting for her. The nurse led her and the cameraman to Dr. Saffre.

Wendy was immediately impressed by Dr. Saffre's size and estimated that he was at least 6 feet 6 inches and 300 pounds. He laughed a lot and seemed very happy. He shook her hand and told her that he was glad to meet her, happy to talk to her and to talk about what a scandal the practice of medicine was at the Veterans Hospital. Wendy was encouraged by his openness and thought that this aspect of the story might be bigger than she had hoped. She called CNN headquarters in Atlanta on her cell phone and told them where she was and what she had. They said they would go live with her in two minutes. She had the cameraman set up by the doctor's desk and got ready. The call came into her earphone, "Ten seconds, and you're on." Wendy walked up to Dr. Saffre and stood next to him. Since she was only 5 feet 2 inches, he towered over her. She heard Dan Williams introducing her through her earphones.

"Thanks, Dan. This is Wendy Trotter, and I'm in Forest Park, Georgia, at the Forest Park Hospital Emergency Room with Dr. Halle Saffre. Dr. Saffre is one of the psychiatrists who has been taking care of Mr. Jumpy Johnson at the Veterans Hospital here in Atlanta. To briefly summarize today's events, Mr. Johnson took two hostages at Pleasant Point General Hospital and is still holding them at gunpoint. Dr. Saffre, tell me what it was like taking care of Mr. Johnson."

"He always seemed to me to be nice person. He certainly come to the Veterans Hospital for help. But my boss at the Veterans Hospital who was supposed to be in charge of the psychiatry residents never took an interest in Mr. Johnson or any of his patients. All he ever did was renew their medications. He could care less."

"Are you saying that this doctor, Dr. Marc Fried, wasn't actively treating Mr. Johnson?"

"Ha, ha, ha, ha. Treating him? If you were to look at the progress notes that he wrote for the last ten years on Mr. Johnson, every note would be the same: patient seen and examined and seems to be doing well. No major disturbances. No active hallucinations. Will renew medications. See back two months. Every patient he would write the same thing. He would spend five minutes, maybe at the most ten minutes, with these patients. Never take care of them. Never do anything to help them. And he would make sure that he would keep the same patients in his clinic so that his clinic would be full so that any new patients would come to my clinic."

"Did you have any idea," asked Wendy, "that Mr. Johnson was about to go on a rampage?"

"Uh, I knew one of these patients one of these days something bad would happen. I jes knew it. Mr. Johnson, no, he was a nice man. I tink I remember his wife being a nice lady and his family a nice family. But they didn't get any help. You can't help people if all you do is refill their prescriptions. All you do is prescribe medicine. You don't talk to 'em. You don't listen to 'em. You don't try to help 'em. You just give them medicine. This is what happened. Yes, these people you know, they crazy, that's it. They're crazy. They come to psychiatrists, and psychiatrists s'posed to help them. That's what medicine is for. We're s'posed to help people. But this man never received the kind of help that he should get."

"Did he ever say anything as far as you know about wanting to hurt people or take hostages or anything like that?"

"Who should know? How could someone know? If Dr. Fried not gonna spend time with him, not gonna talk to him, who should know? We wouldn't know. Dr. Fried doesn't know more than you know, lady. You a nice lady. You seem to have a level head. You could do the same thing he did. And I'm s'posed to be there to learn from him? How'm I gonna learn? He tells me, 'do this, do this, do this! Take care of this patient, take care of this patient.' All I'm doing is taking care of patients. I'm doing his job. I'm a first-year psychiatry resident. I did one year of training, internship…a rotating internship…they needed me for this residency. They came and said to me, 'We need more residents,' so I came here to Atlanta to do this residency. I could be the teacher for all the teaching that Dr. Fried gives me. He goes home in the afternoon. I never see him. And all the patient, they left for me."

"Wow. Well, let me ask you a quick question. I see that you're here in Forest Park Hospital Emergency Room working. Are you working as a psychiatry resident here?"

"Oh, no, no, no. I'm moonlighting here. I moonlight at least two, three times a week as emergency room doctor. I take care of whole emergency room. Anything that comes in, I can take care of."

"So, just doing one year of a rotating internship gives you enough experience to take care of anyone that walks in the door of an emergency room?"

"Oh, yes, don't you see, mon? Even though I'm a psychiatry, I can do surgery, I can do pediatrics. And, if the patient's too sick, I can have them taken by ambulance elsewhere."

"But what about you? What about reading about psychiatry? What about learning more? Don't you need to be studying? Don't you need to be at the Veterans Hospital taking care of the patients there? Don't they have rules that say you shouldn't be here?"

"Ho, ho, ho, ho. Yeah, well, you right. There is a rule in my contract that say…ooh, oh, ooh. I shouldn't have said this… yeah, I'm not s'posed to be moonlighting. No one s'posed to be moonlighting. It's true what you say that. But we all do it. We all just leave and do it. Once we start our training program, the big thing is to moonlight. I have a wife; I have two kids. You know what they pay me as a resident? $28,000 a year. You could live on $28,000 a year? Moonlighting here in the emergency room…one day, I make $2000 to $3000. I mean, I do this two times a week, I make $6000 a week. This is what I need to do. And these hospitals, the same hospitals, they need people like me."

"But isn't it kind of dangerous to have someone who is a psychiatrist sewing you up? I saw a young woman out there with a bad cut over her eye. You are going to be the one to sew that up?"

"I'm the only one here. I can do it. This is what I can do. I know that I can take care of people like this."

"Fascinating. This is an interesting commentary on today's medical system. There are psychiatrists at the Veterans Hospital who, according to Dr. Saffre, take no interest in their patients but just see the patients quickly and get out of the hospital. And even the doctors who are in training, their only thought is to leave the hospital so that they can earn a decent living. We'll be back with more updates, but we understand that there is breaking news from Pleasant Point General Hospital, so we're sending it back to Dan Williams."

Wendy smiled. "Thank you, Dr. Saffre. That was quite an interview you gave."

"Oh, my pleasure, my pleasure. I wanted to be on television."

"Let me ask you a question now that the camera is off. Do you think you'll get into trouble for saying that you're moonlighting?"

"Oh, listen, lady. They need me a lot more than I need them. There's a shortage of psychiatrists. No one wants to go into psychiatry now. Everyone wants to go into big fields, make big bucks. Not psychiatry. They need me. They won't get rid of me."

"Well, thank you again." Wendy walked out the door to her car. Her interview with Dr. Saffre had been an incredible success showing how the system had failed Mr. Johnson. No one had cared enough to take care of him, and now he'd gone on a wild rampage. Wendy was proud that she'd first reported the story and that she had continued to supply great reports throughout the day. As she drove back to Pleasant Point, she hoped that her colleagues would remember her by her work on this memorable day.

CHAPTER 21

Lizzy Chen hated the 6:00 p.m. to 10:00 p.m. shift because she was the only radiologist in the department for those four hours. It hadn't been her turn to work tonight, but she had been told the day before by Thomas Kelly, the Chief of Radiology, that he was going to his son's basketball game that night, and she was going to take his 6:00 p.m. to 10:00 p.m. shift. Lizzy was the newest radiologist at the hospital, so she didn't have a choice. Being the only radiologist there, she had to perform or interpret whatever tests came along. CAT scans, MRI scans, ultrasounds on pregnant women, etc., all were her responsibility for those four hours. No colleagues were around for second opinions or assistance.

Lizzy had just finished her fellowship in pediatric radiology at Emory Medical School and had spent the last two years doing only pediatric radiology. She was planning on a career in academic medicine and had been offered a spot on the faculty at Emory. Then, the offer from Pleasant Point came along and was too good to pass up. The starting salary was $300,000 a year with bonuses based on the amount of work she did. That was a huge amount of money for a single, 31-year-old woman, and she accepted their offer. She had bought a condominium in far north Atlanta and a Lexus sports car, and she had a very active social life, dating at least every weekend and often during the week. She had a date for tonight that was supposed to start with dinner at 7:00 p.m., but she changed it to go out for a later dinner date when she got off work.

It had been a busy shift so far. She had been called three times by the neurosurgeon, Georgio Circelli, about the infamous patient, Mr. Johnson. She had followed the story on the news and knew about the hostage situation. Now, Mr. Johnson was unconscious and intubated with a deteriorating neurological exam, and a STAT CAT scan of the brain had been ordered. Circelli was calling every five minutes to see if the CAT scan had been done yet; just then, the CT tech walked into the reading room with the films. He put the CT pictures on the reading board along with the chest x-ray that had been done to check for placement of the endotracheal tube after Mr. Johnson had been intubated. Lizzy knew that Mr. Johnson was already in the operating room, and Circelli was getting ready to operate, depending on the CT findings.

She looked at the CT scan carefully. It was very obvious that there was a large bleed in the right hemisphere of the brain. She could see that there was no herniation yet, but, with this amount of blood, herniation was imminent. Otherwise, the CT looked OK. No old strokes, nothing else. She quickly glanced at the chest x-ray to make sure that the endotracheal tube was in proper position, and it was. She called Circelli's number in surgery.

"Dr. Circelli, this is Dr. Chen in radiology. I have had a chance to look at Mr. Johnson's CAT scan. He's got a large bleed in the right hemisphere. Hasn't herniated yet, but the amount of blood is huge."

"OK," said Dr. Circelli. "We are getting ready to operate. Thanks for your help."

"No problem," answered Lizzy, and she hung up the phone. She was very proud of herself and the thoroughness of her evaluation of the CT scan. She thought for a second about one of the hospital's doctors who had been complaining about her, Dr. Aaron Bernstein. She hated him. He had brought her name up to Thomas Kelly, saying that, when she was on from 6:00 p.m. to 10:00 p.m., he didn't trust her readings. Or, when she was the overnight person working from 10:00 p.m. to 6:00 a.m., he didn't feel comfortable with the readings she had given him. She told Dr. Kelly that she had never been criticized before, and she asked Dr. Kelly to review her work. Nothing could be found as far as trends of mistakes. True, she had missed one appendicitis, missed a Zenker's diverticulum, and she had called one bowel obstruction that wasn't there, but these were mistakes any radiologist could have made.

No, she thought, I'm a good radiologist. She had Carl take down the CT scan and the chest x-ray.

There is a phenomenon in radiology called fascination error. It refers to times when the radiologist is so concerned or fascinated by one finding on an x-ray that he or she completely misses or ignores something else that is there. Unfortunately, in this case, Lizzy's concern had been so centered on the CAT scan that she hadn't spent much time on the chest x-ray. For if she had, she would have noticed that the eighth and ninth ribs on the right side of Mr. Johnson's chest were fractured, and there was a five to ten percent pneumothorax or collapse of the right lung where the ribs had punctured the lung. All she had done was check the placement of the endotracheal tube and quickly glanced at the lung fields. So, the pneumothorax was missed.

****

In the operating room, Dr. Circelli was prepping Mr. Johnson for surgery. He had his long-time anesthesiologist, Roger Dorme, assisting him. Circelli knew that this was a case that would get a lot of publicity; it had dominated the news that day. He wanted to do as good of a job as possible to save Mr. Johnson's life. He got ready to make the initial incision when Roger shouted, "Wait a second! I'm starting to have some problems ventilating him."

"What's wrong?" asked Georgio Circelli.

"He's getting a little hypoxic. I'm keeping his oxygen saturation in the 90 to 92 range, but he was just 97 to 98 percent before. Is this guy a big-time smoker or something? Or does he have asthma? I didn't see anything on his chart about that."

"Not that I know of." Circelli motioned to the circulating nurse. "Why don't you bring his chart to Dr. Dorme and let him look at it."

All of a sudden, an alarm went off. "Hey, his blood pressure is dropping quickly," said Dr. Dorme. "I'll start giving him some fluids wide open."

Georgio Circelli looked at the blood pressure monitor and saw that the latest blood pressure had registered 80/50. "Roger, wasn't his last blood pressure 120/90? He was hypertensive before we got him down here."

"Yeah. I'm having more and more problems ventilating him. Something else is going on here. Let me think for a second."

The alarm went off again. The blood pressure registered 60/30.

"I'm putting him in Trendelenburg and putting in a central line," said Dr. Dorme.

"What do you think is going on?" asked Dr. Circelli.

"I don't know. I wonder if the endotracheal tube is not in proper position or if the balloon has deflated." Dr. Dorme used his stethoscope to listen to Mr. Johnson's lungs. He heard good breath sounds on the left side, but he didn't hear breath sounds on the right side.

"Holy shit!" Dr. Dorme said. "I think this guy's got a pneumothorax on the right. Get me a chest tube setup quick."

The circulating nurse ran out of the room.

"I'm going to have to make an incision and get this chest tube in," Dr. Dorme said.

The alarms went off again. The blood pressure was 50/20.

"Shit, this guy's gonna die. Gotta get this in here!" Dr. Dorme screamed.

The nurse quickly prepped out the right chest wall.

The heart monitor showed tachycardia at 180 beats per minute.

"Gotta get this chest tube in and get this pneumothorax taken care of."

Robert Dorme got the chest tube in, and a rush of air came out.

"That should get him better quickly. Let me bag him some more," Roger said.

The oxygen saturation monitor read 76.

"Oh, shit, he's going onto asystole! Let's start CPR. Call Code Blue!"

The nurse pushed the Code Blue button. They began to do chest compressions.

"Hook the chest tube up."

The nurse hooked up the chest tube, and more air came out.

"Resume compressions!" Roger barked at the nurse. The monitor still showed asystole.

"Shit," said Georgio. "We've gotta bring this guy back, gotta bring this guy back."

"More fluids, everything going wide open." Roger ran through the algorithm for advanced cardiac life support, and they worked on Mr. Johnson for 45 minutes. They were never able to regain a cardiac rhythm. After 45 minutes, Roger Dorme called the code and pronounced Mr. Jumpy Johnson dead. Dr. Circelli had never made the initial incision.

CHAPTER 22

By the time Aaron got home from work that night, it was 10:30. All three of his children had been asleep for over an hour-and-a-half, and so Aaron tiptoed into each one of their rooms, kissed them and straightened their blankets. Marcy greeted him at their bedroom door with a sad look on her face.

"I heard about your patient," she said. "I heard it on the late news. I'm so sorry that poor man died…I'm sure you did everything you could to help him."

"Never really got the chance to help him. I just feel so bad that I didn't figure out that he was schizophrenic. There certainly were clues, but I couldn't put it together fast enough. This is one of those cases that's going to take me a long time to work through and, hopefully, some day, forgive myself."

"It's not your fault, honey. You didn't make him schizophrenic. Why don't you take a nice hot shower? That will help you feel better. I'm going to check my e-mail on the computer."

Aaron undressed and got into the shower. He let the warm water soak his body. Then, he put his head right under the shower head so that all he could hear was the water rushing over his ears. This had a numbing effect, and it made it difficult for him to concentrate on anything, even Mr. Johnson's face.

Marcy walked into the bathroom and shouted at Aaron several times before he heard her. He quickly turned off the water and stepped out of the shower.

"What's wrong?" he asked.

"Come with me." Aaron dried off and then followed Marcy out of the bathroom and into her office.

"Every time I leave my e-mail to get on the internet, the computer freezes up and takes me back to our home page. Initially, it occurred maybe once a week or so, but now it's happening every time. I can't do anything with it; I have to turn the computer completely off and then start all over once it's warmed up. You know how much I rely on the computer to run our lives. It's a mess."

"I'll get it fixed, honey. Don't worry. Let me call the computer manufacturer and see what we have to do," said Aaron.

Aaron opened a desk drawer and pulled out the operating manual for the computer. There was a 1-800 number to dial for any problems. Still naked, Aaron sat down in the desk chair and dialed the number. After a few rings, the phone was answered.

"I'm Aaron Bernstein calling from Pleasant Point, Georgia. We have a Diamond computer that we bought three years ago, and we're having a problem."

"Describe to me in English what your problem is."

"Every time my wife tries to go from her e-mail to the internet, the computer freezes up and takes her back to the home page. Once that happens, no matter what she does, she can't get off the home page unless she turns the computer completely off and then starts it up again."

"Oh, that sounds like a very disturbing problem. We will have to send one of our technicians to fix it. Let me look and see… you are calling from the United States, you said?"

"Uh, of course, the United States. Where are you?"

"Oh, we are in Mumbai, India. That is where the call center for Diamond Computers is located."

"But I called with a problem six months ago and talked to someone right here in Atlanta, Georgia."

"Oh, yes. Six months ago, the main call center was in Atlanta, Georgia. But they decided it would be much better and much cheaper for them to move the call station to India. We operate the station 24/7."

"So, Diamond Computer, a company from Atlanta, Georgia, that advertises that it's an American-based company and shows an American flag in its television ads, is exporting its jobs to India?"

"Yes, you have got that quite right. Right now, all calls come here. Now, they are building a plant here, and we will be assembling the Diamond computers in India as well."

"My, oh, my. So, can you arrange to have a technician come to our house to fix our computer?"

"Oh, absolutely. Give me your name and address again."

Aaron gave him the information.

"Very good. I will make sure that you will have someone at your house in the next 24 hours. According to my computer, it is now 11:00 p.m. in Atlanta, Georgia. We will have someone at your house tomorrow to fix things. It will be between 10:00 a.m. and 6:00 p.m. Will someone be there?"

"That's a long time to expect my wife to stay at home. Can't you narrow it down somewhat? We've got three kids, and she has a lot of responsibilities."

"We could come next week if you'd prefer. Perhaps your wife won't be so busy then."

"No, no, no. All right. My wife will have to make arrangements. Are you sure it's not something you can tell me how to fix over the phone?" asked Aaron.

"Oh, very few problems can we fix over the phone now. We like to have our specialists come in and take a look at things."

"Very well," sighed Aaron. "I have to admit that I'm surprised to have to call India to get a computer fixed here in Pleasant Point, Georgia, especially when the company is supposedly based in Atlanta, Georgia. But it sounds like you're competent and will get the job done. Thanks for your time. Goodnight."

Aaron hung up the phone and walked into the bedroom where Marcy was sitting in a chair.

"What did they say?" she asked.

"You're not gonna believe it, but Diamond Computers' call center is located in Mumbai, India. The man there took my information but said there was nothing he could do over the phone. He's sending out a technician tomorrow between 10 and 6. You'll have to arrange to be here all day. I'm sorry, but that's the best he would do."

"Thanks, Sweetie," said Marcy. "I'll manage. You get some rest."

"I'll try," replied Aaron as he turned out the lights.

PART 3

CHAPTER 1

Peter Dickman felt he had died and gone to heaven these last five days. They had been the most fantastic days of his life. It had been two weeks since Mr. Johnson's death. Peter felt terrible about causing a man's death, of course, but his grief had ended a week before with a call from Krystal, the nurse he'd rescued. Krystal invited him over to her apartment, and, after some small talk, she told him that she felt obligated to somehow repay Peter for saving her life. They had started kissing and eventually had gone to bed. The sex had been awesome, leaving Peter wanting more. As he left, Krystal suggested that the two of them go on vacation together. Peter immediately booked a package to go to Acapulco, Mexico, and to stay at the Princess Hotel where he had gone on his honeymoon 20 years before. He and Krystal had flown to Acapulco five days ago, and the last five days had been an incredible experience.

First, the Princess Hotel was gorgeous. It was located right on the water with a beautiful beach and four spectacular swimming pools. There had been an abundance of good-looking women in tiny string bikinis, but none of them rivaled Krystal. She had brought a collection of five thong bathing suits and was the only woman at the resort wearing a thong. Peter knew that the eyes of every man at the pool were on Krystal. With her white thong, she wore a white cover-up, which was a tiny see-through piece of cloth that barely covered her butt. She had matching cover-ups with her black, red, pink and orange thongs. He couldn't believe how great she looked, as even the high school and college girls didn't have bodies to match hers.

Krystal had insisted that they make love at least three times a day. When they first got up in the morning, they would have a torrid sex session followed by a big breakfast and then lounging at one of the pools. Then, they would have lunch and go back to the room for what Krystal called siesta, which amounted to sex followed by naps. At night after eating dinner at one of the finest restaurants in Acapulco, the two would again make love and lie in each other's arms until morning. Peter was worn out, but he felt great. Tonight was their last night in Acapulco, and he was taking Krystal to see the cliff divers. He had done it 20 years before and knew it was touristy, but he felt it was exciting and romantic. Earlier that day, he had gone down to the jewelry store in the Princess Hotel and had bought the largest diamond ring they had for Krystal. It was a four-carat diamond ring, VF2G color and cost $50,000. He was going to ask her to marry him that night.

They showered together after getting back from the pool and got dressed. Peter wore a Polo shirt, Polo shorts and sandals while Krystal wore a dazzling baby blue sequined mini-skirt and white halter top. Peter knew that they would be the center of attention at the restaurant, even with the cliff divers performing.

They took a taxi to the hotel where you could have dinner and watch the cliff diving show. It was a 30-minute ride, and the entire time Peter had Krystal in his arms. She kept telling him what a great time she was having and how much she liked him. All he could think about was her incredible body. She was 25 years old, so she was 20 years younger than him. She had a better body than any he had ever seen before. He had gone out with some great-looking women, including Hooters girls, professional cheerleaders and dancers, but none could match Krystal. With her boob job, she had 36D breasts, and she had the flattest, hardest abdomen he had ever seen. She also had the most incredible tight ass. He knew he was in love with her and he wanted to marry her.

It was true he wasn't divorced yet from his first wife, but they had been separated for some time now. The first affair of his that his wife had found out about (which actually was number 13 that he had had) was enough for her to throw him out of the house. He knew it wouldn't be hard to convince her to divorce him now although it would be tough on the five kids. But they were getting older and doing their own thing more and more, so he knew they'd get over it.

They got to the restaurant, and Krystal was immediately the center of attention. There was a group of college boys who hooted and whistled at Krystal. Peter and Krystal sat at the prime table in the restaurant and watched the cliff divers perform. It was a good show with the five divers jumping off the cliff into the turbulent ocean water. At the end of the show, Peter had arranged for the waitress to bring out chocolate cake for Krystal with the engagement ring inside of it.

Krystal said, "I'm really full. Would you help me eat this?"

"Why don't you go ahead," said Peter. "Take a couple of bites, see if you like it. I've heard it's their specialty."

Krystal smiled and showed her pearly whites. She took a couple of bites and said, "Hmmmmm, there's something hard in here."

She reached in with her hand and pulled out the huge diamond ring. At this point, Peter was down on his knee beside her.

"Krystal, the last five days have been the most wonderful days of my life. I love you. I need you so much. I know it was chance that brought us together, but that can be the best way for two people to meet. I want to marry you so that we can spend the rest of our lives together."

"But aren't you married already?" asked Krystal.

"Yes, I am. But I'll get a divorce. We've been separated for some time now. We're married in name only…for the kids. I want you to be the new Mrs. Peter Dickman."

"But, but…didn't you know I already have a fiancé?"

"I know about your fiancé, but when you came on vacation with me, I thought you were done with him."

"Ha, ha," Krystal laughed. "Done with him? He's an actor on a primetime TV show. We're gonna get married, Peter. I love him."

"I thought you loved me," said Peter.

"Oh, I do love you. I love you for what you did for me. You are great. You are a great guy, but I can't marry you. I don't love you that way. I love Quinn. I'm going to Hollywood to live with him. I…felt like I owed you something for saving my life. I wanted to make it up to you and pay you back. That's why I came along. I can't marry you."

Peter was dumbstruck. The greatest five days of his life had come crashing down on top of him. He looked at Krystal. "Ummm, so you don't love me? You don't want to marry me? You did this just to pay me back?"

"Well, not just to pay you back. I really like you. Everyone at the hospital said that you were a Don Juan, so I figured I would have a good time with you…and I did, believe me, I did. It's been a wonderful time."

"Can I have the ring back?" asked Peter.

"Sure," said Krystal. "It's a beautiful ring, and I really thank you. Let's have one more night together. Let's go back to the Princess and let me show you my appreciation."

****

In the taxicab, Krystal was playful, but Peter's heart wasn't in it. They drove back to the hotel and walked into their room. Krystal immediately removed her mini-skirt and halter and stood there wearing only a baby blue thong. She grabbed Peter's shirt and started to pull it off. Peter looked at Krystal and slowly shook his head.

"Krystal, I just don't know about this. I'm really upset."

"I'll get you feeling better in no time," said Krystal. She reached lower and began massaging his penis.

"Oh, I don't think so," said Peter. "I'm just too upset right now. I thought you and I were going to get married. I just can't believe this. Tell you what. Why don't you just stay here tonight, and I'll go down to the front desk and get another room."

"No, no, don't do that," said Krystal as she quickly pulled on her mini-skirt. "I've heard about the nightclubs in Acapulco. Why don't you stay here tonight, and I'll hit the nightclubs? Then, I'll find a hotel downtown to stay in overnight. I'll be back in the morning in time for us to check out." Krystal pulled on her halter top, grabbed her purse from the bed and was out the door before Peter could reply.

Peter sat down slowly on the bed and began undressing. Boy, had he read this situation wrong. He would have to try and return the ring tomorrow and get his money back. With nothing else to do and not feeling particularly tired, he turned on the television. He flipped through the channels, trying to find an English-speaking one. This was the first time in the entire vacation that he had had the TV on. He found CNN and began watching it. The promo announced there was about to be a live interview with Mrs. Sue Ellen Johnson, the widow of Jumpy Johnson who died after taking two people hostage in a Georgia hospital two weeks before. The interview would be conducted by a Wendy Trotter, who had been a reporter on the scene in Pleasant Point when the hostage crisis took place. Peter felt a surge of excitement and lay back in bed to watch.

CHAPTER 2

Wendy Trotter had been shocked when the call came the day before, telling her that CNN wanted her to have a primetime interview with the widow of Jumpy Johnson. At first, she thought she was hallucinating from the Vicodin that she was now taking round the clock to combat the tremendous pain she was having. It had been two weeks since Mr. Johnson's hostage-taking and then death, and, in that time, Wendy's condition had deteriorated. She had seen her doctor the day before; he gave her less than a month to live. She was jaundiced; her eyes and skin were yellow and she peed Coca-Cola colored urine. But when she heard of the opportunity to have an in-studio interview in primetime, she couldn't pass it up. It was something in her 30+ years of reporting that she had never had the chance to do. As it happened, Larry King was on vacation that week, so the network needed something to fill that slot. She agreed to the interview, and, to prepare, she watched tapes of reporting she had done in Pleasant Point. She remembered Mrs. Johnson very well, having interviewed her several times during that fateful day. Her colleagues had told her to stay calm and let the interview have a life of its own and move as it wanted to. They suggested that she use the moorings of people; to try and move from one person to the next and to get Mrs. Johnson to discuss each person involved in her husband's ordeal. By doing so, she would allow Mrs. Johnson to weave the picture of what had happened and what her feelings were then and now.

Wendy showed up at the CNN affiliate studio in Atlanta two hours before the interview was to take place in order to have her makeup done and to be briefed on the logistics of the interview process. The makeup artist gasped when she saw Wendy.

"My...," she stammered, "y-y-you're yellow! Are you sick? What's wrong with you?"

Wendy laughed weakly. "It's nothing infectious. Yes, I am sick. Now make me look beautiful. This is my one last chance."

The makeup artist went to work on Wendy and did everything that she could.

"I can't hide those yellow eyes," the makeup artist said. "I could have given you contacts to change the color or your eyes, but that won't do anything about the yellow where the white should be."

"That's OK," said Wendy. "Maybe no one will notice."

They walked into the room where the interview would take place. There were two comfortable chairs in the room separated by a coffee table, and Wendy sat down in her chair. A few minutes later, Mrs. Johnson came into the room with her two daughters.

"Ms. Trotter," she said, "thank you so much for agreeing to do this interview with me. When they told me they wanted to interview me, I told them I wouldn't let anyone else do it but you. I have admired you through the years, and I appreciate your work the day my husband was killed. Thank you again."

"Thank you," Wendy replied. "This is an extreme honor for me, and we'll make this an interview that no one will ever forget."

****

"Three, two, one…" The director pointed at Wendy as the studio spotlights came on, and the red lights above the cameras came on.

"Good evening. I'm Wendy Trotter for CNN News. I'm here tonight with Sue Ellen Johnson, the widow of Jumpy Johnson, a gentleman who, two weeks ago, took two people hostage in a hospital in Pleasant Point, Georgia, and then lost his life when a doctor intervened in the hostage crisis. We're here tonight to learn more about what drove Jumpy Johnson to take hostages, what could have been done to prevent it and what the future holds for Mrs. Johnson and her family. Mrs. Johnson, thank you for agreeing to this interview."

"Thank you, Wendy."

"Tell me about your husband. What kind of man was he?"

"My husband was a quiet, gentle man. He loved me, and he loved his daughters and grandchildren."

"What kind of work did he do?"

"He was disabled. As you and probably all of America now know, he was a paranoid schizophrenic and was on medication to control his illness. He worked as long as he could as a machinist, but then the illness became too much and then he really couldn't work anymore. It was enough just to take his medicine. But he really managed the household."

"What interests did he have? What did he enjoy doing?"

"He enjoyed watching TV a lot. He probably watched TV ten to 12 hours a day. He loved NASCAR and anything to do with racing. We used to go out to Marietta and other places where they have dirt tracks, and he loved to watch them race. He loved hunting, although he hadn't hunted in probably five years. He loved shooting guns; he would go to the shooting range with his pistol and shoot down there. And he loved seeing his daughters and his grandchildren and doing things with them. He wasn't much of a churchgoer, but he'd go sometimes, and, when he did, he always enjoyed it."

"Did you see any signs that your husband was having problems with his schizophrenia over the last few months?"

"I think the last few months he was slowly deteriorating. He was always up and down, some days better than others, but he was having more bad days. Some days, he wouldn't want to leave the house because he said he was afraid of what someone might do to him or think about him. I told this to Dr. Fried, Jumpy's psychiatrist at the Veterans Hospital, but he just ignored me. He'd spend ten minutes with us and not listen to what I said. Increased his medicine, that was all. Before he was hospitalized, I had left Jumpy for a few days. I always left a list of things for him to do and eat to try and keep him on the right path."

"When you came back, you found him having severe abdominal pain, and you made him go to the hospital, right?"

"Yes. He didn't want to go at first, but I convinced him to go. I thought he might be having appendicitis or something bad. So, I called 911, and an ambulance came out to our house and brought him to the hospital. I knew that, once we got him there, Dr. Conner would take care of him."

"Tell me about Dr. Conner."

"Dr. Conner was our family doctor for the last 23 years. His father, Jeff Conner, Sr., was our family doctor before him. Senior was a REAL family doctor; he did everything for us. He delivered both of our daughters. When Jumpy broke his arm, Dr. Conner, Sr., set it for him."

"And what about Jeff Conner, Jr.?"

"Well, he's been our doctor, like I said, for 23 years. We knew we could always go to him when something was wrong…colds, flu, blood pressure up, whatever. He didn't manage Jumpy's schizophrenia, but he knew about it. Jumpy got that managed at the Veterans Hospital because, down there, he could get his medicines for free."

"Did Dr. Conner take care of Jumpy when he came to the hospital in Pleasant Point?"

"No, and that's probably the most disgusting and disturbing thing to me and my family about this whole thing. Dr. Conner did nothing to help us until it was too late. He told us he had an office practice now; he didn't mess with hospital patients. And so, my daughter said to him, 'What do you mean, an office practice? You mean that, when we get sick, when you're supposed to be our doctor, you're not a doctor anymore? You'll just take care of us when we're well?' He just kinda shrugged and said, 'Yeah, that's about it.' I couldn't believe it. After Jeff, Sr., his father, did such a good job with us…here his son abandoned Jumpy right when he was sick."

"Why do you think that Dr. Conner could have prevented this?"

"Dr. Conner knew his history. He knew that Jumpy was schizophrenic. He was the only doctor in Pleasant Point who knew that. He could have kept Jumpy on his medications and made sure that he was watched closely. When Jumpy got off his medications and then they started doing all those weird things to him in the hospital, you knew there was going to be trouble. Dr. Conner didn't come see him, like I said, until it was too late. By that time, I was ready to spit on him because he cost Jumpy his life, in my opinion."

"Tell me about Dr. Vijay Givagushrai, the doctor who was the attending physician for Jumpy while he was in the hospital."

"Dr. Givagushrai came to see Jumpy in his room after he was admitted. He seemed to be nice. He was a tall, big man. I could hardly understand him, and Jumpy couldn't understand him. And Jumpy always had a fear of foreigners. That's another thing that Dr. Conner should have known: Jumpy never would have wanted a foreign doctor or, pardon me saying this, a Jewish doctor taking care of him. He just didn't like foreigners, and he didn't like Jews. So, once that combination was taking care of him, there was going to be trouble."

"So, Dr. Givagushrai admitted Jumpy to the hospital and then consulted Dr. Bernstein, a gastroenterologist, to see him."

"That's right. One thing I have to say, Dr. Bernstein did try to get in touch with me. He left a message on my answering machine, but I didn't get the message until it was too late because I was staying at my daughter's house. Those two doctors tried to figure out what was going on with Jumpy. They tried to get his pain better, but they didn't do anything about his schizophrenia. They didn't do anything about getting his mind better, and he just got worse and worse."

"How does he have a gun with him in the hospital?"

"He packed it in his suitcase when he left the house. Don't ask me why, although I know whenever he went on trips, Jumpy always used to like to pack his father's German Luger from the Second World War. He always said you never knew who you'd find or what kind of strangers you'd meet out on the road, and it was best to always be prepared."

"So, you've got a man who's schizophrenic, who is off his medication and now has two doctors taking care of him who know nothing about him and who he doesn't know…seems like it is setting up for an explosive situation," Wendy said.

"Of course," said Mrs. Johnson. "Only disaster could happen, and I had to work. I would have loved to have been able to stay at Jumpy's bedside all the time and watch him and watch what was going on. But I couldn't because I earn a living for us. One of us has to work. What Jumpy made in disability was nothing. It couldn't keep our family going."

"How did you find out about Jumpy taking two hostages?" Wendy asked.

"Turned on the news, CNN as a matter of fact, and saw you, Ms. Trotter. Saw you reporting from Pleasant Point, Georgia. You said that there had been an incident at Pleasant Point General Hospital and that a patient had taken two people hostage. When I saw it, my heart sank. For some reason, I thought of Jumpy. Then, a few minutes later, I got a phone call from the hospital telling me that Jumpy had taken hostages."

"Once he took the hostages, it doesn't seem like anyone was able to reason with him. Do you think anything could have been done to talk him out of this peacefully?"

"I'm sure it could have. Jumpy was a reasonable man when he was in the right mind. I just don't think things were done properly. They had helicopters flying over the hospital, policemen there... I think he got scared. And the more scared he got, the more paranoid he got. The more he thought people were trying to hurt him, the more he'd think he'd better hurt someone first."

"Was Jumpy prejudiced against all minorities? You mentioned he didn't like foreigners and Jews."

"No, not all minorities. He didn't like foreigners, Jews, blacks, Mexicans. He really didn't like blacks at all. But other than that, he was OK. We used to go to the "Eyetalian" restaurant down the block from our house, and he didn't mind those people at all."

"Do you think if he'd had American doctors, he wouldn't have been so paranoid?"

"I think if he'd had Dr. Conner there, a man he'd known for 23 years, things would have been different. He might have been a little upset because he wasn't feeling good...and by the way, they never found out why he had such pain in his belly. We'll never know that. He wasn't feeling good, but still he wouldn't have taken those hostages."

"The hostages are taken by your husband. Time is passing, and there is concern that one of the hostages is having a heart attack."

"Yes, I heard about that. Let me tell you something about that. Whatever Jumpy did at that time, he wasn't in his right mind. He was a gentle, loving husband, a good father and a good grandfather. Whatever he did to those people, he didn't mean to."

"You know that the man who had the heart attack is still in the Intensive Care Unit, don't you?"

"Yes, I'd heard that, and my heart goes out to him and his family. My family's heart does, too. We certainly wish him no harm. But what happened next is something we can never forget. They called in a cardiologist, Peter Dickman, whom Jumpy had seen a few times in the last ten years. Jumpy had had some chest pain, and he'd taken care of Jumpy and Jumpy had trusted him. He came into Jumpy's room, supposedly to help this other man, and he killed my Jumpy."

"What do you mean he killed him?"

"Well, you know, he hit him. He hit him so hard, so violently…Jumpy being an elderly man…hit him so hard and I understand this Dr. Dickman is a karate champion…he hit him so hard, he cracked Jumpy's head and Jumpy's brain exploded."

"My understanding is that Mr. Johnson was going to have surgery after that, and there is a good chance they could have saved him but there was a problem. The radiologist missed what they call a pneumothorax…a partial collapse of the lung which led to Mr. Johnson's death."

"Yeah, that's what I understand, too. A pneumo watchamacallit happened to Jumpy also."

"For our viewers, let me explain that a pneumothorax is a collapsed lung. When Jumpy was hit and hit the ground, apparently the injury caused a fracture of one of his ribs which then punctured his lung and caused it to deflate. Eventually, when Jumpy was put on a ventilator or breathing machine for surgery, the pneumothorax got bigger and bigger and eventually led to his demise."

"Yes," said Mrs. Johnson, starting to cry. "It was one error after another." She took a tissue and dabbed at her eyes. "One error after another starting with Dr. Conner and then that Indian doctor and that Jewish doctor who couldn't take care of my husband and get him better and made him crazy. Then, finally, the last nail in the coffin was Dr. Dickman's hitting him and then the doctor not knowing that he'd punctured his lung."

"Are you and your family planning legal action? There have been reports that you have retained the top malpractice attorney in Atlanta and possibly the entire country, Marty Shapiro."

"We have…we have contacted an attorney. The money… it's not the money that it's all about. We just don't want this to happen to anyone else. We want people, when they go to the hospital, to have doctors take care of them that know them, that have taken care of them when they're well. The moral of this story is don't get sick, cuz if you get sick, you don't know who is going to take care of you. From what Mr. Shapiro has told us now, most of these doctors taking care of you in the hospital aren't your best doctors… They're the ones who can't get a practice established out in the community so they have to become hospital doctors and be sent patients from the emergency room in order to earn a living."

"Mrs. Johnson, I wish you and your daughters all the best. Both myself and, I'm sure, all of America wish you comfort in your grief… We're sorry this couldn't have turned out better for you. Thank you so much for joining us tonight. I understand there's a breaking story now. We're sending you to the headquarters of the Pleasant Point Police Department where the Sheriff is about to hold a press conference."

****

A tall, husky blonde man stepped to the podium.

"I'm Sheriff J.T. Garner of the Pleasant Point Police Department. We have now issued a warrant for the arrest of Dr. Peter Dickman in connection with the murder of Mr. Jumpy Johnson two weeks ago. Sources tell us Dr. Dickman has fled the country and was last seen in Acapulco, Mexico. If anyone knows anything about his whereabouts, please contact the Pleasant Point Police Department immediately. Dr. Dickman is a martial arts expert and should be considered extremely dangerous. Again, we are issuing a warrant for the arrest of Dr. Peter Dickman in connection with the murder of Mr. Jumpy Johnson two weeks ago at Pleasant Point General Hospital. Any information leading to his whereabouts and arrest will be greatly appreciated. Thank you."

CHAPTER 3

Vijay had agreed to meet Preeti's father for the first time, and was driving to Atlanta in his new Mercedes Benz 320 Bluetech. Preeti had helped him pick it out – it was black with leather interior. It took diesel fuel which meant better gas mileage and was better for the environment, or so the salesman had said. Vijay had dated Preeti exclusively for six months and was very happy that they were now engaged. Preeti was thoughtful, kind and beautiful; she had become the love of his life and the woman he wanted to spend his life with. But she could be stubborn, strong-willed, and easily hurt, traits which he didn't admire but had found ways to deal with. They'd spent almost every weekend together when Vijay wasn't working in the hospital, and would at least have a quick dinner together when he was on call.

Preeti lived in a high-rise apartment building in downtown Atlanta. Her apartment was on the twenty-ninth floor, and looking out from her windows, Vijay could not only see all of Atlanta but in the far distance on a clear day, he could make out the outline of Pleasant Point. The apartment was furnished in a contemporary fashion and was so exquisitely appointed that it had been featured in Architectural Digest magazine. There were two bedrooms and Preeti's master bedroom had a king-sized bed mounted on a chrome platform. Vijay had never spent the night there; their sexual life had consisted of kissing and hugging only. Both agreed that sex would be saved for marriage.

Vijay had asked Preeti to marry him one week before. He'd told her to dress up since they were going someplace fancy, and when he picked her up, he couldn't get over how gorgeous she looked. She wore a Valentino sequined black floor length gown with a slit up the left side that revealed all of her shapely left leg when she walked. The gown was strapless and around her neck she wore a diamond choker necklace. She wore a Van Cleef and Arpel's watch with a black band and a black coral ring on her right ring finger. Even in his new blue suit which Preeti had helped pick out, Vijay felt unworthy to be with her. She got into the car, gave him a kiss, and on to Atlanta's fanciest restaurant, the Roman Legion, they drove.

Twice on the drive, Vijay's beeper went off – each time it was the hospital nurse to tell him about problems with his patients. One patient, who had just had an angioplasty and stent placement for a blocked coronary artery, now was complaining of a headache and had a blood pressure of 190 over 110. Vijay politely told the nurse to call the cardiologist who had performed the intervention for instructions. The other call came from a nurse who said that the patient in room 405, Mr. Albert, who'd been admitted with diarrhea was now complaining of severe abdominal cramping and wanted medicine for it. Vijay told her to call Dr. Bernstein, the gastroenterologist, for instructions. He also told both nurses that starting at eight o'clock, Dr. Sirha Khan would be covering for him and that he was turning his beeper and cell phone off. He'd already told the answering service the same thing.

They had a magnificent meal at the Roman Legion, and when they were done, Vijay insisted they have dessert. He ordered molten chocolate cake for each of them and two glasses of champagne. When the cake and champagne came, Vijay dropped down on one knee next to Preeti's chair.

"I love you very much. Since the day I met you at the Indian singles event, I have wanted to marry you. You are my heart and my soul, my sun and my moon. You mean everything to me."

He pulled a small black box from his jacket pocket. "Preeti, would you make me the happiest man in the world and marry me?"

Preeti rested her head on her fist as though in deep thought but then turned back to face Vijay. Tears of joy streamed down her face. "Of course, I'll marry you. I love you so, so much. I want to spend the rest of my life with you!" She helped pull Vijay up from the ground and they kissed. The occupants of the tables around them clapped. Vijay sat down, but neither ate their dessert; they were too busy looking into each other's eyes and dreaming.

****

Now Vijay was at another restaurant to meet Preeti's father for the first time. He had asked Preeti whether or not in the twenty-first century, Indian men needed to ask their prospective fathers-in law for their daughters' hands in marriage, and Preeti had laughed that joyous laugh of hers and said that in her mind, it was totally up to the woman herself. She had been born and raised in America, and even though her family clung to many of the Indian customs, this wasn't one she believed in. So Vijay had asked Preeti to marry him and she had accepted, and now Preeti's father wanted to meet him.

The restaurant was in the trendiest part of Atlanta, on a street behind the Peach Tree Plaza Hotel. Vijay walked in the front door and was greeted by the blond hostess. Vijay asked for Dr. Desai and was told he hadn't arrived yet, but had left instructions to take Vijay to the best table in the restaurant. As Vijay walked through the restaurant, he noted that it was narrow, but built on three levels. There were dark iron railings with wooden steps leading from just beyond the entrance upstairs and downstairs. Both stairways made dramatic turns as they led up and down. There were three large chalkboards behind the bar which listed the entire menu. A small chalkboard opposite the bar read "Today's Specials" and listed Vegetable Soup and below it Tomato and Mozzarella Sandwich. The white walls displayed colorful small unframed paintings; some of beaches, others of forests, and others of nothing but slashes of color. The table Vijay was led to was at the very back of the main floor. He sat down facing the huge mirror on the back wall from which he could see the entire restaurant behind him.

Vijay waited five minutes, and then in walked a small Indian man dressed in a grey pin-striped suit. The hostess greeted him warmly, and the bartender stopped mixing a drink to shout out, "Welcome Dr. Desai!" The hostess led Dr. Desai to Vijay's table and Vijay immediately stood up to greet him. He was at least a foot taller than Dr. Desai so he could see himself towering over him in the mirror. Vijay had been exercising daily since he had met Preeti, and his broad shoulders and narrow waist contrasted sharply with Dr. Desai's thin, frail physique.

"So you are the man my daughter says she is going to marry," Dr. Desai said as he put his hand out to shake Vijay's hand. Dr. Desai tried his best to give Vijay a crushing grip but his hand was too small and couldn't reach all the way around Vijay's giant mitt of a hand. Dr. Desai withdrew his hand slightly and settled on squeezing Vijay's three middle fingers as hard as he could.

"Sit down, sit down," Dr. Desai ordered.

Vijay sat down and looked across the table at Dr. Desai. It was quite obvious that Preeti's looks came from her mother who Preeti said had been a model and actress in India. Dr. Desai had a small face with non-descript features and wore tiny wire-rimmed glasses. His skin was mocha and his hair was gray with a few specks of black. He constantly moved his head as if he needed to see Vijay from a different perspective or as if there were something going on in the restaurant that commanded his attention. As his head bobbed up and down, back and forth non-stop, Vijay thought to himself that Dr. Desai reminded him of a squirrel checking out his surroundings.

"My daughter had the opportunity to get married into some of the most successful and wealthiest families in America. She turned them all down. I tried to get her to fly to India to meet even wealthier and more prominent families and she refused. Now she tells me she is going to marry you. Why? You are a poor boy from the streets of Bombay. You have no mother, a father who is in poor health and works on the docks of Bombay, and four brothers and sisters, none of whom read or write. Yes, you are a doctor and one has to admire you for accomplishing that, but as a hospitalist, you will never be rich or able to provide for my daughter in the manner to which she has grown accustomed. Why should I give my consent to someone like you, a schnook off the streets of Bombay, to marry my daughter who is a precious jewel and could have any man she desired?"

Vijay was taken aback. He always tried to maintain his composure and had managed to do so countless times in the hospital when other doctors had lost their cool and had launched into angry tirades when he consulted them on his patients. He took two deep breaths.

"Dr. Desai, you are a very successful doctor and businessman. This restaurant at which we are meeting today that you own,

Preeti tells me, is a testament to your good taste and success. I can only tell you that I love your daughter more than I love life itself, and I will always love her, respect her, and take care of her. I may not be able to provide her with all of the material things she has become accustomed to, but she doesn't feel that is an impediment to marrying me, and neither do I."

"That all sounds very good when you say it, but you have to look ten to twenty years down the line when most American marriages fail. The beauty starts to fade and the passion dims. When you have a family and my daughter wants private schools, long vacations, a large house."

"All of those things are important to us, but not as important as our love. The things you mention are like the tiny grains of sand on a beach, and our relationship is like the mighty ocean which can push the tiny grains of sand away and make the beach take on any shape it desires."

"Preeti told me that originally you wanted her to go back and live with you and your family in Mumbai, but she has convinced you to live in Atlanta."

"When I first came to America, it was the idea of my mentor, Dr. Bissel-Mozel, who was the doctor for our neighborhood. He was born in England and trained to be a physician there. Although he felt I received a good medical education in India, he wanted me to go where I could receive the best training in the world – America. I came here and did a residency in internal medicine with the idea of returning to India when I was done. But as part of the deal for me to get the residency, I had to work in an under-served area in America for four years – they sent me to Arkansas. I worked hard and made some money which I sent back to my father and siblings and to Dr. Bissel-Mozel. After the four years, I realized that if I stayed in America and worked as a doctor, I could not only make more money for my family, but also money to help modernize Dr. Bissel-Mozel's clinic. I found out about this job as a hospitalist and moved to Pleasant Point. Things have gone very well; I am making close to three hundred thousand dollars a year. Still, I was planning on taking over Dr. Bissel-Mozel's clinic in Mumbai when he retired until I met Preeti. My experience with women was limited, but I found her to be the most amazing woman I'd ever met. We fell in love and are going to get married. I asked her to return with me to live in Mumbai; she said no, she wanted to live in the United States and that was the one condition of our getting married that she wouldn't negotiate. After a lot, a lot of thought, I agreed that we would continue to live here. I haven't informed Dr. Bissel-Mozel of my decision, but I will."

"So it is final then. The two of you are going to be married. What religion are you, son?"

"We never really practiced any religion in our household. Any religion in India that sponsored events at which there was free food we would attend and practice that religion at least that day, Budhist, Hindu, Muslim, Christian…"

"My wife and I are Christians, and we raised Preeti as a Christian. In order to marry my daughter, you will need to be baptized and become a Christian. You will celebrate Christmas and Easter with us and accept Jesus Christ as your savior and God."

"Preeti and I have had discussions about religion, and I am willing to be a Christian and accept Jesus Christ as lord and savior."

"Good. I can see why Preeti fell for you. You are tall, handsome, and a straight-shooter. She has had many men seek her, but she only wants you. After you are married, perhaps I will let you come in as a limited partner in some of my business deals."

"How are you able to practice orthopedic surgery and be so involved in business?"

Dr. Desai waved his hand in front of his face as he shook his head from side to side. "I rarely practice orthopedic surgery anymore. That was just a way to make enough money to start buying property near hospitals. Then on the property, I built surgical centers. I got other doctors to buy into the surgical centers and to use them. We made a killing through our facility fees, but I made even more from the monthly rent paid to me by my limited partners. The surgeons eventually all wanted to be equal partners in the centers which I gladly agreed to, but I still owned the land and buildings. I now own twenty surgical centers in Georgia and have plans to build five more in the next two years. I also own doctors' office buildings next to many of the major hospitals in this area."

"So you don't practice medicine?"

"No time. I've expanded into the restaurant business now, but it's more for the real estate. I get junior partners with limited ownership to run the restaurants in locations that I own, like this one. In one deal, in which I may offer you a limited partnership, I now own six Indian fast-food restaurants with plans to expand to thirty. They are doing so well that they are all cash-flowing now. So you see, Vijay, I don't have time for medicine, and I hope that someday you won't either. Why work your brains out and push your body beyond the limits it was meant to go when the insurance companies and the government continue to grab tighter and tighter control of the purse-strings of medicine just like a cobra tightens its grip around the neck of a mongoose? No one will eventually want to take care of any patient, well or sick. Doctors will be paid a salary to oversee a group of nurse practitioners or physician assistants who will actually see and evaluate the patient, and further down the road, will diagnose and treat the patient. Once doctors gave up their duty of taking care of the sick patients and turned it over to the hospitalists, the dye was cast in medicine. First no sick patients, then supervise lower levels to take care of and diagnose well patients, and eventually no patient contact at all or as little as possible. Hopefully, by that time, you will be married to my daughter and have many children and businesses to occupy your time. Welcome to our family."

Vijay smiled. He'd heard everything Dr. Desai said – could he ever not be a doctor? It was what he'd strived for almost his entire life – healing the sick. But look how much he'd changed his original ideals. It seemed it would be easier to accept Jesus Christ as his lord and savior than to give up medicine. He smiled at Dr. Desai and Dr. Desai smiled back. The waitress came by the table and asked if they were ready to order.

CHAPTER 4

The certified letter arrived at Aaron Bernstein's office exactly four months after the death of Jumpy Johnson. At the top of it, it said, "Shapiro and Gold, LLP, Attorneys and Counselors," and had their address in Atlanta, Georgia. It then had that day's date and said, "Aaron Bernstein, M.D.," with his address. Below that, it said, "Regarding the family of Jumpy Johnson v. Aaron Bernstein, M.D."

Dear Dr. Bernstein,

Please be advised that the law firm of Shapiro and Gold, LLP, has been retained by Mrs. Jumpy Johnson and her family for a possible health care liability claim against you as that term is defined under Article 4590I, Section 1.03, Subdivision A, Paragraph 4, of the revised Civil Statutes of Georgia.

More specifically, this claim is based on the fact that, beginning February 10, 2003, Mr. Jumpy Johnson was seen in consultation by you and was treated for his abdominal pain. While under care and treatment by you, he developed symptoms of acute worsening paranoid schizophrenia. The failure to diagnose Mr. Johnson's medical condition resulted in his death. On February 13, 2003, Mr. Johnson died after being assaulted by Dr. Peter Dickman.

As a result of your series of negligent (even grossly negligent) acts, Mr. Jumpy Johnson died, and his family was forced to suffer severe pain and suffering which will continue for the rest of their lifetimes.

As a further result of your conduct and the mental anguish it has caused the Johnson family, they will continue to incur reasonable medical expenses in the hope of somehow reversing the enormous damage you have caused them. In addition, due to the publicity from this case, the Johnson family has suffered severe humiliation and anguish and will continue to suffer the same in the future.

This notice of claim is given pursuant to the provisions of Article 4590I, Section 4.01, Subdivision A, of the revised Civil Statutes of Georgia. If this claim is not settled within 60 days from the date of this notice, all appropriate legal action will be taken on behalf of Mrs. Johnson and her family to protect their rights.

Thank you for your time and attention to this matter.

Respectfully yours.

Marty Shapiro

Aaron read the certified letter twice. It was the second time he had been sued in four months after not being sued in his first

12 years of practice. Colleagues of his had been sued before, and he had heard of the anguish they had gone through. All the time and energy they had had to put into the lawsuit, reviewing the records, reliving the case again and again and then writing summaries of what they had done. Aaron was angry but also felt betrayed. He grieved that Mr. Johnson had died, and he had not been able to help him. But he also felt overwhelming grief for his own situation. He closed the door to his office, leaned back in his chair and looked at the pictures of his wife and children. He knew that this would be a very public lawsuit which would be covered by the press extensively, and he already felt ashamed and humiliated. He put his head in his hands, and, for the first time since his father's death, he began to cry.

****

At the same time, Vijay Givagushrai received the same certified letter, only his name had been substituted for Aaron Bernstein's. He read it through once and put it in his briefcase. It was the 19th lawsuit that he had been threatened with since he had started practice, and it wasn't a big deal to him. Almost all of his lawsuits had been dropped or settled out of court, and only two had gone to trial – he had lost them both. He thought, "It's all part of the business of being a doctor," and went on to admit his next patient.

****

The same letter was delivered to the Fulton County Jail to Dr. Peter Dickman. Peter had been behind bars since his capture in Acapulco, Mexico, three-and-a-half months before. The judge had deemed him a high risk to flee the country and so had jailed him on murder charges without bail. Peter had been miserable in jail. His wife had come to see him once and had served him with divorce papers. His children had come to see him twice, and Krystal hadn't come to see him at all, having moved to California. He read through the letter and knew that it was the least of his worries now. He made a paper airplane out of the letter and played with it in his jail cell.

****

Lizzy Chen received the letter in the radiology department. It was the first malpractice suit she had been involved in, and she was devastated. She had gone through the films with Thomas Kelly, and the pneumothorax had been very evident when it was looked for. Thomas had told her there probably would be a lawsuit attached to this case. But the radiology department was the most sued department in the hospital, he added, and she needed to get used to it. It was the price of doing business, according to Thomas. It still upset her greatly when she received the letter, and she wanted to talk to Thomas about it. Unfortunately, she found that Thomas was on vacation and would be gone for the next two weeks. She would have looked for another colleague to discuss the lawsuit with but then decided it wasn't worth the time now. She had a serious romance going with a wealthy investment banker in Atlanta, and she needed to go home and get ready for their date that night.

****

Georgio Circelli received the letter and wasn't fazed at all. Lawsuits were part of being a neurosurgeon. Unfortunately, lawsuits were what had driven a lot of neurosurgeons to give up their practices after they had made enough money to retire. Georgio had a friend who was a neurosurgeon who had retired at the age of 50 due to an anxiety disorder triggered by the multiple lawsuits he had been involved in. When something went wrong in a neurosurgery case, the patient either died, was left paralyzed or was left with some neurologic deficit. Almost always, whether or not the surgeon was to blame, he was sued. This was why he paid over $200,000 a year in malpractice premiums; he still brought home over $2,000,000 a year in earnings. He did the usual drill; he called his malpractice attorney and faxed a copy of the letter to him. He would have thought about it more, but he was beeped at that moment for an emergency intracranial bleed in an 18-year-old boy who had fallen from a ladder. As he walked to the emergency room, Georgio thought about the irony of medicine: one minute you could be sitting in your office opening the mail and the next minute, you were trying to save a youngster's life. Very few other occupations placed you in such dramatic situations so quickly.

****

Roger Dorme, the anesthesiologist, received his letter also. Working with Georgio Circelli over the years, he was accustomed to getting letters like this, but he had never been involved in a case where the insurance company had to pay out anything on his behalf. This case may be different, he thought. Such a high-profile case and the rumors were that the family was looking for multimillions of dollars. Certainly, they would try and get each practitioner for as much as they could. Roger wasn't on call, so he reached down to the bottom drawer of his desk and pulled out a bottle of Jack Daniels and poured himself a drink. He drank one glass and felt better. After the second glass, he wasn't even thinking about the lawsuit, and, after the third glass, he fell asleep at his desk. An hour later, his beeper went off – it was Circelli paging him from the emergency room to do anesthesia on an 18-year-old with an intracranial bleed.

****

Jeffrey Conner never received a certified letter and wasn't named in the lawsuit. He took that afternoon off to celebrate his wife's 35th birthday, and he took her out on Lake Pleasant Point on his new 45-foot yacht.

CHAPTER 5

Cole Stone had decided to commit suicide because he felt there was no other way out. The humiliation had become too much. First, there had been an article in the *Atlanta Journal-Constitution* about how he had abandoned a young female patient, leading to her death. Then, the story had been picked up by the television show *20/20*. On the show, Cole had been portrayed as an uncaring, unfeeling doctor who had been called repeatedly to see a sick patient after he had put a feeding tube in her, and he had refused. They had medical experts from Harvard and Cornell saying that the injury she had received from the feeding tube going through her colon was easily treatable if diagnosed quickly enough. They had shown the patient's chart where the neurosurgeon, Dr. Circelli, had written notes saying that Dr. Stone had refused to come back and see the patient. Finally, there was a note from the general surgeon saying that the patient had an acute abdomen and was going to be taken to surgery immediately after the CAT scan.

Cole knew he had made a mistake, but he always felt you could make mistakes as long as no one found out about them or at least as long as no one sued you over them. But this case promised to be a huge lawsuit. A week ago, he had gone in to give his deposition at the law offices of Shapiro and Gold. He had never seen anything as luxurious as these offices, even the five-star hotels he had stayed in. The offices looked like something out of a movie set with each lawyer's office as big as a combination of five doctors' offices. The conference room where the deposition took place had a huge wooden table, and the walls were covered with paintings of Andy Warhol and Leroy Neiman. Each chair was big enough to swallow up two people. Cole had been grilled by Marty Shapiro for over three hours. "Why didn't you go back?" "Why did you abandon the patient?" "Have you ever abandoned patients before?" There was a television camera recording everything, and Cole felt that the television camera was probing through his body and into his soul. He had sweated and sweated and sweated.

So, now, this is what my life is going to be like, he thought. To be humiliated, to have all the money he'd ever had taken away from him. Cole knew that they were asking for $30,000,000 to $50,000,000 for a settlement. He knew that he was insured for $1,000,000. He had heard all about Marty Shapiro's reputation and knew that Marty Shapiro would come after him for all of his assets. Part of his assets he had been smart enough to hide in a family trust he had been working on with a lawyer from Atlanta for years. However, there were still things that were not in the family trust that they could take away from him. Financial ruin, public humiliation…it was more than he could take. Cole was driving out to his ranch in east Georgia now for the purpose of killing himself.

Cole's passion was hunting. He hunted deer, dove, and duck, all on his ranch. They were out of season now, but he still had his guns in perfect working order at the ranch house. What he had decided to do on this Wednesday, his usual day off, was to go out to the range, shoot targets and then somehow make it look like he had accidentally killed himself. He knew it was the coward's way out, but, right now, all he wanted was a way out.

He loved his east Georgia ranch. It was over 300 acres of hills and valleys that were covered by trees and had a large lake which he stocked yearly with fish. The huge ranch house could sleep 20 people easily. He had bought the ranch with money he had gotten from buy-ins from the partners he had taken into his practice over the last 20 years. Their buy-ins had paid not only for the ranch, but also for the improvements in it.

Cole had a collection of 20 guns in the ranch house, and he picked out his favorite shotgun and a laser-guided rifle. He walked into the woods with his dog, Sandy. Sandy had been his dog for almost ten years and was trained to retrieve ducks. Sandy would stand by him as he shot targets. He had a target range set up in one woodsy area of the ranch where he had cans and targets to shoot at. He walked for three hours through the woods, shooting the targets and rarely missed a shot. He put down the shotgun and picked up the laser-guided rifle. With this rifle, he could easily hit any bull's-eye at 100 yards. He spent a couple of hours shooting this rifle and felt tired but happy.

He was now ready to commit suicide. He went back to the ranch house and looked over the 20 guns, trying to decide which one to kill himself with. He thought of his wife and three children. They would be left well off; he had almost $10,000,000 in the family trust as well as another $5,000,000 in a life insurance policy, so they would have plenty to live on. He had met his wife in medical school; she had been a nurse at the hospital where he did his first clinical rotation. They dated and had gotten married and had been married now for almost 30 years. She had been a good, dependable wife who had tolerated him and, most importantly, never asked too many questions. He wondered if she ever knew about the affairs that he'd had and just chose to ignore them. If she had known about them, she had been a great actress, for it certainly never diminished her affection for him.

He finally picked out a German rifle, one that his father had brought back from World War Two, and walked back out to the woods. Sandy trotted after him. He decided to make it look like he was setting the rifle down next to him when it misfired and shot him in the chest. He decided he couldn't tolerate a head shot, and he knew that, if he shot himself in the right spot in the chest, being alone in the woods, he would die in a few minutes.

He walked down to where his favorite tree was, an enormous oak tree that was over 200 years old. He stood beside the tree and got the rifle at just the right angle pointing at his heart. Just as he was about to pull the trigger, Sandy jumped up and knocked him over. The rifle fell to the side without firing, and Cole fell on his back.

"All right, girl, come on now!" Cole shouted.

At first, Cole was mad. Then, he thought that maybe this was an omen. Maybe he wasn't supposed to kill himself now. Maybe there was something else for him to do. Sandy kept close to him and barked at him nonstop.

He brought the gun and Sandy back inside the house and locked the house up. The caretaker of the property would be back tomorrow and would let Sandy out. He got into his truck and began driving back to Pleasant Point. It was now about 2 o'clock in the afternoon. Rather than going right home, he decided to drive to the office to see what was going on.

When he got back to the office, he walked into his own office, and Sherry, his medical assistant, came in. She told him that there had been only two messages that day. One was from a patient asking for a refill of Nexium for her reflux disease, and the other was from a patient who had a colonoscopy done the day before and today was having some abdominal pain.

"Must be a nut," Cole muttered under his breath.

He called this patient up. Sure enough, it sounded like she had had some gas pains but now was doing fine. He was going to leave the office, but he first decided to go visit his partner in the adjacent office, Aaron Bernstein. Any way he could, he had screwed Aaron. He had made him pay the $500,000 to join the practice, and, after Aaron had been there for eight years, he told Aaron he would no longer take weekend call. Any patients that he could avoid seeing in hospital consultation, he dodged and sent to Aaron. Anyone who was sick and called the office – patients with Crohn's disease, ulcerative colitis, chronic liver disease - he had always told he was too busy to see and were passed on to Aaron. Aaron had grinned and borne it and had built up a huge practice.

"How you doin', guy?" Cole asked as he walked into Aaron's office.

"Pretty good, Cole. Surprised to see you here on Wednesday."

"Yeah, jes comin' in to open my mail and do some messages. Whatchew been up to?"

"Not too much. These big lawsuits have gotten me down."

"Yeah, tell me about it. You see the news show last night on television?"

"Didn't see it, but that was all they were talking about in the doctors' lunchroom today. That was something, huh? You know, I'm being sued in that case, too, just for being your assistant."

"I know. They get anybody they can. Whoever has got big pockets, they're going to get."

"Speaking of that, look at what I got in the mail today, Cole."

"What is it?"

"This American Cancer Society party. They're having this huge party…"

"Oh, yeah. I never go to any of those things. A bunch of wasted time, people standing around."

"But look, Cole, this one is at Marty Shapiro's house."

Cole did a double-take. "Marty Shapiro...the lawyer?"

"Yeah, he's having this huge party at his house, and he's being honored as the Man of the Year by the American Cancer Society."

"American Cancer Society...Man of the Year..." Cole stammered.

"I guess a lot of doctors will be there. I was thinking about trying to go. I knew him from college. Maybe try to talk to him a little bit on the side. Kind of on a social basis and talk to him about these lawsuits and see if there is anything we can do to work things out so it's not so onerous for me. You think you'd want to go, Cole?"

"Naw, guy, that's not my kinda thing. I don't think I'd want to go to anything like that. But, hey, Aaron, thanks for the info. Gotta go. Checkya later. By the way, when is that party goin' to be? Can you make me a copy of the invitation?"

"Sure." Aaron went to the office copy machine and made a copy for Cole.

"Hey, thanks. Next week, huh?"

Cole walked out of the office. He had a new idea. He wasn't going to end his life now, but someone's life was going to come to an end.

CHAPTER 6

Aaron had never gone to the American Cancer Society Gala before, but this year he wanted to go to talk to Marty Shapiro. The event was being held at the Shapiro's mansion, and, for the week before the gala, the *Atlanta Journal-Constitution* had run a series of articles telling about the mansion and the gala itself. The finest restaurants in Atlanta were catering in different rooms in the house, and there would be live entertainment from some of the top entertainers in the country. In that month's issue of *Atlanta* magazine, there was a 16-page article about the mansion, telling how it was modeled after a French chateau and saying that, at 50,000 square feet, it was the largest house every built in Georgia. It also told about the separate 10,000 square foot party house that was situated on the 20-acre property.

When Aaron's wife, Marcy, found out that they were going to the party, she said that she had to buy a new outfit. They had never been to a party of this caliber before, and she didn't have anything to wear. It was black tie, so Aaron could wear his 15-year-old tuxedo, but Marcy went out shopping and looked and looked and looked. She couldn't find any dresses that fit her due to her obesity. She finally settled on a black pantsuit.

The night of the party, they left the children at home with a babysitter and drove to the Shapiro's house which was located in the Buckhead section of Atlanta. They turned down the street where the house was and saw huge searchlights blazing across the sky. There was a tall iron fence surrounding the property, and there was a guard gate at the entrance of the house. The guard shined a flashlight into their car and asked them for their invitation. Aaron showed him the invitation with their names on it and then showed the guard photo ID's for Marcy and himself. The guard pushed the button, and the enormous iron gate swung open.

It had cost Aaron $1,000 a ticket to come to this party, but he thought that, if he could just talk to Marty for a few minutes and convince him to drop Aaron from the lawsuits, it would be worth it. He had known Marty from Vanderbilt just as an acquaintance, but there had never been any bad blood between the two of them other than that night of the ping-pong game.

Between the guard gate and the house itself was the equivalent of several city blocks, and the road wound around picturesque gardens and magnificent sculptures. Even though it was dark, expert landscape lighting enabled you to see the colors – red, yellows, purples – of the flowers in the gardens. In front of the mansion was an enormous porte-cochere where ten young men dressed in all white stood, ready to valet park the cars. Aaron was driving his Nissan 300 ZX which he had had for nine years. They got out of the car, and the young man who handed Aaron his parking ticket said, "Love these Z's. We've been parking all Mercedes, Rolls Royces and Bmers. This is the first one of these I've seen tonight. It's fast."

"Yes," Aaron replied as he took his ticket, "it's a great car."

They walked to the entrance of the house. Each door was 15 feet high and was made out of solid oak. Inside the house, hundreds of people were milling around, and there was a short receiving line just inside the entrance to greet the new guests.

In the line were four people: Marty and his wife, Jordana, and the Governor of the State of Georgia and his wife. Aaron took Marcy's hand and led her over to them.

"Hi. I'm Aaron Bernstein. This is my wife, Marcy."

"Yes, I know who you are," Marty replied. "I didn't know you were coming. This is my wife, Jordana."

Aaron looked at Jordana. She was a head taller than Marty and was the most gorgeous woman Aaron had ever seen. She had sparkling green eyes, auburn hair and was wearing a stunning white evening gown that was low cut, revealing her magnificent bosom. Around her neck was a choker made up of symmetrical four-carat diamonds, and she was wearing a diamond tiara also.

Marty continued, "It's good to see you here. I haven't seen you in a long time."

"That's right. Boy, your house is beautiful. I've been reading about it in *Atlanta* magazine and the newspaper. It's really incredible."

"Yes," Marcy chimed in. "It's really an incredible house. I can't wait to take a look. I can't wait to see the wine cellar and the bedrooms and the pool and gardens…"

"You folks just look around," interrupted Marty.

"Marty, do you think I could talk to you later? I have a couple of things I want to discuss with you."

"In regard to business, do you mean?" asked Marty.

"Kind of," Aaron replied.

"I'm not here to talk business tonight," said Marty. "As a matter of fact, I don't think you and I have much to talk about. Governor and Mrs. Davis, uh, this is Mr. Arnold, I mean Mr. Aaron Bernstein and his lovely wife."

"Actually, it's Dr. Aaron Bernstein," corrected Marcy.

"Oh, yeah, that's right," Marty laughed. "Ask what kind of doctor he is. Oh, and by the way, make sure you wash your hand well after you shake his hand."

"What do you mean?" asked the governor.

"He's the kind of doctor that puts things into your butt."

"Oh, I see," Governor Davis said as he and his wife and Jordana laughed. "Well, it's nice to meet you, and it's nice to have you both here."

Marty pushed Aaron on the shoulder so that he would move on.

"Sorry, man, you've gotta move on. We have more people to greet."

Aaron took Marcy's hand and walked across the entrance foyer. The ceiling was 40 feet high, and the crystal chandelier was breathtaking. They walked across the foyer to where a table was set up to register. They filled out their nametags, put them on and then walked down a flight of stairs to the wine cellar.

The wine cellar was 5,000 square feet. The table itself was 30 feet long and had 30 chairs around it. Each chair was carved out of wood and had a back that was 6 feet tall. The wood of each chairback had been carved into an intricate scene from the Middle Ages. The walls in the room were decorated with coats of arms which *Atlanta* magazine said were brought back from all over Europe. There were at least 20 coats of arms, representing some of the most prominent European families. There was a long serving table set up with all kinds of Mexican food, and Marcy immediately went over and began filling up a plate.

In the room was a singer who Aaron recognized from television and from seeing articles about her in the newspaper. She was an Atlanta girl who had made it big on the pop rock scene. She was strumming her guitar and singing into a microphone at one end of the room, and approximately 100 people were gathered around her listening.

Marcy came back to Aaron with a plate overflowing with food. Aaron saw Langston Harris on the other side of the room and took Marcy by the arm and walked over to him.

"Hey, Langston, how are you?"

"Hey, Aaron, wasn't expecting to see you at a party like this. How are you? And who's this with you?"

"This is my wife, Marcy."

"Oh, Marcy, hi. I'm Langston Harris. I'm the pathologist at Pleasant Point General Hospital. This is my wife, Christina."

"Hi, Christina," said Marcy. "It's good to meet you."

Christina turned away from the woman she was talking to and looked at Marcy. She eyed her up and down. "Uh, uh, nice pantsuit," she said slowly.

Christina was wearing an elegant aqua gown. She pointed to Marcy's overflowing plate. "You know, ummm…there's food in every room here. They have all kinds. Mexican food here, Italian food – you name it. Each room has different food."

"Oh, I didn't know that," said Marcy. "This will get me started." She began to eat and turned to face Aaron.

Aaron took Marcy by the arm and led her away from the Harrises. The wine cellar was incredible to behold. Marty had a collection of over 5,000 wines. There was a volunteer stationed in one corner who told them the history of the wine cellar – how it had been modeled after a wine cellar owned by the Rothschild family in France. He also told them that the most expensive wine in the collection was worth well over $1,000,000 and was from 1936.

Aaron listened, but, in his mind, he was thinking of ways of getting Marty one on one so that he could talk to him about the lawsuits. He'd never had a lawsuit in all his years of practice, and now he had two. One was ridiculous. All he had done in the case of the young woman who died from the gastrostomy tube being put through her colon was the upper endoscopy. He hadn't put the tube in, he hadn't been responsible for following up on her, so there was no reason he should be sued for $10,000,000 to $20,000,000. The other lawsuit…he had just tried to help that man. He didn't know that Mr. Johnson was schizophrenic, and it wasn't his fault the patient had gone crazy. He thought if he could get Marty alone and could appeal to his sense of fairness, maybe Marty would drop him from these lawsuits.

They walked back upstairs to the first floor and walked from room to room. Each room had a designated guide who would lead you around the room and tell you about it. They walked upstairs to the second floor and into Marty and Jordana's bedroom. Aaron was amazed by the artwork. In the bedroom alone was a Picasso, two Bonnard's and a Degas ballerina statue. Marty and Jordana each had their own 1,500 square foot closet next to the bedroom. Marty had over 150 pairs of wingtip shoes in his closet and 40 different belts. In Jordana's closet were over 3,000 pairs of shoes, and Jordana had 50 pairs of blue jeans. The closets were cedar, and each had a little kitchen complete with refrigerator and microwave in case either of them wanted anything to eat or drink, while they were getting dressed.

Aaron saw a lot of Atlanta dignitaries throughout the house. There were CEO's of companies, star athletes, famous trial attorneys and local television celebrities. Everyone was dressed magnificently and seemed to be having a wonderful time.

Someone came up to the bedroom and said it was time to go to the party house to start the awards presentation. They went downstairs and walked out of the house and crossed the lawn to the 10,000 square foot party house. The party house had been built so that the sides of the building could be open or shut, depending on the weather. It had a ceiling and a marble floor and had white panels going around the sides that could be hydraulically raised or lowered. Because the night was so beautiful, the panels were up, and the house was open. The party house was just one enormous room, and tonight there was a stage set up at one end of the room with hundreds of folding chairs on the floor. Aaron and Marcy sat in chairs at the back just as the Chairman of the American Cancer Society of Georgia walked up to the microphone.

"Thank you all for coming to this incredible evening. Due to your generosity, tonight's function will raise over $1,000,000 to help in the fight against cancer. Words can't begin to convey our thanks to Marty and Jordana Shapiro for hosting this event at probably the premiere house in the entire country. I want to be brief, so I will turn the program over to our honored guest, the Governor of the State of Georgia, Jeff Davis, who will conduct the awards presentation."

The governor walked to the microphone, shook the chairman's hand and then began to speak.

"I'm here tonight to present the American Cancer Society's Man of the Year award for the State of Georgia. This man has done so much and given so much of himself. He is hosting this party at his magnificent house tonight, and this is only a small part of what he does. He's hosted fundraisers in the past for the American Cancer Society and has personally donated millions of dollars to help with research. In appreciation for all that he has done, the new oncology wing at Children's Hospital in Atlanta will be named after him. I consider him a close friend; he's helped me in all of my campaigns. He's also one of the top attorneys not only in the state of Georgia, but in the entire country. For all he does, for his tireless work on behalf of the

American Cancer Society, we are proud to present the 2003 Man of the Year award to Marty Shapiro."

Marty came up on stage. Everyone started clapping, and then everyone gave him a standing ovation. Aaron didn't want to stand up, but everyone else including Marcy was standing, so he reluctantly stood up.

Marty began talking, "Thank you for this award. I appreciate Governor Davis' kind remarks and his being here tonight. Jeff, I've always considered you a close friend and always hoped that one day we would see you and your lovely wife in the White House. All the work that I've done for the American Cancer Society is so worthwhile, just to help one person, to cure one child, or make one adult's life better. It's been my pleasure, and I promise that I will continue to work and do everything that I can to help eradicate cancer in our lifetimes. I welcome all of you to my house. I hope you have a wonderful time tonight. Enjoy the food, the music and the companionship, and thank you very much for this honor."

Everyone stood up and clapped again. Jordana came on stage and put her arms around Marty and kissed him, and photographers' flashbulbs went off all over the room. Then Marty walked off the stage and across the party house. Aaron decided that now was his chance. "Marcy, stay here. I'm going to talk to Marty."

He walked to where Marty was standing at the edge of the party house. Suddenly, two burly security guards walked up to Marty with a man between them. Each of the man's arms was being held behind his back by a security guard, and one of the guards held a rifle with a telescopic lens. The prisoner was dressed in Army fatigues, and his face was painted black. Aaron was close enough to Marty to hear them talking.

"Mr. Shapiro, we found this man perched in one of the trees on your property. Your security system detected him. He has a rifle equipped with a telescopic lens with night vision, and it looked like he was going to try and shoot someone at your party."

Aaron got closer. The prisoner was Cole Stone.

"Hmmm, you look familiar," said Marty. "Where do I know you from?"

"Dunno, guy," replied the prisoner angrily.

"Wait a minute. I know you. You're that doctor I took a deposition from last week. Cole Stone. The doctor who killed that poor young girl. What were you going to do here, try to kill me?"

"I ain't gonna say nuthin' to you, asshole," said Cole. He looked over and saw Aaron. "Aaron, you gotta help me. I don't know what's goin' on here. There's something wrong."

"You know him, don't you?" asked Marty. "This is your partner, isn't he? Was this some kind of plot you guys had to kill me?"

"Uh, uh, I, I knew nothing about it," Aaron stammered.

Marty turned back to Cole, "You were going to shoot me, weren't you?"

"No comment. I want to talk to my attorney."

One security guard spoke, "Mr. Shapiro, we've already notified the police. We'll take him outside so the squad car will take him downtown."

"Yeah, do that. And whatever charges I can press against this guy, trespassing, illegal weapon, attempted murder, tell them I want everything. I'll get one of my firm's attorneys on the case to make sure the prosecutor follows my wishes."

"Yes, sir." The two security guards carried Cole off.

"Marty," Aaron began, "I know this is probably not the best time, but can I talk to you for a minute?"

"I've got nothing at all to say to you, now or ever. This is my party. This is my house. You and your fat wife can eat and listen to the music – you've paid your $1,000, but you leave me alone. We'll see you and your partner in court!" Marty stormed off.

Aaron was in a daze. Cole would be in jail, and Aaron had done nothing to help himself with regard to the lawsuits. He stayed with Marcy in the party house until Marcy had tried all the Italian food being served there, and then they walked over to the swimming pool which was next to the party house. The swimming pool was Olympic sized and in the shape of a giant heart. Jordana had always wanted a heart-shaped pool, they were informed by the guide poolside. There was a large cabana at one end of the pool and at least 50 lounge chairs around it. A small stage had been set up in front of the cabana, and a Latin group was performing. Aaron and Marcy listened for a while, but Aaron couldn't enjoy himself.

"Let's leave," Aaron said to Marcy.

"But we haven't seen the guest house yet. It's a 12,000 square foot house designed by France's top architect."

"I've had enough," Aaron said. "Let's go and get our car."

****

Aaron and Marcy walked through the main house to the entrance foyer. They walked out the front door, and Aaron gave his parking ticket to a valet. Outside the house, just in front of them, Marty and Jordana were saying goodbye to the governor and his wife. There were security guards with the governor, and they got into the governor's limousine with the governor and his wife. The limousine drove off, and Marty and Jordana began walking back to the house. Marty walked past Aaron without looking at him, and Aaron grabbed him by the shoulder.

"Marty, please, can I just talk to you? I really need to discuss these lawsuits with you."

Marty gave Aaron a karate chop to the chest which stunned Aaron. "Keep your stinking hands off me. Don't you ever touch me. I don't want to have anything to do with you. Can't you see…I'm richer than you. You'll never have this kind of money. I've got a gorgeous wife, and you've got a fat pig. I'm going to ruin you, take all your money away and make you wish you had never become a doctor. I win, and you're a loser. And if you ever try to lay a hand on me, don't forget I'm a black belt in karate, and I'll kill you with my bare hands."

Marty in his full tuxedo began demonstrating some karate kicks and punches, pulling them inches from Aaron's body. Aaron stood there frozen in fear. Marty was standing on the edge of the curb, and, just as he started a kick to Aaron's face, he slipped and stumbled off the curb into the driveway. Marty was talking as he was falling, and, just as he said, "With one kick, I could kill you," he lost his balance, and his head hit the driveway. At that precise moment, the valet came speeding up in the 300ZX and the brakes screeched as the car ran over Marty's neck, decapitating him. It all happened so suddenly that it seemed as though the words "kill you" were said by the detached head rolling down the driveway. Blood began spurting from the decapitated body like water from a fire hydrant. Aaron looked on in horror, and Marcy fainted. Jordana let out a huge scream.

There were 40 or 50 other people gathered outside the house at that time waiting for their cars. Even as Jordana was still screaming, ten trial attorneys walked up to her and gave her their business cards.

CHAPTER 7

Yellow Pine Psychiatric Hospital had been built in far north Pleasant Point at the border with the city of Woods. Dr. Sloan Meacham and his partners had purchased 100 acres of land in that area in the early 1980s when it was just pastureland occupied by cows. They had envisioned building a psychiatric hospital as well as surrounding stores, shopping centers and gas stations. Now, the entire 100 acres had been built on, and there were two enormous shopping centers, one of which contained Walgreen's as its anchor store and the other of which had Home Depot as its anchor store. There were four gas stations in the area, many smaller businesses, and there was always bumper-to-bumper traffic.

Dr. Meacham and his partners had made enough money from developing this land to retire; however, he still worked part-time at Yellow Pine Hospital as a staff psychiatrist.

The hospital was actually in the exact center of the 100 acres. It was painted light yellow and had four stories. It was set back from the main road with a long, circular driveway leading to the entrance which was covered by a bright yellow awning. Each floor of the hospital contained 25 private patient rooms as well as multiple interview rooms and one large room for group therapy. There was a huge room in the middle of each of the floors which was used as the dining room and social room and also contained the nurses' station. There was a huge television in this large social room mounted in one corner, and there was a ping-pong table at the other end of the room. Between the television and the ping-pong table were four picnic-style tables where the patients ate.

The lower three floors of the hospital were open floors. They were not locked down, and the patients could leave if they wanted to. The fourth floor, however, which had been nicknamed the "400 Club" or "Heaven" was a locked ward. The heavy wood door at the entrance to the fourth floor was always locked, and there was a television camera over the door, allowing the guard inside to see who was at the entrance.

The fourth floor was for patients who were felt to be a threat to themselves or to others. Dr. Cole Stone had now been a patient on the fourth floor for the last three weeks. His wife had signed the papers committing him to the hospital after Cole had continued to make statements that he was going to kill someone. He only talked about how life had been so unfair to him, how the lawyers were cheating him, how his reputation had been ruined, and how, no matter what, he was going to get revenge.

The three weeks in the hospital had passed very slowly for Cole. The first week, he had been started on one antidepressant medication which had not really helped, so, the second week, a second antidepressant was added. This did not do much either, so, now, in the third week, he was started on a third antidepressant. There were two planned activities for Cole every day in the hospital. At 10 o'clock each morning, he had group therapy, and then, at 1 o'clock each afternoon, he had individual therapy. Each session lasted an hour. The rest of the day was free, and Cole spent most of the time alone is his room lying in his bed reading magazines and daydreaming.

Louis, a large black man who was one of the attendants on the ward, knocked on Cole's door. "OK, Dr. Stone. Time for group therapy. Let's get you down to group."

Cole closed the hunting magazine he had been reading, got out of the bed and followed Louis down the hallway to the large conference room where group therapy took place. There were eight patients in the group and a psychologist who led the discussion. Members of the group were constantly coming and going. On a patient's first day in the group, they were given the opportunity to introduce themselves and to tell about their problems for ten minutes. After that, anyone in the group could speak, with the psychologist leading the discussion.

Cole walked into the windowless room which was painted bright yellow and took a seat in the circle of chairs. The psychologist, Juan McNally, was a short, bald man in his 50s who had a heavy gray beard. The other members of the group were already seated; they were a collection of men and women from their 20s to their 50s who came from varied backgrounds but all of whom were at least middle class or above economically. There was a new young lady in the group today who Cole knew would start off the discussion by talking about herself.

"OK, everyone, it looks like we're all here," Juan McNally started. "We have a new member of our group today. Her name is Cynthia Harberry, and she came in last night. Why don't we go around the circle and have everyone introduce themselves to Cynthia."

The other members of the group gave their names and minimal information about themselves. When it was Cole's turn, he said in a monotone, "Hi, I'm Cole Stone. I'm a gastroenterologist in Pleasant Point. I've been in practice for over 25 years. I've been here for three weeks now."

The new patient began to speak. "My name is Cynthia Harberry. I'm 22 years old, and I'm here because I tried to commit suicide. I have a disease called Crohn's disease which is a miserable disease of my bowels. I've had Crohn's disease since I was 12 years old. You can see how short I am and how puffy my face is. That's from taking steroids all these years. The doctors have never been able to get my disease fully under control. I've had to have surgery after surgery to remove pieces of my bowel, and I have a fistula which is a connection between my bowel and my skin which drains stool all the time onto my skin. My life has been miserable. At age 18, the doctor who took care of me for six years, who was a pediatric gastroenterologist, said I needed to find an adult gastroenterologist to take over my case. My pediatric gastroenterologist referred me to a Dr. Cole Stone."

Cynthia turned and looked directly at Cole and pointed at him. "I remember calling your office and asking for you, Dr. Cole Stone, to take over as my doctor. I remember the conversation with your nurse like it was yesterday. She said you wouldn't take care of any Crohn's or ulcerative colitis patients, that I needed to see a specialist in those diseases. You were supposed to be a gastroenterologist; why wouldn't you see me?"

Cole was stunned. He stammered, "I, I, I don't know what you're talking about."

"Well, I remember your name very well. Finally, when I cried, please, please, I need someone to take care of me, your nurse referred me to your partner, Aaron Bernstein. He's taken care of me these last four years. But ever since that day I talked to your nurse on the phone, I've looked at the sign in front of your office that says, 'Cole Stone, gastroenterologist,' on it, and I've thought about you. What kind of patients will you take care of?"

"Uh, uh, I don't know," said Cole, "but Aaron, now he takes care of a lot of Crohn's and colitis patients. It's just not my thing."

"Aren't you supposed to be a doctor?" Cynthia asked. "Aren't you someone who was supposed to help people and take care of them?"

"Wait a minute," interrupted Juan. "This discussion is getting off track. Cynthia, why don't you get back to telling us why you're here and what's been going on lately?"

"It's not getting off track at all," Cynthia angrily replied. "That man," she said pointing at Cole, "is a good reason why I'm here. People like him who wouldn't help me and just want to leave me to die so I don't mess up their lives. I got married a year ago, and my husband couldn't stand my being sick all the time. He left me, too."

"I didn't do nuthin' to make you sick," said Cole. "I don't take care of patients like you. I do mainly procedures. That's what I do."

"Yeah, you and my ex-husband. You're a pair. You won't take care of sick people even though you're supposed to a doctor, and my husband was supposed to be my husband and soul mate, and he left me after a year. We just finished our divorce one week ago, and I basically decided that life wasn't worth living anymore. I took an overdose of Tylenol, and I woke up in the emergency room at Pleasant Point General Hospital. They saved my life, but I don't want to live anymore. Look how disfigured I am; I look like a freak. I have no job. I have my mom and my sister but no other family and very few friends. Most people treat me like that man over there, Dr...., I guess you could call him a doctor, Dr. Stone. They just want to avoid me because I'm too much trouble."

"Listen, honey," said Cole angrily, "you women always try to take Tylenol overdoses. That's not suicide; that's a suicidal gesture. If you'd really wanted to kill yourself, you'd have gotten a gun..."

"OK," interrupted Juan, "that's enough. I think we've heard about why Cynthia is here. Let's see if anyone can talk about an experience similar to Cynthia's so that maybe we can help her move on from this and help her cope with her illness."

Cole sat back and daydreamed. He never participated in these group therapy sessions. Occasionally, he would glance over at Cynthia. She was a freaky-looking girl. She had the moon facies and buffalo hump that people who had been on steroids would get. She had a very pasty complexion, and her hair had been chopped short. Yeah, Cole thought to himself, let Bernstein take care of patients like her. I don't need them, and I don't want them. All of a sudden, Cole heard his name called again.

"And Dr. Stone, weren't you the doctor who abandoned that girl?" It was Cynthia looking directly into his eyes. "I read about you in the newspaper. I saw you on television. You're infamous, aren't you?" Cynthia was almost snarling at Cole.

"I don't want any more of this group session," said Cole. "I'm getting out of here."

Cole got out of his chair and walked to the door where Louis, the attendant, was standing.

"Sit back down, Dr. Stone," Louis said quietly but firmly.

Cole walked back to his seat and sat down.

"There will be no more fighting among you," said Juan. "Let's try to be constructive. Oops, it's time for the end of group therapy. All right, everybody, let's go to lunch."

The group filed out of the conference room and walked over to the dining room. The dining room had three large unbreakable windows through which the sunlight poured in. It had been painted bright yellow.

Cole sat at a table by himself and ate his lunch. One thing he did all the time in this "nut" hospital was eat. In the three weeks he had been hospitalized, he had gained 15 pounds. His wife was always bringing him donuts and candy which he devoured in his room. He was always hungry; he had no doubt that the antidepressants he was on were the main cause of his hunger, but he also ate out of boredom. When he finished lunch, he watched television for a few minutes and then went back to his room and took a nap.

He was awakened by Louis's voice. "It's time for your individual therapy session now, Dr. Stone," said Louis.

Cole followed Louis down the hallway to the conference room. Cole's insurance was paying for him to have therapy every day with a psychiatrist, but a psychologist met with him six out of the seven days a week. Today was only his third meeting in the three weeks with the psychiatrist who had been assigned to him, Dr. Sloan Meacham.

"Cole, come on in here and have a seat," Sloan cheerily greeted him. "How are you doing?" he asked as he extended his hand to Cole.

Cole kept his hand by his side. "I'm doing OK," Cole said as he sat down.

"Are you feeling less depressed?"

"Yeah, I guess so. I guess I'm less depressed. I think I need to get out of this place. I think this place is depressing me."

"You've got another week to go here," said Sloan. "Your insurance goes one more week. How are you doing as far as your medications? Any bad side effects?"

"Well, I think I'm tolerating it OK. It's messing up my bowels though."

"What do you mean?"

"I'm constantly constipated. I've always got bloating and gas. I'm not having good bowel movements; it's like it's shut my system down. Hell, I feel like one of those irritable bowel "crazy nut" patients that I've avoided all these years. Now that I'm on all these 'nut-type' medications, I can't have a bowel movement, and it's tearing up my insides."

"When was your last bowel movement?"

"Five days ago."

"OK. We'll get you a good laxative today. Don't want you getting impacted. You know, Louis is the one who digs out the impactions," Sloan laughed.

"I appreciate your laxative," Cole muttered.

"Any other problems that you are having? Have you had any more suicidal thoughts or homicidal thoughts?"

"No," said Cole, "I'm not thinking about killing myself or killing anybody else now. I just want to get out of here. I want to go home to my wife."

"All right, well, I actually gotta get out of here quickly today, too. I've got an early tennis game. I just want to make sure you're doing OK. You go back to your room and take it easy."

Cole walked out of the room. The entire session had lasted less than ten minutes. An hour after Cole got back to his room, Louis brought in a laxative for him to take with some water.

"Here, you take these, and you'll be shitting fine," said Louis grinning.

"Thanks," said Cole as he swallowed the pills and then went back to reading the hunting magazine.

****

That night, Cole went for dinner and ate baked chicken, French fries and salad. After he ate, he returned to his room and sat in the chair. He thought that he was no longer homicidal; the one man that he had wanted to kill was dead now. He did not want to kill anybody else, and he wasn't going to kill himself. He just wanted to get through all this and retire and live on his ranch. If his wife wanted to come live with him at the ranch, that was fine; if she wanted to stay in Pleasant Point, that was fine also. He had finally decided to move on and restart his life.

All of a sudden, Cole had a sudden urge to have a bowel movement. He ran down the hallway to the bathroom and tried to open the door, but it was locked.

"Hey, can you hurry up in there!" Cole shouted. "I think I'm getting diarrhea. Hurry, hurry!"

Cole had severe cramping abdominal pain and was bent over at the waist. He was sweating profusely, and his head turned red. He shook the door handle as hard as he could.

"Hurry, you bastard…or I'll mess myself."

"You'll just have to wait your turn," came the voice through the locked door. "I'm having diarrhea myself like I've had every day for the past 12 years, and it can take me 30 minutes to get rid of it. I only hope that you're who I think you are…Dr. Cole Stone."

Cole lay down on the floor outside the bathroom door. That voice he immediately recognized as Cynthia Harberry's. Cole could feel his rectum contract, and then he filled his pants with crap.

CHAPTER 8

Aaron couldn't sleep at night for three months. He would lie down next to Marcy and spend most of the night listening to her snore and fight for air. She snored so ferociously he wondered why it hadn't kept him up before; he decided that he'd always been so tired from work that nothing bothered him once he fell asleep. He marveled at how the children were able to sleep through the noise, even though their rooms were on the other side of the house.

The snoring bothered Aaron, but what really worried him was when Marcy would stop breathing and gasp for air. She would go ten to 15 seconds without breathing, and then, like a car's engine searching for life, would choke, rattle and cough until she started breathing again. A couple of nights, Aaron got out his watch and timed Marcy's intervals between breaths — the longest was 18 seconds. He diagnosed Marcy as having sleep apnea and begged her to be evaluated by a sleep specialist. Marcy refused, saying she was too embarrassed by her snoring to sleep anyplace where people other than her husband could hear her.

Aaron first tried Tylenol PM to help him sleep. He would take it and fall asleep, then wake up one to two hours later and stay awake the rest of the night. He got an internist in Pleasant Point to prescribe Ambien 5 mg at bedtime for him; on this, he slept three to four hours. The internist doubled the dosage to 10 mg and, taking this along with two Tylenol PM, allowed Aaron to sleep through the night.

The combination of Ambien and Tylenol PM gave Aaron more vivid, detailed dreams than he'd ever had before, with most of them ending with Aaron waking up drenched in sweat. On this particular night, Aaron had gone to bed late and had almost immediately started dreaming. In the dream, Aaron was walking through a lush, green forest with the vegetation so thick he could only see a few feet in front and the trees so high they blocked the sky. He walked and walked and walked until he finally reached a clearing. In the clearing stood Cole Stone, with paintbrush in hand and standing next to an easel with a large canvas on it. Over his silver hair, Cole wore a black beret, and his shirt and pants were snow white.

Aaron walked up to Cole, and Cole resumed paining without saying a word to Aaron. He was painting a landscape with the sky the truest of blues and the grass the greenest of greens. Suddenly, Aaron realized that everything that Cole was painting was appearing in the world around him. Cole painted some fluffy, cotton-ball clouds on the canvas, and, when Aaron looked up, he saw the identical clouds floating by. Cole switched to greens and browns to create a thickly-branched oak tree which quickly appeared to Aaron's left. Cole scampered from color to color, adding bluebirds and robins and wrens which nested in the oak tree and flew around it. The birds sang and chirped gaily, breaking the silence.

Cole smiled at Aaron, put his paintbrush between his lips and then picked up the shotgun which lay next to him. He stepped back and began shooting at the canvas. As he shot holes into the painting of the forest, the trees around Aaron began to disappear, and the birds in them disintegrated. When Cole shot the majestically-painted blue sky, the sky above Aaron first dimmed as though it had light bulbs above it that had been turned off and then changed to gray and then black. Aaron yelled at Cole, "Why, Cole, why?" Cole only smiled and kept shooting in the dark.

The sound of shooting was replaced by the sound of a large crowd cheering. Somewhere in his brain, Aaron's neurons were issuing the reassuring message that all the loud noise he was hearing as gunshots and loud cheering was just Marcy snoring. But that analytical part of his brain refused to halt the dream.

The people cheering were in a giant arena, and Aaron found himself at the top row. He looked down to the floor and saw his now grown-up son, David, playing basketball. Aaron almost didn't recognize David because, rather than being nerdy and clumsy, he was handsome and athletic. He was playing basketball on the same team as Thomas Kelly's son, Thomas Junior, so Aaron walked down the stairs of the arena to where Thomas was sitting and sat down next to him. Seated all around Thomas were other members of the radiology department at Pleasant Point General Hospital, and they hissed and booed at Aaron as he made his way to his seat.

At first, Thomas was kind and complimentary. "That your boy out there, Bernstein?" he asked. "He plays pretty good ball."

Aaron and Thomas watched as Thomas Junior threw a beautiful bounce pass to David which clanked off David's hands as though they were covered by iron mitts and went out of bounds.

"Clumsy, huh?" Thomas said. "Just like his father." He shoved his index finger into Aaron's chest. "Your boy shouldn't be out here with the real ballplayers. He's not a man. He should be playing on his computer like the nerds."

Aaron felt anger welling up inside him. It started in his belly and then rapidly went through his chest to his face which burned beet red. He reached out with both hands to Thomas's neck and began squeezing as hard as he could. He heard someone screaming, so he released his grip and looked down in front of him.

Sitting in front of Aaron were people he knew, but he wasn't sure who they were. There was a familiarity about them which made Aaron feel comfortable, and his anger subsided. The two people turned around simultaneously, and Aaron could see that it was his long-dead mother and father.

"I thought you were both dead," Aaron stated matter of factly.

"We are. This really isn't us. We just wanted to check on our grandson. He really did grow up to be quite a nerd, didn't he? Still an ace with the chopsticks, we bet."

"Mom and dad, that's not a nice way to talk about your grandson." Aaron glanced down to the basketball court where, sure enough, David was back to his nine-year-old self. Rather than playing basketball on the court, he was now playing a computer game on the sidelines.

Aaron wanted to talk more to his parents, but, when he looked back to their seats, they were no longer there. They had been replaced by Peter Dickman and Jordana Shapiro.

"What are you two doing sitting next to each other?" Aaron asked.

"You didn't know that we're together now? We're a couple," replied Peter. "After that little squirt, Marty, was killed, Jordana needed someone to comfort her. She came to the hospital with a broken heart, and there was only one person who could mend it."

"We're in love," said Jordana. "And this hunk and I are going to get married."

"Are you going to live in that big house that Marty built?" Aaron asked.

"We're using that house for the big bonfire," replied Peter. "Just like we used to do at Texas A&M before the big football game with Texas. Just before our wedding, we're gonna kindle that mother-fuckin' mansion and have a big party."

"It was all Peter's idea," said Jordana. "Don't you think it's romantic?"

As Aaron was going to reply, gunshots rang out. Aaron looked down at Peter who was lying on Jordana's lap with a hole through his head with blood spurting out of it like lava from a volcano. Cole Stone appeared, carrying an enormous shotgun with smoke coming out of the barrel. He pushed Peter's lifeless body out of the chair and sat down next to Jordana.

"Hey, precious, how about being with a real man now?" he asked Jordana.

Jordana screamed and screamed.

"I'm tired of all of this shit," Aaron said. He walked down to the basketball court and grabbed David's hand and pulled him away from the computer. He and David looked up at the ceiling of the arena. Suddenly, the roof opened, and everyone began cheering.

The PA announcer said, "And now, ladies and gentlemen, for our halftime show, we are proud to present the Goodyear blimp."

A huge blimp flew over the stadium. But rather than being silver with the letters Goodyear in black, the blimp was a caricature of Marcy, Aaron's wife. Aaron could feel the anger inside. How dare they do that? How dare they make fun of my wife, he thought.

Aaron screamed out, "Take it down! Take it down!"

Aaron looked back up to where Cole was standing next to Jordana. Cole had his gun raised again, and it was pointed at the blimp.

"No, no!" Aaron shouted. "Don't shoot her. Please don't shoot her."

Cole didn't hear Aaron's pleas. He shot three bullets through the giant blimp, and, suddenly, Marcy was no more.

Aaron cried, "No, no, no." And then he looked up at the sky where the blimp had been. He saw Marty Shapiro's face, and Marty was taunting him in front of the whole arena.

Marty said, "I'm richer than you'll ever be. I've got a gorgeous wife, and you've got a fat pig for a wife. I've got a children's hospital named after me, and they wouldn't even name a stinking toilet in that hospital after you. You'll never accomplish what I accomplished, even though I'm in heaven now, and you're stuck in hell."

Aaron could take no more, so he forced himself to wake up. He was sweating profusely, and his heart was racing. Marcy was asleep next to him, snoring furiously.

Aaron reached over to his nightstand where he kept many of his most prized possessions. One of these possessions was the last thing Aaron's father had sent him before he had died. Aaron's father had been an avid reader of *Reader's Digest* magazine, and, anytime he found something in the magazine that he thought would benefit Aaron, he clipped it out and mailed it to him. The very last thing he'd clipped out on the day he'd died had been a pocm sent to *Reader's Digest* by a nine-year-old boy. With the poem, Aaron's dad had included a short letter which said, "Even though this boy is only nine years old, he understands the true meaning of life."

Aaron picked the poem off the nightstand and took it with him into the bathroom. He turned on the light and read the poem while sitting on the toilet. The poem was titled "Life."

> Life is something you live
> You must give it all you can give
> No matter what the rest
> You must try to do your best.
>
> If you waste your little time
> Just remember this forsaken rhyme
> The world goes on forever
> When we leave it, we come back never.

It was still an hour before Aaron needed to wake up for work, but he knew he couldn't sleep anymore. He walked over to the shower and turned on the hot water.

CHAPTER 9

August 8, 2003

Dear Vijay,

I hope that you are doing well. I haven't heard from you in a few months, but I talked to your father yesterday. He said that you were continuing to do very well practicing medicine in the United States. I want to again thank you for all of the contributions you have made to keep my clinic running. Believe me, Vijay, your money has saved many lives here in Mumbai, the lives of boys and girls and men and women who live in the slums of our great city. These are people who would have no access to any medical care if it weren't for the generosity of people like you. I know that your father and your brothers and sisters all appreciate all of the money you send them. I see the children of your brothers and sisters in the clinic, and they are all growing up wonderfully. You certainly have a lot to be proud of in your family and in your own accomplishments.

This year marked a milestone for me – it was my 75th birthday. It has been a great life for me, and I have accomplished much more than I ever dreamed I could. I dedicated my life to medicine; to healing the sick, especially those who couldn't afford health care, and bringing comfort to those that I couldn't heal in their times of greatest need. But at age 75, it is getting harder and harder for me to get around and to continue to run this clinic in the way that I want. I now start hospital rounds at 4:00 a.m., and I'm often in the clinic working until 9 or 10 at night. Then, I may go back to the hospital again to check on my sickest patients.

I need someone to help me in the clinic, Vijay, and that is why I am writing you. Would you consider coming back to India and taking over the clinic? I would let you be in charge, and I would be your assistant. I would like to work for at least another ten years in a part-time role before I would consider retirement. Those ten years would give me the opportunity to teach you the ins and outs of the clinic.

I know this is a big request to make of you, but I feel that you are the one for this job. You will have to sacrifice a lot, I am sure, since I know that doctors in America make a great deal of money and enjoy considerable prestige. But some things in life are more important than money. Loving the work that you do and working to save lives are two of those things. I think you will find both of those here in India, and you will be reunited with your father and the rest of your family.

Please consider my offer carefully. I look forward to your reply. May all of your comings and goings be in peace.

Sincerely,

Christian Bissel-Mozel, M.D.

****

August 25, 2003

Dear Dr. Bissel-Mozel,

It was wonderful to hear from you. I know from talking to my father and my family of the great things that you and your clinic have accomplished. Anjay told me how you saved his son's life by diagnosing and operating on his burst appendix. If it wasn't for you, many in the slums of Mumbai would be dead now.

You are the one who inspired and encouraged me to go into medicine, and, for that, I will be forever grateful. However, I am unable to take you up on your offer to return to India and run your clinic. Believe me, it is a great honor for me to be considered by you for this position. But I have my life in America now, and I enjoy this life. You mentioned loving what you do, and I do feel that what I do is important and makes a difference in the lives of many human beings. I love taking care of patients and seeing them get well. In my position as a hospitalist, I may not be the most vital cog in treating the patient, but I still feel that I fulfill an important role. Very few American doctors would be willing to accept the long hours and abuse that I put up with. I have seen many patients come into the hospital near death, and we have brought them back to life. I continue to love being a doctor, and I continue to practice medicine at a high level that you would be proud of.

There is another reason that I cannot accept your offer: I am engaged to be married. I have met a fantastic woman who is Indian, born in America, who lives here in Atlanta. We were engaged not long ago, and we will be married in six months. We will have the wedding here, and then we will have a reception in Mumbai. I want you to come to the reception so that I can see you again and introduce you to my wife.

Life has many strange twists, doesn't it? Who would have thought when I was a 14-year-old boy running through the flooded streets of Bombay looking for you to save my brother's life that you would take me under your wing and help me become a doctor? And even more strange, who would have thought that I would end up here in America working in Pleasant Point, Georgia, saving people's lives. In a way, Dr. Bissel-Mozel, you can take credit for every life that I have saved and for every sick person that I have comforted. I am enclosing a check for $1,000 to be used as you see fit.

Sincerely,

Vijay Givagushrai

EPILOGUE

I t all ended with a letter. Aaron Bernstein went through his daily mail as usual in the afternoon after seeing his last patient. He got to the letter from Denialcare and opened it up. It was addressed to AHC Healthcare Receivables Management, Attention: John Jackson, with the address in Virginia. It was regarding Denialcare 55 member Jumpy Johnson and his dates of service February 10, 2003, through February 13, 2003.

Dear Dr. Jackson,

Your request for reconsideration of the certification of the above-noted dates of service for the above-referenced Denial care 55 member has been received. Based on the clinical information made available for review, the patient was admitted through the emergency room on February 10, 2003, with complaint of severe abdominal pain. The patient's temperature was 98.6, pulse 80, respirations 16 and blood pressure 150/95. His exam was unremarkable except for abdominal pain on palpation. Every laboratory parameter was within normal range, and CAT scan of the abdomen and pelvis was normal. The patient's admitting orders included n.p.o., IV fluids, vital signs every four hours and pain medicine. Over the next two days, the patient continued to receive pain medication, but no other studies were performed, although colonoscopy was contemplated. On the third day of the admission, this patient was involved in an altercation which led to his demise.

Based on available clinical information and autopsy report, it appears that the patient had nothing wrong in his abdominal cavity and should have been discharged to home the day after his admission. Therefore, denial for dates of service February 11, 2003, through February 13, 2003, will be upheld due to lack of medical necessity. The member's family has no financial responsibility for services denied as a result of this decision. Since this case involved a retrospective review of a benefit determination according to the Georgia Department of Insurance and HCFA (Health Care Financing Administration) guidelines, it is not subject to review by an independent review organization. This is the final decision in this matter.

Sincerely,

James Buckman, M.D.
Medical Director

The letter was copied to the patient's family, to Pleasant Point General Hospital, to Jeffrey Conner, his family doctor, and to all the physicians involved in Mr. Johnson's care.

Aaron read the letter and then sat back in his desk chair and put his feet on his desk. Dr. Barbosian had always talked about medicine as being an art, not a science, as he puffed on his pipe in his office deep in the bowels of Ben Taub Hospital in Houston. You needed the science as a foundation to treat patients, just as a painter needs a palette of paints to create a masterpiece. But the art came from listening to people and truly understanding them, wanting to help them and then taking care of them. Aaron shook his head sadly. He tried his best to practice the art, and most of the time he thought he succeeded. A thought came to him: maybe the problems he'd encountered in the last year weren't really his fault, but instead were due to the sorry state of the art. Changes had to be made, he thought, starting with... Just then his beeper went off. He called the answering service and was informed that Dr. Givagushrai had a consult for him to see.

36841378R00205

Made in the USA
Middletown, DE
12 November 2016